Readers love
ASHLYN KANE and MORGAN JAMES

Winging It

"I loved this sweet and sexy story. You don't have to be a hockey fan to enjoy *Winging It* and I encourage readers to give it a try."
—Carly's Book Reviews

"This story was a lot of fun. Great characters. Steamy romance. I highly recommend it if you like any type of sports books."
—It's About The Book

"Take all the elements at play here, the crowds, the teamwork, the plays, and the opposition and media, throw in romance and love. Stir vigorously and out flows *Winging It*, one of my highly recommended reads."
—Scattered Thoughts and Rogue Words

Hard Feelings

"This story was so captivating and entertaining, and so much more than the quick, fluffy read I expected."
—Watch and Word Society

"I liked watching the process with these two men and observing their growth into men with real feelings and the ability to communicate them."
—The Novel Approach

By ASHLYN KANE

American Love Songs
With Claudia Mayrant & CJ Burke: Babe in the Woodshop
A Good Vintage
Hang a Shining Star
The Inside Edge

DREAMSPUN BEYOND
Hex and Candy

DREAMSPUN DESIRES
His Leading Man
Fake Dating the Prince

With Morgan James
Hair of the Dog
Hard Feelings
Return to Sender
String Theory
Winging It

Published by DREAMSPINNER PRESS
www.dreamspinnerpress.com

By MORGAN JAMES

Purls of Wisdom

DREAMSPUN DESIRES
Love Conventions

With Ashlyn Kane
Hair of the Dog
Hard Feelings
Return to Sender
String Theory
Winging It

Published by DREAMSPINNER PRESS
www.dreamspinnerpress.com

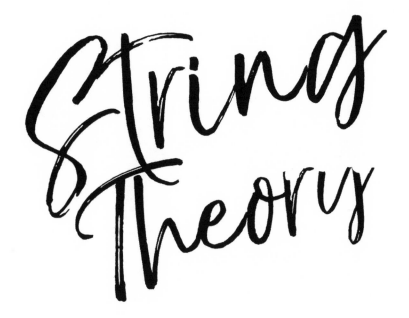

String Theory

Ashlyn Kane & Morgan James

Published by

DREAMSPINNER PRESS

5032 Capital Circle SW, Suite 2, PMB# 279, Tallahassee, FL 32305-7886 USA
www.dreamspinnerpress.com

String Theory
© 2021 Ashlyn Kane and Morgan James

Cover Art
© 2021 Paul Richmond
http://www.paulrichmondstudio.com
Cover content is for illustrative purposes only and any person depicted on the cover is a model.

Trade Paperback ISBN: 978-1-64405-936-4
Digital ISBN: 978-1-64405-935-7
Trade Paperback published June 2021
First Edition
v. 1.0

Printed in the United States of America
∞
This paper meets the requirements of
ANSI/NISO Z39.48-1992 (Permanence of Paper).

Authors' Note

WHEN WE wrote this book in the summer of 2020, we could not anticipate how the next months would play out. We were sad and scared and lonely. Imagining a world where COVID-19 had ended gave us a refuge and a place to make each other laugh, and the characters gave us a vehicle to work out our grief.

String Theory is not an accurate account of how the pandemic played out, but it is the romantic comedy we needed to write. We hope it's as diverting for you as it was for us.

With special thanks to Justin and Katie. They know why.

String Theory

"HOBBES, WHERE are you taking me?" Jax Hall definitely did *not* whine as he followed his grumpy roommate down the sidewalk. On a Friday evening, the downtown London, Ontario, streets were as bustling as they ever got these days. Jax and Hobbes automatically ducked sideways to keep a "safe" distance from another pedestrian. Old habits, Jax thought bitterly.

He shook away the thought.

"Hobbes!" he urged, but Hobbes stayed mum.

Jax lunged forward and grabbed his right hand in both of his and gave it a little shake. "Hobbes!"

"A bar." Hobbes pulled his hand free and jammed it into his pants pocket, stymieing another attempt. Jax wasn't bothered. He hooked his arm through Hobbes's and leaned into him.

The gazes of two women walking toward them lingered on their hooked arms and faces, and they clearly came to the same conclusion. Knowing that some people thought Hobbes's grumpy face was attractive—and having plenty of evidence of his own desirability— Jax leaned into his friend and batted his eyelashes to further the appearance of coupledom. After they passed by, the women whispered together, and was that a coo?

"Why are you so goddamned handsy?" Hobbes grumbled but didn't untangle their arms.

Jax shrugged. "Not enough love as a child?"

Hobbes barked a laugh. "Pull the other one. I've met your mother."

This, Jax reflected with fond amusement, was all too true. His mother had arrived like an avenging angel on the heels of the first lockdown to spend a week presiding over their house and making friends with Hobbes's diabetic cat. Jax's mother had never fussed or

1

coddled a day in her life, but he could tell by the set of her shoulders and the way she glared at Hobbes that Jax's midpandemic roommate acquisition must have had her on edge for months.

Not that she didn't fall in love with Hobbes almost as quickly as Jax had. What could he say? The Halls clearly had soft spots for antisocial pediatricians who grimly risked their lives while complaining at high volume about dangerous working conditions and a lack of professionalism.

"Why are we going to a bar?"

"Because we can," Hobbes said grimly, and Jax couldn't argue the point.

"Which bar? What's it like?"

"That one, and you can see for yourself." Hobbes tipped his head toward the bar at the end of the block—the Rock. The name was written in blocky text across an outline of... Newfoundland?

Hobbes untangled their arms to yank the door open, and Jax followed him into the dim interior. To the left sat the bar, a long counter that spanned nearly the entire length of the room, front to back. To the right, Jax spied a stage with room enough for a small band, currently hosting a piano and a drum kit.

The place was empty at this early hour—it had only just opened, according to the hours on the door—but a few staff milled about.

Hobbes headed for the bar and slid onto a stool. Behind it stood a man with dark stubble and a toque over his hair. He wore suspenders over a plaid flannel shirt with the sleeves rolled up. He was so beautifully Canadian Jax wanted to ruffle his hair. Or suck his cock.

"Calvin, 'ow's she cuttin'?" the bartender asked in a thick Newfie accent, but the next words came out smoother, slower. "What can I pour ya?"

"Whiskey," Hobbes grunted.

Jax leaned into the bar next to him, rested his arms across it, and cocked his hip to display his ass to best advantage should anyone take a look.

"Who's the friend?" the bartender asked Hobbes as he unscrewed the top from a bottle of Hobbes's favorite brand and poured two fingers' worth.

Hobbes grunted. "Jax Hall, my roommate, meet Sean Murphy."

Jax gave his best flirty smile and fluttered his lashes. "My pleasure, Sean," he purred. He had no desire to sleep with Hobbes's favorite barkeep—he wasn't about to make the mistake of getting between Hobbes and whiskey again—but Sean Murphy was a good-looking man with a lumberjack vibe that Jax found all too attractive.

Sean lifted an eyebrow and said, "I'm sure. Call me Murph. Everyone does."

"Will do, Murph. Can I get a beer?" He wasn't supposed to drink much, but one beer this late in the day wouldn't interfere with his medication.

"Sure. What'll you have?"

"Hm." Jax licked his lips. "What's your favorite IPA?"

Murph didn't react to the flirting with any sign of interest, and instead reached for a beer.

"Jesus, kid, would you put it back in your pants?" Hobbes griped.

"But I haven't taken anything out of my pants yet." Jax cast wide no-longer-bedroom eyes at Hobbes and straightened out of his seductive sprawl.

"We serve food here," Murph said dryly. "If anything tries to escape your pants, I'll have to ask you to leave."

Startled, Jax threw back his head with a laugh. "I like you."

Murph placed a bottle of microbrew IPA before him and said, "I'm thrilled, b'y."

After a sip of his unfamiliar but delicious drink, Jax set it on the bar with a sigh. "The things I do for you, Hobbes. I could drown in that accent *and* he knows good beer. I wanna taste."

"I don't think he fancies giving you a bite."

Jax heaved another dramatic sigh. "I guess not."

Murph looked between them with a raised eyebrow. "Hobbes?" he asked, and Hobbes groaned.

"Like the cartoon," Jax explained, happy to elucidate. "Apparently his hockey team thought his outlook on humanity was a little too dim to go on with calling him Calvin. They decided Hobbes suits better."

Murph barked a laugh, topping off Hobbes's drink. "Think they got yer number, friend." He gestured to Jax's glass. "Ya done, b'y?"

"I'm done," Jax said with a grin. "So how does a Newfie end up opening a bar in Ontario?"

Murph poured himself a beer. "Now that's something of a chin-wag."

An empty bottle later, Jax excused himself to the bathroom and, on the way back, stalled as he passed the piano. He hadn't played it in years—not since he was a kid—but his fingers itched at the sight of the slightly battered instrument, and he settled himself on the bench.

Jax wiggled his fingers to stretch them and slowly, softly plucked out the familiar notes of "The Entertainer." It seemed he remembered some of his childhood lessons after all. He paused as he considered. Then, with his eyes half shut, he let his fingers remember the melody to "Mad World." He'd played it on the piano in his mother's living room until she begged him to play something—*anything* else.

"What on earth are you playing?" Murph yelled across the bar. "This is a bar, not a funeral parlor. You'll have any patrons leaving or weeping inta their beer. Play something else, b'y!"

Because Jax was a mature and responsible adult—he coparented a chronically ill cat—he stuck his tongue out at Murph before he turned back to the piano and ran through his mental catalog of songs he could once play. Then he smirked and cast a quick look in Murph's direction—both Murph and Hobbes were watching him—and began to play the opening refrain to "Beautiful Life" by Ace of Base.

Apparently over a decade without practice couldn't erase the chords or the lyrics from Jax's brain. Well, he fudged a few of the lines, but he remembered most of them. And Murph didn't seem to care—he didn't shout at Jax once, even when patrons stumbled in midchorus.

Chapter One

"HE'S LATE." Naomi tapped elegant fingers on the bar top. She was dressed to the nines tonight in a red dress that set off her dark complexion, with nails and lips to match.

"You know a lotta musicians who show up on time?" Jax asked from behind the bar. A keg needed changing out before they could open. "Relax. It'll be fine."

"You don't know Ari."

How would he? As far as Jax knew, he'd never even been in the city at the same time as Aria Darvish, the London-born pop-violin virtuoso who was coming down from on high to perform at the Rock tonight. Apparently it was the coda to his North America tour or something.

"No, but I know *you*. And you worry too much." Jax finally got the keg connected and stood to start tapping off the foam. Then he wedged a plastic pitcher between taps to keep it open and poured her a shot of vodka. "Here. Take the edge off." He waggled his eyebrows. "Unless you'd prefer—"

"I will throw this shot at you," she threatened. Jax counted it as progress; three months ago she wouldn't have given a warning.

"No wasting alcohol!" Murph yelled from the stage.

Jax shook his head. "I still don't know how he does that."

Naomi took the shot. "Amount of time he spent playing professionally, he should not be able to pick up a voice across the room like that."

"Acoustics." Murph heaved a plastic crate of patch cords onto the bar one-handed, the other still in one of those removable splints. The patch cords normally lived by the stage, but tonight everything was pared down—just two violins, the piano, and a drum kit. Practically culture. "Open a book sometime." He elbowed her in the ribs.

5

Acoustics, Naomi mouthed at Jax.

Witchcraft, he mouthed back as he pulled the pitcher off the tap. Perfect timing.

"*Anyway*," Murph said, "if you two're done lollygaggin'—"

Naomi's phone chirped. She picked it up with a look of naked relief.

"See," Jax said, disposing of the foam. "That's probably your piano guy now, right?" They still had half an hour to doors. Plenty of time. Aria himself wasn't even here yet.

But she was shaking her head. "It's Ari. I gotta go let him in."

"What, you're not gonna make him go in through the legion of adoring fans at the front door?" After three months, crowds were starting to feel normal again.

Murph rolled his eyes. "There're twenty people out there, ya drama queen." He shoved the crate at Jax. "See to these, would ya, b'y? Lord knows we'll never find them back if I put them away."

"You can just admit you don't like spiders."

"I like spiders all right. It's the things they eat I can't abide."

Jax suppressed a shudder of his own. Maybe he could convince Murph to send him out to do a supply run next week and he could add a couple bottles of insecticide to his purchases. He wasn't afraid. Just, there was a limit to the number of legs a creature should have, and unless it was an octopus, it was less than seven.

And then there was real work to do—hauling up cases of beer, liquor, and mixer, setting up his station, making sure the bottles of water, disinfectant wipes, and hand sanitizer had been set out behind the stage so the band could access them easily.

You can't be too careful, as Hobbes would say. Or at least that was what Jax inferred when he said things like *Jax, for God's sake, if you have to ride that death trap, at least wear your leathers.*

Jax happily would have worn them every day if he'd had the slightest impression Hobbes might appreciate it the way Jax wanted him to.

6

But Hobbes was straight, and even if he weren't, Jax put the chances of him screwing up anything beyond friendship at about 97 percent. Things were better this way.

Besides, there were plenty of fish in the sea… or the bar, in this case. At least there would be, so Jax had better get back to work.

ARI KNEW something was wrong even before Naomi released him.

"Sorry, sorry," she said as she stepped back, composing herself. She'd grown up a lot in the decade since he'd been her violin tutor, and even though he'd seen her at least once a year in the intervening time, it always surprised him to find a tall, composed woman with flawless skin in the place of the shy, pimply thirteen-year-old. "I know you don't really do hugs. I just—"

"Naomi," he interrupted with a gentle touch to her arm. "It's good to see you too. I don't 'do hugs' with fans. You hardly count."

"Save your judgment till you see my Spotify playlist." But the lingering threads of awkwardness fell away. "Actually, the hug was for fortification—mine, not yours."

He raised an eyebrow even as his stomach sank. He knew he should have taken Afra up on her offer to organize this concert—she managed the rest of his life without a single hiccup—but she deserved time off too. She'd been cagey lately. Something was bothering her. A brother could always tell. "What's wrong?"

"It's Gary, your pianist. He just called to cancel. He's got food poisoning."

Ah. "I see. What about Rosa?"

"Already called her. She's on her way. But…."

Ari hid a wince. "But?"

"You know how they're doing construction on the 401?" She smoothed down the end of a braid. "Well, it's down to one lane. And there was an accident."

That was… not ideal. "ETA?"

"GPS says an hour, hour and a half."

A headache threatened his temples, and he forced himself to unclench his body and breathe deeply so it couldn't take hold. Naomi knew piano. She could play accompaniment. But then he wouldn't have a second violin.

Fortunately they were in a good place to be looking for substitute musicians. "What about Murph?" He hadn't played often when Ari had worked here as a teenager, but he could hold his own.

"Sprained his wrist."

Damn.

"There's another option," Naomi said before he could panic. "One of the bartenders also plays."

That would be acceptable. Ari preferred to play with someone he knew, someone he'd worked with before, but he wasn't in a position to be choosy. They were slated to begin in twenty minutes. While concerts rarely began on time, Ari preferred to be punctual. He respected the people who had paid to see him perform. Just because this concert cost only a fraction of what the larger venues charged didn't make the audience less deserving of that respect.

Still…. Naomi seemed uncertain.

"You have reservations?"

She shook her head. "No, just… well, you'll see for yourself. I'll go get him."

The break room hadn't changed much since Ari had played here—no new paint, just a few new chips in it. One or two of the instruments hanging on the wall had been replaced, though, and the keyboard wedged into the back corner looked new.

At least Murph had thrown out the chair with the cracked seat. Ari couldn't count the number of times he'd pinched his leg on that.

Perhaps a minute and a half passed before the door opened again—just long enough for the tension to start creeping back into his shoulders. He was in the midst of another breathing exercise to relax his muscles when he looked up and completely forgot what he was doing.

One of the bartenders referred to a tall, blond white man in a threadbare T-shirt that highlighted every ounce of lean muscle. Ari barely had time to note startling blue eyes and the hint of a smile on a generous mouth before Naomi nudged the man forward.

"Immovable object, meet unstoppable force."

The bartender laughed. As he held his hand out for Ari, he asked Naomi, "Am I the immovable object or the unstoppable force?"

After the barest of hesitations, Ari took the offered hand and refrained from commenting on the stupidity of such a question. Only five seconds into their conversation and Ari could already tell—no one who knew this man would characterize him as an immovable anything. "Ari Darvish," he said instead.

"I guessed. Jax Hall." Jax's blue eyes flicked down and up, and his lips parted to reveal a tantalizing view of pink tongue.

"Down, boy!" Naomi groaned and hit the back of Jax's head.

Jax released Ari's hand and rubbed ruefully at his hair. "Geez, Naomi, I was only saying hi."

"You can leave the horndog at home tonight. We want you to make a good impression."

"I object to being characterized as a dog."

She rolled her eyes. "I thought the implication that you'd hump anyone's leg very apt."

"Naomi!" He sniffed. "I would never hump anyone's leg—uninvited." He winked at Ari.

At fifty seconds into the conversation, Ari learned Jax was positively shameless. "I will be sure to refrain from giving anything approaching an invitation, then," he said dryly.

Jax fluttered his lashes. "That sounds like a challenge."

Ari ignored the twinge in his stomach. "I'm told you can play piano."

"I do a mean rendition of 'Toxic,' it's true."

Ari did not have time to contemplate that. Instead, he asked if Jax could help them out.

Jax took the offered sheet music and then pulled out his phone. "You're on Spotify, right?" He strode across the room to the keyboard, spread the papers out, and after some searching, pulled the corresponding song up on his phone.

"Let's leave him to it." Naomi hooked her arm through Ari's. "Come to the bar. Say hi to Murph."

Ari didn't usually warm up for shows while standing at bars, but given the circumstances, he followed Naomi out of the room without a backward glance at the strange bartender hunched over his sheet music.

ARI DREW his bow over the strings, and the music vibrated through his body. He'd played this chord countless times; it began the refrain of one of his oldest pieces. But playing it had never felt like this before.

Jax sat behind the piano, head tilted at an alluring angle, a smile on his lips as his fingers flew across the keys in an approximation of Ari's music. It couldn't be expected that anyone other than a seasoned professional could learn so many songs so quickly, and the occasional errors and fudging of complex chords and progressions were to be anticipated. Still, Ari hadn't expected the flourishes.

Jax added in an extra note here, a chord hop there. It should have set Ari's teeth on edge, but instead he wanted to know more. The changes made the music more dynamic. What other ideas did Jax have?

He pulled his bow from his violin as the last notes died out and the audience cheered. Ari set down his violin and grabbed his water—adrenaline was drying his mouth. When he'd swallowed, he said, "Once again I'd like to thank Jax Hall for assisting us tonight while we wait for our regular pianist."

"I'm not exactly on Ari's level." Jax flashed the audience a self-effacing smile. "As some of you may have guessed, I've never played any of this music before. So I hope you're not too disappointed." He winked.

Naomi, finishing off her own drink break, laughed into the microphone. "You're doing just fine, Jax. Just try to keep it up on this next song."

"Oh, darling, I'll always try to keep it up with you."

Ari reset his violin and passed the bow over the strings—a quick hello to the instrument, a habit of long standing.

"I wrote this song when my sister got married." The crowd *aww*ed, as they always did.

Ari looked to Naomi and Jax to make sure they were ready, and so it began.

He had played this song countless times, yet he couldn't help but sneak glances at Jax. His whole body seemed to vibrate with the music, as if he could feel Ari's bars with his body.

When they arrived at the octave jump, Ari expected him to fumble it, but he managed it ably. Jax the bartender did not play the piano "passingly," as he'd told Ari before they took the stage. He didn't have the polished accuracy of a professional performer, but he seemed to have a natural feel for the music and the instrument. He played with his whole body, not just his fingers.

As the song came to a close, Jax gave a little flourish that sent blood rushing through Ari's fingers and ears, and before he could second-guess himself, he mimicked the flourish and added his own.

Jax's head snapped up. Their eyes met. And after the barest hint of a pause, a smirk played across Jax's mouth. Then he bent over the piano once again and responded to Ari's sally. And then Ari answered, and—

And before he knew it they were playing something new, something just for them, leaving Naomi behind, making it up as they went, using the original progressions and chords from the song to build something unique, responding to each other's interpretation. At times they played together; others they waited for a response. It was electric, thrilling. The music poured through Ari's fingers like water over Niagara—too fast, too intense, but perfect, *perfect*—

It barely lasted two minutes, and it left Ari panting and exhilarated, staring at Jax, who stared back over the top of the piano, apparently—at last—unable to counter Ari's musical argument, the audience going wild around the bar.

"And that, comrades," said Murph into the house microphone with an only slightly admonishing glare in Jax's direction, "was the

Rock's own Jax Hall filling in for Rosa Doyle on piano. Rosa's made her way here now, so the musicians are going to take a short break to reset."

Ari set down his violin and executed a bow to the audience, his mind spinning.

He had played with orchestras and professional musicians all over the world prior to the pandemic. He had performed for crowds of thousands. But he had never felt so electrified as he had improvising an ending to one of his songs with a man who'd never played it before today.

As he made his way back to the break room, he tried to untangle his emotions. Under the sheer exhilaration, something felt raw, as though a part of him had been peeled back and exposed to view. How could a casual musician with no formal training read him like that, twist Ari's own music that way? It made him feel unworthy of his education. He should do better.

It made him want to do it again.

"So was it just me," Jax said, and Ari froze as he realized that Jax had followed him, because of course he had. He was one of the musicians, for the moment. "Or was that *completely awesome*?"

Ari wanted to thank him and tell him he had been acceptable. But given the circumstances, that faint praise seemed beyond rude.

Naomi saved him from his dilemma. "Eh, you were all right," she said, nudging Jax with a shoulder.

Good. Let her be the one to damn him.

Jax didn't seem perturbed. No doubt the two of them were used to teasing each other—a dynamic that seemed to grow organically between Murph's employees. "I was at least a little bit awesome. You two are incredible, though. That was *so cool*."

He really couldn't stand still—he was bouncing on the balls of his feet, and his fingers were twitching like they wanted to get back to the keys. His cocksure attitude from the stage had dissipated, leaving behind only sweetly enthusiastic charm.

"Thank you for accompanying us," Ari said. "Your performance was admirable."

Jax opened his mouth, but before he could speak, Naomi stepped on his foot. It didn't look accidental. "It was fun," he said, leaving Ari wondering what he might have said. "I hope I didn't screw up too bad."

Ari, who hated when people didn't respect his work, found he could not say so in the face of such earnestness. Especially not since they had led to that invigorating finale. "No," he said. "Not at all."

Naomi was giving him one of her looks—one that she had once translated for him as "Dial down the intensity; you're scaring the civilians." He recognized that he was staring rather intently and forced himself to blink and take a step backward.

"Please excuse me. I need to go over the revised set list with Rosa." They had switched up the songs in order to put the less complicated piano parts earlier in the show. "Would you prefer the check for your services to be sent here or to another address?"

Now Jax blinked, taking a step backward of his own. Ari must have surprised him. "Ah, you don't have to—"

Ari could not allow any misunderstandings on this point. Especially these days. "Jax. Musicians in my employ are paid. I insist."

Jax quirked a small smile. "Well. All right, then. I guess I'll head back to the bar. You want anything?"

Your phone number, Ari thought, and then was horrified at himself for it. Such an overture would be inappropriate. "No, thank you."

"Naomi?"

"Martini, dirty. Hold the innuendo."

"You're no fun."

"That's a nasty rumor."

"Prove it!" was Jax's parting remark as he about-faced and swanned out the door.

Naomi shook her head and grabbed a bottle of water from the counter. "He does like to make a dramatic exit."

Ari was forced to agree.

JAX MADE 147 percent of his usual tips, despite the low-key nature of the evening, the limited audience, and the fact that he spent the first part of the night on the stage. When Ari's set ended, people seemed disinclined to leave, so Rosa and Naomi took a few requests and the tables were pushed back to make room for a dance floor. Jax kept slinging drinks, looking up every few minutes, hoping to see Ari on the stage.

Jax had hardly had a chance to appreciate the man's incredible talent. He only accompanied him on a few songs, and he'd needed all his concentration to focus on his own part, embellishing here and there to cover the fact that he didn't know the music. Jax had only taken a few piano lessons as a kid. He couldn't sight read fast enough to keep up and had just penciled in the chords at the top of the sheet and hoped for the best.

That last song, though, had his blood pumping. The call-and-answer with Ari happened almost by accident.

Jax loved numbers. He was a math guy. To him, music was applied math.

What had happened with Ari on the stage was the closest thing to magic he'd ever experienced. It was... *heady* was a good word. If Naomi hadn't been there, Jax would've offered Ari a blow job right there in the break room.

But when he got offstage, he was only able to half watch the rest of the concert as he filled drink orders and suffered through a semi for the rest of the evening until Naomi and Rosa took their last bows. Jax didn't even get a chance to say goodbye to Ari.

Jax helped Murph close up the bar and rode his bike home in the wee hours. Thankfully London wasn't big enough to make it a long trip, and soon, Jax unlocked the front door. He was greeted by the sound of the TV and the sight of Hobbes sacked out on the living-room couch.

Jax smiled as he toed off his shoes and crept up to his roommate. The deep circles under Hobbes's eyes, which had moved in before Jax met him, had finally dissipated in recent weeks, but even in the low light of the TV, the newly acquired gray was visible in his beard and at his temples. Jax bit his lip and didn't reach out to smooth the hair away from his face. Instead, he grabbed the throw off the back of the couch and gently draped it over him. It wasn't the first time Jax had tucked his friend into bed.

After one last look at that too-handsome face, Jax turned away and switched off the TV. Then he tiptoed out of the room.

"Meow!" Captain Tribby sat in the kitchen doorway, eyeing Jax with an air of impatience and displeasure.

"Hey, Captain Tubs," Jax whispered.

Tribby lurched forward to rub against Jax's shins, then looked up to loudly demand, *Where the fuck you been?*

"Yeah, yeah, meow, meow. Feed me, bitch. I hear you." Jax checked the feed schedule to make sure he wasn't double-feeding, then filled the kibble bowl with a fresh scoop and the water dish, and left the cat to it.

Teeth cleaned and clothes tossed… elsewhere, Jax climbed into bed clad only in his boxers and settled onto his pillow with a sigh. He could still hear the music he and Ari had played, still feel the buzz in his fingers. Jax wondered if Ari would be that precise and commanding in every situation. The implications sent a shiver down his spine.

Though maybe he brought instead the slight stiffness he had offstage, the faint air of condescension. Jax snickered into his pillow, imagining Ari thanking him for a roll in the hay and offering to cover the taxi fare because he would never let a one-night stand pay for their own way home. The image did little to wilt his semi. He considered rolling over to take care of it, but his limbs felt too heavy to move.

As he dropped into unconsciousness, he felt the bed dip under Tribby's not inconsiderable weight and then the warm body curl up against his hip, vibrating with purrs.

Chapter Two

JAX WOKE to bright sunshine and an empty bed—a stark contrast to his dreams of starlight and a heavy body pressing him into the mattress.

He rubbed his eyes and yawned, then blinked at the ceiling as he realized his dreams had starred Ari instead of—well. In any case, it was a welcome change, but now he needed a nice hot shower. It seemed his dick felt owed after yesterday's long work shift.

Afterward, Jax strolled loosely into the kitchen to find Hobbes at the table, drinking one of his health smoothies and looking at his phone. Tribby sat on top of the fridge and eyed Jax as he moved about the feeding room without approaching the cat dishes.

"Morning."

Hobbes grunted. "Barely."

"I work at a bar," Jax reminded him for the umpteenth time. Jax wasn't going to get up for one of Hobbes's 6:00 a.m. jogs after rolling into bed at two.

"Most overqualified bartender in the country."

Jax pretended the sound of the frying pan hitting the stovetop had drowned him out. It was a tossup, really, who was more upset by Jax's current lack of PhD—his mom or Hobbes.

Jax made eggs and toast with tomatoes, slid into the seat opposite Hobbes, and ignored him as he made his way through a much-deserved breakfast. So he was surprised when Hobbes said, "Jesus, kid, I think you're actually drooling."

Startled, Jax looked up. "What?" He shoved another bite into his mouth.

"Video from last night."

"Video?" Jax said dumbly. Why would anyone take video of him tending bar?

Hobbes shook his head. "Murph sent it." He tipped his head toward Jax's phone, which sat quietly on the counter where Jax had left it last night.

Phone retrieved, Jax found several missed messages in the group chat.

Murph: Hobbes! You missed your boy's debut as musical accompaniment.

He'd linked to a YouTube video. The thumbnail preview titled it *Ari Darvish and Pianist Battle Onstage*. Apprehensive, Jax clicked the link.

The video quality was shit, but damn, their performance was not. The recorder caught them both in the shot, and for the two minutes of the video, it was pretty damn obvious that Jax and Ari were in their own little world. Well, Jax was, at least. His eyes only left the piano keys to glance at Ari.

Hobbes wasn't wrong about Jax's obvious interest.

When the video ended, Hobbes said, "See? Drooling."

"I was not drooling," Jax snipped as he scrolled through the chat comments.

Naomi: It was certainly something. Too bad you couldn't join us, Calvin.

Hobbes: I think I'm glad I didn't if Jax was like this all night.

Hobbes: Only Jax could eye-fuck a stranger on stage and feel no shame.

Murph: Shame! The views are racking up.

Murph: Think of the business!! $$$

Murph: Jax, how much more beer do we need??

Jax snorted and, ignoring that his roommate was right across from him, typed into the chat.

Jax: Easily answered as soon as I figure out how to predict the likely number of new customers per 1000 views.

Jax: Also, there was no eye-fucking! Well... not on stage.

Naomi: Jacob Stirling Hall.

Hobbes: Gross.

17

Murph: you can do all the eye fucking you want, b'y, so long as it brings me customers.

Naomi: Way to make him sound like a sex worker.

Hobbes: Don't give him ideas.

Jax: Snort. I'd be way out of Murph's price range. Have you seen my ass????

"Unfortunately," Hobbes said aloud.

"It's not my fault you're terminally heterosexual." He swiped the last of his toast crust through the egg yolk and popped it in his mouth. "Late shift today?"

After one last text—which must not have been to the group chat, since Jax's phone didn't ping with a notification—Hobbes looked up. "I'm off, actually. Apparently miracles are real."

Jax's eyebrows shook hands with his hairline. "Wow. Lucky guy. Big plans?"

"Wouldn't you like to know."

Jax *would* like to know, which was why he asked, but he accepted the boundary. It was probably healthy; they didn't have a lot of them left. That was what happened when you moved into someone's house to feed their cat when they were in the hospital on a ventilator.

"Well, have fun," he said absently as an email notification popped up on his phone. The sender came up truncated—OFFICE OF REGISTR—

Wincing, Jax cleared the notification. He looked up to see if Hobbes had caught him, but no, he was in the clear. "Think I'm going to call Sam," he offered. "She and George are thinking about visiting sometime. Might be nice to actually meet my nibling."

Sam had given birth at the beginning of the pandemic. After that, she and George moved out of Toronto to his family's Muskoka cabin to wait things out.

"Yeah?" Hobbes smiled. "Well, we've got the extra room. They're welcome to stay."

And that right there? That was the Problem. A guy shouldn't smile at Jax like that over breakfast while inviting Jax's relatives to stay in his house and expect Jax not to fall in love with him. "Thanks,

Hobbes." Then he narrowed his eyes. "You're not going to abduct Alice, are you?"

Hobbes rolled his eyes. "I work with kids all day. Trust me, I get my fill."

Privately Jax doubted that. He had observed Hobbes at work and knew the soft heart that lurked under his lab-coat-lumberjack exterior. "Uh-huh. I'm watching you."

The conversation was over, though. Hobbes stood, ruffled Jax's hair, and moved toward the front hall closet for his shoes. "Have a nice day, honey."

Lord. Okay, he definitely needed to call his sister.

But maybe he'd watch that video one more time first.

"ARI?"

Ari didn't look up from his music, just kept tapping his pencil on the top of the piano, trying to recall the exact notes from the night before. He couldn't ethically use them for anything—not without Jax's permission—but, irrationally, he wanted to remember them, even if it wouldn't recreate the experience.

"There you are."

Finally he looked up from the paper to see Afra striding toward the piano next to the window in his sixth-story loft. She took her customary seat on the ultramodern couch along the wall and set her purse down next to her. "You haven't been answering my calls. *Or* texts."

Ari didn't text much, as a rule. Modern phones made the eventuality of carpal tunnel a near certainty, and he needed his wrists in peak condition. His ancient BlackBerry allowed him to send the occasional text without sacrificing range of movement. "I've been working."

"Oh?" She shifted forward in her seat and cocked her head as he closed his eyes and moved his fingers over the keys. Jax didn't have perfect recall of the music, so perhaps he'd been basing his runs on F instead of C here? Ari tried a few variations. Closer, but not quite....

"That sounds familiar."

"Hmm?" He tried again. There—a different chord inversion, a back-and-forth that walked up the keyboard.

Afra was quiet for a moment while he scribbled down the notes. Then, as he lifted his head, intending to retrieve his violin to attempt to recall his reply, the studio filled with tinny, poor-quality audio.

That's me and Jax.

Startled, he closed the keyboard cover. "Where did you get that?" he asked, barely repressing the urge to snatch up her phone.

Afra didn't answer him as she continued to watch the video. "I thought you said Naomi asked Gary to play for you."

"Gary got food poisoning."

"And Rosa was going to be his backup?"

"Stuck in traffic."

"Huh." She paused the video and raised her eyes. Ari forced his gaze away from her hand. "So who is this guy? Because someone tweeted this video, and it's trending on Twitter in Ontario. Ten thousand views." She nodded at the sheet music on the piano top, and Ari's ears went hot for no reason he could decipher. "And unless my ears deceive me, now it seems like you're trying to catch lightning in a bottle."

His stomach twisted unpleasantly. "I wasn't going to use it for anything." At least now he didn't have to worry about trying to capture the music before it faded from his memory.

A beat. Then Afra opened her mouth, closed it, and frowned. "I didn't think you were. But you didn't answer my question. Who's the pianist?"

"His name is Jax Hall. He works at the Rock." It was safest to stick to bare facts. Every syllable that came out of his mouth would reveal him further. Though really, his sister knew him better than anyone. She'd figure him out eventually. "I was fortunate he was able to step in at the last minute."

"I'll say." Afra hit Play on the video again. "Not a great technical player, but he's got good energy. And he was able to riff on your song pretty well."

"He didn't know it," Ari said, unable to help the note of marvel in his tone. "He only had twenty minutes to learn the songs." Perhaps not impressive for a professional, but Jax wasn't. By his own admission, he'd only taken a handful of lessons as a child.

Afra quirked a smile. "You've got a big musical boner, eh?"

Ari shot her a look. "There is no such thing."

"Uh-huh, sure there isn't. And you definitely don't have one for the gorgeous bartender at the Rock. I perfectly understand you."

Ari scowled and turned to the kitchen. His throat was suddenly very dry. "Would you like a glass of water?"

"Sure." Afra followed him into the kitchen and leaned against the breakfast bar. "So. Since you're trending… I'm going to up the social-media schedule a bit. Maybe you could film some 'in rehearsal' stuff for Insta?"

He scowled. "You know I hate—"

"Yes, yes, boohoo. But you know Noella's going to be blowing up your phone in twenty minutes, because that YouTube video isn't making you any money, but something else could be."

Ari blew out a frustrated breath and drank some of his water. He knew that Afra wasn't simply not wrong but was in fact very right. Didn't mean he was happy about it. It was why she took care of things managerial and he played the music. She was just… better at that stuff.

"Fine. Have her email me a list of what she wants and I'll make it happen."

Afra grinned, triumphant. "Excellent."

Ari waved her back to the couch, and together they settled into comfortable seating.

"So, sounds like the break is helping creativity." She tipped her head toward the piano.

Ari pressed his lips together. Last night hadn't just been an electric connection with another person; it was the first music he'd written in almost six months. When the vaccine finally become widely available, Afra had created an intense cross-continent tour schedule that left Ari exhausted at the end of every day. He had hoped some rest might bring the notes back to him, but the past week had been uneventful until last night.

"Ah. Well. Last night was good, right? You obviously haven't lost it." She tipped over to bump their shoulders together.

"Indeed."

Afra's phone pinged, and she glanced at it before setting it down. "Do you ever wonder if teaching Maman how to text was a mistake?"

"Maman is an extremely intelligent woman who would have figured out the basics of texting without your assistance." Ari took a sip of his water. Shame he hadn't made chai.

"Bitch," Afra grumbled.

Ari didn't smirk. "What does she want?"

"Dinner. She wants everyone to come over tonight." Afra wrinkled her nose and twisted her water glass in her hands.

"Has she been asking again?"

Afra huffed, which was as good as a yes. Ever since Ari came out in college, their parents had focused all their grandchildren desires onto Afra. Once Afra passed her thirty-fifth birthday, the hints morphed into questions edging on demands.

"I'm sorry." He touched her arm gently, and she allowed it for a moment.

Then she pushed her hair behind her ears. "So, please tell me you're coming to dinner with me and Ben? Don't let me be the only disappointing child who shows up."

His lips quirked. "Of course. I wouldn't want to abandon you."

"Exactly." Before she could say more, her phone rang. "It's Ben. Sorry, just— Hi." Her voice softened on the word, and she tilted her head as she listened to her husband on the other end of the line. She had always been that way when it came to Ben. Ari hadn't met many of her boyfriends before him, but right from the start, she had spoken about and looked at Ben like he was something precious. A soft pang of jealousy hit below Ari's heart, but he pushed it away.

"I'm about to head there now…. Yes, Ari is still alive, and he's coming tonight. He says hi." She cast the stink eye in his direction, as if he might change his mind or forget in the next few hours. "Yeah, see you soon. Love you."

"What time for dinner?" He stood with her and followed her to the door.

"Maman says five. So I'll see you then?" He nodded. Once upon a time they wouldn't have eaten until seven or later, but these days his father tired early. "Good. Don't obsess over hot piano man so much that you forget to compose, or that you wear it out." Her gaze flicked down and up, and then she was gone before Ari could scrape his chin off the floor.

He honestly tried to compose something, but he couldn't seem to keep his hands from wandering toward his phone and pulling up that video one more time.

The performance was as electric in the viewing as it had been in the playing. Even through the poor lighting, anyone would be able to see the look of intensity on his face and read it for what it was—profound joy.

And Jax was as captivating in pixelated video as he was in person. The way he played with his whole body, the acute concentration on his face, the looks he kept shooting Ari—

Fuck, Afra was right. He had a massive music boner for Jax Hall. Ari dropped his head onto the piano keys. The discordant notes punctuated his feelings.

He was an idiot. His mother would not be pleased if he brought home a bartender. Which was the least of the issues.

Jax was probably not interested—but before he could finish the thought, an image of Jax giving him sultry elevator eyes flashed through his mind. So Jax was probably interested in *sex*, but judging from Naomi's comments, that was all he was interested in.

Ari lifted his head and let it drop back onto the keys.

His phone rang in his hand, and he raised his head enough to read the screen. *Noella Johnson.*

Shit.

Ari did not want to talk to his producer today, but he should answer. It wasn't Noella's fault that she was contractually obligated to ask him questions about his creative nonprogress.

The phone stopped ringing. A few moments later a text came through.

Hi Ari, just checking in. Why don't we set up a chat next week and you can update me on how things are going. I'll send a calendar invite. Ciao!

Ari lay his head back on the keys.

ARI EASED his white hand-me-down BMW 3 Series into his parents' driveway and thrust it into Park. He wondered if he could find a way to swing the system of ready drivers and hired cars he enjoyed on tour back home in London. Did anyone still have their own chauffeur? And what would that cost? Probably outside his budget, he thought ruefully, and probably for the best. Afra would never let him live down that kind of pretentious douchebaggery just because he hated driving.

He could always take a Lyft, but he hated waiting. Unfortunately, admitting that seemed worse than wanting a chauffeur.

The scent of frying eggplant hit him even before he opened the door, which meant his father was preparing *khoresh bademjan*. The stew had been Ari's favorite growing up. Ari's mother had done most of the cooking, but this was his father's specialty.

It was the dish Ari had prepared when he came out to them at seventeen. He'd wanted the comfort of food he loved in case it didn't go well. Of course, it actually went fine if you didn't count the mortification he experienced when his parents revealed that they'd known for years.

It could have been worse, but the end result was that now Ari associated khoresh bademjan with someone springing something on someone else. He felt like he was walking into an ambush.

Knowing his parents, he probably *was*, but at least it would be the mostly loving kind. Mentally fortifying himself, he took the three steps up to the front door, knocked twice, and let himself in. "Baba? Maman?"

"Befarma! In the kitchen!" his mother called cheerfully.

He found her sitting at the breakfast bar, watching as his father lifted the eggplant, lamb, and onion into the simmering tomato sauce. In the time since Ari had left on his last tour, his father's hair had finished going white, but he seemed stronger now than he had a few months ago. He was recovering.

How much further he'd recover was anyone's guess.

"Hi, Maman." Ari leaned over and kissed both his mother's cheeks, then crossed the kitchen to greet his father. "Baba." He bent so his father could kiss his forehead the way he always had until he turned sixteen and was suddenly too tall. "You look well."

His father gave him a narrow-eyed look. "I'm not ready to shuffle off this mortal coil just yet. Stop looking so surprised."

Apparently he'd been reading Shakespeare again.

"Not surprised," Ari placated. "Happy."

"Hmm." He brandished a wooden spoon at Ari. "Go and make chai for your mother, hmm?"

Ari quirked a smile. "Yes, Baba."

The motions of home comforted him—filling the kettle, locating the correct loose-leaf tea, warming the teapot. "Where's Afra?"

"You know your sister," Maman said, smiling even as she shook her head. "She was born in Iran."

Afra did just fine getting Ari to gigs on time, scheduling his life, ensuring everything was where he needed it when he needed it. She was only ever late for dinner at their parents'. But it wasn't like Ari could tell them that.

"Perhaps they have big news to share and they want to make an entrance," Ari's father put in.

Ari elected to excuse himself from that conversation and paid a lot of attention to measuring out the tea.

"Regardless of what your father thinks, we aren't going to be around forever," his mother said, picking up the thread.

Unfortunately this situation called for something stronger than chai.

"We just want to see you and your sister settled."

A *lot* stronger.

"I have an apartment," Ari said, keeping his voice as level as he could. But it was a losing battle. His parents loved him. They wanted him to be happy, and they accepted that he was gay. It was being *single* that was the problem. Or recently, single and only in town for half the year. "I have a good career. I'm settled."

The kettle whistled an interruption, but he got no reprieve.

"You need someone to look after you," his mother said. "Afra can't run around after you forever. She has Ben. She isn't getting any younger, you know. What will you do when she has children?"

Afra was thirty-eight. Ari didn't even know if she and Ben *wanted* kids, but he was extremely well acquainted with his parents' arguments in favor of them.

"Afra is an independent woman. What makes you think she would quit her job?" He looked pointedly at her. "*You* didn't."

Ari's parents had emigrated from Iran thirtysomething years ago, after the Islamic Revolution in 1978 and the Iraq-Iran war. They told Ari and Afra they wanted a better life for their children, and Ari knew they had never regretted their choice—especially because of what life would have been like for him living there as a gay man. They had both worked at the hospital until Ari began touring at twenty-two.

They'd gone back when the pandemic hit. Ari's mother was a pulmonologist.

"She wouldn't have to quit working to take a job closer to home," his mother pointed out. "She's done other jobs. That law office she managed would kill to have her back. Or she could hire staff!"

That was probably true, but…. "And in the meantime, what?" Ari asked. He reminded himself to breathe deeply while he took down

26

the teacups. "I'm supposed to meet a man, marry him, and make him my tour manager?"

"What about that nice intern?" his father put in, forestalling what was doubtless a comment from Ari's mother that he could just give up touring completely. "What is his family like? Does he have a degree?"

Ari's heart migrated to his toes in an attempt to escape his body. "*Theo?*" Now that was a horrifying concept. "Theo is an infant, Baba." He was what, maybe twenty? He was still too young to be served in the US, that was for sure. "And even if he weren't, I'm pretty sure he's not interested in men. And I'm not going to hit on an employee!"

"Well, you can't expect Afra to arrange your life indefinitely."

No, that's your *job*, Ari almost said, but fortunately he bit his tongue before the words could escape. "Our work is between the two of us." He poured a cup of chai and set it in front of his mother. "It would be disrespectful of me to discuss any changes with you before I talk to Afra, and I won't do it."

It was going to be a long evening.

Afra and Ben did eventually arrive and took most of the brunt of Ari's parents' meddling. Ari wanted to jump to their defense, but he'd exhausted himself deflecting them earlier. By the time the leftover khoresh bademjan was packed into Tupperware for Ari to bring home and the last of the *tahdig* had been eaten, he was more than ready for a change of scenery.

But if he went back to his apartment, he'd only stew. There was no way he'd get any composing done in this mental state. He'd only end up dwelling on the failure of the past few months.

"You don't have to go home, but you can't stay here," he muttered to himself as he slid behind the wheel.

And suddenly he knew exactly where he wanted to go.

Chapter Three

THE VIDEO really must have been a hit, because there was already a lineup to get in the door when Jax got to the Rock at seven thirty. He parked his bike, cut the engine, slung his body off of it, and tucked his helmet under his arm.

"Hey, Bruce," he greeted the bouncer, bumping fists with him.

"Hall." Bruce shook his head. "You know you're supposed to go in the back."

"Bruce. Buddy." Jax nodded at his bike. "Look where I'm parked. To get to the back I'd have to walk through the alley."

Bruce gave him an unimpressed look, keeping one eye on the crowd. "Aren't you the one who's always giving Murph a hard time about the spiders?"

Okay, so the man had a point, but— "Aw, come on. You're not really going to make me walk around, are you? These are new boots!"

Bruce looked, which was when Jax knew he had him. They were nice boots. And with the crowd lined up tonight—looked like about 70 percent women—Bruce's cut of the tip jar was probably looking pretty good. He rolled his eyes and moved over to let Jax pass—not that he wouldn't have anyway. He just liked to give Jax a hard time.

But before Jax walked in, something caught his eye, something that didn't quite fit—a shock of curly dark hair, broad shoulders with posture a little too good for casual standing in line to get into a bar. And a peacoat that looked like it cost more than Jax's rent.

Ari.

Jax clapped Bruce on the shoulder. "Just one sec."

It only took him a few seconds to squeeze through the crowd. Technically speaking it wasn't actually all that crowded, but a year of restricted public gatherings would change your perspective. When he closed his hand around Ari's forearm, the man jumped.

"Sorry," Jax said. "Ari. Hey. Jax Hall, from last night."

Ari looked at him as though he might have lost his mind, which—yeah, okay, maybe last night hadn't been that forgettable. Though it could, in his opinion, have been a lot more memorable. Or memorable for more fun reasons. "Hello."

"Hey," Jax repeated, then immediately felt stupid. "Look, what're you doing waiting here? Come on." He let go of Ari's arm, but he didn't need to check if the man was following him. Jax had a way of getting people to do what he wanted.

"He's with me," he told Bruce as he ushered Ari inside.

The lineup suggested the bar was going to be busy tonight, and inside, everyone was busy preparing for it. The doors would open any moment, and Murph and Naomi were bustling behind the counter, so Jax led the way across the space.

Ari took the seat at the end of the bar, the least desirable one, as it was outside the main traffic route.

Before he left to start slinging drinks, Jax leaned in, his mouth close to Ari's ear—the better to be heard, of course, even though no one was playing anything yet. "What can I get you?"

Ari swallowed. "Ah, why don't you pick for me?"

Oh, what a delightful offer. Jax licked his lips. "Any allergies or dislikes I should avoid?"

"No."

"Good." After a quick deliberation, Jax settled on the most obvious choice. He slipped away and quickly mixed the necessary ingredients.

A few minutes later, he slid a blood-orange drink across the bar top.

"What is it?"

"Coconut rum, orange liqueur, lime juice, grenadine, 7-Up, lemon and lime, with a splash of Irish cream."

Ari lifted an eyebrow and took a cautious sip. "It's good." He licked his lips. "Surprisingly good." He drank some more.

Jax grinned, rapped the bar, and stepped back. "Doors're opening, so I've got other people to serve. But don't go too far, yeah?" Hope bubbled in his belly. He really wanted an opportunity to see where things might go.

Jax made the rounds with a few stacks of coasters as the patrons came in, but then he got back behind the bar to fill orders. Table three needed beer, and then he took a large order from an adorable hipster with pigtails, thick-rimmed glasses, a toque, and a too-big flannel. Jax kind of wanted to take her home and snuggle her. Any other night, he probably would have leaned in and offered to help her finish off her drinks. But her allure didn't hold a candle to Ari at the end of the bar, quietly sipping from his glass.

Jax licked his lips. He knew himself pretty well, and he doubted he'd be looking at anyone else anytime soon.

As soon as he was able, he slid back down the bar and leaned in. "Still enjoying that drink?"

"Hm." Ari took another sip, which Jax took as an affirmative. "So, I owe you something." He pulled a folded paper out of his pocket and handed it over.

Jax snatched it, lips quirking. "Are you passing notes? Will I have to check yes or no?"

"It's a check," Ari said dryly. "For your… services the other day."

Jax grinned and slipped it into his pocket. "Thanks. Not necessary, but thanks."

"I told you—"

Jax waved that off. "That you always pay your musicians. So thanks."

Ari licked his lips—an unconscious echo of Jax's deliberate flirtation?—and leaned forward. "I was wondering—why did you become a bartender?"

Not a surprising question. Everybody always wanted to know that, especially once they learned more about him.

"Well," Jax drawled. He crossed his arms conspiratorially on the bar top, and Ari did likewise. "Years ago, a small baby was left in a basket on the back steps of this very bar." He tipped his head toward the back door. "Poor Murph—scared the living daylights out of him when he found it in the morning. What could he do but take the child in and raise it as his own?" Ari narrowed his eyes, and Jax grinned. "As I'm sure you've guessed by now, that child was me, and now I help out around the place in repayment."

Ari gave Jax the flattest of looks. "It's truly amazing. First, that Murph was running a bar at the age of twelve or thirteen." Jax's grin grew. "Second, that I never noticed you in all the years I worked here."

"Did I mention that I'm very good at keeping a low profile?"

"Now that," Ari said, an actual smile threatening the corners of his mouth if Jax was not mistaken, "is the most blatant lie I have ever heard. And I just heard you mythologize yourself as a barkeep's Moses."

Jax laughed and threw one hand over his heart. "A direct hit."

The smile did come out now, and it was every bit as devastating on Ari's sharp features as Jax had suspected. Despite his stiffness and formality, Ari had a rather expressive face. "I bet."

"More seriously," Jax said with a shrug, "I like making people happy, giving them what they want."

Ari nodded and, to his credit, accepted the rather vague answer. Thank God, because the truth was embarrassing and frankly no one's business but Jax's.

Still. Jax smiled and fluttered his lashes. All things considered, his seduction of Ari was going very well indeed.

ARI'S PULSE jumped as Jax leaned into his space. His startlingly blue eyes shone with interest, and when he lowered his lashes, shadows played across his sharp cheekbones. Ari wanted to caress those shadows.

"What about you?" Jax asked. "Why music?"

Ari took another sip of his drink as he pondered how best to answer. "I like making people happy."

"Touché," Jax murmured with a pleased little half smile. Ari's heart skipped a beat.

31

Before Ari could figure out what to say next, Jax ducked away to pour another customer a drink.

Ari's seat provided an excellent view of Jax as he worked, and it was a magnificent one. Not least because he was so frequently afforded a very favorable view of Jax's not inconsiderable ass.

Said viewing was interrupted by Murph, who was apparently taking a break from pouring beers.

"G'day. Been a while since you were here for a drink." He eyed the cocktail glass. "Not exactly your usual fare."

True. It was a far cry from a gin and tonic. "I decided to live dangerously and let the bartender pick for me."

Murph hummed and gave the half-finished drink a closer look. "Is that rum, orange, and 7-Up?"

Ari tipped his head. "Among other things. It's actually not as terrible as it sounds."

"I bet it's not," Murph laughed. "That there is Sex with the Bartender."

Ari nearly choked. "I'm sorry?"

"The name of the drink." His eyes were dancing, and he did nothing to hide his grin. "Not very subtle of Jax, but then again, subtle has never been his métier."

No, that much was obvious. Ari had to admit there was a certain refreshing charm in being pursued so boldly, even if it was outside his realm of experience. He opened his mouth to ask about him— how long Murph had known Jax, what he was doing here—before he realized that would be invasive. He'd already asked Jax. If Jax wanted him to know the truth, he would tell Ari himself.

In the meantime he shouldn't pry.

"Show's about to start," Murph commented, nodding toward the stage. "Oi! Jax!" He swatted at him with a bar towel. "You're up."

Jax ripped off a lazy salute, unslung his own towel from his shoulder, and leaned forward with his elbow on the bar to drop a paper umbrella in a patron's cocktail. "That's my cue."

A general cheer went up as the house lights went down until only the stage was illuminated.

Naomi stepped up to the stage first, wearing heeled cowboy boots, jeans, a white top, and a red guitar slung over her shoulder. As she was plugging in her patch cord, Kayla, the redheaded drummer, stepped up behind the kit and twirled a stick in her fingers.

Jax jogged up last. Ari let himself appreciate the view of his lanky body and broad shoulders, the way his jeans clung to the curve of his ass—who could blame them?—and long legs. The second the spotlight hit him, he seemed to grow three inches taller. He pushed up the sleeves of his Henley and grinned at the crowd as he made his way to the piano on the left.

His eyes met Naomi's across the stage. She rolled hers, and Jax grinned wider.

"How's it going, London!" Naomi half shouted into the microphone. Ari winced. He knew she had to hype up the crowd—he'd taken his share of turns doing the same when he worked here. He'd just always hated it.

The crowd cheered in response. Sometimes it was difficult to get much energy out of them so early in the evening, before the music had actually started and the alcohol flowed more freely.

"Unless I miss my guess, half of you are first-timers." Naomi plucked out a few bendy notes. "So I'm Naomi, and that's Kayla on the drums."

Kayla hammered out a quick solo and ended with a cymbal crash. "Hey."

"And if you're here because of last night's viral video sensation, you probably recognize Jax Hall tickling the ivories."

Jax picked out a quick, light melody that sounded suspiciously like "Strangers in the Night."

Naomi huffed a laugh at him, but fondness seeped into her feigned exasperation. "Jax's a man of many talents, the most obvious being his ability to flirt with an entire room of people at the same time."

Jax inclined his head in acknowledgment of her glowing praise.

"Since we've got some newcomers tonight, I'll give you the 411. This"—she picked up the request jar from Jax's piano; it already held several slips of paper and five-dollar bills—"is where

33

you put your requests. You can find the slips on your tables or at the bar if you run out. Keep in mind this is a lighthearted entertainment set, and bored people don't buy alcohol, so if you request Leonard Cohen you're probably gonna be disappointed. We've got a couple more musicians who'll rotate in over the course of the evening. Happy hour starts at nine." She glanced at Kayla. "Did I forget anything?"

"Guitar pick?"

"Got it."

"Sound check."

"Done it."

"Ritual shaming of Jax."

Naomi turned from Kayla to Jax, then shook her head. "Well, I tried."

Kayla grinned. "Reminder to tip your bartenders?"

Naomi pointed at her. "Yes. *That*." Then she returned her attention to Jax. "Anything to add?"

Jax played a quiet F chord and a B flat. Then he settled his hands against the keyboard and leaned into his mic. "Welcome to the Rock!"

After this expert buildup by Naomi, the cheers came even louder. The act had chemistry. Ari, who normally kept himself carefully reserved when he watched other musicians lest he accidentally betray anything that might be interpreted as condescension, found himself clapping in encouragement.

When the noise quieted, Jax nodded to Naomi, who adjusted her capo and then glanced at Kayla for the count.

The guitar part came in first, a cheerful riff of twanging strings that seemed familiar. Ari knew this song. So did everyone else in the bar, apparently. But he couldn't place it until Jax licked his lips and leaned into the mic again.

Oh my God.

"'Party in the USA'?" Ari said, glancing down the bar at Murph, who had taken over. A third bartender had brought up another keg and was installing it under the bar. Henry—Ari remembered him from his own days working here.

Murph shrugged. "What can I say? B'y enjoys flouting expectations."

Another understatement,'Ari thought, and he shook his head as Jax bounced out the chords, singing his heart out and apparently having the time of his life. "That he does."

Ari quickly realized he ought to have taken a seat closer to the stage. But he also realized he would not be safe there. Jax's sheer magnetism drew him from across the room. Ari wouldn't trust himself within ten feet of the man when he was playing.

He was so *different* from Ari—lively, unrestrained, almost wild with enjoyment. In just a few moments, his cheeks flushed with exertion.

It was… captivating.

In only a few songs, Ari's fingers itched for an instrument of his own. But he didn't want to play along with Jax right now. He wanted to capture Jax in song the way Jax had captured him—the fluidity of his movements, the way his lips twitched as he skipped past a mistake, throwing out a wink in case someone in the audience had noticed. The way he drew the other musicians into his orbit and played off them and they him. If Ari could encapsulate that energy, that movement….

Hastily he shook himself out of his trance and glanced at his drink. He'd finished it at some point while he was watching.

Sex with the Bartender. If Naomi were to be believed, this was likely a perfectly serious overture, but one Ari was not going to respond to tonight. Instead he slipped out his wallet, left a twenty on the bar, and nodded to Murph as he slid off the stool.

Ari tapped his fingers against the steering wheel as he drove and hummed along with the beat. Once finally inside his loft, he tossed his wallet and keys without seeing where they landed and beelined for the piano. He played the bars running through his head. No, not quite right. He shifted into a suspended fourth. Better, but… maybe the key should be G instead?

Hours later several pages of sheet music were covered in scribbles and Ari was rubbing bleary eyes. He stood from the piano and shuffled into the bedroom, where he undressed, quickly passed his toothbrush over his teeth, fell into bed, and passed out hard.

Chapter Four

JAX PULLED out of warrior's pose and into mountain. He pressed his palms together and breathed deeply, enjoying the moment to just feel the warmth in his muscles.

He was still cooling down with his bottle of lemon water when the doorbell rang.

"Surprise!"

"Sam!" His sister stood on his doorstep, her husband, George, behind her, holding Alice. "You're early."

"We are. We were able to get away earlier than expected." She stepped close and wrapped her arms around Jax in a tight hug.

God, it had been well over a year since he'd last felt her arms holding him, and the smell of her perfume made his eyes sting. He squeezed her tighter. Memories of their childhood overtook him—his small hand in hers as she brought him to school for the first time, a giantess of nine years to his four; Sam at fifteen gently cleaning his scraped hands, knees, and face after he'd been in a fight; resting his head on her shoulder and asking if she still loved him even though she'd found him kissing a boy—and Jax pressed his face into her neck and inhaled.

"Not to break up the moment," George said, "but I need to pee."

Jax stepped back with a choked laugh and ushered them into the house. "Come in, come in."

Sam took baby Alice from her husband's arms and pressed her into Jax's as Jax directed George to the bathroom. Then, his hosting duties discharged, he curled his arms around the baby and stared at her beautiful face. Alice stared back.

"Hi, Alice."

"Jax?"

"Yeah, I'm your Uncle Jax."

"Jax!" Grinning, Alice pressed forward and touched his face with her tiny hands. "My Jax." She stroked his face and wrinkled her nose to feel two days' worth of growth.

His eyes prickled, and he pressed his face into her soft baby curls. "Yes, your Jax." Their frequent FaceTimes had been a poor replacement for getting to hold this precious baby girl. Alice squirmed, and Jax loosened his grip so she could lean back to see his face again.

George returned from the bathroom, and Jax shook himself out of his reverie. "Sorry. Come, sit." He brought them into the living room. Jax and Alice kept their eyes locked on each other. He wasn't sure how many minutes were lost to their stare down, but Jax never wanted to take his eyes off her again.

Though when Sam suggested Alice was in a need of a diaper change, Jax gladly handed her over to her dad.

"You're looking good, Jax." Sam shifted closer on the couch.

"You too."

She touched his hair as though she couldn't help it—it was getting long, but he'd gotten out of the habit of regular cuts. "How are you doing? Really." Her eyes were searching. Jax doubted that she missed the premature gray in his beard—plague stress. "Please tell me you've taken a proper rest now that your big brain isn't needed to analyze an international crisis."

He exhaled shakily. "I'm trying."

"Good. Still working at the bar?"

"Yeah. It's nice."

"I bet." Her lips twitched with a smile, but her blue eyes stayed grave. "Getting to show off. You used to love playing piano for Mom's guests."

"I can't say that's a lie."

"Attention whore."

"Maybe."

They smiled at each other, and for a moment, Jax enjoyed the silence and the weight of her presence. His big sister was here.

"What about your PhD?"

38

Jax pressed his lips together and looked away.

"Jax...."

"I can't." Jax hadn't been back to Cambridge since the day they closed the campus. Even now that it was open again, he couldn't bring himself to return. He hadn't been able to bear the thought of Grayling's empty office, and he'd avoided it for the past year, but the thought of the office being occupied by someone new hurt even more.

"Can't or won't?"

"Either? Both?" What did it matter? The result was the same.

She said nothing for a long moment, probably studying his face. She did that a lot. "You're almost done—"

"I know." Jax was all too aware of how close he was to finishing his PhD. The only thing left was his defense. But talking about his mathematical program for predicting the growth of various populations in ecosystems seemed pointless after spending a year modeling pandemic spread and death rates. "I'm just... tired."

"I know." Sam ran her hand over his head again. "But you can't tell me you want to stay an ABD forever." *All But Dissertation.* Once upon a time, he'd mocked people for failing to go the distance—privately, in his own head. He wasn't *that* much of an asshole.

"I'm not twenty anymore," Jax pointed out. Having the paper didn't seem important somehow.

"Jax, Grayling wouldn't want—"

"Don't tell me what he would have wanted. You didn't know him." Sam had never visited him in Cambridge.

"Maybe not in person, but I knew him through you. And everything you have ever told me leads me to believe that he would want you to finish what you started."

A sharp pain seized his heart, and Jax scowled. He would not feel guilty. But before he could open his mouth to reply, the front door opened.

"Jax? Whose car is in the driveway?"

Hobbes was home. Saved by the doc.

Or maybe not. Sam took one long look at Hobbes—the slightly hangdog face he had, like he'd just been scolded for leering at a waitress or something, the thick groomed beard peppered with gray… the lollipop still tucked into the pocket of his scrub top.

Jax was so incredibly busted.

Oh my God, Sam mouthed at him. George turned his face away to disguise a laugh, and Jax sighed resignedly. "Hey, Hobbes."

"Oh my God," Sam whispered, out loud this time.

"Shut up!" Jax hissed back. This whole arrangement depended on Hobbes remaining blissfully ignorant of Jax being even remotely capable of sincere romantic attachment. If Hobbes started feeling guilty, it'd ruin everything.

Hobbes looked at Jax—raised his eyebrows at Alice, which, fair; Jax did not strike most people as the comfortable-with-children type, except in the sense that they thought he still was one—and then got a look at Sam.

Those hazel eyes widened and then—

"Hey!" Jax said reflexively. "Eyes up here!"

"Oh my God," Sam said loud enough for everyone to hear this time.

Hobbes ran a hand over his face in obvious and deserved mortification. "Hi. Sorry. Dr. Calvin Tate, Jax's roommate. You must be Sam?" He held out his hand to shake, drew it back, offered it again. "Wow, I made that awkward. Jax's told me a lot about you, although he didn't mention the uncanny resemblance."

Sam shook his hand and accepted his explanation. "Nice to meet you. This is my husband, George"—they shook too—"and the little barnacle hiding in Jax's sadness beard is Alice."

Jax felt rather than saw Alice turn her face out, then back in toward him. He hoped his beard didn't give her a rash.

"She does really seem to love the stubble," Hobbes commented, taking off his shoes. "That's nothing, though. You should've seen it in the winter. Thought the birds were going to nest in it."

Almost overnight, Jax had gone from a near complete inability to grow facial hair to the kind of guy who could use a shave again at five o'clock, so he didn't think it was fair of Hobbes to pick on him for wanting to experiment. Especially since—"You could scrub pots with yours, old man, so don't be casting stones."

"Speaking of pots. Did you offer our guests a drink?"

Jax started, guilty. "It's possible I got hung up on baby cuddles?"

Hobbes's expression softened. "Yeah, that'll happen. Can I get anybody anything?"

Sam and George exchanged glances. George said, "That'd be great, actually. Let me help."

Then he abandoned Jax to Sam's less than tender mercies. Rude.

"Well, at least now I know why you never bothered looking for your own place," Sam said lowly.

Jax hid behind Alice, who wouldn't judge him. "It's not like that."

"Oh, so you didn't intentionally attach yourself to someone who could never want you back, thus saving you from experiencing the potential disappointment of a failed relationship?"

God. Now Jax was mortified. "Nothing about this was premeditated."

"Uh-huh." Sam bumped his shoulder. "You always did fall in love at the drop of a hat. But he seems nice anyway. By which I mean he seems like an asshole, but in a way that's good for you. Aside from the obvious."

"He is." On all counts.

"*However.*" And her eyes were sparkling, which meant Jax was about to catch even more shit. He couldn't wait. God, he'd missed her. "Word is there's more than one tall, dark, and handsome in your life."

This was more stable ground. Given the choice of examining his feelings for his roommate or his obvious hard-on for a guy he barely knew…. Hell, Jax would've talked about Ari voluntarily. He was *fascinating.* "Truly it's an embarrassment of riches," he agreed.

"Embarrassment my—butt," Hobbes said, returning from the kitchen with George and a tray of glasses and iced tea. "You're medically incapable of that."

Mostly true, so Jax let that slide.

"Have you seen the video?"

"I've been waiting to watch it with Jax for his commentary."

"I've seen it," George said.

"You're in for a treat." Hobbes took his phone out of his pocket. A second later the smart TV came on. "Assuming you enjoy watching Jax make a fool of himself."

"Hey, I make good money making a fool of myself."

Sam gave him a look that said *not as much as you would if you finished your PhD*. Hobbes joined in. George and Alice seemed not to notice or care. Jax liked George more every moment.

"I feel like I should've made popcorn," Hobbes said, "but that would take longer than watching the actual video, so…." He hit Play.

The video had less charm on the big screen, and the sound quality was noticeably worse when played on the built-in TV speakers.

"So, hold on," Sam said before it really got started. "How'd you end up playing in this guy's show anyway? I love you, little brother, but an orchestral quality pianist you are not."

"Dumb luck," Jax admitted cheerfully. "The first pick got food poisoning, and the backup was stuck in traffic."

On the screen, Jax raised his eyes and grinned as Ari responded to his first deviation from the song with an improvised echo, then a longer, more involved challenge.

In his arms, Alice turned toward the screen.

"Oh, you like the music, huh?" Jax asked, bouncing her a little and holding her around her middle so she didn't squirm onto the floor. Their place wasn't exactly babyproofed. The corners of the coffee table were sharp. "Good taste."

"You can't resist, can you?" Sam said, shaking her head. "Someone says 'I dare you to keep up' and it's like they're talking directly to your… disco stick."

George made a noise like he was dying. Hobbes looked at Sam, raised an eyebrow, and tilted his iced tea toward her as though in a toast. "I like you."

In the video, Jax's eyes flickered from the keys to Ari. It was innocent; he hadn't had time for more than a glance, and he'd *needed* to look—had to see where Ari was taking the song, see if

42

he could catch a cue—but it looked for all the world like he was batting his eyelashes.

Which, fair enough. He'd done that too, when Ari came to the bar. But Ari had left without saying goodbye while Jax was in the middle of a set, so it looked like he'd have to work a little harder.

Jax really did love a challenge, dammit.

"You should come out and see the show sometime," he said when the video ended. Maybe she'd let up about his ABD if she could see he was happy doing what he was doing. But of course she'd need a babysitter, and it wasn't like she lived in the area, and—

"We would love to," George said.

"In fact," Sam said, "we'll be getting more chances in the future."

"Oh?" Jax's heart leaped in anticipation.

"As you know, we've both been working almost exclusively from home for the past year, and George's office has officially announced that they won't be reopening—"

Jax swallowed, his mouth suddenly dry.

"—and I've been looking for a change…."

"Put the poor man out of his misery," George suggested.

Jax shot him a grateful look.

"We're moving to London."

"What?" Jax whipped his head round to stare at her. "What? When? Why?"

Sam laughed. "I got a new job here in town. As soon as we can. Actually, that's why we're here this weekend—house hunting."

For a long moment, Jax fish-mouthed in her general direction, too stunned to say anything. Then he lurched across the couch, Alice still in his arms, and wrapped both ladies into his embrace. "Fuck, tell me you're not joking."

"I'm not joking," Sam repeated, her voice sounding suspiciously choked.

"Good."

Alice squirmed, and Jax pulled back. "Hey, hear that, Hobbes? My sister is moving to town."

43

"I heard. We'll be glad to have more friendly faces nearby," he added with a raise of his glass.

"Thanks," George said. "It was a long time coming. Sam's always thought about moving back, and now that Jax is based out here… no-brainer."

Jax beamed at his brother-in-law, then at Hobbes, then Sam, who laughed at him and ruffled his hair. Nothing could get him down right now.

ARI SPREAD his notes out on his closed grand piano and then lifted his violin to his chin, ready to try to make sense and order out of the chaos.

He was still at it—alternating between scribbling on the pages and testing the notes on the strings—when Afra arrived.

"Come in, Theo. Don't worry about him. If you wait for an artiste to be ready for you, you'll grow old and die."

Ari scowled at his music but refused to otherwise acknowledge her or her digs. She was interrupting him in the early morning when he was working. What did she expect?

"Noted," Theo said softly. "Where should I put…?"

"On the table. I'll get the starving artist."

Ari set his violin on the piano and leaned in to make various notations on the page, perfecting the line. Still, his eyebrows climbed up his forehead even before he turned to her. "I'm hardly poverty-stricken."

"No," Afra agreed. She put her bag down on the coffee table and inched up to the piano so she could see his work. "But you're probably hungry. It's after one."

He blinked at her and then looked at the clock. His stomach gurgled, pleased to have an audience.

It also earned him a big-sisterly look of contempt. "Did you even eat breakfast?"

Not wanting to answer that minefield of a question—did one leftover eggroll count?—Ari put down his pencil and followed her to the table, where Theo was setting out plates and cutlery.

"So what brought on this splurge of writing?" Afra asked him over their lunch of takeout Chinese.

"I felt inspired." How could he tell her that another encounter with the subject of his music boner prompted him to write for hours in an attempt to perfect the piece humming through his veins?

"Inspired." Afra took a bite and chewed it slowly. Then she looked at Theo, the intern she had picked up at the university job fair. "That's basically Ari code for 'I'm writing an opus for the pretty face I met at a bar,'" she said in the teaching tone she had adopted for him.

Theo, who had the babiest of faces, widened his dark brown eyes and nodded very earnestly. "I have seen the video. It is a very pretty face."

"Isn't it? Maybe we should go meet it in person. See the muse for ourselves."

Theo nodded enthusiastically.

After months of working with the pair of them, Ari was not charmed by their double act. "You have jumped to conclusions regarding my inspiration. Your ideas are unsubstantiated."

"Uh-oh, Theo. He's going debate club on us. Better run for it." Her eyes twinkled at Ari: *I see through you.* "Did I ever tell you about his stint on the high school debate team?"

Theo's lips twitched. "No. I bet he was... a formidable opponent."

"Damn right, he was." Afra grinned and launched into one of her favorite stories—the time Ari absolutely destroyed the MC and judges at a formal debate for suggesting the topic of repealing the newly legal gay marriage act. She had never been prouder of him than when he ignored the timer to continue speaking about the damage such debates could have in a high school setting.

"Very cool, Ari," Theo murmured quietly to him as they gathered up all the dirty dishes and cleaned the kitchen.

"I don't know what you've done to do that"—Afra pointed at the piano—"but keep it up." She hugged him tightly and then dragged Theo out of his apartment and left Ari to it.

Only… the piece was almost finished—at least the first draft. It would need tweaking and input from others, but for the moment, Ari's work was nearly done.

And he suddenly felt like he was back where he started— needing to write music and unsure where to begin. But he knew where he could get inspiration.

Hours later, as he sat at the bar watching Jax ham it up while he played "I'm Just a Girl," with Naomi glowing by his side and Kayla behind him on drums with a grin on her face, a lightness filled Ari once again, and he knew more writing would follow this visit too.

He had arrived late enough that he caught the tail end of the first set, the musicians breaking after only one more song. But that hardly mattered, since he'd managed to procure a small table near the stage, and he caught Jax's eye on his way to the break room.

Instead of continuing toward the back, a grinning Jax took the stool opposite Ari. "You're back." The grin segued into a smirk. "Couldn't stay away?"

"Perhaps I'm merely a glutton for punishment," Ari answered wryly, but he could feel an answering smile trying to creep out.

Jax threw his head back and laughed, mouth open wide enough Ari could've counted his fillings if he'd had any. He didn't.

Ari wondered at the extreme enjoyment Jax seemed to get from Ari busting his chops, but perhaps it was all part of the game for him.

"Fair enough." He shook his head. "Well, I can't stick around for too long, because I really do need to go figure out some songs for the next set. But I have enough time to atone for some sins of the past. Just—give me a sec?"

Ari spread his hands. "I am at your disposal."

Jax laughed again, softer this time. "No, you're not. Not yet. But that's okay. You might have noticed I like a challenge."

He slipped away from the table and eeled behind the bar, moving around the other bartenders with familiar touches to waists and shoulders, making space for himself. Ari had never been that at ease in his own skin unless he was playing an instrument, but Jax inhabited his body and the world so seemingly effortlessly, in tune with everything and everyone.

Ari could already hear the melody of it—the smooth tied eighth notes in an arpeggio skipping up and down the scale for violin, the piano always ahead or behind, never quite touching it, as though the violin were playing hard to get.

Perhaps not so appropriate for Jax. But then, maybe it was.

Jax returned a moment later, never seeming to spill a drop or miss a step despite the crowded bar. He deposited a tall champagne flute of sparkling pink liquid in front of Ari. "Voila!"

Ari pulled the drink toward himself, bemused. "Are you going to tell me what this one is called, or do I have to wait for the translation from Murph?"

"Murph wouldn't know anyway. That's prosecco, Bitter Truth Pink Gin, and pink limoncello."

That didn't sound like any cocktail Ari had ever heard of, but he wasn't exactly a connoisseur. He picked it up and took a sip. It had a light fruity flavor, and the sweetness of the limoncello perfectly balanced the bitterness of the gin.

Ari liked it even better than the first drink Jax had made him. "It's delicious. You just came up with it?"

Jax lifted a shoulder like it was nothing. Maybe it *was* nothing; Ari didn't know the first thing about mixing cocktails. He'd only ever played music when he worked here. "I've been thinking about it for a couple days."

That was nice to hear. Maybe *too* nice.

Ari was treading on dangerous ground. He didn't want to lead Jax on. One-night stands simply weren't his style, but he was too intrigued to blow him off. And if he asked to spend time with Jax because Jax inspired him to write sweet, sweet music—well, *someone* was going to get the wrong idea. "Why?" he asked, to distract himself from the direction of his thoughts.

Jax shrugged and ran a hand back through his hair and over his neck. He seemed flushed, maybe even genuinely abashed, but he had so much natural charm it was hard to be sure he wasn't playing it up for Ari's benefit. "Well, based on the fact that you left without saying goodbye last time, I figured you weren't ready for Sex with the Bartender. This seemed more your speed."

Ari went warm all the way through, cool refreshing drink notwithstanding. This man *was* dangerous. "And what *do* you call it? Since no one here will be able to enlighten me."

The question earned him a grin and a waggle of Jax's outrageous eyebrows. "I call it a Sparkling Conversation."

Ari startled into a laugh. Maybe he *didn't* have to explain anything to Jax.

But he still couldn't keep him to himself all night. "I really do need to go cram a few more chord progressions into my brain." Jax tapped on the table as he stood. "But I'll see you?"

He didn't wait for Ari to give an answer.

Ari knew he should go home. He already had the idea for another song, or at least a good chunk of one. Yet it felt rude to leave so soon after Jax had brought him this drink and when Jax was clearly hoping he'd stick around... even if it was only for his conversation.

Besides, he'd hardly gotten to hear Jax play.

He stayed where he was.

After the break, the live show started up again without Jax, with one bubble-gum pop standard, an alt-rock classic from the '90s, and "Friends in Low Places." Eventually Jax returned to the stage and nudged Rosa off to the bass guitar. He flexed his hands a few times, cracked his knuckles, then flashed the audience a smile. "Bear with me on this one. I've never gotten this request before, but I like it too much not to give it a shot."

He nodded at Naomi, then at Kayla, who rapped out a quick, almost militaristic beat on the snare. Jax matched it with staccato chords, picking out a familiar tune Ari couldn't quite place. He sat forward anyway, enraptured, and when Naomi played the guitar riff on violin instead, he shivered.

He *did* know this song.

Up until now, he'd only seen Jax perform silly, irreverent things—enjoyable songs, but not particularly challenging ones, lyrically or musically. This, though—"White Rabbit"—was challenging even for Grace Slick to sing live, and Jax was giving it everything he had. It was far from perfect, but when he sang about the men on the chessboard getting up, the hair on Ari's arms rose. He couldn't have torn his eyes away for anything.

The song was short, but for two or three minutes, Ari was enraptured. As the last notes faded away and the crowd cheered, another set of notes filled Ari's mind and some lyrics danced tantalizingly out of reach.

Ari had a complex relationship with lyrics. Usually he figured the music could stand on its own, carry the emotion without an artist having to explain it. Additionally, he didn't think much of his own singing voice, so he had to bring in someone else on tours to sing for him. But sometimes he wanted to fill pages with poetry. It would be another late night tonight.

At least Noella would be happy. Pop stations were happy enough to pick up his work if it had lyrics, but otherwise he was relegated to XM and AM radio.

On the stage, Naomi and Jax bantered, and then Naomi belted out a goose-bump-inducing version of "Feeling Good" that had the whole crowd swooning. After the applause died, she reached into the request jar, read the slip, snorted, crumpled it, and tossed it at Jax's head.

"This one's all you," she said, leaning into the mic.

"Oh?" Jax uncrumpled the paper and laughed. "But it doesn't have any piano in it," he said, mock innocent.

Naomi snorted again. "As if you'll be sitting still."

"Touché," Jax said with a flirty grin. He stood and passed the paper to Kayla and pulled the microphone out of the stand.

The ladies began to play. The crowd cheered as they recognized the song, and Jax all but glowed under the approval. He swished his hips and winked.

Of course Jax knew all the dance moves to "Single Ladies." He moved with an ease and grace of long practice. Ari was assailed by a sudden mental image of a gangly young Jax hiding in a bedroom and watching the video on repeat on YouTube for the purpose of mastering the moves. The thought was unbearably charming.

After the song, Naomi called for a break, claiming Jax needed a cool-down from that, and Jax didn't argue.

A moment later, water bottle in hand, Jax slid into the seat opposite Ari and leaned on the table. "Enjoying the show?"

Ari hummed. "I'm wondering just how many hours of practice went into that routine."

Jax laughed his no-holds-barred laugh. "More than you're guessing, I'm sure. I was obsessed with the song at sixteen."

"Of course. Beyoncé is a cultural icon."

"Definitely. And my idol. Part of me will always want to be her when I grow up." His teasing smile made his eyes crinkle, and Ari's lips twitched with an answering smile.

"While you may not be able to *be* her, I'm sure she would be honored by the… tribute your performance paid this evening."

"Aw, Ari, is that your way of telling me you like the way I swing my hips?" He licked his lips, and Ari followed the movement with his gaze and then lifted it to catch Jax's eyes.

"Perhaps," he conceded, and Jax's eyes sparkled with clear delight.

Ari was definitely in trouble.

Chapter Five

NOT LONG after Jax's break, someone he didn't recognize filled Ari's seat, and Ari didn't come back. He suspected crowded bars weren't really Ari's scene, and the fact that he came and stuck around just to talk to Jax—well, that said a lot.

Jax sighed as he remembered the look of approval and appreciation in Ari's eyes when Jax explained about the drink. He was reasonably sure that if he played his cards right, he could get more than one date out of Ari. Hopefully more than a few orgasms as well.

"Stop mooning and help me with these chairs," Kayla said. They were the last two left in the bar, except for Murph in the back room.

"I," Jax said with overacted dignity, "am not mooning."

She scoffed. "No? What else do you call staring into space and sighing at regular intervals?"

"Reflecting." Jax flipped another chair upside down onto a table.

"Reflecting? Interesting euphemism for contemplations about the beauty of a man's ass."

Jax fluttered a hand over his heart. "Kayla, you wound me! I would never." She rolled her eyes. With a rueful shrug, Jax admitted, "I'm much more intrigued by the dexterity of his fingers and the practical applications thereof."

That made Kayla pause. "Oh, damn you. Wow, I'm gonna be thinking about—Jax, why have I never slept with a violinist?"

"You live with Naomi." Kayla made a contemplative face, but Jax didn't mention how poorly that could end. "So I honestly have no idea. *But* I call dibs on this one." He moved on to a new table.

Kayla cocked her head. "One, don't say *dibs*, that's gross. Two, *everyone* is aware. Three, even discounting that Naomi would probably kill me for trying, I'm pretty sure nothing about this"—she waved a hand to encompass her five-feet-six-inches of curves and red hair—"is his type."

Considering that Ari appeared to be both gay and not into one-night stands, Jax suspected that was true.

"My darling, how could anyone say no to you?" He stepped closer and took her into his arms for a quick spin about the floor. Since the tables hadn't been placed to accommodate dancing beyond gyrating in place, it did not go smoothly.

Laughing, she pulled herself from his arms. "Idiot. Tell me you're coming to the party. Naomi and I are putting together a backyard shindig."

"What's the celebration?"

"It's a 'Big Fucking Party Because We Can' party." She glowed. "And we want all our favorite people there, which includes you. So you better come over and eat barbecue, mister."

Touched that she considered him a favorite person, Jax grinned. "I wouldn't miss it."

"Good."

"Besides, I love a barbecue—so many sausage-and-bun jokes just waiting to be made."

"You better make those in front of Murph and Hobbes—otherwise it's all wasted potential."

"Done."

ARI CAME back the next night, missed the one after, but came on the third.

Jax stopped telling himself that he wasn't looking for him whenever he walked into the bar or took the stage.

Every time Ari came in, he ordered a Sparkling Conversation from Jax and stayed long enough to get the other kind.

And did their conversation ever sparkle—it sizzled and popped and left Jax high on adrenaline.

Someday soon, Jax would kiss that smirking, sassy mouth.

Between sets and serving drinks, Jax slowly learned all about Ari. The "oops" baby of immigrant doctors from Iran, Ari had an older sister who acted as his manager and a difficult time keeping his supportive and well-meaning parents out of his personal life. Jax hadn't had much to offer to that—his own mother stayed out of his, not because she wasn't interested or didn't care, but because, he thought, it didn't really occur to her to ask. Instead he talked about Sam and George and Alice, named for his and Sam's favorite storybook character growing up.

He learned Ari had attended the New England Conservatory of Music, where he double-majored in strings and composition, and that he still had friends in Boston. Jax wondered briefly what it would have been like if they'd ever run into each other in the city, but Ari would have graduated long before Jax started at MIT.

"Did you always know you wanted to be a musician?" he asked between sets one night, chasing droplets of condensation down the sides of his water glass.

Ari raised an eyebrow, and Jax realized they'd had a version of this conversation before. "Did you always know you wanted to be a bartender?"

Jax did his best to maintain a smile, but the words stung. He wasn't ashamed of his job; it was the unfinished PhD he was ashamed of. But he couldn't put it into words. Telling people about his degree opened him up to questions he'd rather not answer. On the other hand, keeping his mouth shut made it impossible for people to actually know him—the whole of him—and sometimes led to him feeling like he'd been reduced to a stereotype. Ari wasn't doing that—he didn't seem to care as long as Jax was happy—but Jax still couldn't make himself fess up.

But before he could say anything, Ari shook his head and the eyebrow went back down again. "I didn't always know, no." He lifted a shoulder, then his drink. "But when I was younger, I sometimes had a difficult time expressing myself. A teacher suggested to my parents that I might find an outlet in music. And I did. It helped me process my emotions and think about what I was feeling."

That was a gift, Jax knew—a real, honest, vulnerable answer—not something he should use to build a cheap line. With a gentle tease in his tone, hoping that the *thank-you* would come across, he said, "And of course, you were a prodigy."

Ari inclined his head. "And I was a prodigy," he agreed.

Silence fell for a moment, waiting for something to fill it, and for the first time in what felt like years, Jax found it within himself to be brave. "I won a province-wide math competition when I was fifteen."

He watched the words land. Ari barely blinked, only tilted his drink and gestured for Jax to go on.

Somehow the silence seemed to pull even more words from his lips. "My mom's a professor of applied mathematics at Queen's," Jax explained. "I used to want to be just like her."

Of course it was the *used to* Ari found interesting. "But now?"

What a loaded question. Jax shrugged awkwardly and swallowed half the truth. "Ah, I realized academia's just not for me."

Ari didn't probe any deeper, but Jax didn't think he'd totally bought the line either. Shortly after that he had to go back up on stage.

When the song was over, Ari was gone.

ARI HAD two songs sketched out now—whatever the elusive Alice piece turned out to be and the one he thought of as Jax's theme song, with the remixed notes of "Strangers in the Night." That was two songs more than he'd managed to write on the entirety of his tour, and though he knew they weren't perfect—not ready, not polished—he did actually need to prove to the label that he had *something* to show. So he spent the week recording a no-frills version in his simple home studio, just piano and violin with no vocals for "Alice," because Ari was a lot of things, but a gifted singer was not one of them. Then, with great trepidation, he sent them off to Noella.

The trouble was, after that, he still had to *do things*. He had dinner with his parents again, and this time they invited not only Afra and Ben but Theo too, saying that home-cooked meals were important for students away from their families. He went grocery shopping and cleaned his apartment. He found a tai chi class taught by the same instructor he'd had fifteen years ago, when he'd needed a physical outlet so he could focus on things beyond teen angst and his own ever-present erection.

These days Ari would have preferred sex as a means to focus his mind, but he liked the way tai chi kept him limber. He needed a full range of movement to perform up to his own standards.

But as Monday edged over into Tuesday and Wednesday and finally Thursday, he had to admit that the one thing he was not doing was being inspired to write anything else.

On Thursday afternoon Noella called.

"Ari," she said without preamble. "I got the tracks you sent."

Music executives, Ari thought, should know better than to open without giving artists some inkling of what they thought. "And?"

"I like it. The first one's a little technical, but that's typical for you. Your audience expects that. The one with vocals—are we calling it 'Alice' for short? I like the metaphor. I can see the devices you're using in the song."

Ah. "But," Ari prompted, hearing everything she had not said.

"But," Noella said, proving him correct, damn her, "they're very… cerebral."

That was one of the words critics used to describe his music, it was true. And it *was* cerebral. Ari liked his music to make people think. But making people think didn't sell records. Making them feel did. "They're still in early stages," he hedged.

"Mm-hmm. Afra tells me you've hit some kind of well of inspiration?"

Damn it. "Something like that," he agreed.

"Well, dig deeper," Noella ordered. "I like where this is going, don't get me wrong. The bones are there. The flesh is there. Just… it needs some heart. You know? So whatever you're doing that's bringing this into your work? Do that, but more."

More spending time with Jax and being inspired by whatever was building between them? Ari didn't have to be told twice.

He went back to the Rock.

It turned out to be a wise decision because that evening Naomi cornered him during his visit and insisted he attend her barbecue. "Everyone on staff will be there," she said with a twitch of her lips. Ari didn't acknowledge the hint but promised he would see her on the weekend.

Naomi and Kayla lived just outside the city proper, in a house on Dundas Street that Naomi's grandparents had left her when they passed away.

On Sunday Ari arrived at the barbecue with a couple of bottles of wine in hand. At Naomi's insistence on the more, the merrier, he also brought Afra, who brought Ben and Theo, an enormous stack of homemade flatbread, and a vat of hummus.

Ari arched an eyebrow at his sister when he saw her intern, and she shrugged in response. "I've grown fond of him. Besides, he needs more food in him."

Theo cast large, adoring eyes at Afra and didn't dispute the need to be fed. Ari remembered those undergrad days well, constantly hungry and always happy for free food.

They walked around the house and into the backyard, where the party was in full swing.

Ari spotted Naomi standing near the food table and headed in her direction, confident the entourage would follow.

"Naomi," he said by way of greeting, handing over the bottles of wine and accepting her hug gracefully.

"Thanks for coming," she said with her face pressed to his shoulder. "Good. You brought Afra. How are you?"

The women greeted each other with hugs and exclamations of how long it had been.

"Have you met my husband?"

Ari surreptitiously scanned the crowd, telling himself he was not looking for a particular blond head as Afra made the introductions for Ben and Theo.

"You're adorable," Naomi said after she got a good look at Theo's wide dark eyes and curly hair. He was in fact adorable, and people tended to greet him with motherly affection. "And I can't think of any higher recommendation than being coopted into this family."

Ari didn't inhale sharply, but only because he'd spent years controlling and monitoring his every reaction for the stage. Theo had no such training and couldn't suppress his flinch. At least Naomi had turned away and missed the unhappy look on his face.

Theo didn't often talk about being adopted or how he felt about it, but he'd dropped enough hints for Ari to know he had complicated feelings born out of being visibly brown and raised by white parents. Ari had often suspected that Theo was so drawn to him and Afra because they understood what it meant to live in brown skin. Though he also suspected spending so much time with no-nonsense Afra and child-psychologist even-keel Ben would be restorative and calming for any twenty-year-old.

"Ari!"

Ari turned to see Jax loping across the lawn, looking like something out of a summer catalog or a Hollywood teen drama. He wore a fuchsia Sun's Out, Guns Out tank top with a pair of board shorts and flip-flops. His blond hair shone in the sun, and as he stepped into the shade, he slipped his aviators onto the top of his head.

"Jax," he said, suddenly acutely aware of Afra, Ben, and Theo behind him. Why had he ever thought it was a good idea to put Afra in the same backyard as Jax?

"It's good to see you in the sunlight," Jax said with a cheeky grin and some elevator eyes. "It suits you." Afra was no doubt laughing it up.

"I couldn't turn Naomi down," Ari said diplomatically instead of one of the many observations he wished to make about Jax being much more suited to the sun.

Jax laughed. "Definitely not. Though I'm more worried about Kayla's wrath. She knows my weaknesses." Something about the way his lips twitched at the last word threw Ari. What exactly did Kayla know, and more importantly, how did she know it?

"Wise to be wary, then," Ari agreed.

As Afra cleared her throat, Jax glanced over Ari's shoulder and his eyes widened.

"Oh. Hi." He lifted a hand to wave. He didn't appear to wish to crawl into a hole out of embarrassment, like Ari, but he seemed uncertain what to say. He probably didn't want to make any assumptions.

Best take the plunge. "Jax, meet my sister, Afra, her husband, Ben, and her pet intern, Theo."

Jax grinned broadly at them and shook their hands. "I'm Jax."

"No introduction necessary," Afra said. "I've seen the video."

"The video?" Mischief danced in his eyes. "I'm almost afraid to ask which one."

Thankfully Naomi had moved on and was not near enough to hear.

Ben chuckled. "The one with the piano. If there are any videos of you involving less clothes, I don't want to know about them." He cast a look at Ari.

"None that are on YouTube," Jax shot back, all good humor.

Ari managed not to blush, but only because Jax implying in front of Ari's sister that he'd made a sex tape made all his blood want to hide in his toes.

Before he could muster any kind of response, someone shouted at Jax from across the yard. "Hey, Hall! Are you going to waste what might be your last day this year to get your ass handed to you or what?"

With no small amount of trepidation, Ari realized the man was wearing swim goggles and an enormous water tank strapped to his back. There was a pump-action spray gun resting on his shoulder.

Jax gave them a mock-somber look. "Sorry, it looks like my title is in jeopardy from a thirty-five-year-old pediatrician with a Super Soaker." He winked at Ari. "If I fall on the field of battle, I trust you to avenge me." Then he jogged off.

"Wow, hate to see him go," Afra quipped.

Ari's face burned. "Afra." Her husband was right there!

"No, I agree," Ben said. "The back view is almost better." They fist-bumped.

Ari glanced at Theo, hoping to appeal to him, but he just shrugged. "Do you actually want to argue?"

That was a fair point, unfortunately. Ari sighed and made himself turn away from the scene lest he be forced to watch as Jax's shirt, which already revealed his delectably muscled round shoulders, got wet and clung to his chest.

Instead, he clapped Theo on the back and pushed him toward the grill at the rear of the house. "Come on. Let's go see what we can feed you."

It had been too long since he'd attended a party, and for the first twenty minutes or so, he felt off-kilter, even though he'd spent the past few months touring. But finally, as Theo polished off his second hamburger, nodding vigorously along with whatever Kayla was telling him, Ari let out a breath and realized the tension had fled from his shoulders.

Of course, that didn't last long once Afra caught up to him again.

"So," she said, nudging him in the hip just hard enough to slosh the liquid in his red Solo cup. "Noella said she's heard a demo?"

"Two demos," Ari said, resigned to talking business.

"And Naomi said you've been by the Rock just about every day they do live music for the past week," she continued blithely.

Oh no, it was worse than business.

From somewhere toward the back of the yard, there was a triumphant shout and then an actual yell, which interrupted what Ari felt sure would be the most uncomfortable moment yet. He glanced over just in time to see Jax turn the hose on the man who had taunted him earlier, to laughter and applause from their audience and a good deal of cursing from the doctor.

Ari told himself he wasn't disappointed it wasn't Jax who'd ended up soaked to the skin.

Afra cleared her throat. "Noella seems to think you might have a muse."

Noella was a damn gossip. "Is that such a bad thing?"

"I didn't say it was," Afra soothed. "I only want to catch up. You've been buried in work this week."

Ari took another drink of his questionable beverage, wishing it were something else, and tried to relax. "He's just... interesting." How could he explain it? Did he even have to? Anyone who looked at Jax would surely see the way the world bent into something a little more joyful around his edges. Or maybe that joy was coming from Jax. Either way, it was addictive. Of course Ari wanted more of it.

Jax and his sparring partner were returning to the main yard— Jax laughing, his friend not so much.

"Oh my God," Naomi said as she came out of the house behind Ari and Afra and looked past them. "Calvin, what happened to you?"

The soaking-wet man—Ari assumed he must be Calvin— glowered halfheartedly and jerked his thumb at Jax. "This overgrown child in a frat-boy costume happened to me."

"Weren't you the one who issued the challenge?" Ari asked before he could help himself.

Calvin turned the soggy glower on him.

Naomi looked at Jax, who gestured to Ari and Afra. "What? Look, there were *witnesses*!"

Afra raised her hands. "I wish to be excluded from this narrative."

Naomi snorted, then opened the back door again. "Come on, Cal. I'll find you a towel... and maybe a T-shirt."

They went inside, and Jax wandered over to the drink table. Calvin *had* shot him with the water gun at least once; the tank top was plastered to his back over his left kidney, and his shorts were wet too, highlighting the perfect round curve of his ass.

"Interesting is one word for him," Afra allowed.

Ari didn't facepalm, because he had never facepalmed in his life, but he might have tried to hide his face in his tumbler of lemonade.

Afra gave him a look but kindly said nothing else.

Theo, on the other hand, munched a chip and asked, "Does he know about your music boner?"

Really, getting covered in Ari's spit-take lemonade was the least Theo deserved for that.

60

Naomi returned with a less hangdog-looking Calvin and introduced him to the group. Then she hurried off to take care of other guests.

Calvin graciously shook Afra's and Theo's hands and was practically a gentleman, even when Afra dragged Theo away to find a bathroom to clean off the lemonade.

"So," Calvin said with a long, slow look at Ari. "You're Ari."

"Indeed." Ari wasn't sure what to make of this man. He had already deduced him to be Jax's roommate, "Hobbes," who had a stamp of approval from Murph for being a "good'un."

"You look different in person."

Ari arched an eyebrow. "You've seen my picture?"

Calvin snorted. "Your video. Mind you, the quality on that thing isn't great, but…." He shrugged.

"I assume you're referring to the video with Jax."

"Yeah, that one." Calvin gave him another assessing look. "You ever own a puppy?"

What? "No."

"Puppies are cute and lovable, but they're also a lot of work, vulnerable, and get easily attached. And the thing is, you can't just get rid of the puppy when it chews on your favorite shoes, right? You have to keep it because it needs you to survive."

Was this really happening? Surely Calvin didn't think of Jax as a puppy?

"So you better be sure that you want that puppy before you take it home, all right?" His gaze was intense.

"If I fully understand your meaning, you are comparing one of your closest friends to a dog."

"Well, he did follow me home one day," Calvin grumbled. That was rather unshocking news, though it did raise the question—had they slept together? *Were* they sleeping together?

No, they couldn't be. No one could sleep with Jax and be this blasé about Ari's obvious interest in doing the same.

Ari opened his mouth to pry more of the story out of Calvin, but a cup with a familiar-looking drink appeared in front of his face.

"I had to make some adjustments based on supplies, but here." Jax sat down in the vacant chair at Ari's right and looked back and forth between Calvin and Ari. "So, you two have met. That's great. I'm sure you have plenty to talk about and all of it is about me. Do I want to know what was said, or should I just move things along and live in ignorance?"

Never one to waste an opportunity so neatly presented to him, Ari smiled and said, "Calvin was just about to tell me the story of how you met."

"Oh, was he?" Jax shot a suspicious look at Calvin, who didn't dispute Ari's claim. "Well, it's not that interesting a story—"

"That's a lie," Calvin cut in.

"No, it isn't. We met when I was doing some research, and then Hobbes got sick—" A shadow passed over Jax's eyes, and Ari had a fair guess what sickness that might have been. "—and someone had to look after Captain Tribby—that's the cat—so I said I would do it. But Tribby's diabetic, so it's kind of hard to just pop by."

"What Jax is trying to get at is that he moved in while I was weak in the hospital, and I haven't been able to get him to move out."

Jax laughed. "Squatter's rights, old man."

"The cat likes him better anyway," Calvin said heavily. "So we're stuck with each other now."

"He loves me, really," Jax said.

Ari believed him. It would be difficult not to.

"He grows on you. Like a fungus." Calvin gestured at Ari's hand. "What'd he make you?"

Ari opened his mouth to answer, then realized how embarrassing that would be and raised the cup to his lips instead.

Naturally Jax had no such compunctions. "It's a Sparkling Conversation, Hobbes. You should try it sometime." He gave the man a gentle shove. "Somewhere else, maybe."

Calvin made a face like he'd just sucked a lemon. "What, you think I wouldn't recognize that as my cue? I'm going. Nice meeting you, Ari."

"Likewise." Ari raised his hand in a halfhearted wave. His head felt like it was spinning—not, he suspected, an unusual sensation for people who spent a lot of time around Jax. The man was like a tornado full of razor blades. It took a lot to keep up with a mind that sharp, but Ari enjoyed the challenge.

Only now that they were alone, some of Jax's edges bled off. "So. You and Naomi know each other, obviously?"

"I used to be her violin teacher," he admitted. "But actually I've known Kayla longer. We went to school together."

He should say hello, except—no, she was setting up her pails to do a guerrilla drum demonstration, and he enjoyed those too much to delay her. He'd talk to her afterward, and maybe she'd be willing to let him borrow a rhythm if something struck him just right.

"Yeah? Kayla is awesome. We would be deeply in love if it weren't for the whole aromantic thing." Jax sighed gustily, clutching at his chest, full of drama yet completely oblivious to the fact that, to Ari, the world had just suddenly flickered into black and white. "Alas." When Ari didn't respond right away, Jax looked over and touched his shoulder. Color flooded back in. "You all right? You look a little wan."

Somehow Ari managed to clear his throat. "Fine," he said, taking a healthy sip of his drink to give himself some breathing room. It worked—he found something to change the subject, at least. "You're not drinking?"

"Oh." Jax shrugged as they made their way back to the drink table, where he fished a bottle of water out of a cooler. "Sort of? Downsides of moving in with a doctor. Twenty-six years old, and last year I got an unlooked-for ADHD diagnosis. Surprise!" He cracked the top off and chugged half of it, condensation running down his arm. Ari watched his throat work and debated just climbing into the cooler. "Anyway, being medicated is mostly great, but alcohol interferes with the time-release mechanism, and let me tell you, when your resting heart rate jumps from sixty to eighty-seven it is *not* a fun adventure. So I've got a strict two-drink limit, and I pretty much can't start until after dinnertime. No day drinking."

That was the most Ari had learned about Jax in a single conversation, and it left him reeling. "I see."

He'd been operating under the assumption that Jax was trying to seduce him as a game. Ari had been holding out because sex without intimacy wasn't his style and falling into that with Jax would be ruinous for his heart. He'd thought maybe, if he were patient, Jax might take him seriously. Maybe they could have something real.

But if Jax didn't feel romantic attachment, then—what?

The smart thing to do would be to walk away. He was playing a game he couldn't win. He could cut his losses and struggle through the writer's block on his own. Eventually the music would return. He knew enough about himself to know that.

Or he could follow through. He could let Jax flirt with him until he couldn't take it anymore, until he gave in. Ari would fall in love with him—he was already halfway there.

It would end with possibly the most beautiful album Ari could ever dream of composing and Jax breaking his heart.

"Well," he said, reaching out for the first time and consciously touching Jax at the waist, so that he turned toward another table, "if you can't drink, how do you feel about refined sugar?"

Chapter Six

JAX HEFTED another keg out of the supply room and brought it to the bar, enjoying the strain in his muscles—one of the better distractions he'd had all day. He hooked the keg up to the tap and tried to ignore the nagging feeling in the back of his brain.

He didn't want to think about MIT right then.

He turned on the tap to prime it and watched the foam collect.

The email had been easy enough to ignore, to put off for another time. But there was something about a letter.... Jax had to read it.

Frustrated, Jax cut the tap and wiped down the clean bar—no customers around yet to make it dirty. He cast a glance at the clock and wished the next seven minutes would pass so he might at least have work to distract him, to keep him from remembering.

... should you elect to continue your studies, tuition is due no later than January 3. If, instead, you choose to defer completion of your doctoral thesis, the fee for nonresident studies....

As customers trickled in, Jax gladly accepted their requests for alcohol and song, and soon he mostly drowned out the dread and nagging.

When Ari arrived around eight thirty, Jax was stuck at the bar, filling drinks. He barely had time to talk when he dropped off Ari's usual Sparkling Conversation.

Pulled away to make up a collection of cocktails for a group of ladies near the stage, Jax had to give up Ari-watching for several minutes. When he turned back, Ari was gone and his glass was empty.

Heart falling, Jax grabbed the glass and the twenty tucked underneath it and quickly put both away. Then he turned to the next customer. He had thought they were past the stage of leaving without saying goodbye.

He was pouring some vodka with a service-person smile pasted on his face when he heard the opening violin strings of Coldplay's "Viva la Vida." Rosa must be doing the piano, but he wondered who Naomi had found to sing.

Except that *was* Naomi singing. Jax glanced at the stage and—

Ari stood on it with Naomi, her violin tucked under his chin.

Jax couldn't tear his gaze away as they tore through the song as a duo. Naomi had to glance occasionally at some lyrics, but Ari managed not only the song's established violin work but also some modified bars to make up for the lack of other instruments. Ari knew the song by heart.

Suddenly Jax was very grateful for the bar between him and everyone else, as it now hid his semi.

Naomi shimmied, and a fond, indulgent smile quirked Ari's lips, though he didn't miss a step.

The crowd loved it.

"Thank you! We're a bit short-staffed tonight, so a dear friend has graciously agreed to give us a hand. The request jar is still open, but we don't want to overwhelm our newbie."

Ari arched an eyebrow. "I taught you everything you know."

The crowd hooted.

"That sounds like a challenge, old man, one that we need a second violin for. I'm going to take a short break, and Ari is going to entertain you." Naomi ducked off the stage.

Ari stepped up to the microphone and, without a word to the audience, launched into a violin remix of "Thriller," Rosa and Kayla following his lead. It sent chills down Jax's spine, and he began to wonder how he would get out from behind the bar without breaking public indecency laws.

Naomi returned from the break room with her backup violin, and they proceeded to kill their way through a set, Naomi alternating between violin and vocals.

"This next one is an old favorite of mine," Naomi said, beaming. "You see, Ari was my first violin teacher." The crowd cooed. "And we learned to play this song together."

"You insisted," Ari said dryly.

Jax wondered if their gangling young act was as adorable or enthralling as this.

"You were the one who wrote the arrangement." Naomi smirked and lifted her violin to her chin. Then, with barely a glance at each other and a few subtle foot taps for rhythm, the duo launched into Taylor Swift's "You Belong With Me."

Jax couldn't decide what was cuter—a thirty-two-year-old Ari playing this song with a chagrined smile or the image of a twentyish Ari listening to Swift on repeat to arrange it for his preteen student.

After, Naomi excused them both for a break and dragged Ari to the back. Jax silently cursed them for putting the patrons in such a good drinking mood, as he was trapped mixing drinks and unable to follow. He wanted to climb Ari like a tree and kiss him into next week.

Naomi returned first and slipped behind the bar. "Jax, we need you on piano."

He gave her a look and pointedly moved his gaze to the shaker in his hands.

"Yes, yes. But we have an idea, and we'll need a piano player/singer for it."

Intrigued, Jax said, "Explain."

She did.

"You," he said and pointed at her, "are so lucky that I decided to learn that one because I figured it was only a matter of time before someone requested it, what with you being on violin and all."

Naomi beamed.

"Okay, talk to Murph, see what can be done about this—" He waved a hand at the busy bar. "—and I'll join you on stage."

She hurried away.

Jax figured their trio would be first up after the break, so he was surprised when he heard the violin once again. Ari stood on the stage alone, slowly pulling out the melody and vocals of Elton John's "Your Song."

Jax's mother had never had a broad taste in music, but she'd had favorites. He had grown up listening to Elton John and had always loved the earnest simplicity of "Your Song."

When Ari reached the line about eye color, he looked over at Jax and winked.

Jax swallowed and reprimanded himself for wanting to swoon. Surely Ari wasn't playing "Your Song" as some sort of message for him.

Not that it wasn't working as a seduction technique, deliberate or not. God, Jax was so ready. He wondered if Ari would forgive him if he dragged him into the break room and gave him a blowjob.

Probably. Jax's blowjobs were legendary.

The song finished, and Ari announced there'd be a short break while they prepped to rotate in another musician. That meant a sudden surge of patrons at the bar. Murph appeared from somewhere, and Bruce the bouncer came in to help out as well. Jax spent a few minutes on autopilot, elbows-deep in liquor and mixers.

Then he looked up and found Ari watching him with the hint of a smile. It was a good look for him—like he knew something Jax didn't. That expression on Ari? Made Jax want to learn all his secrets.

"Hey, stranger," Jax said, leaning forward across the bar. "Your usual?"

"Hmm, I don't think so." Ari tapped his fingers on the bar top, eyes dancing. Oh, was he going to turn the tables tonight? Was it Jax's turn to be teased? Jax couldn't wait. "I'm looking for something different tonight."

Jax grabbed a glass and filled it with ice. "Yeah? You want to tell me about it?"

Ari wet his lips. Jax's heart stuttered at the quick flash of tongue, but then it was gone. He *was* teasing. "Well, it's got coconut rum."

Oh boy. Was he going to order what Jax thought he was going to order? "Uh-huh," Jax said, grabbing the bottle. "What else?"

"Orange liqueur."

Jax skipped right past the triple sec and the Cointreau. Only the best for Ari. He snagged the Grand Marnier. "Got it."

"Grenadine for sweetness." Oh God. "And some citrus." Ari gave him a wry look, as though he were almost ashamed of what he was going to say, but he said it anyway: "It should be a little tart."

Well, he wasn't wrong. Jax wanted to laugh, but he was so turned-on he could barely pour the alcohol without spilling. He topped up the glass with 7-Up like he was supposed to—it wasn't like he didn't know what he was making—but then asked, "Anything else?"

He just had to know if Ari would *say* it. "A splash of Irish cream."

Fuck. Jax's dick did not have a *prayer*. He was going to be hard through the whole set, but it'd be worth it. "Coming right up," he said hoarsely.

God. Tonight's set was going to be interesting, to say the least.

With three of them working behind the bar, it didn't take long to clear the backlog, and soon Murph was shooing Jax up toward the stage. The crowd let out a cheer as Murph switched off the Spotify playlist and the house mics went live again.

"Friends, Romans, countrymen—" Jax began, sliding into his seat at the piano. Behind him, he could hear Naomi laughing. At the other side of the stage, Ari smirked and raised his violin. "I've been freed from the bar, thanks to the relief efforts of Bruce the bouncer. Everybody say 'Thank you, Bruce.'"

Everyone dutifully thanked him, including Ari and Naomi.

Jax walked up a bunch of arpeggios, D minor, C, down to B flat, then A. "I think we've all been wanting to play this since the first time Ari showed up. I hope you'll like it too."

He glanced at Kayla, and she nodded. Ari lifted his bow. Jax didn't need to check Naomi; she was always ready.

"Here goes."

Kayla counted them in for "The Devil Went Down to Georgia."

The song was heavy on fiddle, with the piano a thumping, driving backbeat. Ari took the introductory lead at a blistering pace, and it was all Jax could do to keep up and keep the lyrics on-key. As he laid out the terms of the wager between the devil and Johnny, he wondered which of his band mates would take on which role.

It probably shouldn't have surprised him that Ari chose the devil.

Thank God Jax had practiced the piano part to back the fiddle solos until his fingers ached. It meant he could watch Ari in his element, eyes blazing, slightly sweaty curls flying around his face as he burned through a solo that sounded absolutely nothing like any recorded version of the song Jax had ever listened to. He'd never heard a fiddle that sounded like it wanted you to do a line of cocaine and then drive your motorcycle off a cliff before. Hell, if the devil were real and half as convincing as Ari, Jax's soul was as good as sold.

He was so distracted that he had to go through the bridge part twice to get to the next verse, which was fine; the audience was still cheering for the first one. But Jax couldn't just *go on* with the song. He kept his fingers moving and said into the microphone, "Hey, Ari. You know the devil's supposed to lose the bet, right?"

Naomi kicked the piano bench, which was fair.

"All right, all right, you'll get your turn," Jax grumbled, but his face wouldn't stop grinning.

When the song ended, the crowd roared their appreciation, and Jax made sure to direct that applause at Ari and Naomi specifically. "Wow, I am seriously outclassed," Jax said with a shake of his head.

"Good thing you're cute," Kayla agreed.

He reached into the jar for a handful of requests—something a little less intense, maybe, but also something that would keep the energy high. The night was pretty well shot, and he wanted to end the evening with a bang.

In more ways than one.

"What do you think?" he asked Naomi.

She leaned over his shoulder and scanned the offerings. Then she smiled and tapped one with an immaculate nail. "Oh, make Ari sit this one out. He should get the full effect."

"You're on this team too, eh?" He grinned, then leaned into the mic. "Hey, Ari. Naomi says take five, we got this one."

Ari raised his eyebrows, lowered his violin, and bowed off to the side. "I look forward to it."

"I can't believe you're helping me get laid," he muttered to her, sotto voce.

She snorted. "Not *you*, idiot." Then she took center stage.

This time they all waited for her signal. Jax took a deep breath, feeling like he really *had* done a line of coke. He fixed his eyes on Ari, who was looking at him like he was—Jax didn't even know. A Maraschino cherry stem he wanted to tie a knot in with his tongue.

Naomi bowed the sharp staccato notes of the intro, and the bar roared.

Jax didn't even pretend to look at anyone else as he let his voice go high and breathy. Was it absolutely ridiculous to sing "Toxic" to the man you wanted to take you home? Yes. Had that ever stopped Jax before? No. And by now Ari knew that.

From the look in his eyes, he was into it.

By the end of the song, Jax was dizzy with wanting it; he had no idea how he made it to the end of his shift.

It was possible that he was shoved out the door early for being gross, but Jax didn't care because Ari stood next to him and leaned down to husk into his ear, "Tell me you're coming home with me."

"Yes," Jax breathed, and they stumbled into a cab. Jax might not have had anything to drink, but he wasn't sober. His bike would be safe for the night. Probably.

Ari's loft wasn't far. He guided Jax into the building with a hand on the small of his back, and the gentle sweep of his thumb over Jax's spine ratcheted his arousal up more and more.

They didn't talk on their way up or as Ari was unlocking his front door. As soon as they were inside, Jax spun, pushed their bodies together, and kissed him.

Ari's mouth was wide and giving under Jax's eager press. Ari placed a hand on the back of Jax's head, his keys clattered to the ground, and the other hand settled on Jax's hip. He hummed into the kiss and licked Jax's lips, and Jax didn't think he'd ever had a first kiss this good.

He opened for Ari's tongue and pushed back, pressing into Ari's mouth, testing, tasting. Ari scratched his nails over Jax's scalp, and the noise that escaped Jax then could only be classified as a whimper. Judging by the sharp forward thrust of Ari's hips, he was into it.

Ari trailed his lips up to Jax's ear. "What do you want, Jax?" The low tone sent shivers through him.

"Fuck. Everything. Anything. God, Ari—" He cut off with a strangled moan as Ari dragged his teeth across the tender skin below his ear.

Ari purred and said in the same husky voice, "You tell me if I do anything you don't like."

"Yes, yes," Jax breathed. He might be drunk on lust, but he was aware enough to recognize that for the negotiation it was—*let me guide you*. Jax was nothing if not predictable in that regard.

Ari hauled him into the bedroom, yanking Jax's clothes off as they went, getting his mouth on all the newly exposed skin. Jax did his best to return the favor but found the buttons on Ari's shirt difficult to work with Ari's mouth on his collarbone and one of his hands pinching his nipple.

He was naked when Ari pushed him down onto his bed, and Ari was shirtless, revealing a moderately hairy chest. He shimmied out of his jeans and prowled onto the bed, over Jax.

Jax grabbed his head and pulled him down into a kiss. He spread his legs and hooked one over Ari's thighs, trying to pull them closer. Ari resisted—*Why?* Jax pulled, and Ari pulled back, nibbled Jax's lip. Then, after Jax stopped pulling, as if to prove Jax couldn't make him do anything, Ari pressed forward and their hips collided. The press of Ari's cloth-covered cock against his own was delicious, and Jax moaned into the kiss. Then Ari thrust his hips and made it better. *Yes!* Jax arched into the friction, hooked his other leg around Ari's hips, and let him set the pace.

Then Ari stopped thrusting. Jax whined into his mouth, scratched at his shoulders, arched his back, trying to entice Ari into movement, but his hips stayed still. He pulled his mouth off Jax's and kissed his neck, his collarbone, his chest. He worked his way south and stopped at Jax's nipples for a nibble and at his belly button for a lick, but he was clearly a man on a mission.

He pushed Jax's legs wide, loosening their grip around his back, and shimmied down until he was head to head with Jax's dick. Without further ado, he leaned in and licked, base to tip. Then he took Jax into his mouth and sank all the way down.

Jax shouted and arched off the bed, but Ari pulled off with a growl, pinned Jax's hips, and went back to work.

He sucked Jax like he was starving for it, working the base while he sucked the head, pulling off to lick all over, rolling and tugging at Jax's balls, taking him all in, to the back of his throat. Jax hadn't been sucked off this enthusiastically in—ever, maybe. He clutched at the sheets, Ari's hair, covered his mouth to stifle some of the loud moans. He hardly knew what he was doing.

Ari placed two fingers behind his balls and pressed, and Jax's legs spasmed and tried to shut until Ari wrestled Jax's thighs flat against the mattress. He looked up at Jax, his dark eyes black under his sweeping lashes, and Jax gasped and just about came, even though Ari's mouth was not currently on his dick.

"I'm gonna come," Jax breathed in warning.

"Good." Ari deep-throated him in one go, his eyes still on Jax's.

Granted permission, Jax couldn't hold back, and when Ari once again pressed on his perineum, he shouted, slammed his eyes shut, and came, his fingers twisted in Ari's hair. Ari hummed and swallowed and didn't release Jax until he was gasping and tugging his hair. "Please!"

Ari finally pulled off, and Jax collapsed into the sheets, quivering and panting, a puddle of sated goo. Ari gave him a few cleaning licks, then crawled up Jax's body. Was it too cliché to compare his lover to a wildcat? The look in his eyes was certainly predatory. Jax shivered in delight and pulled Ari to him for a sated grateful kiss.

Ari wiggled his hips, his hand brushed against Jax's, and then the cotton briefs separating them were gone.

"I can suck you," Jax said between kisses. He made a move to get up, to roll them over, but Ari laced their fingers together and pressed Jax's hands into the pillow.

"Later." Ari settled himself comfortably over Jax and started to thrust, rubbing his dick into the cut of Jax's hip, his belly bumping Jax's sensitive cock, and God, Jax might just get hard again.

He wanted to protest that he *wanted* Ari's dick in his mouth, had wanted it for weeks, but he got the feeling Ari had a plan. Jax was happy to call the shots at the bar and just as happy to take a back seat in the bedroom.

Especially when taking a back seat meant rolling his hips up to meet Ari's, lifting his head to catch Ari's lips in another kiss, and angling his body until their cocks slid together.

The contact was almost too much on his oversensitive skin, and he unintentionally bit Ari's lip. If the noises Ari made were any indication, he didn't object.

But it was only a moment before Ari pulled away, scraping his stubble against Jax's cheek. "Not too sensitive?"

They both glanced down at the same time. Their cocks nestled alongside each other, Jax's still glistening with saliva, Ari's uncut one leaking on Jax's abs. They were both hard.

"Pretty sensitive," Jax admitted, "but turns out I'm into it?"

Ari's eyes went dark—darker—but he didn't lower himself all the way. Instead he raised his hand to Jax's mouth. "Lick."

Jax's dick jerked in approval. No way Ari didn't feel it. He looked like he wanted to eat Jax alive.

Jax licked, thick and sloppy, because he was into the sensitive thing but chafing was still a hard no. Real lube would've been better, if it hadn't meant stopping.

Fuck stopping.

Ari wrapped his hand around them both, then slotted his mouth back over Jax's.

Jax was right about violinists' hands. Ari was playing him expertly.

It didn't take long with Ari stroking them together like that. One minute Ari groaned into Jax's mouth as Jax fisted one hand in his hair and dug the other into the flesh of his ass. The next Ari was tearing his mouth away, sitting back on his heels to watch as he came all over Jax, splattering his chest and stomach. Hot liquid coated his fingers too, and Jax's cock, until Ari was jerking Jax off with his come for lube.

"*Fuck,*" Jax said weakly.

Ari rubbed his thumb under the head. He looked wild, his tangled, sweaty curls framing his face, his lips swollen. "Jax."

"Uhh," Jax said as his orgasm ripped out of him.

For a moment he lay still as Ari knelt above him, both of them breathing hard. Jax's mind was blissfully blank. After the night he'd had, he knew sleep was lurking right around the corner. Probably within the next five minutes.

Their eyes met, and oh no, were things going to get awkward? Was it too soon for sleepovers? Should he leave?

Ari blinked first, when he broke eye contact to rake his eyes down Jax's chest and stomach and—

Jax cleared his throat, flushing despite the fact that he'd been writhing shamelessly under Ari's touch forty seconds previously. "I appreciate your appreciation, but I need at least an hour if you want me to get it up again, and I'm about three and a half minutes from unconsciousness. Do you want me to leave?"

Ari blinked again, his brows drawing together slightly. Jax felt very naked. "Absolutely not."

"Oh," Jax said faintly, instinctively burrowing deeper into the mattress. It was a nice one, with nice sheets too. "Okay."

"Stay here," Ari said, voice suddenly warm. Jax couldn't see his face anymore; his eyes were closing. "I'll get a washcloth."

"Mm-hmm," Jax agreed.

He was so comfortable.

Ari was gone for a moment, and Jax drifted into a haze of post-orgasmic bliss. The next thing he knew, something soft and warm was between his legs, wiping over his chest and stomach.

Then Ari climbed into bed and curled an arm over Jax's waist, and wasn't that nice.

It was *so* nice.

Jax slept.

Chapter Seven

ARI WAS six pages deep in the music of the third track, playing the electric keyboard with the volume down low, when the door to his apartment swung open.

"Ari? Are you home? I heard music…." A pause. "It smells like a bordello in here."

Lifting his head, Ari scrambled for his phone. What time was it? Why hadn't he heard the knock? What was she doing here? Oh God, was it really almost ten?

"What the hell have you been up to? You better not be naked."

"I'm—" He cut himself off. He'd put pajama pants on, at least, because having your balls stuck to the piano bench was never a good time. "Please be quiet," he said resignedly instead.

Afra paused in the act of taking off her shoes and actually looked at him. Her eyebrows rose and her mouth opened. She stood on one foot for a handful of seconds and then finally recovered. "Shit, shit, I knew I should have called first. Is this a bad time?"

On the contrary. It was a very good time. Emphasis on *was*. But if Afra was here without warning, obviously something was up.

Ari stood up and crossed to the bedroom door. Jax was passed out in the bed, half tangled in blankets, chest rising and falling steadily. Ari had never seen him so still.

Reluctantly, he closed the door and gestured Afra to the couch. "What's going on?"

"I could ask you the same question."

He ignored her. "Did we have an appointment I forgot about?" It wouldn't have been the first time.

Her face shuttered. "Not exactly. I mean, *you* don't have an appointment." She sat, shoving her hands between her knees in an obvious tell.

77

Okay, now he knew it was serious, if she wasn't asking about who he had in the bedroom. Though who was he kidding—she obviously knew it was Jax. Time to make a shitty decision. "You want to get coffee?"

He watched in horror as her eyes filled with tears, though thankfully they didn't overflow. "Yeah," she said, her voice cracking. "That would actually be great."

Okay. So he needed to get dressed… and wake Jax and let him know he was leaving. Not how Ari wanted the morning to go, but Afra wasn't a crier by nature. Whatever was going on with her was serious.

"Just… give me a minute."

Jax was stirring when Ari went into the bedroom. Afra was right—it did reek of sex.

Ari sat on the bed next to him and wondered what was appropriate, considering Jax probably wasn't for messy entanglements. Jax had stayed last night, for Ari, which was thoughtful. Would it be pushing things too much to stroke his cheek to wake him up?

"Ari?" Jax groaned and stretched. His lashes fluttered, and he gazed sleepily up at Ari. "Morning."

"Good morning." Ari licked his lips and took in Jax's bare torso, which boasted more than one bruise from last night. He would have to remember that Jax bruised so easily. "I had hoped to feed you this morning and see what else we could get up to in bed"—Jax grinned and wriggled his hips—"but I will have to ask for a rain check. My sister is here, and I don't know why she's upset but—"

"Say no more." Jax sat up. "Family comes first. I think I legit kicked a guy outside in his underwear once for my sister's sake." He gave a shy grin. "So, do you want me to grab my stuff and go? Or am I hiding until your sister leaves?"

Impulsively, Ari said, "Neither. My sister and I are about to leave for coffee"—he glanced down at himself—"once I'm dressed. Take your time cleaning up. I'll leave you a key to lock up behind you." He licked his lips. "I'm not attempting to hide you from my sister, but I'm guessing you don't want to meet her again in this state."

His eyes flicked down once again to the many bruises—hickeys—on Jax's torso.

"Erm, yeah, maybe not. I mean, I'm not shy about taking a quote-unquote walk of shame, but not usually around sisters and not usually while half naked. You sure about that key, though?"

"Jax, I know where you work."

"Right." Jax gave a small smirk.

"I trust you." After all, they knew almost all of the same people. "Now I really should go."

"Yes, yes." Jax waved him off and watched silently as Ari collected clothes and stepped into the en suite.

He took the fastest shower of his life and quickly dressed in his black jeans and T-shirt. When he emerged, Jax was still lounging in the bed and playing on his phone.

"Take your time," Ari said, because he felt like he should say something.

"Don't worry about me. Get back to Afra. I'll text later." Jax waggled his phone.

Tenderness swept through Ari, and he could not curb the impulse to lean down and kiss Jax's mouth. "Thank you," he breathed, "for understanding."

"No, uh, no problem," Jax said somewhat breathlessly. Had Ari made him uncomfortable? Was that too romantic?

Ari stepped back. "Right. See you later, Jax."

Afra got up from the couch when he emerged and said nothing as Ari led her to the door.

Once outside on the sidewalk, Afra led him toward their favorite local café, where Ari bought them drinks. He waited until they were settled on a relatively isolated park bench to ask, "What's wrong?"

"So, kids." She fiddled with the straw in her iced coffee. Ari waited. He'd never understood how his mother couldn't see the extent to which the topic pained Afra. "We've... we've been trying. For a while."

"I didn't know." He reached out, and she took his hand and squeezed it.

"I know. We never said—first because we wanted to surprise everyone, and then…." She took a deep breath. "We've been doing IVF, but… the first one didn't take."

His chest ached. He didn't know what to say. "Afra…."

"I have an appointment today to try again, but if this doesn't work… I think—know—they'll tell me we've reached the end of the road." She gave a weak smile, her eyes glassy.

Ari pulled her into a tight hug. "I am sorry. I wish I could fix this for you."

"I know," she said, her voice muffled in his shoulder. He buried his face in her hair. As children, she had been his hero, the brilliant older sister who could do anything. She often still was; his life would be an utter shitshow without her influence. Seeing her this upset barely computed, so he vowed to hug her for as long and as tight as she wanted.

A few minutes later, she untangled them and gave him a tiny smile. "Thank you for understanding."

"You're my sister—"

"I know." She patted his knee, straightened her spine, and cleared her throat. "We've been talking to an adoption specialist. We didn't—" She stopped, and her mouth twisted into a wry smile. "We didn't want to put all our eggs in one basket. Ha-ha. So if this doesn't work out, our prospects look good. I mean, Ben's a child psychologist, so…. I'm just not sure how to tell our parents."

"Ah." As doctors, his parents would understand logically that infertility was beyond Afra's control, especially at her age—that neither she nor Ben were to blame and that adoption was a lovely way to expand a family. Surely they must have some idea by now that it might not be in the cards for her to get pregnant. But Ari had no idea how they would respond emotionally. "They'll understand. Eventually."

"Yeah, *eventually*. I've been debating whether to tell them now or when we're matched with a potential mother. You know?"

Ari did know. Surprises were often easier to handle when they were a done deal instead of a hypothetical, but….

"Adoption can take a while."

Afra nodded, her eyes unhappy but her mouth a firm stubborn line.

"But in the meantime... I don't know. Every time they mention the kids thing, it hurts you. I hate that."

"They do the same to you," she said weakly, but Ari shook his head.

"No, they meddle and make me feel uncomfortable, but I'm okay with being single. It's not the same."

"Thanks." She cleared her throat. "And speaking of being single...."

He groaned; he'd really walked right into that one. Though in the interest of cheering Afra up, he could submit to a few awkward questions and some innuendo. "Yes, all right. Let's hear it."

Afra leaned forward, watching his face. "Okay, well, first of all, since when do you take men home without first wining and dining them until even *I* have blue balls—"

Well, he asked for it.

"—and second, you're dating bartenders now?"

Ouch. That particular flavor of skepticism stung. "Is that really what you think of me? That I'm shallow?"

Afra rolled her eyes. "Come on. It's not shallow that you're generally attracted to guys with genius-range IQs. I don't think you're *shallow*. I think you only date guys you'd bring home to Maman and Baba."

"And Maman and Baba—" would not approve of Ari bringing home a bartender.

"Are kinda shallow."

Fair point.

"Well, we're not *dating*," Ari said, trying to keep the tone light and failing completely.

"What!" Afra yelped, sitting up straight. "Why not?"

Ari could not tell her about Jax being aromantic. For one thing it wasn't his to tell, and for another she'd insist he stop seeing Jax, which he had no intention of doing. "Well, like you mentioned, Maman and Baba...."

She rolled her eyes. "Oh, so what? You're thirty-two years old! You can date who you want."

Sure, he *could*, if he wanted to defend his choices to his parents for the rest of his life. "You believe that?" Just because she'd found a guy their parents didn't intentionally drive away didn't mean it was easy. She *happened* to fall in love with a guy who had multiple degrees and came from a perfect nuclear family.

Sighing, she melted a little. "Well, I'd *like* to believe it. I think they'd come around eventually."

"Maybe."

"Anyway, let me get this straight." Afra didn't look amused anymore. Actually she looked like she wanted to kick his ass. "You can't take Jax home to Maman and Baba, so instead of dating him you're just using him for sex?"

Okay, that did sound terrible. "Maman and Baba not approving is incidental to the reason. It's Jax."

"What about him?"

"He's…." Ari grasped for straws. "Kind of skittish. I thought if I tried to date him first it might scare him off."

Afra pursed her lips in a way that meant she was attempting to hide a smile. "So you're, what, incepting him into dating you? You've got an awful high opinion of your skills."

Now Ari allowed himself to give in to the satisfied smile that he deserved. "After last night, so does Jax."

She barked a laugh, finally. "All right, all right. I hope you know what you're doing."

"Not the slightest idea," Ari said. "But it's kind of a refreshing change."

Afra raised her iced coffee and waited for him to do the same. "I'll drink to that."

JAX RAN out of flour during the seventh recipe.

The sixth batch was still in the oven, so he couldn't just leave and buy more. And in point of fact, he probably shouldn't be making *these.* Excessive baking was wasteful. And he was going to need every extra dollar.

Unless, of course, he sucked it up and cracked open his laptop.

Jax didn't want to suck it up. Not the *it* in question, anyway.

He could put off thinking about his PhD if he had more flour.

Oooor he could think about Ari.

He hoped Afra was okay. He got the feeling Ari didn't exactly leave men in his apartment alone the day after ruinously good sex that barely got past first base, which meant whatever had happened, she'd needed him.

Meanwhile, Jax could indulge himself in daydreams of when he might see Ari again while surrounded by the scent of two hundred freshly baked cookies.

Aaaand he was spiraling. He shouldn't have stayed over at Ari's. He'd forgotten to take his meds this morning, which explained the hyperfixation on baking, as well as the headache blooming in his frontal lobe. He needed caffeine.

Maybe he should text Ari.

"Jax?"

He must've missed Hobbes coming home.

"Hey. In the kitchen."

"Yeah, I can tell." Hobbes appeared in the doorway a moment later. "So, first you don't come home at night, and now you're apparently starting a side hustle in refined carbs. Do I dare ask if you want to talk about it?"

Jax swatted him with the spatula when he reached for the chocolate chip. "Those just came out. They're still too hot."

"Was that a no to talking about it?"

"It was a 'please test the cream-cheese chocolate swirl, I think I might've put the sugar in twice.'" They sat at the kitchen table with a plate of various cookies and cups of coffee.

"So." Hobbes picked up a cookie and examined it in the light. It must have passed inspection, because he continued, "Ari," and then took an enormous bite.

"I could draw you a diagram," Jax offered.

"Pass." Hobbes hummed in gratification at the cookie. "Right amount of sugar, by the way."

Jax mentally congratulated himself. Considering the medication slipup, he was definitely going to have to taste-test every type of cookie. "Thanks."

"Uh-huh." Hobbes dusted off his hands and picked up his coffee mug. "I take it the night went… well?"

"Playing with fire, Hobbes," Jax warned. "Unless you want to hear about all the things Ari can do with his tongue." He paused, derailed. "Well, not all of them, there's only so many hours in a night—"

He raised his hands in protest. "I yield!"

"I do actually need your help with something," Jax realized. "Which one of these cookies says 'I'm into you the exact amount that you're into me' without reeking of premature devotion?"

Hobbes blinked at him, then looked at the cooling rack. "Well, it's not the macarons."

Fair.

What was an appropriate number of cookies for a "the sex was great, but how about I make you breakfast next time" gift?

"Jax?"

He rubbed a hand over his eyes. "I hate when I forget my meds."

"That does explain a lot," Hobbes said. "Maybe you should keep some on you if you're going to be having impromptu sleepovers."

Jax took out his phone and willed himself to have received a text from Ari, but still no luck. "I'm still sort of hoping it'll be less impromptu next time."

"Hey." He looked up at the suddenly serious tone. Hobbes was watching him steadily. "If he doesn't call you, he's a fool."

Now there was irony for you. Jax cracked a feeble smile. "Thanks, Hobbes."

Jax's afternoon didn't perk up. He still felt jittery and untethered when he got to work—only a few minutes late, and still wearing his Never Wear a Red Shirt T-shirt, whoops—and discovered that for him, a bar shift with unmedicated ADHD was a unique brand of hell.

Murph kept shooting him looks and, after his third drink mix-up, shoved him out from behind the bar and told him to put the energy to good use.

At least he couldn't drop the piano.

Ari hadn't called or texted all day, and Jax's romantic pessimism was engaged in battle with his trust in Naomi and Murph, who wouldn't have let him get involved with an asshat. Afra's problem must have been bigger than Ari had anticipated.

Though if that was the case, surely he would have answered Jax's late afternoon text of *Hope Afra's okay.* Right? Or the follow-up, *What can I do with your key?*

After an hour, he was behind the bar once again, this time filling drinks as Murph ordered, when Ari arrived. He was still dressed in those sinfully tight jeans, and he wore a messenger bag cross body, which made his shoulders look wider and his torso longer. Jax wondered if he was drooling on the bar.

The crowd moved for him, but Ari didn't seem to notice. His eyes were on Jax as he made his way to the bar.

"I'm an asshole," Ari said by way of hello.

"Oh?" Jax's heart thumped.

"I should have called or texted today."

"Yeah," Jax agreed. He had seven kinds of cookies to find a home for.

"I'm sorry that I didn't." He glanced away, then met Jax's eyes once again. "Sometimes I go full-on flighty artist when I'm writing. Forget everything. But I shouldn't have let myself do that today."

Okay, not an asshat. "Definitely not gentlemanly behavior." Jax let himself lean into Ari's space.

"Indeed." Ari gave a tentative smile. "I really am sorry, Jax. I came here as soon as I lifted my head and saw the time."

Jax glanced at the clock—almost nine. "That must have been some writing binge."

Ari blushed dark enough to be seen in the low lighting of the bar. "Yes, it was." He cleared his throat. "That doesn't excuse my idiocy, though." He reached into his bag and pulled out something soft and lumpy. "I'm hoping this might get me back into your good books."

Curious, Jax took the object. It was cloth—a nice T-shirt, judging by the feel. He unfurled it to get a good look—and burst into laughter.

The majority of the chest was occupied by a large pi symbol with a cartoon drawing of a bushy mustache pasted on the crossbeam. Underneath, it read *Magnum Pi.*

"A Tom Selleck math joke. It's almost like you know me."

A smile tugged at Ari's lips. "I'm getting there."

Jax's heart melted. *Definitely* not an asshat. "Okay, you're forgiven. But only because this shirt is amazing."

"Good." Ari smiled at him, and his eyes were soft and tender. Jax's heart hammered against his ribs, and he clutched the shirt tighter. A guy could get used to being looked at like that.

Unfortunately the look was maybe too addicting. Within ten minutes, Murph was glaring at Ari, and Jax had to chase him away.

"I'm unmedicated today, and I can't mix drinks with your face"—Jax waved his hands in the general direction of Ari's head—"doing that."

One eyebrow went up. "Doing what?"

"Looking at me. Just… go sit somewhere else and let me work."

So Ari stood slowly, and with one last lingering look that had Jax almost breathless, he disappeared into the break room. Probably for the best. As long as Ari was within eyesight, he would be a distraction.

Not that it helped much, Jax thought ruefully as he fumbled a glass and watched it shatter on the ground. At least it was empty.

"Right, that's it." Murph threw a cloth onto the bar top and gave Jax a long look. "You're useless tonight. Honestly, b'y, the next time you forget them, just call in sick."

"I didn't want to leave you in the lurch," Jax said guiltily.

Murph sighed. "We're full up on staff. We'll manage without the great Jax Hall for the rest of the night. Go find your fanboy and get out of my bar."

Meekly, Jax stepped around Henry, who had arrived with a broom, and darted to the back. He found Ari hunched over the keyboard, headphones in, scribbling something in a notebook.

Jax cleared his throat, knocked on the wall, and then knocked on the keyboard.

Ari jumped. "Jax! Are you done already?"

"I've been sent home early for being a danger unto myself and others." Ari arched his eyebrow, and Jax rubbed his own, somewhat sheepishly. "I, uh, broke a couple of glasses. Forgetting a pill leaves me worse than I was before medication."

"I see." He cocked his head and took Jax in fully. "I had hoped, if you forgave me, that you might be willing to join me again tonight."

The thought of another night in that comfortable bed with Ari curled up nearby was so tempting, but....

"As much as I'd like to get acquainted some more," Jax said slowly, "I'm kind of exhausted. Another side effect, unfortunately. I'll probably be asleep within the hour." Just thinking about bed made him yawn.

"That is understandable. Would you like a ride home?"

Jax had picked his bike up on his way home from Ari's, but he hadn't taken it to work today. It didn't take a genius to realize that scatterbrainedness and motorcycles should not mix. "A ride would be great."

Ari gathered his notebook and headphones and slid everything into his messenger bag. He finger-combed his loose, riotous curls away from his face. For a second, Jax nearly threw the plan out the window and asked Ari to take him home for another kind of ride. But his chemical-induced exhaustion was no joke, and Jax wasn't exactly in the mood after a day spent spiraling.

That didn't mean he wouldn't feel differently after a full night's rest.

"Hey, Ari?"

"Yes?"

"How about you treat me to brunch tomorrow, by way of apology." A soft slow smile was curling Ari's lips. "At your place."

"For you," Ari said with that wonderful fond look in his eyes, "that can definitely be arranged."

Chapter Eight

ARI HADN'T expected Jax to be so upset with him. He didn't have experience sleeping with someone who didn't feel romantic attachment, but he supposed ignoring text messages was rude no matter the circumstances.

But he'd finished off the first three songs now, at least, and rerecorded them for Noella. Which meant that when he dropped Jax off—with the world's most awkward nonkiss good night because Ari couldn't figure out if it was inappropriate—he didn't need to go straight home to compose.

He needed to go to the twenty-four-hour grocery to shop for brunch.

Fresh fruit was a must. He debated champagne for mimosas, but Jax couldn't drink alcohol before dinnertime, so he nixed that idea and bought fresh-squeezed orange juice—and the nicest loaf of bread he could find, farm-fresh eggs, the softest, freshest prosciutto, heavy cream for whipping, real vanilla, maple syrup, feta, cucumber, parsley, orange blossom jam…. Was he going overboard? This was an apology brunch, not a romantic one.

Shit.

On the other hand, if he bought enough food, he could justify Jax staying for dinner too, and *then* they could have champagne.

He woke up at quarter to seven, wide awake, and his brain was already in the kitchen thinking about which fruit he should cut up first when he realized his phone had woken him.

The text was from Jax.

I'm so sorry! I guess it's my turn to be a dick. I have to cancel brunch.

Ari's heart sank. A second text came in.

I'm really super sorry, and I would never cancel without the best of reasons! Sister needs help with the kid, though.

Tucking his hurt away, Ari wrote back *That is understandable. Brunch can wait.* Besides, it would be the height of hypocrisy to complain.

Ugh! But *I* don't want to. :(

His lips quirked. Knowing Jax had been looking forward to today as much as he had soothed his disappointment.

Me neither. But brunch will still be here after you have helped your sister.

Good.

Ari waited for more—Jax was rarely taciturn—but after a few minutes of silence, Ari put his phone back on the nightstand and rolled over for a few more winks.

When he woke again, it was almost nine and his phone was vibrating on the nightstand once again.

Breakfast with my new date isn't nearly as enjoyable.

I should hope not.

He dropped his phone and headed for the shower. Several minutes later, clean and hungry, he brought his phone to the kitchen. He was nibbling on some of the fruit he'd bought the night before when he checked his phone again.

At least she's entertaining, Jax had written and then shared a series of pictures—a Caucasian toddler sitting at a kitchen table with her face smeared in a combination of crumbs and berry juice, the same toddler sitting in Jax's lap for a selfie, her fluffy golden hair and bright blue eyes a match to Jax's own. *This is Alice.*

God, they were cute. He tapped to enlarge the photo. Jax was smiling at the baby, ignoring the camera, while she was reaching for it, clearly eager to play with the toy. A few old friends had complained about their kids' desire to play with the phone, and it looked like Alice was no different.

Alice. Huh. What a coincidence.

Ari looked at the adorable chubby face. The sizzling, popping sensation of creative inspiration bubbled in the back of his brain. He crossed the room in quick strides, searching for his notebook. He needed to make some adjustments to his lyrics.

JAX WOKE up early, deliberately took his pill when his phone chimed, and was contemplating the best outfit for a booty-call-slash-brunch-date when his phone rang.

"Hi, George. What's up?"

"Are you doing anything today? I mean, I know you're working later, but what about right now?"

There was a tinge of desperation to his voice, and Jax bit his tongue. "Why? What's going on?"

"Sam's at work, all sorts of new employee stuff, and I was meant to be taking it easy today so I could watch Alice. We don't have a day care yet." He huffed.

"And?"

"And someone fucked up—at my work, I mean. Royally. And the client is baying for blood, and my boss needs me on it, only it's several hours of work and I can't—"

"Say no more. Do you want me at yours or to bring her here?"

"Jax, you're a life saver," George said eagerly. "Normally our place would be easier, but there are boxes everywhere.... Calvin won't mind you having a kid at home all day?"

"George, if you didn't figure out that Hobbes won't mind a kid, then I don't know what to tell you."

He laughed. "Good point. Okay, give me a few to pack her up and I'll be there soon. Like, thirty minutes?"

"Do you need me to come get her?"

"Your bike doesn't exactly have room for a car seat, not to mention the several bags a toddler comes with."

He had a point. "See you in thirty, then," Jax laughed and hung up.

Only now he had to cancel on Ari. *Fuck.* Last night, Jax's dream self got plowed into the mattress with his ankles around his ears, but it looked like his waking self would have to keep waiting.

He texted Ari and was careful to make the message sound appropriately apologetic and disappointed. Then he went to the kitchen to find breakfast for himself and a baby.

George looked ready to kiss him when Jax accepted Alice and her bags. "I can't thank you enough. Normally I might tell him to deal without me, but they're a bit nervous about me having moved so far away, even though it was their decision to go remote permanently."

"Hey, don't worry about it. That's what brothers-in-law are for. It's why you moved so close, right?" They'd found a temporary rental not ten minutes away and were searching for something more permanent.

"Exactly. Okay, be good for your uncle Jax and I'll see you at the end of the day. One of us will be back to pick her up as soon as we can."

Jax squeezed his precious niece and pressed his face to her downy head. "Like I said, don't worry about it. I'm sure you'll be back before my shift at seven. Now go—make money and wow your bosses. Say bye-bye to Daddy, Alice!"

She lifted a chubby hand and waved at George as he backed away and then dashed to his car.

Jax shut the front door and then stared at Alice. "Alone at last," he said as it dawned on him that he was indeed alone with his niece for the very first time and it had been years since he last took a babysitting job. "Well, today should be interesting," Jax told Alice. She nodded seriously. "Do you like strawberries?"

She clapped. "S'awberries!"

"Let's go find some, then."

At least she wasn't afraid of him. Otherwise it'd be a really long day.

George had texted a tentative schedule—when he could expect her to be hungry, when she'd want a nap. One of the texts was just a poop emoji followed by *10:30*. Alice beat the clock by three minutes.

"Your dad is kind of scary good at this," Jax told her while he changed her diaper on the living room table. One good thing about living with a doctor—they always had plenty of bleach wipes to disinfect the furniture.

"Good," Alice agreed. Then she attempted to kick him in the face.

By nap time—eleven—Jax was ready to sack out with her. He put her down for a nap in the middle of his bed, pillows piled on either side so she couldn't roll off, closed the curtains to make it at least *sort of* dark, and crept back toward the door. But as he was closing it behind him, something got caught underneath, and he stopped to pick it up.

Dear Mr. Hall,

Pursuant to our email of September 3....

Jax bit back a curse and crumpled the paper in his fist. Then, in a fit of uncharacteristic rage-induced determination, he went back into the bedroom, dug under his desk for his school laptop, and crept out again. If this was the universe sending him a sign, fine. It could maybe take a lesson in subtlety—Jax didn't need to be babysitting his niece to be reminded that he had adult responsibilities—but *fine*. He needed to confront reality. Message received.

The laptop hadn't been powered on in months, and it took half an hour to run a bunch of updates before he could do anything. In honesty, it didn't have much software to update—just the antivirus and the operating system, a web browser, and the two programs Jax had written, which took up most of the memory.

It still had Excel, though, and he pulled that up, along with his bank account information. It was time to take a look at the facts.

Fact one: He'd been ready to defend for more than a year. His thesis was based on a computer program that modeled population growth and decay within biological systems. Grayling, his advisor, had pronounced it ready to defend in March of 2020, just before the world imploded, when Jax had been conscripted as his assistant on a modeling project for the Massachusetts Department of Health.

Fact two: He'd already paid thousands of dollars to *not finish his PhD*, because if he withdrew completely, it would cost him forty grand to go back and finish, even if all he had to do was sit in front of the committee.

Fact three: Jax didn't pay a lot in rent, but he also didn't make enough money to justify continuing to spend thousands of dollars in "nonresident graduate tuition" per term.

It wasn't sustainable. He knew it wasn't. He could've done the math on this when he was ten. If you factored in scholarships, he'd spent more money *not* going to MIT than he had actually attending four years of classes.

The problem was that the idea of returning to Cambridge, walking through the Simons Building, knowing his advisor wouldn't be there… sucked.

Also, he needed, like, thirteen thousand dollars.

Grimly, Jax opened Excel and began entering numbers—expenses, estimated income, assets. He might not be able to do anything right now, but he at least needed to know what he didn't know—a bottom line, a final figure, a stretch goal.

Twenty minutes later he blew out a long breath and closed his laptop, ready for a different kind of distraction.

Hopefully Alice would wake up soon.

ARI SPENT the majority of Thursday fussing with "Alice," until it became less wonderland and more psychedelic musings. He moved the piano melody down an octave and transposed it to a minor key. Then he took a pen to the lyrics.

It seemed so obvious now that Jax wasn't some innocent who'd fallen down a rabbit hole into a nonsense world. No, Jax was the grinning Cheshire Cat—an outsider who understood the illogic of the world but didn't belong to it. Not *really*. He was holding too much of himself back.

Ari wanted to see beyond the grin, but he had the suspicion that if he tried, the whole of Jax would slip away bit by bit, just as the cat did in the book.

When he'd reworked it to his satisfaction, he sat down to rerecord, first the piano and then the violin. He even took video of the violin part so Noella would have something to post to Instagram. In a separate file, he recorded the vocals too, even though he hated his own singing voice, and packaged the whole thing off for Noella.

Got them, her reply email read three minutes later. *I want to share these with Bill and Yaron, and they're going to want to talk about them. Tomorrow good for you?*

Tomorrow said like that, with no given time, likely meant he'd be in video meetings all day. He winced, but his album was already behind schedule, so he didn't have much room for complaint. *Fine*, he wrote back.

Then he pried himself off his piano bench to get some exercise, since he was going to be sedentary all day tomorrow.

HE TURNED out to be right about the meetings.

"Stop fucking around with 'Alice,'" Noella told him right away. "It's done."

Ari blinked. She'd never been so satisfied with one of his tracks that quickly. "Okay?"

Fortunately Noella had plenty of experience with artists and knew what he needed to hear. "Look, is it your typical blockbuster track? No. Is it going to be the emotional powerhouse behind the album? No. It's introspective and kind of thinky, which, let's face it, is your milieu. And I know I'm always harping on you to inject some emotion, but it's also beautiful the way it is. Do you have a vocal artist in mind for it? With the caveat that Leonard Cohen is not an option."

She reminded him of that every time he wrote a song that came off as weird and kind of fucked-up. "Bon Iver, maybe?" he hazarded, and she hummed, so she must not have thought it was the worst idea.

He had a grand total of twenty-three minutes between the first call with Noella and the subsequent call with her, Bill, and Yaron.

So of course his phone rang right in the middle of it.

"Hey," Jax said, and Ari could hear the grin through the phone, even if it sounded like it might be fading away. "What're you up to today? Got time for that rain check?"

Ari sighed. "I've been on conference calls all morning, and I have"—he checked the clock on the microwave, remembered the microwave was in the process of reheating his lunch, then looked at the oven instead—"eleven minutes before the next one."

"Take that as a no," Jax sighed.

"We could do dinner instead?" Ari suggested. "If you're not okay with french toast after 6:00 p.m., we could go out somewhere." Even though he'd rather have quick access to a bed.

"Breakfast foods are all-day foods, but I work at seven. Picked up an extra shift." Well, crap. "What about tomorrow?"

"I'm free all day."

"Not anymore."

JAX SHUFFLED out of his bedroom and stifled a yawn. Picking up extra shifts at the bar might be good for the bank account and his Finally Acquiring the PhD—a plan that he was basically approaching from the side because he wasn't ready to face it head-on—but his body was not a fan and now insisted on afternoon naps. He passed out only an hour or two after his call with Ari.

At least Murph had been relieved when Jax approached him looking for more hours.

"To be honest, b'y, you're pulling in enough business these days that we need more staff almost every night. I'd rather give more work to my people than start advertising for new folk." He pulled his phone from his pocket to look up the schedule. "Did you want to work every night?"

Jax did. The sooner he scraped up the money, the sooner he could put the PhD and everything that came with it behind him.

In the meantime he had Hobbes to deal with. "Again?" he asked when Jax announced he was on his way to work.

So Jax was probably going to have to tell him the truth, sooner rather than later, because the way things were going, he wasn't ever going to *see* him unless he came to the bar.

He let himself mull it over in the back of his mind as he worked his shift, thinking of what to say. But when he got home just after midnight, the lights were still on and Hobbes was sitting in the living room, eating one of the rare cookies that hadn't made its way to the doctors' lounge at the hospital.

"Hey," Jax said quietly as he closed the door behind him and locked it. "You're still up."

"I don't know what I've ever done to make you think I turn into a pumpkin at midnight." A glass of brandy sat on the table next to him, and a mug of tea steamed on the coffee table, obviously for Jax. "Come sit down for a sec?"

Hobbes was less than a decade older than he was, but sometimes his dad vibe was too much. But maybe that was just because Jax hadn't ever had one. Either way, Jax dutifully climbed the stairs and took the seat opposite him on the couch. "What's up?"

Wordlessly, Hobbes held up a crumpled piece of paper.

Ah. That. Jax vaguely remembered leaving that in the kitchen. "Oh."

"Yes, *oh*," Hobbes said, tone laced with any number of complex emotions—anger, humor, exasperation, grief. "Seems like someone's been getting hate mail from his would-be alma mater. You want to tell me about that?"

"Not really."

Hobbes closed his eyes and massaged the bridge of his nose. "Kid—"

"Give me a break. I'm seven years younger than you."

"Yeah, the same age as my little sister. Who will *always be a kid*." He huffed. "Jax. Just tell me what's going on."

Fuck it. Jax's eyes felt like sandpaper, and he wanted to go to bed so that it could be tomorrow already. "I'm going to finish it, okay? Next semester. I'm going to go back to Cambridge and defend and just… close the chapter. Move on."

"This is a bill for four thousand dollars," Hobbes said pointedly.

Jax sighed. "Yeah, it is. I paid it."

"You paid four thousand dollars to *not attend*?"

"Closer to twelve, total." He shrugged, not bothering to hide the wince. "It was that or drop totally and then pay forty if I ever decided to go finish."

Understanding dawned on Hobbes's face. "Jesus, that's disgusting. This is why you're working Sundays now?"

"Every shift Murph'll give me," Jax confirmed. "Tuition's due again in January." No measly four grand this time either.

Hobbes schooled his expression into careful neutrality, but Jax had known him at his lowest. Hobbes couldn't fool him. "You know I don't—"

Jax raised his hand. "Don't make that offer, please. I know you don't, but I want to and I will. I'll pay rent or I'll find a new place."

Unhappy acceptance writ large on his face, Hobbes sighed and sank into the couch. "Jax. You were there for me when I couldn't even get to the john by myself. Would it kill you to let me help?"

It might. Jax's sense of self-worth was fragile as it was. He didn't need to grind it into dust. "You *are* helping," he said instead. "You charge well below market rent. You pay all the utilities and won't even ask me to do yard work in return." Jax did it anyway, because he needed to have *some* pride, even if he hated pulling weeds. "Plus my rent includes access to a therapy animal."

Hobbes glanced at the Captain, who was snoring gently in front of the fireplace. "He's a therapy animal now?"

"I was talking about you."

"Of course you were." Hobbes sighed. "Okay, fine. But if you're going to be working seven nights a week, I'm hiring somebody to cut the grass."

Jax huffed, but he hated cutting the grass. He was pretty sure he was allergic to it. Every time he finished, he found himself wheezing. Besides, it was already fall; there'd only be a few more cuttings this season.

He could make up for it raking leaves. "Fine," he agreed.

"Fine," Hobbes echoed. "Great. Drink your tea."

Chapter Nine

ARI WOKE up once again to unread text messages, this time with the addition of missed calls, all from his mother, wanting to know when he would be available for a dinner party. The last time he'd spoken to her, she'd suggested he take up internet dating—*That's how people your age find dates these days, isn't it?*—so he was inherently suspicious. He ignored the message and rolled out of bed to start brunch prep.

By the time he had the fruit cut, the cream whipped, and the table set, he had just enough time to shower before Jax arrived.

Should he have changed the sheets?

Then again, they were just going to dirty them.

In the end he didn't have time to make a conscious decision. As he was buttoning his shirt, there was a knock on the door.

Jax.

Ari brushed his palms quickly over his jeans to smooth them out and strode toward the entryway.

"Hi," Jax said, smiling a charmingly sheepish smile, his head bent.

It took Ari a moment to realize he was doing it to call attention to the shirt Ari had bought him, which he now wore. He'd guessed the sizing right exactly. It fit snugly across the chest and shoulders, and the mustache—

Ari reached out to touch it before he could stop himself, somehow hypnotized by the ludicrous fake fur between Jax's pectorals. Only when he had his palm flat on Jax's chest did he realize what he was doing.

He jerked his head up and met Jax's gaze, an apology on his lips, but before it could gain any traction, Jax stepped into his space and kissed him.

Brunch could wait.

When Jax walked him backward into his bedroom, they were already half naked, tearing at each other's clothing. Jax tripped out of his jeans, but he landed on his back on the bed, and Ari followed him down, preventing as much as helping Jax disrobe. Jax bit at his lip again, groaned when Ari tightened his hands on his hips.

"Ari," Jax gasped as Ari mouthed down the line of his neck, determined to gauge the color of the bruises he'd left two nights before. "You gotta do something for me."

Ari would write him a symphony. "Name it."

Jax fisted a hand in his hair—Ari's dick jerked—and yanked until they were eye to eye.

Then he said, "Take off your pants and fuck me."

Well. Ari did owe him for accidentally ghosting him, after all.

He leaned in and kissed him, hard. "It would be my pleasure." He untangled Jax's hands from his hair and briefly pressed his hands into the mattress. Jax let out a delicious moan that Ari filed away for later. He knelt and undid his pants and pushed them off as quickly as he could. Beneath him, Jax wiggled out of his own clothes, and they came together again, kissing frantically.

"Like this?" Ari asked, meaning *On your back?* Jax panted openmouthed in approval. Ari had never been much for talking in bed, but Jax's reaction inspired him... and perhaps the uncharacteristic dialogue would remind him he shouldn't form a romantic attachment. "I could bend you in half. I bet you like that, knees around your ears?" Jax pushed up into him, desperate and hungry, like he couldn't get Ari's dick into him soon enough. "Or," Ari said, "maybe on your stomach or your hands and knees." Jax dragged his nails down Ari's back. "Me on my knees behind you, plowing into you, gripping your hips until they bruise."

"God yes," Jax said fervently. "Please, that. Do that."

Ari didn't need to be asked twice, but he was pretty sure Jax would do it anyway. He knelt to give Jax room to move and reached for the nightstand drawer.

But when he returned his attention to the bed, he could barely process the image in front of him: Jax with his knees spread, the firm, round bubble of his ass pushed up for Ari's appreciation. His skin was tanned to the waist, as though he'd spent a great deal of time shirtless out of doors over the summer, but his cheeks were cream pale. And—

Oh God. Ari traced his fingers over the dark ink on Jax's right cheek, which he had somehow missed in their earlier encounter. "What's this?"

"A story for after," Jax promised, undulating under the touch. "You're killing me."

Ari flipped the top on the lube and generously coated his fingers, then wasted no time sliding two of them deep.

Jax arched his back on a moan, and his body yielded immediately. Ari knew logically that Jax's temperature wasn't any warmer than anyone else's, but the heat around his fingers still sent a shock of lust through him. He thrust gently, mostly to distribute the lube since Jax didn't seem to require stretching. But then he nudged Jax's prostate and Jax's spine went positively liquid. He made a noise that began deep in his chest and ended curled tightly around Ari's cock, and Ari had to add another finger and make him do it again.

Finally Jax said, "*Ari.* Are you going to fuck me like you promised, or do I have to do it myself?"

Ari pressed into his prostate again—hard. Jax's elbows buckled and he fell to them with a grunt.

"Fuck," Ari breathed. Jax's ass looked even more inviting with his shoulders pressed lower. He grabbed a condom and yanked his fingers out of Jax's ass at the same time, eager to move things forward. As he slid the condom onto his dick, Jax scrambled back onto his hands. It somewhat ruined the view, but....

Impulsively, Ari leaned down and followed the swooping curve of the tattoo on the meat of Jax's ass with the tip of his tongue. The design was unfamiliar to Ari but was clearly a letter of some kind. A shocked noise—part moan, part whimper—flowed from Jax, and Ari licked the design bottom to top, then, after another look at the appealing curves, bit it.

"Oh my God, Ari." He sounded drunk with lust and impatience. "Later you can show me everything you can do with your tongue, I promise, but please, I need—ungh!" His begging turned into incoherent moans as Ari pushed his dick in deep with one unerring thrust. Jax pressed his knees wider and his belly down, apparently eager to get more of Ari, faster. Fuck.

"Bossy," Ari admonished. He resettled his hands on Jax's hips and assessed his balance. If he was going to give it as hard as Jax wanted, he didn't want to fall over.

"Only when I need to be." Jax squirmed delightfully, perhaps in an attempt to entice Ari into movement. Or maybe he just couldn't stay still when full of cock—he certainly couldn't manage it at any other time. Another avenue to explore later. "Jesus, are you going to just stay there? I thought you were going to *fuck me*."

"As you wish," Ari said drolly. With a light squeeze of Jax's hips, he pulled out and slammed forward. Jax yowled and arched his back, trying to press into Ari's thrust, so Ari tightened his grip and began in earnest. Now that he knew Jax could take it—*loved* taking it—all bets were off.

Time blurred as Ari thrust hard and fast, doing his best to meet Jax's many demands for harder, deeper. His elbows buckled and he fell to them a second time. The curve of his back, his trim waist, round ass, like the most beautiful violin, was a sight to behold, and Ari didn't want to take his eyes off the flexing muscles under smooth skin, or his own cock moving in and out.

But those shoulders made a tempting offer Ari couldn't ignore. Shifting forward, he planted his hands on the mattress next to Jax and, once curled around him, applied his mouth to Jax's trapezius. The soft moan-filled *ah*s that pushed out of Jax were music to Ari's ears.

He sucked hard below Jax's jaw. Jax fell forward, and his face hit the mattress. The new angle pushed a series of turned-on moans out of him, but it didn't allow Ari to indulge his new obsession with that delicious neck. He snaked an arm around Jax's chest and hauled Jax with him until they were both on their knees.

"Fuck," Jax moaned as gravity pushed him farther onto Ari's cock. The increased sensation deserved a reward, and Ari sucked a mark into the unbitten side of Jax's neck as Jax squeezed down hard.

"Jax," Ari groaned. Retaking his hips, he began to push at a brutal pace. Jax got even louder in this position. Ari slid his hand across Jax's chest and up under his chin, the better to get a strong hold, and Jax moaned at every touch.

"How—how do you want to—" Ari pushed out between gasps, his thrusts erratic now. He wanted Jax there with him.

"I'm close," Jax gasped, which wasn't an answer. Then Jax craned his neck and tilted his head back, his mouth open and seeking, a clear invitation for a kiss.

Ari might be surprised by the request for something so intimate, but he wasn't a fool. He took Jax's lips in a filthy, panting kiss and Jax's dick in a sloppy hand job, and Jax came, moaning into his mouth. Ari followed after, his mouth pressed against Jax's, their moans mingling with their breaths.

"Fuck," Jax whimpered, a boneless sprawl across Ari's lap. "I don't think I can actually move."

Ari didn't want to break the moment, but he figured Jax might feel drastically different about still being connected. He gently tipped Jax forward onto the bed, helping control the fall, and carefully slid his dick out. Jax sighed and burrowed his face into a pillow.

Ari was more than happy to linger over the view, one of superb ass and defined shoulders littered with bruises. Only... would Jax want to cuddle? He hadn't minded staying the other night, but Ari didn't want to make him uncomfortable. Besides, the condom needed tossing, and Jax would probably appreciate a washcloth.

Ari got up to accomplish both tasks and returned to find Jax flipped over onto his back. He smiled at Ari when he returned and held up the warm cloth like a peace offering. He took the cloth and cleaned his belly and cock of the remaining evidence.

"You know," Jax said, shifting his hips and wrinkling his nose, "me and these sheets might need more intense washing intervention."

Ari snorted. "I'm happy to share my shower with you. Jointly or individually." The sheets were a lost cause, but if they were going for round two—or three—there didn't seem much point in stripping the bed now.

Jax held out a hand to be pulled upright. "Well, with an offer like that."

ARI TURNED out to have a very nice shower and a knack for brunch. Jax could get used to both.

"So this is where you do your composing?" He wandered over to the piano, which sat on a colorful woven rug. Ari's living room overlooked a park, with the Thames just visible in the distance. Of course, the piano faced away from the window, so maybe he didn't even look at it. Maybe he looked at the coordinating wall hanging, or the framed picture of the couple who must be his parents standing in front of a beautifully tiled building with the perfect high arches he associated with Persian architecture.

"When the mood strikes me and I'm home, yes." An electric violin and bow hung on the wall, and a conventional case sat underneath the piano, probably for a wood instrument. Jax would bet that one had some kind of humidity control. You wouldn't just leave an expensive instrument outside of a carefully controlled climate.

Something in Ari's answer made Jax look up. "Trouble?" he asked.

"Of a sort." Ari joined him at the piano bench, and they sat down shoulder to shoulder. Jax had never played a piano this nice. The ebony wood gleamed in the light from the window. "I have an album due soon."

Ah. Good to know he might be disappearing into a hole for the next little while. "How soon?"

Ari looked over, lips quirking. "I'm supposed to start recording next month."

Wow. October was more than half over. "So, really soon. Why do I sense a 'but'?"

"I expect because you're entirely too perceptive." Ari moved his fingers over the keys, gently coaxing out a tune that felt warm but melancholy, like a rainy summer day without your lover. "Technically I should have the songs written and greenlit by now and just be rehearsing and booking session musicians to record with. Normally I get a lot of writing done on tour. But this last tour didn't feel like any other tour, and I didn't get any writing done."

"I can see how that would happen." Jax fumbled out a few notes, trying to follow along with what Ari was doing. "Are you having any better luck now that you're home?"

Ari stopped playing and watched Jax's fingers for a moment. "Some," he admitted. "More than I hoped for. Less than my producer would like."

Jax wondered what had changed. Maybe he needed different scenery, or to be around his family. Maybe he needed to decompress.

But either way it was probably pretty personal, so Jax didn't ask. "Will you play one for me?" he asked instead, placing his hands in his lap.

Strangely—sweetly—this made Ari flush, though he must get asked all the time. "Ah, not yet." He smoothed a hand over his hair— totally unnecessarily, as he'd tied it back with an elastic. "I'm... superstitious about them, I guess you could say. They're not done yet. I let Noella put bits of one on my Instagram, but only because she insisted. To have someone hear it live...."

"I understand. When they're finished, though?"

Ari flushed again—a sweet dark pink washing over brown. "We'll see."

Jax nudged him in the side. "Tease." Then he caught sight of the time. "Damn. I have to go." He stood, relishing the slight ache in his muscles. "I have to run a couple errands before my shift tonight."

Gracefully, Ari stood as well. "I thought you worked Thursday through Saturday nights?"

He'd memorized Jax's schedule? Jax forced down a wave of warmth. It was far too soon for that. He knew better than to put the cart before the horse. "We've been busy lately, what with the publicity from your show and the university and college being back in session. Murph needed extra help. I was available." *And I need the money.*

"A mutually beneficial arrangement," Ari said. Jax wondered if he was imagining the innuendo there—but what would he be implying? It didn't make sense.

"It does make having a social life a little challenging." Jax offered a small smile as he toed into his shoes. "But there's plenty of room at the bar if you get bored."

"I may take you up on that."

He had just enough time to hit the pet store to take advantage of the sale on Whiskas and then go home to feed the Captain before his shift.

WHEN JAX strolled into the break room, Kayla was already there, doing her makeup. In retrospect, he might as well just have worn a sign.

"Oh, honey," Kayla said, turning away from the mirror. "Come here and let me look at you."

Jax submitted to inspection with a rueful smile. "Hi, Kayla."

She whistled low as she took him in from head to toe. "Great shirt, by the way."

"Gift from Ari."

"Oh?" She leaned in close to him, touched her fingers to his chin, and tilted it to the left. "And what about these?" She walked her fingers down the side of his neck, eyes sparkling. "Are these gifts from Ari too?"

Jax grinned. "He's very generous."

"Well, he'd better be." She patted his cheek. "You deserve it, sweetie. Make sure he's good to you or I'll break off all his fingers one by one and feed them to him, okay?"

"Jesus, Kayla." Talk about a graphic threat. "You'll forgive me if I don't pass on that particular message."

"You're no fun. Now come here." She yanked him closer and shoved him in front of the mirror. "You can't go out there looking like someone's been using you as a chew toy. Someone else will think they can have a bite." She picked up her makeup palette and dabbed foundation on Jax's neck. "So tell me. What's our opening number tonight, hmm? 'I Just Had Sex'?"

Jax snorted and tried not to squirm at the tickle of the brush. "'Side to Side'?" he suggested. "'Dirrty'? 'She Wolf'?"

"You and Christina." Kayla tilted his head to the other side. "I can't believe you're neglecting Beyoncé like this. 'Rocket'?"

"Ooh."

"Think you can manage something that sultry?" Kayla asked as she put the finishing touches on Jax's neck.

Jax shot her a sassy look. "Please, this is me." He dropped his lashes. "I can do sultry."

"Now you're just trying to tease. Put that face away when you're not going to follow through." She flicked his nose with her brush.

Jax grinned. He loved how well he and Kayla understood each other. "If you insist." He watched her put her makeup away, then clapped. "You gonna help me play 'Rocket'?"

"Hell yes!" She tossed her hair and grinned. "Don't suppose Ari's coming around tonight?"

Jax laughed. "One can only hope."

ARI WROTE late into the night after Jax left. Then he slept in and wrote again the next morning. He hadn't felt this possessed since the early days, when he was attempting to get all the songs that had ever lived in his head out at once.

At least this time he remembered to check his phone during water breaks and had promptly responded to a query about what Ari had been up to that evening, complete with a lascivious smiling face.

Ari was tempted to put on shoes and head to the bar, but he knew better than to ignore his muse at times like these.

He was elbow deep in sheet music after lunchtime the next day when a knock came at the door.

A quick check through the peephole revealed Theo. What was his sister's intern doing there?

"Hello. Did Afra send you?"

Theo stuck his hands in his pockets and gave a rueful smile. The kid was entirely too adorable for someone halfway through university. "Yeah. She had an important meeting but felt that someone should come check on you."

Ari rolled his eyes but let the kid come in.

"Drink?"

Theo took one of the Cokes hidden in the fridge for guests. He popped the tab and took a long slurp. "Thanks. The walk here was longer than I expected." His cheeks were chapped from the October wind, and Ari almost wanted to scold him for not having worn a hat. But that was probably crossing some sort of employer-pseudo-employee boundary, so he cast about for something else to say. His piano sat open, the top propped up on the support bar. Right—he'd been about to take care of that.

"Want to help me tune the piano?"

Theo paused with the Coke can halfway to his mouth. "Really? Okay. What do I do?"

"Just sit on the bench and play the keys one at a time, please."

Theo hit the lowest A note, and Ari checked the note and tightened the string until it registered the proper vibration. Satisfied, he asked Theo to climb to A-sharp and repeated the process. They had climbed all the way to the first F-sharp before Theo spoke. "You like doing this."

"Hm?" Ari gave the bolt another twist. "Try that." Perfect. "I guess? I like knowing I can fix the problem. And there is something therapeutic about the process. Normally I do this alone, so it takes longer, but I can zone out when I do it."

"Oh. Sounds peaceful."

"It is. G, please."

They came around to A again. "I wish I could play music like you do."

"Have you ever tried to learn? Play again."

Theo hit the key, and Ari motioned for him to move on. His brow furrowed as he played the next one. "Not really. I mean, I had to play the drums for a while in school, but I couldn't quite manage the dual rhythm thing."

"Ah, not an easy feat. Kayla, who plays at the Rock, can manage three rhythms, hands and feet, in a manner that I find pretty enviable."

Theo gave him a little smile and replayed the note when requested. "I guess it's something of a unique talent. Though wouldn't playing the piano…."

"It's not dissimilar. Though there is a reason I prefer the violin."

"My parents were super worried about falling into parenting traps and clichés," Theo admitted. "I'm not sure if it's because they didn't want to be the rich white parents who forced their kid to take piano or if they didn't want to make their brown kid into a stereotype, but they were against making me take any music lessons." His lips quirked. "I could have asked. They'd have given me whatever I wanted."

Ari finished tightening the current string. "It sounds like they were doing their best to love you."

"Oh, definitely," Theo agreed. "They definitely did. I know they love me. They, uh, couldn't have kids but kept hoping and got started on the whole adoption thing pretty late." He played the next note, looking distracted. Ari glanced at his tuner and tightened the bolt. "They were almost fifty, so I was their miracle baby, you know?" He cast a look Ari's way. "If I told them I wanted to tattoo myself purple and dress only in tutus they would have taken me to a tailor to get a custom tulle wardrobe."

Ari chuckled. "I guess you should be grateful you didn't want to, then."

"Yeah." Theo played the note once more and moved on to the next one.

"Was it difficult, growing up with white parents?" Ari asked tentatively. He didn't want to pry if it was an uncomfortable subject, but Theo had brought them up—maybe he needed to talk about it.

Theo smiled wistfully. "Sometimes. Especially when they forget that I look like a 'terrorist.'" He barked a humorless laugh. "Though I guess I mostly miss the worst of it since I dress like a white guy."

Ari nodded. He got the same kind of Islamophobic BS even though his family wasn't Muslim, so he had the same mix of prejudice and privilege to deal with. "I get it."

Theo gave a wan smile, then turned back to the keys. The moment was apparently over. "So. Which note is next?"

JAX WAS still in bed when the phone rang, which was probably the only reason he answered it. If he'd seen the Caller ID—

But he didn't.

"Hello?"

"Oh, so you're taking my calls now."

Shit.

Jax swallowed, suddenly wide-awake. He scrambled upright, the sheets pooling around his waist. "Mom. Hi."

"Hi, he says. Like it's good to talk to me. As though he hasn't been dodging my calls since June."

"I haven't been dodging your calls." He'd been dodging her calls since January.

His mother did not dignify that with a response, and guilt sneaked in to fill the silence until Jax couldn't take it anymore. "Sorry," he mumbled.

"I get it, kiddo," she said gently. "The past eighteen months haven't been easy on any of us, you know? I just want you to talk to me."

Ah yes. More guilt. "And say what?" Honestly, where could he even begin?

"I don't know. That's why I'm asking you."

He took a deep breath and scrubbed a hand over his hair. He needed a haircut again. That seemed so strange, since just last year he'd gone three or four months without one. "Okay, let's start over, I guess. We can pretend. Hi, Mom. Long time no speak. How are you?"

Whatever shortcomings his mother might have, she loved her children. Jax counted himself lucky that right now she seemed to love him enough to humor him. "Well, you know. School's back in session, so I'm living the dream."

This was an old, well-worn conversation between them, so he let himself relax into it. "Let me guess—the freshmen get younger every year."

"They are like little babies," she confirmed. "Most of them not as little as you were, though."

Jax had been only sixteen when he started university and hadn't hit his growth spurt until he was twenty-one, so that didn't surprise him. "Lucky for them," he said. "You teaching undergrads this semester?"

"Just the one session, thank God. Linear algebra."

"At least it's a fun one."

"You'd be surprised how many of my students don't think so."

He snorted. "And you wrote the textbook for them and everything. Ungrateful."

"They have the nerve to bitch about paying fifty bucks for the copying fees."

Jax shook his head. They'd bitched about that when he was in undergrad too. "Some things never change, I guess."

"I guess," she agreed. But apparently he ought to have offered more, because she took advantage of the natural pause in conversation to say, "What about you, Jax? How're things with you?"

And this was where things got sticky. "Oh, you know me. I'm always fine."

"Hmm," she said noncommittally. "That does seem to be the consensus of the comments on this video."

Fuck. "You saw that?"

"Half the Northern Hemisphere's seen it, kid. You really didn't want to tell your mom you finally got internet famous?"

"It wasn't on purpose," he protested. "It was a last-minute thing. I was just having fun."

"Sure," she said too easily. Jax sensed a trap. "So listen. I've been asking around."

Jax was immediately on high alert. He rolled out of bed and paced barefoot beneath the window. "Mom—"

"Hear me out. I know you know Western has a math PhD program. I spoke with Dr. Singh—"

"Mom!"

"Jax!" she echoed. "I'm sorry, but what do you want me to say? That it's okay with me if you waste your talent playing second piano in a bar three nights a week?"

Jax bit down on his tongue in order to avoid telling her it was every night now. "A little empathy might be nice. It's not like I didn't finish on *purpose*. Sorry there was a global pandemic and I had to leave the university and while I was gone my thesis advisor fucking died!"

"I know," she said, and already the anger had leached out of her voice. It always did, not that it made it better. "Shit, I know that. I'm sorry. I know Grayling meant a lot to you."

Grayling had been like the father he'd never had, though Jax had never felt the loss of one when he was growing up. His mother was aromantic and had always been single, but she made sure he and Sam had plenty of role models of all genders. That didn't mean he didn't fall in love with Grayling's family, his wife and two teenage daughters, who invited Grayling's grad students to family barbecues and gave him a home away from home.

And then the pandemic hit, and everything shut down. Grayling got conscripted to work on some software for the Massachusetts Department of Health, and Jax was his right-hand man. Then he crossed the border into Canada, called home by a prime minister who'd seen the writing on the wall. Two months later Grayling was dead.

"How can I face them?" Jax whispered. "I abandoned them."

"Jax… honey. You don't have to go back. That's what I'm trying to say."

"You're right. I don't. I'm happy doing what I'm doing." He was good at bartending. He was mediocre at playing piano. But he was *excellent* at making sure people had a good time.

"I mean in order to get your doctorate."

Jax stopped, bowled over. "So, what? You think I should abandon my years of research and start over because it's more important for me to have a PhD than...." Than what? Whatever the fuck he was doing now? Than dealing with grief and PTSD and a brand-new ADHD diagnosis in the best way he knew how? Finally forming friendships that felt like they'd last, with people who cared about more than Jax's enormous, beautiful brain?

"If you had chosen a Canadian university in the first place—"

The surge of rage that washed through him then made him wind his arm back to throw his cell phone at the wall. But he couldn't afford to replace it, and that was a childish impulse anyway.

"If I had chosen a Canadian university, there still would've been a pandemic. But I wouldn't have worked on a computer model that predicted viral spread in human populations. That was actually *useful*."

His mother was silent for several long moments. "You know I'm proud of that work."

Jax took a shaky breath.

"I just want you to be happy, Jax. To live up to your potential." And there was the kicker. Jax's mouth twisted.

"I'll think about it, okay?" he lied. He was already thinking about it, just not the way she wanted. "But I'm done talking about it now. If that changes, I'll let you know."

"All right," she said softly. "If that's what you want."

"Thanks."

"Jax, if you ever need money...."

Oh Jesus, what now? Was she going to try to bribe him into going back by offering to pay for it? "I'm fine," he said firmly.

"I'm just saying—"

"Look, I should, uh, get going. I'm working tonight and I've got things to do."

113

"All right," she said after a long silence. "I love you. And answer your phone now and again."

"I will, Mom." He might.

He hung up and flung himself back on his mattress. A glance at his phone said he would have to get moving soon if he had any errands today, but he pressed an arm over his eyes and wondered if a nap would be a bad idea. Or maybe he could see what Ari was up to?

Jax retrieved his phone from the mountain of blankets and texted, *You busy today?*

The Captain jumped up onto the bed and stomped toward him. Jax reached out and tickled the cat's chin and stroked his ears.

Pressing into Jax's hand, he chirruped and purred, and eventually settled his heavy body across Jax's chest. It looked like someone was voting for more sleep.

"You win, Captain Tubby-pants. We'll stay in bed just a little while longer." Ari hadn't texted back yet, and a bit more sleep would be helpful to get through anything strenuous.

Chapter Ten

ARI HUMMED as he selected an outfit for the evening. He'd been somewhat shocked by Jax's texts just before noon asking if Ari was free that day and would he mind if Jax came over? Jax was rather eager to try that other thing Ari had suggested.

That I suggested?

Something about my knees and ears.

Well. If you insist.

Jax had been ravenous when Ari opened the door, and Ari indeed learned what Jax looked like bent in half and begging for it. He looked especially appealing draped over Ari's expensive couch, his pale skin contrasting with the slate gray fabric.

And it was as brutal and frenzied as the first time.

Later, when Jax had to leave for work, he kissed Ari goodbye, hard and grateful. "Thank you. I really needed that." He ran his hands over Ari's chest and then pressed another hard kiss to his mouth. "If you come to the bar tonight, I'll sing something just for you." He winked and hurried out the door.

As always after seeing Jax, Ari was desperate to write. Especially with that parting blow. Jax obviously meant something salacious. It was all too easy, though, for Ari to misremember it, to believe he intended to make a romantic gesture. It hurt, but it was the kind of hurt that led to productive time with his instruments.

Still, he set an alarm on his phone. He didn't want to miss a personal performance.

At the Rock, Jax was already on stage. Ari greeted Murph at the bar, ordered a ginger ale, and settled in to wait.

He didn't have to wait long.

"I promised a friend," Jax said, leaning into the mic like he was trying to seduce it, "that I would sing this next song. I hope you like it." Their gazes caught, and Ari's breath hitched.

Behind him, Murph muttered, "I'm gonna have to put a leash on that b'y."

Kayla took the lead, bashing out an '80s beat on her drums, and soon Jax and Naomi joined in with their instruments and ahhs. Thanks to his older sister, Ari recognized the refrain. "Holding Out for a Hero"?

Ari didn't understand this man, but Jax clearly enjoyed playing it. All three of them went hard on the instruments, and Jax brought the same intensity to the vocals as he begged the universe for a man to come save him. The song suited his brand of ham, certainly.

As always, the crowd loved it, and Jax glowed under the attention. Ari wanted to bend him over the piano.

He wondered how much damage that might do to his own instrument.

Naomi called for a break after Bonnie Tyler, and they left the stage in different directions. Jax bounced up to him and asked, "So, what did you think?"

"As enjoyable a performance as always," Ari teased.

"I knew you'd like some '80s synth rock." He pressed two fingers to Ari's knee and fluttered his lashes, a positively tame flirtation.

"Yes, you have spotted my musical weakness."

"Well, then, you better stick around for the next number."

Ari hummed his agreement. "I have nowhere else to be."

"Good! Now I have to run to the bathroom because I've been stuck on stage forever. Rosa has the night off." He grinned and hustled away. Ari watched him go.

"It really is a stunning view," a familiar voice said next to him. Ari looked over and saw Kayla behind the bar, a sweating beer in her hand.

Jax had suggested once that he and Kayla had some sort of past entanglement, but since Ari didn't know the details, he wasn't sure how to proceed.

116

She turned to Ari. "You know, you two really are disgustingly cute together. Like I totally wanna barf about it, but it also makes me super happy for him."

"Should I apologize or thank you?" Ari asked dryly.

Kayla grinned. "He told you we slept together, right?" Ari inclined his head. Not in so many words, but…. "Anyway, it was damn good, and Jax is sweet. It almost made me wish I could give him what he wants." Ari clenched his fists in his lap. "But well, relationships aren't my thing, and Jax is the marrying kind." She shrugged.

Ari's mouth dropped open.

If it weren't for the whole aromantic thing, Jax had said.

Kayla. He'd meant *Kayla* was aromantic.

So did that mean…. Was Jax looking for Ari to be his hero in a romantic sense? Was that what the song was about?

Well, at least he'd figured it out before he managed to let on to Jax that, as far as he was concerned, they were casual sex partners. He'd only known Jax a little while, but he could guess how well *that* would go down.

"Ari?" Kayla waved her hand in front of his face. "I didn't break you, did I? You're not regretting your life choices? Wondering how long before you can make a break for it? Because Jax won't have a chance to kill you. I'll do it first."

"No," he said quickly, shaking himself. "Forgive me. It just… it seems like you know him well."

She leaned her elbows on the bar, affording him an ample view of her cleavage, should he wish it. He kept his eyes on her face. "I mean, I know him about as well as he'll let anyone, except maybe Hobbes."

So Ari had been right to believe Jax was holding pieces of himself back. "Maybe you can tell me, then…."

She dimpled at him and finished her beer. "Maybe. If it's not too personal."

Ari lowered his voice. "Why does he play so many songs by female artists?"

117

The dimple became a full grin. "Jax was a gender studies major in another life."

Before Ari could decide if she was serious, Jax slung himself around Ari's shoulder and onto the barstool next to him. "Is Kayla telling lies about me?"

Ari looked from Jax to Kayla and honestly couldn't tell. "I have no idea."

"I'm a mystery wrapped in an enigma," he agreed with an irreverent smile as Kayla passed him a beer.

"You're needed on the stage," Murph corrected. "What's-his-name's request, remember?"

"How could I forget? Guy leaves a hundred-dollar tip *per musician*? You better believe we're gonna get that right." He took a long swig of his beer, then wiped the condensation on his jeans. "I hope this guy knows what he's doing or he's gonna kill the mood for at least two songs." He shook his head and loped toward the stage.

Ari blinked, looking from Murph to Kayla and back.

Kayla patted his arm. "I told you. The marrying kind." Then she followed Jax up to the stage.

Jax slid onto the piano bench opposite Naomi as Kayla twirled her drumsticks. "This next song is by extra special request from a regular. We don't normally do this, but I actually heard him sing and can personally vouch that your eardrums are safe."

The crowd parted to allow a slender fortysomething with salt-and-pepper hair and a leather jacket and sunglasses over a Depeche Mode T-shirt to ascend the stage, where he grabbed a mic stand and set up between Naomi and Jax.

Suddenly Ari understood what was going on—and Jax's cryptic comment from earlier. It hadn't happened *often* while he worked at the Rock, but it was always memorable. Sometimes for the wrong reasons.

"It's fine," Murph said. "I make them fill out a questionnaire now."

Ari eyed him wryly. "Is there also a waiver?"

But he didn't have time to hear Murph's answer, because Naomi started an upbeat synth piano that Ari immediately recognized as "Just Can't Get Enough."

Well, that explained the T-shirt.

It seemed that tonight, the only thing the Rock liked more than paid musicians going all out to entertain them was a member of the audience spending money to do the same. Depeche Mode Guy had a better singing voice than Jax and the energy to carry off a song that had a lot of repetition without seeming self-conscious, but for Ari, it simply wasn't as enjoyable as watching Jax.

Still, Ari applauded along with everyone else when he stepped off the stage near the end of it and knelt in front of a pretty, plump woman with crow's feet at the corners of her eyes and she said yes.

Naomi retrieved the mic before anything could happen to it, and then she and Jax caught eyes as she picked up her violin from its stand. At the same time, Murph, Bruce, and Rosa began to disperse from the bar, carrying loaded trays.

"Thanks for your indulgence, folks," Jax said. "The happy couple have asked me to invite you to celebrate with them. Servers will be coming around with shots of mastic. Let's all raise a glass"— Jax seemed to have one too, and Ari suddenly realized so did he—"to putting a little love in your heart."

As one, the bar raised their shot glasses and tossed back the alcohol, which smelled and tasted strongly of pine.

On the stage, Jax made a face at the taste of the liquor, then made a show of shaking himself and cracked his knuckles. "And now if the soon-to-be newlyweds would like to indulge us... a song for you."

He tipped his head at Rosa, who strummed a light, simple rhythm on the electric guitar. Jax and Kayla joined in a moment later, and Jax and Naomi took turns inviting the audience to "Kiss Me."

Ari desperately wanted to take Jax up on it.

The newly engaged couple swayed together on the floor, faces pressed close together, holding hands by their chins as though they couldn't bear to part. It was an emotional scene, but Ari could hardly tear his eyes away from Jax, who seemed to have gone soft around the edges. It looked as though he was glowing in the spotlight.

Maybe it was just the mastic.

As the evening wore on, Jax returned to the bar and Ari every chance he got, and Ari became certain of one thing. He wanted everything with Jax that he'd been denying himself, and he wanted it now.

JAX BOUNCED off the stage at eleven and practically fell into Ari's lap. "My shift is over," he murmured into Ari's ear.

Ari squeezed his arm and said, "Collect your things and come back to mine?"

"Yes," Jax breathed. "I have my bike. Meet you at yours?" He shimmied out of Ari's embrace—was Ari handsier tonight?—and hurried to the back room, grateful that he'd thought to throw extra underwear and pills into his bag, just in case.

Ari was waiting by his car when Jax pulled up and parked his bike behind the bumper, out of the way. He held out his hand, and Jax took it and followed Ari upstairs.

Inside, Jax put down his bag, turned to Ari, and caught him in an exploratory kiss, so unlike any kiss from Ari before. Jax twined his arms around Ari's neck and opened his mouth, eager to see where Ari would lead him.

It turned out Ari wanted to lead him in a very slow shuffle across the apartment, to touch Jax everywhere, over his clothes, and then carefully remove each item.

By the time they were both naked, Jax was panting and desperate. He looped his legs around Ari's waist and pulled him down into a kiss. "Oh my God, please say you're gonna fuck me again."

Ari didn't answer aloud, but his actions proved more than reply enough.

"Oh my God," Jax moaned several minutes later, his head lolling on the pillow, when Ari finally pushed inside.

Hovering between his legs, Ari tangled their fingers together and leaned in for a long, slow kiss. Jax pushed into it and tried to buck his hips up into Ari's cock, but Ari used his weight to pin him.

Gasping, Jax pulled out of the kiss and ran his lips along Ari's cheek. "Please."

Ari would not be swayed. He kept his movements slow and steady.

"Oh my God," Jax gasped again on another excruciating thrust.

Ari pressed their foreheads together, their eyes locked, and fucked him until Jax couldn't remember any words, until he was shaking and coming so hard he thought he might never recover.

After, they lay together in a tangled heap as they touched and kissed, neither of them ready to break contact. Ari rolled them to their sides and kissed Jax long and slow again. He pulled back and pressed their foreheads together.

"I," Jax said, "have no idea what got into you tonight, but feel free to get into *me* like that again anytime."

Ari snorted. "Noted." His eyes were fond, though, and he cupped Jax's face and swept a thumb along the cheekbone. "And nothing in particular got into me this evening. But I've been wanting to do that."

A slow grin stretched Jax's face. "Yeah? Well. Anytime." He wiggled closer, wanting more contact, and with a little nudge, he got Ari onto his back and rested his head on his shoulder. "Seriously. That was awesome."

"Good to know," Ari whispered as he tangled his hands in Jax's hair.

They couldn't stay there forever, though. Cleanup was needed. Jax pulled Ari into the shower, and they soaped each other under the steam.

"Can I ask," Ari said as he washed Jax's back, "what this means?" He trailed his fingers over the tattoo on Jax's ass.

"Oh, it's the Greek letter phi. In math it's a stand-in for a universal constant." He shot a look over his shoulder. "Like pi."

"And what constant does phi represent?"

Jax turned so they were face-to-face. He soaped up Ari's chest, playing some with the hair, and turned into lecture mode. "Well, numerically speaking, it's one point six one eight et cetera. You might've heard it called the golden ratio?"

"That sounds familiar."

Jax nodded eagerly. "It's just so…. Okay, so say you have a line, A, and you break that line into two separate lines, B and C, so that line B multiplied by phi is equal to line A—you with me?"

"I believe so."

"Well, the remaining bit of the line, line C? If you multiply C by phi, then you will get the length of line B."

"Oh. How unusual."

"And you can keep doing it! And it appears everywhere in nature too, the ratio of the spirals in a snail shell and so on." Jax beamed, pleased that Ari seemed to be following his mini lecture. "And when I say it's everywhere, I mean it's everywhere. It's in music. Like, you can write music using it, sure, but it's also just in there, you know? Like some pop songs, when you find that high point, that crescendo, and multiply the time marker by phi, you get the song's total run time!"

Ari listened with his head cocked to the side and a small smile on his face.

"Am I rambling too much?" Jax asked. "I know not everyone finds math this fascinating."

"No," Ari said, wiping at Jax's forehead. A line of shampoo suds that had been headed for Jax's eyes fell to the shower floor, and Ari nudged him into the spray to rinse it off. "I like listening to you."

Jax closed his eyes and let the water wash away the rest of the bubbles, grateful for the excuse to close his eyes. He didn't know what had changed with Ari, what he'd seen in Jax in the past few hours that he hadn't seen before, but something was different. The way he was treating Jax was different. Not that he'd treated Jax poorly before, but there was something to this newfound tenderness. It was dangerous and seductive.

A man could fall in love.

"You'd be the first," Jax quipped after a too-long pause.

"I doubt it." With a gentle hand on his waist, Ari pulled him out of the spray again. "Considering how busy the bar is every time you lure me there."

He didn't sound displeased about being tempted, and when Jax met his eyes, they held no trace of teasing.

"That's different. That's people paying me to sing what they want to hear." Jax knew he was a lot to handle. His interests bounced from one extreme to the other, many of them only for a few days, and Ari wouldn't have been the first to find that annoying.

"I can hardly blame them for that either."

Ari was too much for Jax's ego. He wanted to believe his sincerity, but it was a lot all at once, so he pressed a kiss to his chin. "Bed?" he suggested. "I'm beat."

It was true, after all.

"Bed," Ari agreed.

They lay down in a tangle of limbs and blankets and pillows. It should have been uncomfortable, Jax thought, except he was exhausted and couldn't do much except close his eyes. Ari turned his head just enough that his cheek brushed Jax's crown, and that was all Jax knew.

Chapter Eleven

A WEEK passed in the blink of an eye, and the next followed suit and brought November with it. Ari regretted not seeing Jax as often as he might, but with Jax's work schedule and Ari well past his original deadline, they often didn't have time for more than a phone call or some text messages.

When he felt especially pathetic, he put away his music and went to the bar, where Jax's wide smiles and unabashed love of good fun and pop music drew him out of his funk even before Jax was able to take a break to spend with him.

Sunday through Wednesday soon became his favorite nights of the week, since the bar closed early and he could claim Jax to himself for a few hours.

Unfortunately, by the time his weekly family dinner rolled around on Saturday, Ari had already decided he'd much rather spend his evening with Jax.

There was a logical response to that, of course. If he told his parents he was dating someone, surely they would want to meet him as well. Jax would be invited to dinner, or more likely lunch, since his working hours would prohibit him staying much past an evening meal. But Ari didn't know if he was ready to share Jax.

Besides, his parents were… his parents. And Jax was Jax. He had no doubt that his mother had only suggested he try online dating so she'd have a natural opportunity to put forward her own candidate when it failed. He'd have to be careful about how he introduced them.

It was with this in mind that Ari parked in his parents' driveway— behind an unfamiliar Audi—and let himself inside.

"Ari, is that you?" his mother called when he closed the door behind him.

Ari hated yelling through the house, so he took off his shoes and followed her voice. "Maman?"

"In the courtyard!"

The leaves still on the trees were brilliant red and orange, but today the weather was fair. His parents sat outside at their patio set, under the wide cantilevered umbrella, with a spread of lavash, feta cheese with grapes, watermelon, and fresh herbs laid out on the table. A large pitcher of water with lemon and cucumber sat next to it.

But it wasn't only the unusual appearance of appetizers that brought Ari up short as he stepped onto the patio.

His parents weren't alone.

"There you are!" his mother said warmly as she gestured him forward as though she hadn't planned an ambush. "Come and meet everyone."

By *everyone*, Ari assumed she meant the middle-aged couple casually holding hands on the table and the younger man who, from his features and age, was obviously their son.

He should have seen it coming.

With no way to back out without being inexcusably rude, Ari forced himself forward and greeted the guests. "Salam," he said belatedly, offering his hand first to the older man. "As you must have guessed, I'm Ari."

"It is good to meet you, Ari. I'm Armin, and this is my wife, Jaleh."

Ari shook her hand as well and inquired after their health.

Then, of course, there was nothing to do but face the elephant in the room.

"And this is our son, Sohrab."

Sohrab looked slightly abashed to be meeting Ari this way, but they shook hands and went through the social prerequisites without either of them actually dying of mortification.

"Armin worked with me at the hospital," Ari's father said before Ari had even sat down. Oh good, they were already at the "look, an eligible gay man from a good family" portion of the evening.

125

Ari smiled politely and offered everyone refills of their water glasses. Then he poured his own. "Oh?"

"My husband is a cardiologist," Jaleh said proudly. "Sohrab is finishing his residency in oncology."

Trust his parents to attempt to set him up with a doctor. What did they think was going to happen when Ari went on tour? A doctor couldn't very well follow him, and he was gone for months at a time.

Not that it mattered in this case, since Ari was not interested in dating anyone who wasn't Jax, no matter how accomplished or— he could admit it—attractive. "Very impressive," Ari said evenly, meeting Sohrab's gaze. "You must be very dedicated."

Sohrab smiled. "I've always wanted to follow in my father's footsteps."

Ari froze with the most pleasant expression he could muster, wondering if Sohrab's insult was intentional. Neither Ari nor Afra had elected to follow medicine, despite not-occasional prodding when they were growing up. Eventually their parents had accepted that they would pursue their own interests, and they were supportive. But Ari knew they were still disappointed—and that some would see it as shame.

Awkward.

"Well," said Ari's mother, "I am sure your parents are very proud of you, just as we are proud of our children." She shot a look in Ari's direction.

He wished he didn't doubt her sincerity—that the glow of pride under her look wasn't tainted under the suspicion that her praise was aimed at Sohrab, hoping he'd see Ari as worthwhile. Feeling miserable and guilty for being so uncharitable, Ari pushed those thoughts away and sipped his water.

It didn't take long for their parents to send them off together. "Ari, we need chai, but that's so many cups to carry. Sohrab, why don't you help him?"

They stood awkwardly in the kitchen, waiting for the kettle to boil.

"So," Sohrab broke the silence, "shall we address the elephant?"

Ari blew out a breath. "I suppose we must."

"I'm not against a dinner date," he said with an encouraging smile.

Embarrassed, Ari flushed and rubbed at the back of his neck. "Actually—I mean not that you're not, but I...." Why was this so hard?

"Ah, there is someone else. And since I'm here, your parents either don't know or don't approve."

"Shit. Sorry." He cast a glance at the windows and saw all four parents still seated outside. "I haven't told them yet. It's new, and as you may have guessed, they'll have opinions."

"Really? I wouldn't know what that's like." Sohrab's lips twitched.

Casting his unexpected ally a dry look, Ari pushed away from the counter and began collecting everything he needed to serve chai. "Quite. It's new enough I'm not sure he'd be able to deal with... overbearing, meddling Persian parents."

"Ah," Sohrab said all too knowingly.

Ari wondered if he'd faced a similar struggle when dating men who were culturally Canadian.

"Well, if my parents are to be believed, meddling in their children's love lives is one of the great pleasures of retirement."

Ari controlled his own smile, but barely. "Mine have not said so, but I have surmised as much." He put the tea leaves into the pot and poured the hot water over top.

"Well, feel free to blame everything on me not being interested."

"Throw you under the bus?" Ari arched an eyebrow.

Sohrab nodded, looking coy with his hands shoved in his pockets. In another lifetime, where Ari and Jax's orbits hadn't collided so spectacularly, Ari would have found this man appealing. "Why not? It's what I plan to do to you." He grinned, and Ari chuckled softly in surprise.

"Well, fair's fair."

"Yup. Now, how about I carry those cups out there while you finish brewing?" He stepped forward to gather up the tray with the mugs, and Ari watched him go. Sohrab was going to make someone very lucky someday.

His phone vibrated, and when he pulled it out of his pocket, he found a message from Jax. *Someone ordered this from Naomi last night and she made me make it for them. Not nearly as fun as making it for you. :(* A second later, a picture of a Sex with the Bartender cocktail uploaded.

Chuckling, Ari typed back, *Miss you too*, and was warmed to receive a string of heart-eye emojis in return.

The timer sounded, and Ari put his phone away to deal with his chai.

Sohrab might be lucky someday, but he would never be as lucky as Ari.

WHEN THE door finally shut behind Sohrab and his parents, Ari cast a reproachful look at his own. "That was so awkward."

"It really wasn't," his mother said blithely. "Sohrab is lovely, and so are his parents. It was a pleasant evening."

"I felt like a fattened calf at auction." Throughout dinner his parents had expounded loudly and at length about Ari's musical accomplishments. The only things that lessened Ari's embarrassment were the equally obvious comments from Armin and Jaleh and the shared looks of misery with Sohrab.

"Don't exaggerate," his mother said.

"I'm not. You kept pointing out my good qualities like you were trying to get Sohrab to buy me."

"Now you're just being vulgar," his mother sniffed and bustled into the kitchen to clean up. "And so what if we were trying to sell you a bit? We're just trying to help."

Ari frowned. "I know, Maman, but no one asked you to."

"I don't need an invitation to help my children," she said, hurt coloring her tone.

Great, now she was guilting him for being upset. "Look, you know I appreciate your support, but I don't need your help finding a boyfriend."

"And why not?" She scraped some leftovers into the trash and let the lid fall back down with a clatter. "You haven't brought anyone to meet us in years." True, but it wasn't like Ari hadn't been dating. He just hadn't dated anyone long enough to attempt that hurdle. "And you should have someone who makes you happy."

And more guilt. "I know you're doing it because you love me, but I didn't ask you to. If I ever want you to play matchmaker, I'll let you know."

"And what will you do in the meantime? Be miserable and alone? Run yourself ragged? You're not a boy anymore. You're thirty-two. It's time that you settle down, stop jet-setting around the world, and instead take care of family."

Ari swallowed against the hurt clogging his throat. As if his music, the tours, his life's work, were just a way of passing time until he found someone to occupy him. "And then what? I just stop doing what I love and sit at home waiting for my doctor husband to return to me?"

"Ari," his father cut in.

Ari frowned and shook his head. "That's not the life I want. I like the one I have." Then he turned around and left the house. He had the sudden desperate urge to see Jax.

FOR THE first few moments when he regained consciousness, Jax couldn't have said what woke him. By all rights he ought to have been down for the night, after a long shift at the bar followed by a frantic but thorough shift in Ari's bed. His eyes felt like sandpaper and his body was an overcooked noodle, but when he took a deep breath and decided to continue sleeping, the soft notes of the piano drifted in again, and he couldn't resist.

Quietly, he climbed out of bed and padded to the doorway, the better to observe Ari in his natural habitat.

He sat at the piano, backlit by the streetlight and the moon shining in the floor-to-ceiling windows. Aside from that, the room was dark as Ari measured out careful notes, occasionally pausing and backtracking, his head tilted to the side.

It was beautiful, Jax thought—not at all conventional, halfway between a ballad and a lullaby. C, C, D, E, G, C, an experiment, a scattering of perfect chords, then the same notes out of sequence.

"C4, E4, G4, C5, G5," Jax murmured. "One, three, five, eight, thirteen. The Fibonacci Sequence. Did someone fall down a math rabbit hole?"

Ari looked up, his features outlined in stark relief. He was gorgeous in the moonlight, the smooth line of his back highlighted in glimmering silver that also kissed his hair and limned his eyes. "Did I wake you?"

"Yeah, but it's okay, I don't mind." The view was worth it. Getting to hear Ari compose was worth it.

Though Jax half expected him to get up now that he knew Jax was there, he remained at the piano, coaxing out a sweet, fanciful tune, almost hypnotic. He was working in a spiral, Jax realized with a soft smile.

"I'm impressed that you noticed," Ari admitted. His shoulders had hunched in as though he didn't want to be seen, but he didn't stop playing.

Jax rescued a pair of boxers from the bedroom floor and slipped them on before joining Ari on the piano bench, their thighs pressing together. He watched Ari's hands for a moment and then copied the tune up two octaves. Ari let him and shifted to an accompanying set of chords, incorporating complex harmonies that added a mournful undertone.

He felt like he owed Ari something of himself for letting Jax see him like this, when he was obviously at his most sensitive, his most vulnerable. He'd been having trouble writing music, and he didn't like anyone to hear things until he was ready—but he was letting Jax.

Jax could respond in kind.

"I'm pretty good at hearing numbers, I guess," he started. But Ari would know that much from Jax's work at the bar and what he'd already admitted from his youth, so that didn't really count as sharing. "Pattern recognition—that's one of the things my mom and I used to do together when I was a kid. She'd make it a game." He paused. "She's a professor of mathematics and cryptology at Queen's."

There. That was as good a start as any.

Ari stopped playing for long enough that they both faltered, but eventually he started again and Jax followed, both of them a little slower this time. It was easier to have something else to pretend to focus on. "You don't talk about her much."

Jax let out a long breath. Here was his opening. His heart beat a little too fast, out of sync with their song. "Yeah, well, we haven't exactly been on the best of terms since I chose MIT over her university for my PhD."

To his credit, Ari only missed one transition, but the disharmony resonated unpleasantly through the room. He corrected immediately. "You have a PhD in math?"

Jax sighed. "No. That's another point of contention. I'm ABD. All but dissertation."

At that Ari stopped playing and turned his attention fully to Jax, who put his hands in his lap. Ari closed the keyboard cover. "Why didn't you finish?"

Jax tried a smile, but it felt anemic, so he let it slide away. "Same reason as everybody else who was supposed to graduate in 2020. The pandemic hit and I came home." He knew it had been the smart decision regardless of what had followed. "I always planned to go back, but I...."

After a moment of silence, Ari placed his hand on Jax's knee. Their thighs were still touching, and now that Ari wasn't working the piano pedals, their ankles were too. "You don't have to tell me, but I'm willing to listen."

Jax hadn't even talked this out with Hobbes or Sam, but the words seemed to bubble out of him. "I wanted to go back. My project is done; my advisor had verbally approved me to defend before everything….” He gestured to the room to indicate *went to absolute shit*. “And then he died, in April.” He took a deep, shuddering breath. “It feels shitty to say, because my mom was a great single parent and I never felt like I needed a father figure, you know? She’s aromantic, she chose to raise kids alone on purpose, and she was good at it. But he was like a father to me.”

His voice cracked.

Then Ari took his hand, and everything suddenly got much harder to swallow. If he said he was *sorry*—

But he didn’t. “May this be your last sorrow.”

Jax blinked at the sentiment, then managed a small quirk of his lips. That must be a Persian thing. He liked it. “Thanks.” He finally managed a breath that didn’t make his lungs shake. “Anyway. I’m dealing with failing to live up to parental expectations. Not like the whole world doesn’t have PTSD right now, but how dare I bring shame on the Hall family name by failing to complete my doctorate. Like extenuating circumstances count for nothing, or all the work I did during the pandemic. Or like the highest and best thing a person can do is get a PhD in applied mathematics.”

Ari squeezed his hand. “It’s never easy to disappoint parental expectations.”

Understatement. Jax squeezed back. “Our conversations are kind of… fraught these days.” He huffed. “This is not great conversation for three a.m.”

“Maybe, maybe not.” Ari stood and, still holding Jax’s hands, urged him to follow. “Some things are easier to say at three a.m.”

The understanding and compassion in his gaze were too sweet, too much. Jax pressed forward and kissed him, deep and quiet as the night. Slowly, Ari guided him back to bed, not breaking the kiss until they settled back on the mattress. They rolled into each other and arranged their heads on the same pillow. They kissed some more, but it never turned heated. Not that Jax wanted it to.

He fell back to sleep between one kiss and the next, Ari’s arm around him grounding him as he drifted away.

Chapter Twelve

ARI PUT the last touches on his recording of the latest song—working title "Golden Ratio"—sent it off to Noella, and stretched. He hated the computer side of composing.

A glance at the clock told him it was almost noon. Afra would be there any minute.

He contemplated the contents of his fridge and wondered if Afra would want a beer. It seemed like a beer kind of lunch.

Afra arrived with sushi and headed straight for the couch and coffee table. She said yes to the beer.

"What happened?" she asked once she was comfortably curled up with food in her lap and her drink within reach.

"They set me up. They brought over this doctor Baba knows."

"They didn't!" Afra's eyebrows flew up.

"They did." He stabbed at a tuna roll. "It was awful. They invited his parents too. And then everyone sat around and pretended like both sets of parents weren't trying to sell us to each other."

"Oh my God." She pressed a hand to her cheek and shook her head. "Tell me he wasn't terrible."

Ari groaned. "No, at least he wasn't that. I might have actually been interested if I'd met him elsewhere and, you know, two months ago."

Afra smiled. "Yes, there is *that*."

"He was pretty understanding about that too." He shoved the tuna roll into his mouth and chewed.

Afra sipped her beer and watched him. "What did they think would happen?"

"I don't know," Ari did not wail. "It's not like I'd ever want to date some guy they brought home for me, even if Jax weren't an issue. And a doctor? Seriously? It's not like we'd have time to see each other. Our careers are totally incompatible."

"True." Afra shook her head. "Considering you never even liked it when someone else picked your ice cream flavor for you, I'm not sure why they thought you'd let them pick your boyfriend."

Ari groaned and chewed another bite aggressively. "Then, when I told them how, how... not cool the whole thing was, I got another lecture about being old and single." He pulled a face. The tune was wearing thin. Afra was lucky to have largely avoided that lecture, since she met Ben in her midtwenties, but she'd had to endure years of "So, grandchildren?" instead. He wasn't sure he'd trade.

"Like most people aren't getting married in their thirties these days."

"Right? But even if they weren't, even if I wanted to stay single for the rest of my days, that's up to me."

"Hear, hear," Afra cheered and lifted her glass.

Ari's mouth turned down, and he looked at his plate of rice and fish. "She said I needed to get a husband so I'd stop touring."

Afra sat up straighter. "She did not."

"Apparently all these years I've just been... killing time, waiting for a doctor to make me his househusband."

"Ari, you know I'm sure she didn't—" Ari gave her a look. "Okay, maybe she did mean it about the touring, but she probably doesn't expect you to never play or work again. Just...." Afra shrugged.

Ari nodded. It wasn't like he didn't understand that his parents were getting older and worrying about how much time they had left to see Ari happy, but it didn't make the judgment any easier to deal with. He'd wanted to tell Jax about it, but he didn't want to take Jax's moment, to make him feel overrun. And explaining why his parents thought he was single would take more than a few lines of explanation. Despite Jax's issues with his mother, Ari wasn't sure Jax would understand how intense his parents could be. It wouldn't be out of character for them to show up at the bar to meet Jax should Ari fail to introduce him soon enough.

"I don't know why I'm trying to defend them," Afra huffed. "I know they love us, but you can't just expect your kids to want what you want, to fit into the boxes you give them. That's not how kids work—it's not how people work!" She took an agitated gulp of beer. "And the more you push them to fill those roles, the more they either bend and contort themselves to fit in and lie and make themselves unhappy, or the more they rebel and—" She pressed a hand over her eyes.

When she didn't continue, Ari prompted gently, "Afra?"

"Or the more they do both—rebel just for the sake of having something of their own, and then when they hit trouble, they hide the consequences and lie just to avoid disappointing my parents." Her mouth trembled, and Ari felt on the edge of something important.

My parents?

This wasn't like her. Normally she was sharp, sunny, not prone to outbursts of emotion. He knew she was likely still reeling from the aftereffects of IVF, both hormonal and emotional, the second of which had only been confirmed a failure two weeks previous. But something told him this went deeper than that.

He licked his lips and stalled for time. "It… it sounds like you're speaking from experience."

What had she done? He tried to think back to when she was a teenager. That was when children rebelled, wasn't it? He would've been what? Eight? Twelve at most during that stage of her life. Had she ever been in trouble? Had she come home late? He didn't remember.

She laughed, but it was a brittle, humorless thing. "Yeah, you could say that." She set the beer bottle down, empty. It thunked on the table with resounding finality.

Ari decided to tread carefully. "Do you… want to talk about it?"

"I have been, sort of." She took a deep breath and blotted her face with one of the clean sushi napkins. "Though I guess you didn't know it at the time."

Ari had no idea what she was talking about. "Okay?"

"Okay," she echoed. "I'm going to have to do better than that, I know." She tapped her nails on the arm of the couch, biting both lips. "I had a boyfriend in high school."

Ari wanted to make a smart comment—what a rebel she'd been, dating a boy at the age girls generally dated boys, when their parents had had no strict rules against it—but it didn't seem like something he should tease about right then. "I don't remember that."

"Yeah, well. Maman and Baba didn't know. He wasn't exactly someone they'd approve of. He didn't take enough academic courses, and he wasn't going to go to university. You know what they would have said."

"That he wasn't a good long-term investment, emotionally," Ari surmised. "He had no ambition. He would not be able to support a family."

She flashed him a quick, mirthless smile. "Wow, it's almost like we grew up in the same house. But yeah, that's exactly what they would have said. And I know, because they said it anyway, even though they had no idea I was seeing him."

Ari winced.

"And you know what the funny thing is? He got a great job after graduation, working with Hydro One. Now he's got a wife and two kids and, like, seven dogs. Guess he showed them."

Ari still didn't know where this was going. "So he was your boyfriend…?"

"Yeah, he was. And I… I was dating him in part because I knew it'd piss Maman and Baba off, because their expectations made me so angry I could scream. I thought, you know, we moved to Canada so we could have more freedom, not so we could recreate the expectations of Iran in another country. Which is way harsher than they deserved, but I was a teenager. But also… he made me laugh. He was kind, in a goofy way. He didn't care that I was smarter than he was, which let me tell you, that is rare. A lot of the guys I dated after were *really* sensitive about that."

That, at least, was one dating pitfall Ari had managed to avoid by being male. "I apologize on behalf of my gender."

"Thank you, I accept." This smile had a little more emotion behind it. "Anyway. We broke up right before I left for university, and I was… heartbroken. But I couldn't come to Maman and Baba about it, because they didn't know I'd even been seeing anyone."

Ari relaxed a little. "That must have been difficult," he tried. Surely there had to be more to the story to support her reaction to telling it?

"Yeah. I went off to school in September stupid and hurt and angry at Maman and Baba, like it was their fault it didn't work out, and of course frosh week was just one long party and I went a little off the rails…."

So there *was* more to the story. Only now Ari didn't know if he liked where it was going. "Understandable."

Finally Afra laughed. "Ari, just… bless you for not being willing to jump to conclusions."

He felt himself flush. "Not enough to go on."

"Not for you," Afra agreed, not unkindly. But she seemed to have gathered strength somehow, because she finally cut to the chase. "When I didn't come home right away the next summer, I said it was because I was busy moving into student housing and getting ready to start my new job. Which was true—I did move, and I did have a part-time job there for the summer. But the *whole* truth is that I needed to stay there. I couldn't come home right away. Because a week after exams, I…."

He waited.

"I had a baby."

His mouth dropped open. "You…."

"I got pregnant frosh week like a stupid after-school special," she confirmed. He expected her to sound bitter or tearful, but she actually seemed calm. Maybe a little rueful. "I wasn't showing yet by winter break, but by reading week I knew I needed to figure out what I was doing instead of coming home, because my obstetrician wasn't about to approve a nonessential C-section for a nineteen-year-old, and I could not come home nine months pregnant. Maman and Baba would never let me leave the house again, and there was no

137

way they'd give me any option about keeping the baby. Actions have consequences, family first, blah blah blah."

"So you gave it up," Ari filled in.

"It was an easy decision," she assured him, finally dry-eyed. "It was the right call. I'd do it again."

"Afra." He wondered if she'd let him hug her.

"But I also knew I couldn't…. Open wasn't an option, because how could I be a part of the baby's life when it wasn't even supposed to exist? And now I can't go looking, I can't ask." And she would spend the rest of her life wondering about the only natural child she would have.

"I'm sorry you had to go through that… are going through that. The past few years must have been really hard."

She shrugged. "Yes. Not being able to get pregnant hadn't occurred to me." She gave a wobbly smile. "But that is all in the past, and there is nothing left to be done but to move forward, right?"

"Right."

"And to make sure you're making decisions just for you. You're not a dumb eighteen-year-old. You're thirty-two, with your own bank account, and you know you've got me and Ben in your corner."

Ari was in his last year of high school when she first brought Ben home, and he had spent all of his twenties knowing that Afra and Ben were his safety net, always. He'd run to them after the messy end to his first serious relationship. "I know. Likewise."

Afra smiled. "Now, finish your sushi, because you and I are going to go for a walk. I could use some sunshine, even if it is cold as balls. And you probably could too. Noella says you've been sending stuff regularly, which means you've probably spent most of your time locked up with your piano."

"Maybe."

After they finished their food and tidied the coffee table, Afra stepped into her sensible flats and Ari his favorite slip-ons, and they put on their coats and headed out the door.

"I need to buy something at the pharmacy." Afra turned them to the right. Having no opinion to the contrary, Ari followed her.

138

As they went, they avoided the topic of their parents and focused instead on fun things. Afra talked about Ben's new origami hobby—"He says it's useful when talking with kids and getting them to open up, but he's actually kind of terrible at it."—and how weird it was that Theo was back at school and not underfoot anymore.

At the pharmacy, Afra picked up Band-Aids and a bag of Starburst—Theo's favorite—and stuffed her purchases into her sensible bag. "He's stressing about finals already," she said, shaking her head. "I guess he missed his target mark on one of his midterms."

They were meandering toward a park when a familiar blond head caught Ari's eye. Jax was walking slowly down the path, a backpack over one shoulder and a chubby toddler waddling before him.

Ari must have given something away, because Afra said, "What—" and then followed his gaze. "Oh my God. Ari, tell me you're going to put a ring on it."

Ari spluttered. "Afra," he hissed. But he was frankly relieved. He thought it might be difficult for her to be around children.

She laughed loudly enough to draw attention.

Jax lit up when he saw Ari—how had Ari ever thought Jax wasn't emotionally invested?—and waved.

"I need to see this close up," Afra said, and they made their way to Jax and Alice together.

Jax made the introductions. "Alice"—Afra jerked and looked at Ari—"meet my friends, Ari and Afra." He pointed to them and prompted Alice into a wave.

Alice gave a clumsy flap of her hand and said, "Hi."

"Hello, Alice," Ari said seriously.

"Hi." She smiled, showing off her chubby cheeks.

"Hi," Afra said. "Lovely to meet you, Alice. Good to see you again, Jax."

The smile he gave her was genuine and sweet. "You too. How have you been? Keeping Ari in his place, I hope."

"Oh, always. Today's job was to get him out of the house. He's been composing too hard."

"Don't I know it." Jax grinned.

Afra gave Ari a look. "Oh, I'm sure you do."

Ari elbowed her gently and said, "She dragged me out for a walk."

"Well, my gain," Jax said. "Alice and I got bored at home—I'm on babysitting duty—so we decided to see what thrills central London had."

Alice squirmed, and Jax put her back down. "We'll have to follow her," he said apologetically, but Afra waved him off.

"Is your sister busy again today?" Ari asked.

Jax hummed. "Yeah, some growing pains involved with a new job and moving to a new neighborhood, so I got conscripted for another afternoon of niece-minding." His expression turned hopelessly fond. "Not that I mind."

"No, I bet not. She's pretty adorable."

"You're just saying that because she looks just like me."

Afra smiled. "She does. Looks like she could be yours."

Jax laughed. "Yeah." He rubbed the back of his head as he stepped to follow Alice a few feet down the sidewalk. "I'm probably giving off all the dad vibes right now." He cast Ari a mischievous grin. "What do you think, Ari, DILF or Weird Dad vibes?"

Ari glanced at Afra, then at Jax, and said, "I plead the Fifth."

"He's fishing for compliments anyway," Afra advised.

Jax acknowledged the hit with a grin and allowed Alice to lead him to the playground, where she patted the slide in an obvious sign. Jax scooped her up and helped her "climb" the ladder to the top.

Afra clapped Ari on the shoulder. "You are completely fucked, bro."

Ari nodded. "I think you may be right."

They watched Jax with Alice for a few moments, during which Ari was uncomfortably aware that they had just picked the scab off a deep wound from Afra's past and now they were getting awfully close to it with the salt. "Do you want to head back?"

But when he turned to look at her, she didn't seem upset. She was smiling gently. "I do have to go, actually, but I'm fine. Weirdly fine. I think…." A shrug, a wry twist of her lips. "I think it's easier now that I have a final answer, in a way. I'm not going to get pregnant. No more

IVF, no more fertility treatments, no more waiting and wondering. We've already started the courses for foster to adopt."

"If you're sure," he said doubtfully.

She ran a hand down his arm, squeezed his wrist. "I'm sure." Then she jerked her head over her shoulder at Jax. "Say goodbye from me, will you?"

He promised, and she set off with her purse full of sugar, leaving Ari to pine helplessly over Jax's adorable uncle act. Though he felt a little strange watching from afar—maybe he was coming across as a creeper? A quick glance around proved that no one was paying him any attention, but he stepped up to Jax's side anyway, drawn inexorably into his orbit. "Afra had to run."

When Alice shrieked with glee as she slid down into Jax's arms, Ari understood the sentiment.

Jax lifted Alice onto his hip and nuzzled a kiss to her cheek. "Guess it's just the three of us for this date, eh, Alice? You okay with Ari being the third wheel?"

"Ba!" Alice agreed.

"You're right, he *is* handsome. We'll allow it."

"Thank you, Alice," Ari said.

She patted Jax's cheek.

Alice wanted to try the swing next. Jax produced a bleach wipe from the diaper bag. "Would you mind?" he asked, handing it to Ari. "New-old habits."

Ari dutifully sanitized the plastic over the chains and the swing, but he was still thinking about the word *date...* and the fact that they had never actually been on one. "Speaking of dates...."

Jax wrangled Alice into the baby swing, making silly faces at her all the while. When he looked up at Ari, he was still cross-eyed with his tongue sticking out. He uncrossed them and raised his eyebrows. "Yes?"

Oh, so he was going to make Ari work for it. "It occurs to me that I have been remiss in taking you out and showing you off."

"I do thrive in the spotlight." Jax gave Alice a little push, and she waved her hands in delight. "What are you proposing?"

141

That was the question. "Dinner would be traditional," he said. "But that seems like it might not be possible with your work schedule."

Jax smiled. "Well, I do have a day off coming up. Someone rented the bar Monday night for a private party."

Perfect. "So may I take you to dinner on Monday?"

Jax grinned. "It's a date."

"Date!" Alice shouted.

Ari smiled. He was excited too.

ALICE WAS clearly a spy sent to Jax under the guise of cuteness to gather information about his life for Jax's meddling sister. She spilled the beans about the date almost as soon as they walked into the house.

"Date!" she yelled and ran headlong into her mother's legs.

Sam lifted her into the air, kissed her face, and asked, "You're a bit young for that, aren't you, sweetie?"

"Date!"

"I think she just likes the way it sounds," Jax said as he unloaded the diaper bag from his shoulder.

"I see." Sam looked at Jax, then back to Alice. "And where did you hear about dates?" The tone of her voice suggested the question was for Jax, but Alice was obviously in a helpful mood.

"Ari."

Sam stilled, but then a wicked grin took over her face. "Oh, Ari, eh? Jacob Hall, did you use my baby to woo your new man?"

"Not intentionally."

Sam laughed. "You are shameless. Fortunately for you, I'm all too happy to let you use my kid to get in there. Now tell me everything while I make you dinner." She placed Alice in a playpen and returned to her cutting board. George stood at the stove, stirring sauce.

"I might be shameless, but it wasn't actually a deliberate ploy. I ran into Ari at the park, and we had some fun together. Alice took a bit of a shine to him, which is understandable."

"Hm, he is kind of shiny," Sam agreed.

Jax chuckled.

"But," George said, "when do we get to meet him?"

"Don't push. You sound meddlesome." She tossed a carrot top at him, and he yelped and dodged.

"Like you weren't lamenting it last night," George defended.

Jax rubbed the back of his head and said, "Soon I hope." It wasn't like Jax wanted to keep Ari away from his family—well, his sister's family, at least. Ari and George would get on like a house on fire, sitting back and watching the Hall Sibling Show like it was the most bingeable streaming entertainment available. And Sam would love him. She hadn't always been fond of his dates and crushes and tended to fuss every time he fell for someone new, but Ari was serious and earnest, and most importantly, he was serious and earnest about Jax.

Sam grinned. "Excellent. How about dinner some weekend?"

"Make it lunch and you have yourself a deal. Bartender."

Her mouth twitched like she wanted to say something but bit it back.

He clapped his hands together. "Now, what can I do to make food happen, because I am hungry, and I have to be at work in an hour and a half. Why did no one tell me that watching a toddler was so much work?"

Chapter Thirteen

NOW THAT Operation Finish the Goddamn PhD so Everyone Would Shut Up About It was underway, Jax remembered how much schoolwork was simply boring. First, Jax contacted MIT and declared his intention to return.

The bursar and registrar offices were all too happy to send him forms to fill out and tabulate tuition fees. The only snag being the answer to the question, Who is your advisor?

So began a lengthy email chain with the registrar offices, the math department administrative director, and Jax, as they all debated how best to handle that. Did he need a new advisor? Surely since Grayling had said he was ready, Jax could defend without an advisor. He didn't need a replacement for Grayling. They could just add one more faculty member to his committee. Did Jax have evidence that Grayling had signed off on the project? Perhaps it should be reviewed by someone else. Now that almost two years had passed; it was possible that changes in the field of statistics and mathematics had impacted the results Jax would wish to defend.

Jax slammed his laptop shut and went outside to aggressively murder some dandelions.

Two days later Jax opened his program and began rereading every single line of code. If he was going to defend this sucker, he needed to know it as well as when he had written it. And apparently he needed to be able to defend his decision not to change it even before his defense.

The work was slow going.

Jax loved math, loved the way it spoke to him, the simplicity of some numbers, the complexity of others. Math had been a way of coping with or escaping from most of the difficulties of his life. Hell, half the work he'd done during the pandemic had been done during late-night panicked sprees as he attempted to stop his brain from thinking about how the data and statistics could—did—affect him personally.

But the project didn't provide any comfort, not when he heard Grayling's voice in his head as he reviewed every line, his soft tones as he calmly questioned Jax's decisions so Jax would be forced to carefully and thoroughly reason them out, the pride in his face whenever Jax answered a question so completely Grayling couldn't think of anything else to ask. Reading the program hurt, and Jax's eyes burned and twitched until he was tempted to throw his laptop in the Thames.

When it got to be too much, Jax found vegetables to massacre in the kitchen instead and made pots of soup or pasta.

Hobbes found him grating a carrot with such force one afternoon that he snapped, "Careful. I don't fancy eating grated you in my dinner."

"You should be so lucky to get a piece of me," Jax snarled back, but he flung down the carrot anyway because he needed his hands intact if he was going to be slicing lemons in a few hours.

Hobbes raised his hands in surrender and backed up a single step. Jax noted the dark circles under his eyes. They were working him too hard at the hospital again. "Whoa, hey. What did the carrot ever do to you?"

"The carrot is just a metaphor." He picked it up from the floor and tossed it into the Garburetor.

There was a pause as Hobbes eased himself into a kitchen chair, watching Jax closely. "Yeah, I got that," he said finally. "And all the other elaborate healthy meals you've made in the middle of the day this week—I'm assuming those were also metaphorical?"

"Those were *delicious*," Jax corrected, pulling the final carrot from the bag and peeling it with extreme prejudice. Though with Hobbes to vent to, his frustration was waning. "And they weren't so much a metaphor as a productive distraction." Jax had spent too much of his life thinking Hobbes might die, and when he got out of the hospital, he was weak. Jax had gotten used to cooking for him, partly because Hobbes couldn't do it himself and partly because Jax hadn't had anything else to distract him. Then Hobbes went back to work. And Jax wasn't an idiot; he knew doctors ate too much takeout, but he still maintained that if Hobbes hadn't wanted Jax to worry about his cholesterol, he shouldn't have left his bloodwork results piled in with Jax's sheet music.

"All right, I'll bite," Hobbes said easily. "A delicious, productive distraction from what?"

Jax put down the grater again, debating.

Aside from Hobbes and those contacts at MIT, he hadn't told anyone he planned to go back to school. He carried the weight of enough expectations. The decision to return to Cambridge had opened a sucking stomach wound, and Jax was walking around with both hands pressed over it to keep from bleeding out. He couldn't let anyone look at it in case they made it worse.

But Hobbes already knew, and he deserved to know what had prompted his roommate to turn into Neurotic Jax, with whom he'd have to live for the next six weeks while Jax obsessed over his work. It wouldn't be fair to leave him in the dark.

"Jax?" Hobbes prompted.

Well, now or never. Jax cleared his throat and met his eyes. "I've been going over my thesis program."

"Ah." Hobbes nodded, and Jax could see him get lost in his head for a moment as he ran through a replay of Jax's actions and attitude over the past few days. "Yeah, that tracks."

Jax swallowed. "I need to do it if I'm going to go back and finish. But it's… hard. It keeps bringing up unpleasant memories. Well, actually, most of the memories are good, except that then I remember Grayling is dead and I'm a failure—"

"Jax—"

"Yeah, I know, blah blah, not my fault, whatever." He huffed. "The good news is the freezer is full?"

"As long as you're not going to make seven kinds of cookies again." Hobbes patted his stomach. "I'm still working off the last ones."

"No cookies," Jax promised. Maybe zucchini bread. Banana muffins? "Actually, speaking of stuffing myself—"

"Please don't."

Jax stuck out his tongue. "I wanted to let you know Ari and I have a *date* on Monday. So you're on your own for dinner."

"Yeah? Nice, kid. No sweat, though. I was going to go to Naomi and Kayla's. They're having that thing for Naomi's birthday."

"Oh, yeah, the potluck. Naomi mentioned it."

"So, a date... I take it this is serious?"

Oooh, he didn't like how Hobbes asking that made him feel. Like he was talking to a parental figure, but it was also Hobbes, the best friend he had a weirdly codependent relationship with and who until recently he'd sometimes thought about naked. Jax never had daddy issues before Grayling died. Just one more way Covid had screwed him over. "Cautiously optimistic yes?"

"Wonders never cease." Hobbes looked at him shrewdly. "You really like this guy, don't you?"

Like was certainly one word for it. By now Hobbes had heard enough stories of Jax's misspent youth—and seen his phi tattoo, which had begun life as a *Y* for Yolanda—to know all about Jax's habit of falling in love too hard, too fast. "I do," he admitted. "And for once, we seem to be on the same page."

"Yeah? Glad to hear it." Then he cleared his throat and put on an authoritative voice. "You just make sure he treats you right and has you home by ten."

Well, if the intentional dad impression didn't kill off any lingering sex feelings, nothing would. Jax shuddered internally, but he couldn't let on that some part of his brain was screaming *augh, no* and reaching for the bleach, so he batted his eyelashes instead. "Don't worry, we'll be sure to get to bed early."

He was gratified when Hobbes groaned and tilted his face skyward. "Can't believe I walked into that one."

ARI HAD only just changed into his good clothes—dress pants he'd been reliably informed showed off his assets at their best and a wine-red cashmere sweater—when Jax knocked on the door.

Jax looked positively delectable in a blue button-up the same shade as his eyes and gray slacks Ari wanted to peel off with his teeth. Jax gave him slow elevator eyes. "Yum."

"The sentiment is reciprocated," Ari said. Then he pressed a sensual kiss to Jax's mouth.

Jax was tangling his fingers in Ari's loose curls when Ari pulled back. "As much as I would love to rip you out of these," he murmured, "we did talk about doing a proper date this evening."

With a groan, Jax stepped back and straightened his clothes. "Okay, right. Date. Not starting with the bed."

"I made a reservation at Pepitas. If we leave now, we should arrive within plenty of time."

Ari guided Jax from the apartment with a hand to the small of his back and led him to the sidewalk. "I thought it might be best to walk. It's only five minutes."

Jax waved for him to lead the way. "So how did you manage to get a reservation at this place on such short notice?"

Pepitas was one of London's hottest restaurants. "I know a guy."

"Being mysterious, huh? All right. I can wait."

Jax asked after Ari's family as they wound their way to the restaurant. Not wanting to talk about the awkward meal he'd spent with them on the weekend—Afra had invited Theo—during which his parents cast unhappy looks in Ari's direction but refused to discuss the tension in front of a guest, Ari shrugged and said they were fine.

Jax accepted the answer and, to Ari's relief, didn't ask any more questions. Instead he launched into the story of the time he met Hobbes's parents for a home-cooked meal, which took them the rest of the walk.

At the restaurant, Ari gave his name, and Hello, I'm Sophie gave a cheery grin.

"Right this way, Mr. Darvish. As I'm sure you're aware, the chef's table is located in the kitchen."

Jax jerked and looked over at Ari with wide eyes. "Chef's table? Someone wanted to impress tonight."

"Perhaps." He shot Jax a sly look. "I know I promised to show you off, but... would you think less highly of me if I admitted that it was the only table left?"

Jax tapped his chin. "Nah. Just more charmed."

Sophie led them into a hot, busy kitchen and guided them to a corner and a slim countertop with barstools behind it.

"Here you are." She motioned for them to have a seat and poured two fresh glasses of water. "I won't be asking your drink order because Chef can be picky about that. She'll be with you in a moment." She gave them one last smile, wished them a pleasant dinner, and ducked back out of the kitchen.

A fortyish woman with crinkled eyes and a bright pink ponytail mostly hidden by a wrap stepped up to the table. Paloma finished drying her hands and flung the towel over her shoulder. "So you made it, I see."

"Of course, Paloma. I said I would."

"Yes, you also mentioned bringing a date." She gave Jax a long up-and-down look. "But you didn't mention he was so handsome. You sure you want to waste your time with this idiot?" she asked Jax, jerking her thumb at Ari.

Eyes wide, Jax grinned. "Pretty sure. His is the best offer I've gotten so far." He winked at Paloma, ever the flirt.

She barked a laugh. "Is that so? Well, I own this restaurant, handsome, and could afford to keep you well-fed."

"Judging by the smell in this kitchen, that is a highly tempting offer."

Her kitchen always did smell heavenly. Ari couldn't blame Jax for being tempted.

"I like you." She patted his hand. "So, any requests or food aversions I should know about before I start seducing handsome here with my amazing food?"

"None for me," Jax said agreeably.

"You know I will eat whatever you make for me, Paloma," Ari said. He knew better than to argue.

"Good. Stay where you are, and I'll bring an appetizer and something to drink." She rapped their table and shuffled away.

Jax watched her go, then turned to Ari. "All right, please tell me everything."

"Everything? Everything I know does encompass rather a lot—"

"Everything about her," Jax laughed. "How do you know her?"

Ari inclined his head. "She's an old friend of Afra's."

"Oh, I see." Jax's grin turned wicked, suggesting he did indeed see, and all too well. "Has she known you since you were in diapers?"

Ari's nose twitched. "Not quite, but very nearly. Her family moved here shortly after I began school."

"And she and Afra would have been, what? About to start high school?"

Ari hummed. "Grade six, I think."

Still smiling, Jax propped his chin on one hand and eyed Ari almost sleepily. "I bet you were an adorable kindergartener. All those curls and big doe eyes."

"Oh, he was as cute as a button," Paloma said as she settled two small glasses of white wine and a plate in front of them. "Of course, all of Afra's friends were absolutely smitten with him. We didn't exactly have to be talked into babysitting. Probably because he was just so agreeable." She nudged the plate of food forward, then followed it with a linen-covered basket. "Imported manchego cheese, and a selection of house-made preserves—candied tomatoes, pickles, and olive tapenade. With fresh bread, of course."

She swooped away, and Jax turned sparkling eyes on Ari. "Agreeable, eh? What happened?"

Ari picked up a piece of cheese by its toothpick skewer. "I can be agreeable when I want to be." He shot Jax a look and then unloaded the cheese onto a slice of bread, topped it with the tomato, and bit. He'd forgotten how delicious Paloma's creations were.

"Apparently I just need to learn how to butter you up?" Jax raised an eyebrow over his wineglass, but he couldn't hide his smirk.

"What else is a date for?"

The wine was perfect—crisp and dry but a little fruity—a nice complement to the tapas. Jax made rapturous noises over the tapenade, to the point where Ari just pushed the little ramekin toward him and let him go to town.

"At least try one bite," Jax protested, loading up a slice of bread with spread, manchego, and the last tomato. "Here. The sweetness of the tomato and the bitter salt of the olive and the richness of the cheese...." He held it out for Ari.

Ari jolted, realizing Jax might actually mean for him to bite the bread out of his hand. He wasn't sure he was ready for that level of intimacy with another person present, even if Paloma was mostly busy, so he carefully held Jax's wrist steady with one hand and plucked the piece of bread from him with the other.

Jax was right; the combination worked perfectly, like three-part harmony. Four, if you counted the bread.

"I think it's a hit," Ari heard, but he still had his eyes closed, savoring the flavors. When he opened them again, Paloma was back, this time with another plate.

"Grew the tomatoes myself, even." She traded out their antipasto plate—empty—for one of artfully folded sliced cured meat with a lovely fatty layer. Ari's stomach growled.

"Did you grow the pig too?" Jax reached eagerly for his fork.

She laughed. "No. It's *jamón ibérico*—imported. And this...." She produced two more wineglasses, red this time. "Is my personal favorite rioja."

Oh—damn. Ari had forgotten about Jax's alcohol restriction. The glasses were small so that they could be paired perfectly with each dish, but still, he wouldn't be able to taste all the wines.

When Paloma left again, Ari murmured quietly, "I'm sorry. The chef's tasting menu comes with drink pairings. I forgot you're only allowed two."

Jax lifted a shoulder, unperturbed. "It's all good. I don't mind having a sip of each. You can finish them off since neither of us has to drive."

At least the wine wouldn't go to waste.

Still—"Excuse me," he said, and slipped away from the table to beg a favor from Sophie under the guise of using the restroom.

Ten minutes after his return, Paloma brought the next course and two wineglasses once again. But she then turned around and produced a large martini glass filled with something pink and fizzy. "I heard you're a bartender," she said conversationally, sliding the drink in front of Jax. "Certified virgin cocktail. Though I'm not sure I caught the name of the beverage…?"

"That's—thank you." Jax took it, flushing slightly, and glanced sidelong at Ari. "The version I make him's called a Sparkling Conversation."

Paloma laughed. "That's fabulous. I might have to bribe you out of your recipe. But what would you call the no-alcohol version?"

"Hm." Jax tried a sip. "A Diverting Discourse?"

"Needs work," Paloma noted, but she left them to their next course.

"You didn't have to do that," Jax murmured.

"I wanted to."

He wanted everything to be perfect.

"THIS IS the nicest first date I've ever been on," Jax commented as they walked back toward Ari's apartment. The original plan had been to take a walk after dinner, but the forecast called for rain. The sky was rumbling, and the winter chill had finally arrived.

"I'm glad," Ari answered, squeezing his fingers. "I was nervous."

Something warm fluttered in Jax's chest. "Yeah? I'm kind of a sure thing, you know."

Even without looking, he could feel Ari's wry side-eye. "Perhaps. But I… it may shock you to know that I'm not actually very good at dating."

This information caught Jax so off guard that for several seconds, his mouth hung open and nothing went in *or* out of it. At length he managed, "Well, you're faking it very well as far as I'm concerned. A chef's table for a private tasting menu? With wine pairings?"

"Wine pairings I forgot you wouldn't be able to enjoy," Ari pointed out.

"Still impressed."

A moment of comfortable silence passed before Ari volunteered, "In fairness, it's not usually the actual dates that are the problem."

Jax glanced over, but he couldn't glean anything from Ari's face—not enough light, and the man could play professional poker if he wanted to. "No?"

"It's a lot of things. People sometimes find me a bit cold."

What? Jax thought of the softness of his eyes, the way he said Jax's name, the tenderness of his touch, and the passion he put into his music. "Have these people met you?" He rarely felt as warm as he did under Ari's focused intensity.

"Unfortunately a different me, I think." Ari tugged on their hands, consciously or not, and Jax stepped closer, until their shoulders were brushing. "I don't always find it easy to connect with people. I often express myself through music instead of words or actions."

Okay, that made sense, and Jax could maybe forgive some of these hypothetical past lovers for missing the larger picture. Maybe. "But not with me?"

"*Also* with you," Ari corrected. "But you understand the music, I think, and...."

Jax's pulse beat high in his throat. "And?" Why was he holding his breath?

"And unlike anyone else, you're worth putting in the effort to remember words and actions too."

There was that warmth Jax was talking about. It practically flooded through him as they reached Ari's building.

Jax cleared his throat. "You know, I'm not actually great at dating either. I mean, sometimes it's not my fault. Just because when I'm not in a relationship I'm a promiscuous pansexual doesn't mean I'm a cheater, but try telling that to assholes. Maybe that's why, ever since I was a kid, get me in a relationship that doesn't suck, and I...."

Ari waited patiently, tugging Jax's hand again until they faced each other in the glow of the streetlamp.

It was harder to say this while looking straight at him. Jax cut his gaze away and looked down the block at the quiet street. "I just go all in way too fast, you know? My sister says I fall in love at the drop of a hat." His voice broke a little on that all-important word, and he quickly added to cover it up, "It freaks people out."

Sometime in the past twenty seconds, his hands had gone clammy. He hoped Ari didn't notice.

"It's just really nice," Jax went on, babbling helplessly with no way to stop himself, heart pounding, "to be on the same page for once."

Ari dropped his hand. In the dim light of the streetlamp, his eyes were very dark and velvet soft. He raised his palms to Jax's cheeks and held his face gently as he kissed him slowly and toe-curlingly deep.

When he broke away, it took Jax a moment to gather enough spare vocabulary from the couch cushions of his brain to make a sentence. He licked his lips, chasing Ari's taste. "So." His voice came out in a warm rasp. "Do you put out on the first date?"

Ari hummed. "For you? Definitely."

Chapter Fourteen

JAX WOKE the next morning feeling pleasantly used. A glance at the clock said it was past eight already.

He shuffled into the bathroom for a pee and to brush his teeth. They had showered last night after getting thoroughly dirty. Of course, they did get dirty again in the shower, but the water was handy.

In Ari's bedroom, Jax slipped on his boxers and then, after some consideration of last night's trousers, raided Ari's closet for soft pants and a T-shirt. Maybe he should stash a couple of items here for mornings after.

Yawning, he went into the kitchen, poured himself a mango juice, and took his pill.

After another sip of sugar, Jax looked around and realized he'd walked right past Ari, who stood next to his piano with his electric violin under his chin, running the bow roughly over the strings. He was frowning, pressing the bow in rough jerks.

Not wanting to interfere, Jax clutched his glass and waited.

Ari yanked the bow away with a discordant sound, and for a moment, Jax thought he might throw it across the room.

Instead he dropped both arms and let out a gusty sigh. The instrument almost looked sad, hanging limply from his grip.

"Having trouble?"

Ari jerked and turned toward Jax. He smiled, his gaze tender and then heated as he took Jax in. Not doing much to hide his pleased smile, Jax sipped his juice. Ari cleared his throat and turned to put away his violin.

"So," Jax said when Ari stepped toward him. "Trouble?"

Ari shook his head. "Composing has not come easy this morning. But that is not unusual."

"Ah. Writer's block. How did you shake it the last time?"

The poker face was back. Ari gave nothing away, even as he leaned in to kiss Jax. "It's nothing, I'm sure. Only I have been incredibly spoiled recently and forgot what a difficult piece feels like. Now." He ran one hand down Jax's arm and threaded their fingers together. A sense memory of last night flashed through Jax. He squeezed back. "How about we get you some breakfast."

"Breakfast sounds great," Jax agreed and followed Ari back to the kitchen.

Ari pulled fruit, cheese, and eggs out of the fridge, and a loaf of bread—some sort of baguette?—out of the cupboard. It struck Jax that Ari was feeding him yet again, and maybe he should even that score, though Jax's roommate, and Ari's lack thereof, made dates and sleepovers somewhat impractical. He'd have to think on it.

"What can I do?" He set his glass aside.

Ari gave him a knife and free rein over the fruit and turned his attention to the eggs.

Starting with half a cantaloupe, Jax cut off wedges, sliced into them, and then ran the knife along the rind to detach the pieces. As he worked, he considered the problem of a date in which Jax provided food.

He couldn't take Ari home, not without coordinating with Hobbes, who'd been hollow-eyed with exhaustion lately. Jax wasn't going to risk interrupting his sleep when Hobbes was already not getting enough of it. Not to mention, why sleep in Jax's old queen-size when Ari's plush king sat waiting for them? Equally, Jax couldn't really afford to take Ari out. Well, he could afford a McD's feast, but that seemed inappropriate. He certainly couldn't afford the chef's table at one of the city's best restaurants.

Jax washed the grapes and considered the apples. Should he cut those too? A glance at Ari showed that he was scrambling the eggs still. Apple slices it was.

And sure, you didn't *need* money to make a date special, but *special* usually involved a place of meaning or something of significance. Jax and Ari didn't really have that yet. Well, other than the bar, since that's where they met. But what was Jax going to do? Serve Ari homemade meals on Murph's bar top?

Jax paused, the knife halfway through an apple.

Huh.

"Done," he said as he finished with the apples.

Ari pulled the pan off the stove and divided the eggs between two waiting plates. "As am I."

They put the plates of eggs and fruit on the table. Ari added slices of bread, the cheese, a pot of honey, and a pot of tea. Then they settled in to eat.

Breakfast was comfortably quiet. Jax didn't even feel the need to fill the silence. It struck him once again how well matched they were.

"So," Jax said, picking up a grape, "what are you up to this week?"

Ari cleared his throat. "Actually, Noella has asked me to come to Toronto."

Jax tilted his head. Noella was... "Your producer?"

"Yes. She wants me to come up for a few days so we can discuss my next album in person. I believe she's also interested in recording some of it and talking to potential vocalists." Ari sighed. "They called this morning. I leave early tomorrow and won't be back until Sunday."

"Oh. That sucks."

"Succinctly put," Ari said wryly.

Made worse by the fact that undoubtedly Ari would be working while Jax was free, and vice versa. Jax huffed. "Well." He pasted on a smile. "We'll just have to make the best of today."

ARI HAD spent enough of his life in hotel rooms that their impersonal nature no longer registered. A part of him found it soothing to be in a space with no memories and no distractions. It usually put him in the right mood to compose.

Or it had, before this last tour.

His record label had put him up in the Fairmont, one of Toronto's most exclusive hotels. In fairness, this one was decorated well beyond what anyone would call *impersonal*. It was warm and inviting and spacious, and the room service menu left nothing to be desired.

Ari missed Jax before he even started to unpack.

A car picked him up just before lunch and brought him to the label's corporate offices, where a receptionist so fresh-faced she could've been Theo's younger sister directed him to a conference room. Noella was there, along with Julia, her boss, and Tom, her assistant.

"You made it." She raised her eyebrows. "I was afraid we were going to have to send out a search party."

She basically had—they'd hired a car to retrieve him from London. Ari's distaste for driving was well-known. "I always honor my agreements," he protested.

"Uh-huh, save it for someone who didn't already extend your album deadline."

Before Ari could defend himself, the necessary pleasantries intervened—handshakes, and then Tom offered to procure refreshments. Ari would make do with the water on the sideboard.

The business luncheon was productive. Ari approved the usual session musicians he preferred to work with. Paul from the art department came in to talk about album art. Ari and Paul batted a few concepts back and forth, and Paul went back to his office to make magic happen.

And then Noella called for a car to bring them to the studio.

"I want to get the majority of 'Alice' recorded," she said. "I think it's going to be huge for you to do so many songs with vocals, but we need music to bring to potential vocalists, and the sound quality of what you sent is going to give people the wrong impression."

Ari would have been the first to admit his recording technique wasn't up to snuff—he usually didn't even bother with a proper mic. He certainly didn't have any sophisticated software. He was kind of a Luddite.

"Fine," he agreed.

He and Linsey and Brian had worked together on his last album, and they were both consummate pros and easy to get along with. It only took an hour to get a good cut ready for sound mixing.

"This is different from your usual," Linsey commented during a short break caused by the failure of one of the patch cords. Noella was fetching a replacement.

"Yeah," Brian agreed. "I like it, though. It suits you. Very 'still waters run deep.'"

For some reason, that made Ari think of the first time he'd met Jax—*unstoppable force, meet immovable object.* If Ari was still waters, Jax was a tempest in a teacup.

He vaguely remembered a lesson from high school physics about equal and opposite reactions. But if he and Jax were equal and opposite forces, didn't that mean they added up to nothing?

Oh—damn, it was his turn to say something, wasn't it? "Thank you—"

"So," Linsey cut in. "New muse?"

Ari's ears heated. "Is it very obvious?"

"I think a couple of literal hearts floated out of my guitar during that solo," Linsey said wryly. "When you get a vocal artist in here, you're going to need, like, a fainting couch."

Brian nodded sagely and twirled a drumstick. "You should mention it to Noella."

"I'll take that under advisement."

When they finished the session, Ari bid the two of them goodbye and went back to the office with Noella, who sat down across from him with a portfolio. "So. I have a short list."

"Are you going to tell me Bon Iver isn't available?" he said ruefully.

Noella snorted. "Just keep an open mind, okay?" She hooked her phone up to the Bluetooth speaker in the lounge and flipped the folder open to the first page.

Noella had curated ten artists, six women and four men, for Ari to choose from, and she had audio samples for all of them, though three were artists he'd heard on the radio. He didn't need to hear samples for those.

He'd been waffling about the artist's gender. He'd originally wanted a man, but the fourth woman on the list had a dreamy, raspy quality to her voice that made him reconsider. It suited the song almost perfectly.

"Should I stick a pin in this one?" Noella asked.

Ari nodded distractedly and glanced at her CV. Maxi Greene. Only twenty-one, a rising star, or so the label was hoping. Her voice and headshot suggested a maturity beyond her age, with large dark eyes and pale skin over cheekbones that could've sliced cheese.

"We should definitely keep her in mind," he said. The CV noted an album release slated for January.

He put two more in the Maybe pile, both men, but he was pretty sure he was going to end up going with Maxi. It wasn't exactly how he'd thought the song would turn out, but he could already almost hear it, and he couldn't say he was disappointed.

But when Noella was putting her phone away, she must have hit the wrong thing, because music played from the speakers again, and all the hair on Ari's body stood on end.

"Who is *this*?"

Noella pulled her phone closer and touched the screen. "Aiden Lindell, apparently."

"It—he?" Ari asked. The voice was androgynous, lilting. It was a deep alto, but smooth, lacking any gruffness or cracks.

Noella tapped at her phone and, after a pause, said, "Yes. He's—I can't believe this—Canadian and based out of Toronto." She looked up. "I'm guessing you want—"

"Yes." The voice was everything Ari wanted for the song but hadn't known to ask for.

Noella smiled. "I'll make some calls." Ari might have felt bad for putting her on the spot if he didn't know that "I'll make some calls" was Noella's battle cry, and she was as bloodthirsty as any Klingon.

WITHOUT ARI in town, Jax found time to get bored. On Friday, before his shift, he slumped into the couch and pulled out his phone.

Even mindless scrolling of an Instagram feed was better than staring at the ceiling.

Jax had followed Ari's official account months ago. Ari didn't do social media for himself, really—his phone, an antique BlackBerry he insisted on using to avoid straining his wrists, had an appalling dearth of apps—and his accounts were actually PR vehicles run by someone else. But Jax wasn't going to stop following his boyfriend's official account just because Ari didn't actually use it.

Over the weeks, Jax had largely ignored the updates to Ari's account, since they tended to be pictures and video stockpiled during the tour or reminders about events, products, or endorsements. Today's picture was different.

Ari stood with his violin in one hand, gesturing with his bow at some sheet music with the other. Next to him, a slight young man with large dark eyes and fine features, somewhat obscured by a fashionable toque, was obviously listening intently. *New collaboration. Aiden Lindell @AideL and Ari discuss vocals for Ari's upcoming studio album. #dreamteam #thecountdownbegins*

Jax started at the picture, at how Ari practically loomed over Aiden, but the kid didn't look intimidated. Instead his body language and his fierce look of concentration spoke of something else entirely. He was eager to collaborate with Ari and make it successful.

It wasn't that Jax doubted Ari. Even if he didn't trust his own instincts—which, given his past, maybe he shouldn't—Naomi loved Ari, and Murph admired him. Ari was a good man and would never betray his trust. Also he was pretty sure Afra would do permanent injury to her brother if she ever discovered that he'd done something as crass as cheat.

But that didn't mean Jax was delusional enough to think Ari had suddenly lost the ability to recognize an attractive man when he saw one. Ari might, and was perfectly within his rights to, look at another man and think, *Yeah, I would if I could.* That was life. That was human nature.

And Aiden Lindell was definitely attractive.

Knowing it was a bad idea but unable to stop himself, Jax clicked on the Instagram profile.

The profile picture was artsy in the extreme—a black-and-white silhouette too tiny to be studied. The biography listed him as a singer/songwriter and gave links to the usual suspects—website, Twitter, Facebook, Bandcamp. Jax turned to the recent posts.

Some food, artsy pictures of instruments... a close-up shot of his face. Jax clicked it and swallowed. The promotional shot was head-on and showed him to great advantage. The large eyes were centered in a heart-shaped face with a cute nose and delicate but sensitive mouth. His hair was fashionably cut—the left side above his ear was shaved close, and the top was long and swept across his forehead and right cheek. In this photo, his lips were parted invitingly, suggestively, as he eyed the camera.

Fuck.

Jax would proposition him in a bar.

He scrolled down to see more photos.

It turned out that spending almost an hour internet-stalking the cute boy your boyfriend was doing a music collaboration with was not good for your mood.

At work, Jax put all his feelings in a tiny box and focused on what needed doing. First, he needed to talk to Murph about next week. Ari should be home on Sunday, and Jax had a plan for his return, but he needed Murph's cooperation if he was going to pull it off. Cute singers notwithstanding, Jax wanted to show Ari that he wasn't the only one who could plan a romantic date.

Fortunately, Murph would agree to just about anything if you asked him while lugging kegs around, though the look he shot Jax made it clear he knew Jax was exploiting his weakness. "I'd have said yes anyway," he huffed as they wrestled in the replacement keg.

"Yeah, well, I'm a mathematician." Jax grunted and nudged the keg the rest of the way into place with his shoulder. "I like to stack the odds."

As Jax knelt to connect the tap, Murph stood and prepared the pitcher for the head. "Next Sunday soon enough? It's getting cold enough that crowds are slowing, and the college kids are buckling down for exams. We're probably going to have to go down to six nights a week."

Jax hid a wince even as he nodded. That was one less night a week to line his bank account. On the other hand, at least he'd have time to see Ari and a way to host a romantic date without breaking the bank. "Next Sunday. Thanks, Murph."

The doors opened at seven and brought the usual rush of students who wanted to get in early enough to avoid paying the cover charge but would end up spending as much on drinks. Jax scrupulously checked IDs and toned down the flirting, suddenly feeling his age. They weren't there to flirt with him anyway; they just wanted to unwind after their midterms.

Well. *Most* of them weren't there to flirt with him. That didn't stop them from adding it to their agenda. He filled orders for a Slippery Nipple, a Blowjob, and a Screaming Orgasm for a sophomore with a blond bob and a T-shirt that read *Geologists Do It in the Ash*. She took the shot before she left the bar, no hands, licked the cream off her lip, and winked as she walked away with the other two.

"They get younger every year," Jax muttered, trying and failing to feel less like a dirty old man.

Someone at the bar let out a sharp laugh. "What are you, twenty-five?"

Jax turned toward the voice and smiled reflexively. "Twenty-seven," he said defensively. Well, close enough.

The man who'd spoken was handsome in a refined way, like a *GQ* model, and wearing a watch that belonged in one of their ads. If Jax's estimation wasn't too far off, he was at least in the ballpark of thirty. Now this guy Jax could flirt with.

"Oh, well, huge difference," the guy said. "One foot practically in the grave."

Jax's turn to laugh. "All right, Kierkegaard. Can I get you a drink?"

"Beer," the guy said agreeably. "Cold."

"Coming up."

There was a lull in bar traffic as Bruce started to charge a cover at the door, slowing the influx of patrons, so Jax had a few minutes to make small talk. "First time here?" he asked as he slid the guy a coaster.

"What gave me away?"

"I didn't recognize your face," Jax said dryly. "I'm in every day. Kind of a giveaway. What brings you in? Drink specials? Thirst for live music?"

"Coworker." The guy nodded thanks as Jax set the beer on the mat. "This is his chosen watering hole, not that he's had time to make an appearance lately with the shifts he works. When I mentioned my sorrows, he suggested I come here to drown them."

"Well, you're in luck. Drowning sorrows is our specialty. Anything in particular?"

The customer leaned his elbows on the bar. "What do you do for a guy whose romantic prospects are so pathetic his parents set him up on a blind date with another guy. Chaperoned—" He paused for dramatic effect. "—by both sets of parents."

Jax whistled under his breath and reached for a shot glass. He filled it with vodka and slid it next to the beer. "Start with that, then wait for the show, I think. I'm Jax, by the way." He wiped his hands on the bar towel and held one out to shake.

The man smiled, reaching out. "Nice to meet you, Jax. I'm—"

"Sohrab."

Both Jax and his customer—Sohrab—turned at the sound of the familiar voice.

Jax grabbed a highball glass and a chunk of ice and poured Hobbes's usual. "Hey, Hobbes. This one of yours?"

"Unfortunately." Hobbes slid onto the stool next to Sohrab and accepted his drink with a nod. "Dr. Sohrab Hosseini, may I present Jax Hall. This reprobate is my roommate."

"Reprobate, wow. You get that from your Word of the Day calendar?"

"Shut up."

Jax ignored Hobbes and returned his attention to Sohrab. "I take it the blind date didn't work out so well."

Sohrab shrugged. "Well, he was nice, hot, and actually gay. The problem is I'm not sure what possessed my parents to believe he'd actually be available. The guy's kind of a local celebrity." Jax was peripherally aware of a dawning look of horror on Hobbes's expressive face. "Actually I heard he hangs out here sometimes. Ari Darvish? Shit, I hope he doesn't think I'm stalking him."

Jax's stomach suddenly felt like it was full of liquid nitrogen. He forced himself to smile. "You're safe. In Toronto until Sunday, or so I heard."

Hobbes kept trying to catch his eye, but fuck that. Jax needed a break from this conversation, and for once, time was on his side. "I gotta go—almost showtime. You want to settle up, or should I start a tab?"

He took care of their bills on autopilot, the other 90 percent of his available brainpower spinning through a loop of what this might mean. Why had Ari's parents set him up on a blind date? Did they not know he was seeing Jax, or did they just not approve? And why hadn't Ari told Jax about it?

Jax didn't have any answers.

But he didn't have time to dwell on it. He needed to get his head in the game. He sat down at the piano and waited for Naomi to come over.

After the set, Jax took a bathroom break, then found himself at the bar once again. Hobbes was nowhere in sight, but Sohrab hadn't moved.

"So, I guess I put my foot in it."

Jax gave a tight smile. "No, not really. Okay, maybe a bit. Mostly it was just awkward."

Sohrab wrinkled his nose. "Still. I didn't mean—" He sighed. "Honestly, considering I know he comes here, I probably should have held my tongue around cute white boys."

Jax cocked his head and poured a beer and a water. He handed the beer over.

"Thanks."

"Why hold your tongue around white boys?"

"Oh, Ari mentioned he was seeing someone. He was pretty vague on details, but that came up."

"Ah." Jax's stomach churned. Why would Ari mention that? Unless it was to explain why Sohrab—whose skin suggested he too had Middle Eastern heritage—was an acceptable choice and Jax was not.

Sohrab sipped his beer, licked his lips, and said, "Anyway, it was nice to actually meet the guy that's got Ari so... gaga."

"*Gaga?*"

Sohrab chuckled. "He's crazy about you. I never stood a chance. Anyway, I'll let you...." He lifted his beer in salute and slipped away.

Jax gave a distracted goodbye and tried to focus on drink orders before he had to head back on stage. So a stranger thought Ari was gaga for him, but Ari's parents didn't know about him. Or didn't think Ari was gaga enough to not leave Jax—

Fuck. Jax needed more music to get himself out of his head.

It was going to be a long night—and a long week until Ari returned.

Chapter Fifteen

ARI DID his best to remember to text Jax often throughout the day. He might hate texting, but he was learning that Jax appreciated it. So Ari sent him pictures of his food, the view from the hotel room, and the ridiculous bathroom in it—Jax offered to drive over to help him test the tub and even added a splash emoji—and he tried to send updates about his progress when he could.

I hate meetings with advertisers.

?? they trying to sell you stuff?

No. Trying to sell me.

HAH! I wanna make so many sex-worker jokes I don't know where to start. Also that's kind of dehumanizing and I feel bad now.

I just had to sit through an hour-long meeting with executives asking questions about my unfinished album so they can make "marketing plans."

Aww, poor baby! The suits are so mean to make artists think about business. Is all that left-brained thinking hurting you?

The idea that left half of the brain is reasonable and the right creative is a ridiculous myth and I'm ashamed of you for indulging in it.

1. I know it's a myth. 2. It's a metaphor.

Not a very good one.

3. I have listened to your music and know it's not even a good metaphor to describe your process. 4. Stop sulking.

The long text chains created by Jax's talkative nature couldn't compare to actual conversation, but since their work schedules were incompatible and the "suits" kept Ari busy until well after dinner, they could never find the time for a phone call.

Ari threw himself into his work as a distraction and to ensure he wouldn't be asked to stay longer.

"What do you think?" Aiden asked as the music faded on the latest cut of "Alice." They'd spent the past two hours rehearsing and recording. Aiden was young and eager. He had introduced himself the first morning with a bright smile and, "Thanks. I was so honored when your people called and said you wanted me. Getting pulled for one of your songs is a bit of a coup. I hope I do it justice."

He was easy to work with—listened attentively to everything Ari said and offered thoughtful suggestions.

"I'm not sure. What do you think of that second bridge?"

"Too fast, right?" Aiden nodded.

"Yes. That second line needs to be—"

"Half a beat slower." Aiden smiled, stood, and trotted back into the studio.

Ari pulled out his phone and texted Jax. *Making progress. I think I'll actually get out of this city on Sunday as promised.*

When Aiden left, it was with Ari's number and an agreement to talk more collaboration in the future. Ari was pretty sure he'd take the kid up on the offer. He thought Jax might like to meet him if they were ever in Toronto together. Jax would probably appreciate the kid's style.

On Sunday Ari threw his things in a bag and almost bolted out of the hotel. Once comfortably ensconced in the back seat and on the 401, Ari pulled out his phone and messaged Jax.

On my way. Should be home within 3 hours. Want to do lunch? I could.

Great. Come to mine? I want you to myself.

Sure.

Ari puzzled at his phone. Perhaps Jax was busy.

At home, Ari eyed the contents of his fridge and sniffed a dubious-looking container. Then he called in an order at his favorite Greek place. He could do with some comfort food after the past week, especially comfort food that came without disappointed parents.

Jax was a beautiful sight for sore eyes, and Ari didn't curb the impulse to wrap him in his arms and kiss him thoroughly.

"Hi to you too," Jax gasped when Ari finally pulled away.

Ari blinked. "Did I forget to say hello?" He couldn't keep his hands from slipping under Jax's coat, then another layer deeper until he could rub his thumbs up and down the lines of Jax's iliac crest.

Jax licked slightly swollen red lips and said, "You know what? We can skip the pleasantries this once," and let Ari drag him further inside.

Everything was that much *righter* with Jax pressed against the bedroom door, panting as Ari dismantled him with his mouth. "Fuck," Jax said as he squirmed against Ari's hands and reflexively tried to push his cock deeper. "I guess you missed me too."

That was such an obvious fact it didn't bear commenting, especially when Ari's tongue was busy. He flicked his gaze up to Jax's face—flushed, pupils blown, sweat trickling down his temple because he still had his coat on—and pointedly rolled his eyes.

Then he relaxed his throat and enveloped him to the base.

"*Fuck.*" Jax slammed his head back against the door. Ari reveled in it, in the taste and feel of him, but mostly in how easily he came apart under Ari's touch. "Ari, I'm—"

Ari pressed his fingers behind his balls, and that was it. Jax made a sharp, high noise without any vowels and came in his mouth, his thighs shaking.

He thought he'd have at least thirty seconds while Jax recovered, but apparently he'd underestimated Jax, because he'd barely wiped his mouth when Jax sank to his knees beside him and pushed him onto his back on the floor. He was about to protest that the bed was three feet away, but Jax already had his jeans open and really, this wasn't going to take long.

Ari really had missed him.

An embarrassingly small number of minutes later, Jax rolled his head off Ari's lap and lay next to him on the floor. "Hi, Jax. Nice to see you, Jax. How was your week? Couldn't stop thinking about you, Jax."

Ari huffed, duly chastised. "Hello, Jax. I missed you." He turned his head to look at him, but Jax was staring up at the ceiling. He had a streak of come on the corner of his mouth. "How was your week?"

Jax took a few breaths—enough that Ari started to tense, worried something was wrong. Although what could be wrong? Surely if something were bothering him, he wouldn't have responded so eagerly when Ari jumped him.

But maybe that *was* the problem? Jax had said he often had difficulty keeping his partners on the same page with him, relationship-wise. Had Ari made him feel used?

Before he could spiral too far into a panic, Jax took a deep breath and shook his head slightly. "Long," he said finally as he turned to look at Ari. The muscle at the corner of his jaw was bunched. "My week was long. Kind of lonely."

Ari turned onto his side so he could reach for Jax's hand and lace their fingers together. "I'm sorry." He wished Jax could have come along.

Jax looked at their tangled hands and swallowed. Then he looked up. Whatever he was holding back, it was still bothering him, and it had something to do with Ari.

Why didn't he say something?

On the other hand, why couldn't Ari just ask? He cleared his throat. "Is something the matter?"

Jax bit his lip, then shook his head. This time the tension in his body seemed to melt away for real. "It's nothing. I was just thinking."

Thinking hard enough for a small crease to form between his eyebrows, which Ari reached up to smooth away. "About?"

Jax captured his hand again, but he didn't interlace their fingers, just held it loosely between their bodies. "Well, you met Alice. And Sam's been asking about you. I thought maybe we could do lunch sometime? Just the three of us, I mean. Well, we could ask George and Alice too, but that's logistically more challenging."

Was Jax worried Ari wouldn't want to meet his sister? "I would love to," he said honestly. "We could make something here, or would it be better to go out?" Would Sam like him? Did they need to be on neutral ground, just in case?

Something flashed across Jax's face, but it was gone before Ari could catalog it, never mind decipher it. "She'll probably want to cook for us, but we should talk her out of it. She doesn't get out for a lot of socializing. Perils of being a working mom."

"I understand." Ari pulled Jax's hand to his mouth and kissed his knuckles. "You'll ask her and let me know when she's free? I don't have anything scheduled this week, so my time is yours."

Especially since he was up against the wall again with writer's block. Having Jax around more often could only be good for his creative process.

He hoped.

"Are you sure?" Jax asked. "You were gone for a week. You don't need to go see your parents or anything?"

"Well, we do have standing dinner plans on Saturdays." A truly absurd time to have a commitment with one's parents when one was dating conventionally, but it didn't matter to Ari since Jax wasn't available anyway. "But no, I don't need to make a special effort to see them during the week. It's... actually, it may be better if I stay away until the weekend."

Now Jax was frowning again. "What? Why?"

Ari pursed his lips and debated how to phrase it delicately. "My parents... are supportive of me to a point. They're proud of me. But I think they think that I should give up touring and stay in London to take care of them until—" *Until they die.* But that was too morbid to say out loud.

"And you don't want to do that," Jax filled in. That shadow in his eyes was back, the tension in his face.

"I can't do that," Ari corrected. "Music—not just writing it but performing live, especially my own music, for an audience—is cathartic for me. It helps me process things. It might seem trivial, but I need it."

"That doesn't sound trivial to me." The squeeze of his hand and the light in his eyes said he understood. Ari wondered if Jax felt the same about singing... or math. "Have they been pushing you lately?"

Ari sighed. "Yes. They had me at home for a long time when I couldn't tour. And when my father got sick, I was around even more to look after them. I think they hoped it might be the"—he smirked unhappily—"'new normal.' But I can't go back to that. I... barely wrote the entire time."

It was Jax's turn to offer understanding affection. He looped Ari's arm around his shoulder and rested his head on Ari's. "They don't want you to leave again."

"They do not. And our visits have become... fractious."

Jax snorted. "Big word."

Ari hummed and buried his face in Jax's hair. His ass was starting to hurt sitting on the floor, but he didn't want to move yet.

On the other hand, while he couldn't give up touring, spending four and a half days apart from Jax was a terrible idea. He would do whatever he could to make sure it didn't happen again.

THE PROBLEM with fishing, Jax reflected, was that if you came home without catching anything, you couldn't be certain if that was because the fish just missed you, if the fish was wily and escaped you, or if there were no fish to begin with.

Ari had effectively dodged the conversation about family introductions, leaving Jax no further ahead.

Another long week followed. Jax had spent the past month using Ari as a distraction from the stresses of extra work hours and time spent reviewing this thesis project. But hiding from stress was difficult when Jax couldn't stop worrying that, despite what he'd said, Ari wasn't taking their relationship seriously.

Not that Jax denied himself Ari's company. They slept together and then fell asleep and *actually* slept together several nights. He tried not to read anything into Ari's actions, tried not to spend their time together watching. Ari was sweet and attentive as ever. On Wednesday they met up with Sam for lunch. At Jax's insistence, they took her out. At Ari's, they went to a trendy bistro where he picked up the tab.

As expected, Sam and Ari got on almost distressingly well. Sam teased Ari for wooing Jax with his violin. Ari cocked his head and said, "I see the family resemblance. And Jax did most of the wooing. With his piano." When Sam laughed, announced that she liked him, and demanded to know everything about him, Ari obliged with a charming grin.

It was unfair of Ari to charm Jax's sister so well when he wouldn't even talk about his parents in the context of his relationship with Jax.

On Thursday, after a night spent in his own bed because Ari had an early meeting and couldn't wait up for Jax to get home, Jax baked five dozen muffins. The only upside to his baking freak-out was that Hobbes didn't show up to ask questions, though Jax did wonder where his friend had been lately. Then again, maybe he shouldn't look a gift horse in the mouth—Hobbes hadn't had the chance to grill Jax about Sohrab's blind-date bomb, and at this rate, Jax could hopefully put him off until the New Year when he left for Cambridge. Or at least until Jax got up the courage to ask Ari about it himself.

He packed up two dozen muffins for his sister—she wouldn't say no to free food that Alice would eat—and brought another dozen to Ari so as to leave less incriminating evidence.

He spent the rest of the week planning and fretting about the date. Jax wanted everything to be perfect and tried not to think too much about why he was so desperate for the evening to be so romantic.

On Sunday Ari arrived at the bar at seven as requested and texted Jax that he was just outside.

Jax nervously checked the setup one last time and then hurried to unlock the door. Ari's hair was tied back, and he was dressed—fuck—in those sinful black jeans and a crisp white shirt with the sleeves rolled up. Jax tried not to drool at the sight of those forearms, which looked just as lovely when pining Jax to the bed. Or the wall. Or the floor.

Ari smiled and stepped in close to kiss him hello. "Why are we meeting here when it's closed?" he asked when he finally pulled away. "You've been very secretive."

Jax grinned. "Maybe a little. But I wanted to cook up a surprise." He stepped farther inside and waved toward the bar top, set for two. "I thought we could have dinner together in the place where we first met."

Ari's expression went soft, and he cleared his throat. "Technically, we first met in the break room."

"Shut up," Jax laughed. "We're not eating there; it smells like fart. Besides, the bar is where we had our first real conversation and where you let me mix you drinks. Now come on." He grabbed Ari's hand, determined to make the night perfect.

At the bar Ari settled into a seat, and Jax pulled over some appetizers. He'd put his day off to good use, made the stuffed prosciutto-wrapped dates himself, and had more food waiting at the bar. Their entrees were in the kitchen so they could stay warm.

Jax poured them both half glasses of wine to sip. "I might not be chef at one of the best restaurants in town—"

"Jax."

"—*but* I'm not without skills when it comes to making dinner and finding wine pairings."

Ari bit into a date and made a noise of delight. Then he washed it down with a sip of wine—and made a face like he'd just bitten into a lemon.

Uh-oh. "Not a good wine pairing?" Jax asked, heart sinking.

Ari eventually swallowed his mouthful, then picked up the bottle and examined the label. "This is usually a good bottle, but…." He sniffed the neck, then winced and held it out for Jax.

Dutifully, Jax took a whiff. "Oh. Wine shouldn't smell like that."

"Perhaps the cork shriveled and let air in the bottle."

That would explain the vinegar bouquet. "Sorry," Jax said, trying not to let on how upset he was. He wanted tonight to go perfectly— he'd *needed* it to go perfectly so he could finally get an angle on the question, "Hey, Ari, when am I going to meet your parents?" Which was really just a cover for "Hey, Ari, do you promise you're really serious about us?" Now it seemed like the prospect was doomed from the get-go. "I'd offer to make you something else, but…." He gestured to the liquor shelf, which was kept under a locked gate when the bar wasn't open.

Why couldn't Jax do anything right? Murph would've given him the key for that if he'd asked. Jax could have paid for anything they used.

"Jax." Ari's hand covered his. "It's only a bottle of wine—a drink you can only partake of in limited quantities anyway."

Jax allowed himself to be comforted. Still— "I just wanted everything to be perfect."

"If I required alcohol to enjoy spending time in your company, I would not do it."

Smooth talker. Jax had no choice but to let it go. "All right, you make a valid point. Flatterer." They could have a nice meal without alcohol.

Ari smiled, and Jax's tension disintegrated further. "I have my moments."

They made do with sparkling water, and Jax tried to relax into the conversation, catching up on what they hadn't managed to talk about over the week.

The problem was that after a while, all Jax's musician-bartender stories started to sound the same. Ari knew all his coworkers, so there wasn't much Jax could tell him about them. And Jax was still puzzling out how to work *so I met the guy your parents set you up on a blind date with* into conversation without it sounding accusatory. Probably because it *was* accusatory.

So conversation turned from shared stories of working at the Rock to Ari's trip to Toronto and the album's progress.

Jax scowled at his pasta, chased an errant noodle through a puddle of too-acidic sauce, and tried not to grit his teeth as Ari spoke fondly of Aiden Lindell and his sweet voice, his emotive expression, his—okay, Jax stopped listening. A man could only take so much.

"...collaborate with him in the future." Ari paused. "Jax. The noodle is dead."

So was the mood, Jax thought sourly. "Yeah," he forced himself to say as he put down his fork. "Sorry." But before he could excuse his distraction or even change the subject, Ari nodded and went on, apparently oblivious.

"Noella thinks she might be able to set up a synchronized tour so that Aiden's available to perform live with me. That might depend on finding another artist he'd be a suitable opening act for—"

Jax dropped his fork in his pasta plate and finally let his mouth get the better of him. "Jesus. If he's so great, why don't you just go on a blind date with *him*."

Whoops.

When he looked up, Ari was staring at him with his mouth slightly agape, his eyes wide, two spots of color high in his cheeks. So much for finessing the conversation. Outright confrontation was always more his style. He should've known better than to try to be subtle.

Ari cleared his throat. "Jax, something is obviously bothering you. Rather than avoid the issue, could we... talk about it?"

Ugh. Jax had caught him in a lie—one of omission, but still—and he was still going to make Jax play the jealous lover? *Fine.* Jax would play the jealous lover. "I met a friend of yours last week. A Dr. Sohrab someone? He told me a story."

"Ah." Ari took a deep breath and set down his own utensils, not that he'd been using them since he'd been talking about Aiden for the past five minutes instead of eating the meal Jax labored over. "You *are* angry with me."

"No," Jax denied. Off Ari's infinitesimally raised eyebrow, he amended, "Fine, yes, I'm a little annoyed. Obviously you can't control other people's actions, but you should have told me about it after the fact. Do you know how it feels to have to work in a public-facing job all night after one of your customers tells you his parents set him up on a date with your boyfriend? And your boyfriend didn't mention it?"

"You're right that I should have told you." Ari reached for Jax's hand, and Jax grudgingly, against his better judgment, let him take it. "I didn't think… well, I didn't think."

That wasn't an apology, but Jax wasn't finished airing his list of grievances either. "And speaking of other people's actions." He knew Ari's parents were a challenging subject, but if Jax didn't bring it up, he was going to drive himself to multiple root canals from all the tooth grinding. "I guess I don't understand why your parents were setting you up on a date in the first place."

Ari's expression froze, but Jax could see the emotion in his eyes even if he couldn't identify it. Fear? Guilt? Ari swallowed. "Jax…."

Yeah, Jax didn't like where this was going. Would it be the thing that broke them? He'd thought they were on the same page, but he was learning they really, really weren't. And that hurt.

Suddenly he couldn't stand to be in the room with Ari. "I… excuse me."

Not wanting to deal with the people he might see on the street proper, he went out through the break room. The exterior door stuck, and Jax had to throw his shoulder to get it open. It banged against the brick when he finally succeeded, and Jax stepped out into the November chill.

Ari stepped out behind him. "Jax," he said softly.

Jax clenched his fists and bit out, "I'm guessing, from your reaction, you haven't told your parents about us."

"They've probably seen the video, so—" Jax shot Ari a look. "No. They don't know I'm seeing someone."

Even though Jax had been expecting it, it was a blow to the ribs that left him breathless. He shut his eyes and forced himself to inhale deeply, but when he opened them again, it still hurt. "What the fuck, Ari," he said, his voice rising. He turned to get into his face. "You've met my sister. *I've* met *your* sister. Why the hell don't your parents even know I exist?" He was yelling now.

Ari looked stricken, his mouth tight and his eyes wide. "Jax. It was never my intention to hide you."

"Then what *was* it!"

"They're…." He cast about as though searching for words. "They're judgmental and nosy! They have ideas about what my life should look like, and they would want to see if you measured up."

"So what? You don't think I would?" Jax snapped. He wrapped his arms around his chest, feeling the cold for the first time.

"No!" Ari shouted. "Of course that's not what I think. But they would want to meet you immediately. They've chased men off before."

A reasonable-sounding fear, but— "So your parents will hate me. That's great. What the fuck?"

"I didn't say—"

"You didn't have to."

"Would you let me finish?"

"Why? So you can spout more bullshit? God, I'm starting to wonder what the fuck we're even doing here."

Ari flinched. "Don't say—"

"What? How I feel?" Jax scrubbed his hands over his face and hair. "Fuck this." He turned and started to walk.

"Jax!"

"I need some fucking air, Ari. Just… go home."

Jax strode through the parking lot and out onto the street. It was too cold to be out without his jacket, but he didn't want to turn back. He needed space from Ari, from the bar, from the date he had worked so hard to make perfect and which had ended so disastrously.

His eyes burned. Fuck, fuck, fuck. For the first time in Jax's life he'd felt in sync with someone, and Ari hadn't thought Jax was good enough to take home to Mom and Dad.

He stalked aimlessly around central town, dodging pedestrians and doing his best to avoid crowds. He had no desire to interact with anyone else, and he probably looked like a dangerous tough guy, wandering around wearing a scowl instead of a jacket.

Sometime later he dragged himself back to the bar. Thank God he'd left the keys in his pants pocket. Otherwise he'd also be locked out in the cold without a way of getting home.

He trudged across the parking lot toward the back door and stopped dead in his tracks when he spotted it. Standing open.

Please tell me my eyes are deceiving me. Jax hustled across the lot and slowed as he approached the door. He took a deep breath and stepped into the building to look around. There was no one else in the break room, and the locked door into the restaurant was still shut. Jax breathed a sigh of relief. Then he took another look and groaned.

There were no people… and no guitars either.

Could this night get any worse?

Chapter Sixteen

ARI STOOD dazed in the Rock's back parking lot for several long minutes, trying to process what had happened. The evening had started out so promisingly. Jax had seemed happy to see him. And then… everything went horribly wrong.

Ari shut his eyes and breathed deeply. The memory of Jax's face in the bar and outside as he processed what Ari had done—or rather what he *hadn't* done—flashed before him. He had really fucked up.

The problem was, Ari thought miserably as he left the parking lot in a different direction from Jax, that Ari wasn't sure not telling his parents about Jax wasn't the right call. His parents' brand of meddling leaned toward actual action on their part. As soon as he told them about Jax, they would want to meet him, and if Ari didn't bring Jax to them fast enough, they would go to Jax in the only place they could be sure to find him. And no matter how lovely Jax was, doing the meet-the-parents thing at the Rock would end disastrously.

But not telling *Jax* that… that was inexcusable. If Ari was going to keep his parents in the dark for Jax's sake, he should have told Jax ages ago, explained that he couldn't throw Jax to the wolves during the early stages of a relationship.

Especially since Jax had expressed how happy he was to be with someone who was on the same page as him. Who took what they had seriously.

Ari rubbed his face and sighed. He definitely should have told Jax about Sohrab. There probably would have been a way to even make it seem funny if he had told Jax when it happened. If Jax hadn't found out about it from Sohrab weeks after the fact.

The hurt in Jax's voice when he snapped "Why don't you go on a blind date with him" stopped him cold. Jax looked embarrassed and hurt and angry at all once. For the first time it occurred to Ari that maybe Sohrab wasn't the only thing to push Jax over the edge. He'd been talking about Aiden at length, comfortable in the knowledge that Aiden was in no way his type, but maybe Jax wasn't so sure.

Ari might be the dumbest man alive. This was why his relationships crashed and burned. He wasn't good at seeing what other people needed or predicting what they would do. He thought he was making it work with Jax. Apparently not.

"Ari?" Theo stood a few meters away, a reusable bag in one hand and his phone in the other. His head was cocked. "What are you doing here? Are you okay?"

Ari looked around. In his distraction, he'd apparently wandered into a student neighborhood. "Oh," he said. No, he wasn't. But he wasn't going to say that to his sort-of intern. "Hey, Theo. You live around here?"

Theo looked at Ari, then at the grocery bag he was plainly carrying down the sidewalk. "No," he said dryly. "I like to carry groceries miles out of my way and risk my ice cream melting."

Well, Ari deserved that. He'd been exceptionally stupid this evening. "Ah...."

Theo's brow furrowed. "Ari? Seriously, you seem, um, distracted."

That was one word for it. "I'm fine," he lied. "Sorry. I...." But he couldn't come up with anything to say. "I'll let you get back to your groceries," he finally managed. "Have a good evening, Theo."

He had the feeling Theo's eyes were boring holes into his back as he walked away, but he didn't turn around. He couldn't see anyone he knew just then. They would ask questions he didn't want to answer, and when he inevitably did, they'd tell him what he already knew.

That he brought this on himself.

And what was he going to do about it?

Jax had told him to leave. Even if Ari could properly formulate an apology, Jax wouldn't hear it right now, and Ari should respect that. When he did apologize—and he had a feeling it should involve groveling—he wanted to have taken some kind of action that would show he meant it, that he took Jax's concerns seriously and was attempting to do better.

So, hunching his shoulders against the November chill, Ari walked back to the Rock, got in his car, and went home.

By the time he was unlocking his apartment door, he'd ignored three calls from Afra. Theo must have tattled. If past actions were any indication, Afra would invite herself over if he kept it up, so he texted her that he was safe at home and he'd call her in the morning.

Then he turned off his phone.

Against the backlight of the window, his piano was a hulking, imposing presence, but its lines were familiar. And tonight, for the first time in weeks, it was calling to him. He took off his shoes and poured himself a glass of water. Then he arranged himself on the bench, back straight, and lifted the key cover.

The music he coaxed out of the instrument was dark, discordant, and angry. But no. A song couldn't start there. It had to have somewhere to go. Ari backed it up sixteen measures. What was the song before the anger? Before Ari screwed up one of the best things that had ever happened to him?

Content. Warm. Harmonic. Resonant. *Sweet.*

That was what Ari had destroyed.

He hoped the soundproofing in his apartment was as good as the contractors had promised, because composing this on an electric keyboard would feel wrong. He took the violin from its case, tuned it quickly, and sketched out the story he was telling. Two lovers, two instruments, together in harmony. A sweet, slow, smooth dance of twisting notes, phrases that echoed and repeated.

And then a screech of violin. That was Ari, falling out of harmony, betraying his partner.

He flicked on the light above the piano and scribbled down notes, composing furiously. The violin and piano would work almost in a round at first, catching each other *here* and *here*, as if to say that together they could reach infinity. And then the faltering violin. A change into a minor key.

The piano part would crescendo gradually as the violin struggled to keep up, repeating a variation of the same phrase, increasing in pitch and desperation. And then finally—

The piano would thunder. It would drown out the strings. Ari tried to keep his fingers light on the keys as the emotion stormed through him. He was feeling what Jax felt now, layered on top of his own self-loathing. He deserved this pain. He had been completely spineless. Worse, he'd made Jax feel—

Your parents would hate me?

I'm starting to wonder what the fuck we're even doing here.

He'd made Jax feel like he was in this alone. The way Jax had felt so many times before. "I fall in love at the drop of a hat," he'd said.

Had Jax loved him? Had Ari ruined that forever?

These were questions the violin now had to ask, since the piano had thundered itself into acceptance. *Forgive me*, Ari thought, raising his violin to his chin. He had no idea how to earn Jax's forgiveness in real life. He could make the arrangements with his parents, he could try to prepare Jax for what meeting them would be like, for the scrutiny and backhanded compliments. But would it be enough?

He didn't know. But the violin's part—that he could write. He coaxed, he wheedled, he begged, he serenaded.

He let himself believe the piano would forgive him, and the two parts dovetailed again. But the music couldn't go back to what it had been. The key had changed, the time signature too. The shine had worn off. The music was still beautiful, but now it had a scar. It was haunting.

When Ari put down the bow, it was nearly two in the morning. He knew instinctively that the song was finished. He wouldn't edit it, not beyond refining the length of the notes, playing with vibrato in the shakier sections. For better or worse, the song was done.

Was his relationship with Jax over too?

IT TOOK Jax almost two hours to clean up the bar before he crawled home to bed.

Monday he woke up with a feeling of dread and lay in bed for several long moments remembering why he was angsty. Right. Last night he and Ari had an epic fight and then Jax lost Murph several guitars.

Jax thought about his savings account. The police weren't likely to find the guitars. They couldn't even stop the spate of robberies in the neighborhood. Jax had little confidence that this would break the case. But he didn't exactly have a spare thousand or two lying around to replace the instruments, so he'd never have enough money by January to return to MIT. He'd have to delay until the summer semester.

Jax's plan had been solid—make enough money by January, defend and return home before Ari went on tour. Maybe, if Ari wanted him, go with him for a while. If he waited until May, he'd have to leave around the same time as Ari....

But maybe that wouldn't matter. Maybe all of his careful plans for the future, working his life around Ari's, would be for nothing after last night. Were they even still together? Did Ari even want them to be? Or had Jax been fooling himself the whole time?

Jax got up, showered, got dressed, and mechanically choked down a bowl of oatmeal. Then he swallowed his pride and called Murph.

"I fucked up. The back door didn't latch properly, and someone got in. They took the guitars. But I'll totally pay for new ones," he rushed to get out before Murph could say anything. "It was totally my fault. I should have been more careful."

"Damn, b'y. Breathe."

Jax did, but only because he needed to.

"So. No guitars?" Murph blew out a breath. "Not convenient."

"I'll pay for them," Jax said.

"B'y. You don't have to. That's what insurance is for."

"They'll hike up your premiums. I can't let you do that, not when it's my fault." His pride wouldn't allow Murph to suffer the consequences for his stupidity.

"Jax." Murph had pride of his own, damn it.

"Murph, I was an idiot who got distracted. I shouldn't have…
I should have made sure the back door was shut." Ah, shit. There it
was, that feeling of shame. Jax Hall, too flighty to be trusted to lock
a stupid door. The only thing that would assuage it would be to get
Murph to accept the money.

So he said, "Ari's going to cover half of it anyway. All right?
You know he's got money."

Ari is never going to find out about this.

Sometime later Hobbes found him staring at his spreadsheet,
trying to recrunch the numbers, but no way could Jax get the money
by January—not unless he found another source of income or sold
something of value. Not that he owned much. He eyed the old laptop,
but even it would probably fetch more as scrap metal than as a
machine. The motorcycle, maybe, but who would buy one of those
with winter coming?

"Didn't think I'd see you this morning," Hobbes said, standing
awkwardly in the doorway.

Jax shrugged.

Hobbes narrowed his eyes. "You said you had a date. You were
planning that date. Why are you not currently curled up in Ari's bed?"

Jax's mouth twisted. He couldn't lie to Hobbes any better than
he could to Sam. "We fought."

Hobbes blew out a breath and headed for the coffee maker. He
flicked it on and turned back to Jax. "What about?"

Jax shut the laptop—it couldn't tell him anything he didn't
already know—and met Hobbes's eyes. "What do you think?"

"So. Finally asked him about that blind date."

The laugh that broke out of Jax was bitter and shocked him a
bit. "Turns out he never even told them he was seeing someone. Here
I thought—and he never even told his parents." Jax wrapped his arms
around himself.

Hobbes scowled. "Well. That's… shitty."

"Tell me about it."

"What an ass. He met your sister."

"I know," Jax said.

"So." Hobbes poured some coffee and sat down at the table. "Where does that leave you?"

"Fuck if I know. Mad and hurt and waiting to see what Ari does?"

Hobbes made a noise of neutral consideration. Jax's phone chirped.

A message from Ari. He took a deep breath and looked at it. *I am an idiot. Can we talk? I would like to apologize and explain and apologize.*

Jax swallowed. If Ari wanted to apologize—badly enough he'd mentioned it twice—that was a good sign, right? Maybe Ari wasn't a total loss.

Not today. I'm busy before work. Maybe tomorrow.

Okay. Until then know I never meant or wanted to hurt you.

Okay.

Tomorrow then.

"So?" Hobbes asked.

Jax exhaled. "We'll talk tomorrow. I have shit that needs doing today." He stood and cleaned up his breakfast things.

"For what it's worth, kid," Hobbes called as Jax was about to leave the kitchen, "I didn't think you were alone in this."

"Thanks, Hobbes."

Jax had to visit three different shops, but by the time he made his way to work, he'd found and bought replacements for everything. At least as he was running around the city, trying guitars and looking for the best deals, he couldn't think about Ari and his bruised heart.

Much.

ARI SET his phone aside and stared into space. So, he'd fucked up badly enough that Jax didn't want to see him today, but not so bad that Jax was denying him the chance to apologize. So that was good.

Maybe.

God. Why was he so bad at this?

He stood ruminating in his kitchen for he didn't know how long before Afra arrived.

She kicked off her shoes and marched up to him. "Well. You're alive, I see. You know you scared the shit out of Theo. He said you looked miserable."

Ari made a face. He *felt* miserable. And he didn't exactly want to tell his sister what happened, but she wouldn't let him escape the conversation. "Jax and I had a fight."

"What about?"

Figuring he'd better pull the bandage off quickly, Ari confessed, "About the fact that Baba and Maman do not know about him. And that I did not tell Jax this fact or that they attempted to set me up with someone a few weeks ago."

Afra raised her eyebrows and opened her mouth, but it was another moment before she found the words to come out of it. "Wow," she said. "I should slap you myself. I had no idea you were such an asshole."

Ari winced. He deserved that. "Yes, well. Neither did Jax, and now he does. Which is the problem."

"It's too early in the day to start drinking, but you're gonna owe me at the end of this. Not beer either, I need something harder." She kicked out a chair at the kitchen table and dropped into it. "But actually, you're wrong about the problem. Or you're wrong about the first problem."

Ari was getting used to the idea that he was wrong about a lot of things, so he poured two cups of coffee and sat down. "Since I'm incapable of using the sense I was born with, would you care to enlighten me?"

"The first problem is," Afra said, pulling her mug toward herself, "*you* didn't know you were an asshole."

Grimacing, Ari stirred a half teaspoon of sugar into his drink. "I can learn to live with my own mistakes." Well, that wasn't the whole truth. "Provided Jax can forgive them."

"At least *now* you've got your priorities straight." She blew out a long breath and picked up her mug. "So what's your plan?"

"Grovel?"

"That's a good start. Vague, though."

Yes, that was a problem. "I'm still working out the details." How did you make up for something like that? He could amend his behavior going forward, but he couldn't undo the mistakes he'd already made.

And any apology was going to have to include addressing the original issue, which meant telling his parents the truth and introducing them to Jax.

Ari needed a few hours and a lot more coffee to work up to confronting that fact.

"Uh-huh." Afra sounded skeptical. "Just don't put it off too long. I mean... you were happy. I have never seen you like that. Don't fuck it up any worse."

"Your encouragement is heartwarming," Ari said morosely.

"You're damn right. Now." She sat forward in her chair and pulled her tablet out of her purse. "We've got four months until the tour begins. It's time to start looking at scheduling. I talked to Noella, and she's got a list of venues and festivals she wants you to hit."

Grateful for the distraction, Ari sank into several hours of planning and worked up a list of potential venues so Afra could start putting the tour together. By the time she left, he felt almost okay about what he had to do next.

Key word being *almost*.

He made a sandwich for lunch and ate it standing next to the piano, looking out the window at the view but not really seeing it.

He needed to call his parents—possibly even go over there and explain in person so they could see how serious he was. And then he needed to open his mouth and say, *Maman, Baba, I know you have dreams of me settling down with a nice Persian doctor, but I'm dating a white bartender and I need you to pretend to be okay with that.*

There should be a song for that. And maybe he was still in procrastination mode, because he brought his sandwich plate back to the kitchen and then sat down at the piano, pulled his notepad toward himself, and started to scribble.

You say you won't be
my dirty little secret.

Oh, but everybody knows.
You say I'm singing solo,
But this is half of a duet
I've been trying to transpose.
How can I tell someone what you mean
When I haven't got the words?
How can I sing a song unseen
If I might also go unheard?
If you have an accusation, honey,
I've got the perfect excuse.
And if you have a broken heart, baby,
I've got a matching set of blues.

It wasn't the song he'd intended to write, but he could see where it was going, and maybe that was enough of a sign. He put down his pen and sighed as he reached for his car keys. Time to see if his parents were home.

Chapter Seventeen

It was Jax's idea to meet at a coffee shop, even though he didn't drink the stuff. Neutral territory, somewhere they could each storm out if the mood struck. And because Jax was a practical man, he'd chosen Starbucks. He wasn't sacrificing his good memories of his favorite pastry place on the altar of their relationship if the shit hit the fan.

He arrived fifteen minutes early and ordered a mint tea, hoping to calm his nervous stomach. Then he sat at a table in a corner and made himself as small and unapproachable as possible.

He expected a disaster.

Ari came in five minutes before the appointed time and ordered a London Fog. The drink suited him—looked nice, smelled better, unexpected depth of flavor. Jax raised his head and made eye contact to acknowledge he'd seen Ari, and ignored the butterflies attempting to stage a coup in his belly. They could keep their fluttering to themselves.

Finally the drink was ready and Ari sat down, glancing around as though to gauge their privacy. Shit, Jax hadn't thought of that. He'd never dated anyone kind of famous before. He hoped it wouldn't become an issue.

"Thank you for agreeing to meet with me," Ari began formally as he ran his long fingers along the edge of his cup lid. For a moment he watched his own hands, and Jax wondered if he was going to keep talking to them, but then he lifted his gaze and met Jax's eyes. "I treated you abominably. You deserve better."

Unless Ari was a better actor than Jax gave him credit for, he meant that. He looked like he hadn't slept in two days, and his eyes were shadowed with guilt as well as exhaustion.

Maybe they could salvage this. "Yeah, well." Jax wrapped both hands around his cup and tried to draw strength from the remaining warmth. "Either you're going to earn a second chance or I'm going to get closure, I guess." He didn't like that it came to an ultimatum, but some things could not be compromised.

Ari swallowed. "I understand. It was inexcusable of me to keep our relationship from my parents without at least explaining my reasons to you. I shouldn't have made you feel as though I'm ashamed of anything about you. Nothing could be further from the truth."

Jax let out a slow breath. Ari still had a ways to go, but he was on the right track. Jax could acknowledge that and attempt to explain the strength of his own reaction. "Thank you." He cleared his throat. "It hit a nerve, you know? Not just because of things with my own mom, but." He rubbed at a little run of spilled tea dripping down the side of his cup. "One of the things with ADHD, it can make you feel like you're not good enough, being left behind. So anything that seems to confirm those feelings is a big deal. I'm telling you now because it'll come up again." It was easier to manage now that he had medication and a diagnosis, but twenty-seven years of baggage didn't unpack itself overnight.

Especially since the PhD was on indefinite hold.

Ari looked stricken. "Jax… I regret that I hurt you."

Jax nodded and lifted his cup. Lukewarm tea proved a poor distraction.

"Also, I should have told you the truth about Sohrab when it happened." Ari put his cup down, flexed his hands into fists, then released them and twitched his fingers as though he were warming up for the piano.

"Why didn't you?"

He sighed. "I was embarrassed and ashamed I hadn't told my parents about us, and that it led to such an absurd situation." He made an abortive motion toward Jax's hand, and after a moment's hesitation Jax reached out and allowed him to take it. "I don't ever want you to doubt my loyalty or my feelings for you."

Two for two, Jax thought. "Apology accepted."

That left the restitution, though. Ari could apologize all he liked, but— "So what are we going to do about it?" He should've said *you*, but he'd used up his assertiveness.

Ari took a deep breath. "I have told my parents about you and they wish to meet you."

"Oh." Jax hadn't expected Ari to fix that so quickly. "Okay."

Ari squeezed Jax's hand. "I want to warn you... I wasn't exaggerating when I said that my parents have chased away men."

"It's okay. I've got excellent meet-the-parents game." That was probably an exaggeration—Jax hadn't met a lot of parents in this context—but he was great at charming people.

"I am aware of how charming you are. But Jax, I need you to understand something. There is a reason my parents picked Sohrab. Remember when I told you about them wanting me closer to home? Well, mostly they want me to marry a rich Persian doctor and be his househusband. They have probably already gathered information about surrogates and adoption."

"That's, uh, a very specific wish list." Surely his parents couldn't be that restrictive? Then again, Jax's mother's dream for him involved a PhD in math at a Canadian university.

"Indeed. And yes, they love me, but they also love the image they've created of my future. And you are definitely not a Persian doctor."

"Ah. Right." So Jax was starting on the back foot. That was fine; in a manner of speaking, he'd been on the back foot most of his life without knowing it. He could work with that. "I guess that means I have to try extra hard to be lovable."

Ari frowned and looked not entirely convinced. Jax squeezed his hand.

"Also, sorry, but do your parents think you're a girl in the early twentieth century? Why marry you off to a doctor?"

"My parents are doctors and neither of their children are. It's their last chance to get a doctor in the family. Or so they think."

That made a weird sort of sense, Jax supposed. "Wait, isn't Ben—?"

"He's a psychologist. Not quite the same as an MD."

"Ah." Again, weird sense. "So when is this meet happening?"

"Well, my parents are available to meet you this weekend. We could do Sunday dinner?"

"Okay. Yeah. Let's do that." Jax sipped his cooling tea and wondered if it was too soon to brace himself for the meeting. He looked up and caught Ari looking back at him. His eyes were fond, and a little smile curled his lips. Jax wanted to kiss him. "How do you feel about PDA?"

"At this very moment? I think I feel almost favorably about the idea. But creeper pictures of me have found their way to the internet, and I'm not overly fond of the idea of any moment with you being treated that way."

"That is… totally fair. Also, how did you make 'Don't kiss me' sound sweet?"

"If you like, we could go back to my place for that kiss?"

Jax wasn't sure how far he wanted to take things. He was exhausted from the uncertainty of the past few days, but he really wanted to kiss Ari. "Okay. Let's do that."

AT ARI'S they barely made it through the door before Jax cupped Ari's face and gently kissed him. Ari hummed and wrapped his arms around Jax and held him almost tenderly.

They didn't stumble to the bed or start taking off clothes. Instead they curled up together on the couch, close and touching, kissing almost chastely. It kind of felt like high school, and Jax couldn't say he disliked it.

"I think I'm too tired to move."

"You will have to move eventually when you go to your shift."

Jax groaned. "Don't remind me. Can't I just hide on your couch forever?" He tried to burrow into the cushions and ended up pressing his face to Ari's chest. His chuckle made Jax's head vibrate.

"I would gladly give you safe harbor from all the evils in the world," Ari murmured. His soft, deep rumble sent shivers down Jax's spine. "But I am not sure Murph counts. In fact, excepting his atrocious habit of using thick Newfie slang solely for the purpose of getting out of conversations, I can't think of anything very dastardly about him."

Jax hummed. Thinking about Murph made him want to blush and squirm with embarrassment as he remembered the trouble his stupidity had caused, but he shoved those thoughts away and focused on Ari's warm body. "He does make me carry kegs. From the basement. With the spiders. And the things with more legs than spiders."

"The horror." Ari's voice was dry as kindling. "Very well. I shall keep you safe here in my ivory tower." He curled an arm around Jax's shoulders and held him close. "I will defend you from marauding arachnids and unreasonable barkeeps for as long as you like."

Jax snickered. "My hero. Can you also protect me from drunk patrons who just want me to sing 'Piano Man'?"

"Oh, definitely. I have been known to stop Billy-Joel-requesting drunkards in their tracks."

"Good." Jax snuggled closer, and then his stomach reminded him he'd been off his food for two days. "Hey, Ari, does your ivory tower have any food in it? Because I could really go for some lunch."

Ari pressed his face into Jax's hair. "There is some. But I think today is a 'Screw it, let's support a local business' day. How do you feel about gyros? There is a place down the road that makes some excellent sandwiches."

"Hm, depends. What kind of sides come with it?"

Ari whipped out his phone. "Let's see."

An hour later they had decimated their lunch and were watching TV, though Jax wasn't so much watching as staring in its general direction. Ari had put on *The Golden Girls*, and Jax had lost track of the plot about five minutes in. He wiggled and settled his head on Ari's shoulder. He would close his eyes for just a minute, and then maybe he'd be able to keep them open.

But when he opened his eyes again, the credits were running, Ari's fingers were threaded in his hair, and he was chasing away the memory of—

"I'm guessing there's no *Golden Girls* episode about string theory?" Jax said groggily, blinking away the last traces of the dream, in which Betty White had moonlighted as a theoretical physicist.

Ari paused with his fingers tracing the shell of Jax's ear. "Not that I'm aware of." His voice radiated amusement. "Although it sounds intriguing."

"Oh yeah?" Jax tilted his head back to look into Ari's eyes. "Are you secretly into unifying theories of physics?"

"Are you telling me that string theory has nothing to do with pianos and violins?"

Jax laughed, snuggled his head back, and stretched out his legs. Ari got the memo and resumed carding his fingers through Jax's hair. "No. Well, not more than it has to do with snails or real estate. String theory is... complicated, but it intends to describe a unifying theory of physics. Someone thought, 'Okay, well, what if the particles we think we know of are actually tiny vibrating strings. Two kinds—one that's open on both ends, and one where the ends are connected so it forms a loop.'"

"I'm with you so far."

"You're doing better than most, then." Jax flexed his toes. "Anyway, you'll like this part—strings vibrating at different frequencies constitute different particles. So, like, say a G4 gives you a graviton."

Ari ceased running his fingers through Jax's hair and rested his hand on his chest. "Why do I feel as though you're oversimplifying this?"

With a snort, Jax admitted, "I'm an applied mathematician, not a theoretical one. True understanding of it is beyond me. The thing that got people excited about string theory is it could describe both gravity and quantum mechanics, which had never happened before. People were hoping for a unifying theory—that means something that can describe all the forces that act on particles with a single framework of these strings interacting."

"C, E, G," Ari murmured.

"Yeah. And scientists think that the way these strings interact with each other, these open strings are just out there, and sometimes they join with other open strings." He threaded his fingers through Ari's. "And then they might join at the other end too and become a closed string."

"That sounds… very theoretical."

It sounded downright *romantic* to Jax, but Ari wasn't wrong. "Understatement," he agreed. "But it's an interesting field, and it's led to some breakthroughs that linked previously discrete branches of mathematics, for example. They had to discover, like, seven more dimensions to get there, though."

Ari rubbed his thumb over Jax's breastbone. "I admit that I have trouble imagining that."

"Yeah, me too. I sort of envision them as pitch, color, temperature…." He shrugged.

"I think perhaps I'll stick to *Golden Girls*."

"Maybe *Golden Girls* episodes is one of the dimensions."

Maybe Jax had spent a little too much time reading up on mathematical journals before bed in preparation for a PhD defense that had been delayed yet again.

"Hmm."

"What?" Jax asked.

Ari nudged him. "Sit up."

Bemused, Jax slid his feet off the couch and turned toward Ari. "What—"

Ari recaptured Jax's left hand and held out the other one, beckoning.

Jax let him have that one too.

Ari ran his thumb over the back of Jax's hand and smiled softly. "Closed loop," he pronounced.

Jax went warm all over, but while part of him wanted to melt back into Ari and the couch, instead he stood up and pulled Ari with him.

"Where are we going?" Ari's voice held a note of laughter.

"Where are we going?" Jax echoed. "It's three in the afternoon and you just made a romantic math overture. We're going to *bed*, Ari."

Ari flushed. "I thought maybe you wouldn't want... I made several mistakes."

"And you apologized, and I forgave you," Jax said. "Are you saying you're not in the mood?" *Yeah right.* Jax had had his head in Ari's lap for the better part of an hour. He knew a mood when it was right next to his face.

"Just acknowledging my good fortune," Ari said, pulling Jax close by their still-linked hands.

Jax tilted his face up into a very promising kiss and danced Ari backward.

After, when Ari had his head pillowed on Jax's shoulder and was idly walking his fingers up and down Jax's bare chest, Jax laced their hands together again. "C, E, G."

If Ari could speak Jax's language, Jax could learn his too.

ARI HAD originally intended to pick Jax up at home prior to their dinner with his parents, because his parents' neighborhood was a hopeless suburban tangle of streets that Google was still only guessing at and because the weather had turned cold and was threatening to snow. Also, his mother would shit a brick if Ari's boyfriend showed up on a motorcycle. He wasn't going to sabotage himself.

Unfortunately Jax messaged him about needing to run something to the post office, so Ari waited for Jax at his apartment. They could leave from there instead.

"Hey," Jax said when he came in, his helmet tucked under one arm. He set it on the counter along with his keys. "I'm not late, am I?"

"No." Ari leaned over and kissed him, first a quick peck and then a firmer, deeper one that felt a little desperate. Jax had said he would be fine, and truly, if anyone could survive Ari's parents, it was Jax. But.... "Are you sure you want to do this?"

Jax cocked his head. "You don't want to back out, do you?"

Yes. But it was irrational. He'd prepared Jax as well as he could. "If I did, they'd think I invented you, and I'd have to endure another blind date." He grabbed his car keys from the hook by the door. "I'd rather not have to cut them out of my life completely, so...." *This is for the best.*

Jax followed him out of the apartment. "Should we come up with a safeword?" He hoisted a container Ari hadn't noticed. "I made cookies. Just say 'chocolate chunk,' and I'll fake a family emergency and you can be my hero."

Despite himself, Ari laughed. "Hopefully we won't need such drastic measures."

At his parents' place, Ari sat in the driveway for a long moment without turning off the car.

"Ari?"

"It would be irrational to turn the car around and simply run away forever." He cut the engine.

"Probably," Jax agreed.

They went into the house.

"Baba, Maman?" Ari called out, and his mother arrived from the kitchen, drying her hands and wearing her polite "we have company" expression.

"Ari, hello. Introduce us, dear," she prompted.

He swallowed. *Right.* "Jax Hall, meet my mother, Nasreen Darvish. Maman, this is Jax."

"Pleasure to meet you, Nasreen." Jax smiled his charming smile and held up his Tupperware. "I brought cookies."

"Oh, how lovely." She took the bin and peered inside. "Did you make these yourself?"

"Yeah. I love to bake."

The look she gave Jax when she lifted her head was almost promising, but Ari refused to be lulled into a false sense of security. "These look delicious. I've always said anyone who can bake is worth keeping around. Now come into the kitchen. Baba is fussing over the stew."

"It smells amazing," Jax said.

Ari's maman smiled at him. "It's one of Nader's specialties."

In the kitchen, his father stood at the stove. When they entered, he stepped away to greet Jax with a handshake. "I hope you brought your appetite with you." He waved to the bar. "Feta with spicy fig sauce. Try some on a cracker."

Ari cut off some cheese for a cracker and passed it over to Jax, who took a bite. "God, this is fantastic."

"Good! It's even better with chai."

They stayed in the kitchen as Ari's father kept babying one of the dishes, and the rest of them stayed gathered around the food. "I should get this recipe. My niece would love it."

"Your niece?" Ari's mother asked, looking politely interested.

"Yeah. My sister's kid. She's cute as a button, and she loves figs. They're her favorite treat. Her parents have to ration them out."

"How charming."

Ari couldn't believe it. Was this actually going to work? Maybe he should've told Jax to bring the baby along.

Jax grinned. "I started stocking Fig Newtons in the cupboard as a bribe, though they seem to be disappearing when I'm not looking." He shot Ari a look filled with humor. "Don't tell Hobbes I spilled about his secret passion."

Ari could not imagine the grumpy man eating Fig Newtons. Then again... maybe he could picture him sneaking them.

"Hobbes?" His mother looked baffled.

"Oh, my roommate. He's a pediatrician. Maybe that's where he got a love of Fig Newtons from."

"Ah, I see." Her lashes fluttered, and Ari's stomach tightened. Was she going to get after him for having a roommate? Lots of people had roommates.

Of course, lots of people weren't dating Ari—

But then she smiled. "It's clear you love your niece very much. Do you just have the one?"

"Oh yeah, just the one nibling." Jax sipped his chai, not quite a slurp but enough that Ari twitched internally. Fortunately his mother let this pass. "I only have the one sibling, an older sister."

"Just like Ari," his father said cheerfully from the stove. "Are you and your sister as close as our two?"

"Well, I'm not sure we'd survive tour cohabitation, but we're pretty close. I really missed her the past year. She was in Muskoka and I was stuck here."

"I am sorry to hear that," Ari's mother said compassionately. "We were so blessed that Ari and Afra managed to get home and were near us. I can't imagine being so far from family during such a time."

Jax gave a somewhat wobbly smile, and Ari reached out to gently touch his waist. Jax swayed into the touch.

"Happily, Jax's sister has recently moved to town, so Jax gets to see her and his niece regularly." Ari portioned another bit of cheese onto a cracker and slid it toward Jax.

"Oh, how lovely! Did she or her husband find work here?"

Jax hummed around his bite and nodded. "Yes, she did, actually. His company switched to remote working, so when she was looking for somewhere new, she picked London to be closer." His smile turned almost bashful.

His mother's expression was open as she asked after Sam's job and whether she liked London. Ari was starting to feel almost good about the meeting, which was probably why he thought nothing of saying, "Sam seemed very happy about her new employment."

"Oh?" His father had drifted over to grab some of the appetizer. "Have you met her already, then?"

"Just last week," Ari said carefully, but his doctor parents could do that math all too well, and they were not pleased.

"How nice that you have met Jax's family," his mother said with a quiet edge of steel to her voice.

Ari swallowed against the guilt.

"Well, he hasn't met my mother yet," Jax said brightly.

Ari shot him a look, trying to say *thank you* with his eyes.

"Is your mother not in London, then?"

"No, she's in Kingston. She teaches at Queen's." Jax wiped his hands on a napkin and shifted his weight.

"Oh." Maman's eyes softened. "And what does she teach?" Both of Ari's parents had clearly warmed to this topic—a mother with a PhD could only mean good things.

"Applied mathematics." Jax smiled as he gave the layman's explanation of his mother's work.

"She sounds quite accomplished!" His mother smiled. "She must be a very busy woman. What about your father?"

Jax shifted his stance again. Ari wondered if he was biting back a retort about heteronormative assumptions. "No dad. Just Mom, Sam, and me. And George and Alice, now."

"Oh, I'm so sorry to hear that." Ari's mother clearly thought she'd brought up feelings of grief for a dead parent.

Jax waved away her concern. "Don't be! I mean, he never existed." He shrugged. "There's a man out there who I owe for 50 percent of my genes—Sam too—but he was never our dad, never Mom's anything."

"Oh." Ari's parents looked stunned. They had clearly understood the subtext and did not appear to know what to make of it. "Well, what, uh, what an unusual choice."

Jax's eyebrows twitched. He'd always seemed proud of his family and his mother's choices. Ari doubted he was impressed by the word *unusual*. "I think it was a practical one, Maman," he cut in smoothly.

"Totally," Jax said with a small smile. "Mom wanted kids, but no husband."

"Well." Ari's parents exchanged another look, and Ari knew exactly what they were thinking. They had always believed children needed two parents because parents were the model for the relationship the child would grow up to emulate. Old-fashioned, but they would only point to statistics that showed a close relationship with one's father as a child was a predictor of successful intimate relationships later in life.

He had a feeling Jax could school them on the shortcomings of that math.

Should he have warned Jax about this? On the one hand, he didn't plan on breaking up with Jax, so his parents were eventually going to find out he'd been raised by a single parent. On the other hand, maybe it would have been better to avoid the subject until Jax's charm worked its magic.

Maybe Jax sensed the doubt this had introduced, because he added, "Mom's parents were always in the picture too, and if you count the faculty Mom roped in as aunts and uncles, we probably had the world's most overqualified babysitters."

Ari had to hand it to him—he really was good at reading people.

"I can imagine," Ari's mother said warmly, glancing over at Ari. "We were lucky to have a similar support system when Ari was a child. Though Afra did the majority of the babysitting once she was old enough, of course."

"Of course," Jax agreed, smiling out of the corners of his eyes as he too looked at Ari. He seemed to be saying, *See? Told you I'm good at this.* "I bet Ari never gave her any trouble either."

If that wasn't a leading question, Ari had never heard one. But parents loved to talk about their children, and his were no exception. Ari's father got up to put dinner on the table, and as they ate, he cheerfully recounted the greatest hits of Ari's childhood.

Ari would put up with any number of embarrassing stories if it meant his parents and Jax developed a rapport. He was starting to feel silly for having doubted him.

"It is so strange that Ari kept you from us," Maman said to Jax, though there was an edge to her voice and she was looking at Ari. "He's never hidden things from us before."

And things were going so well. Ari wasn't sure which of them that was intended to be a dig at, but either way, it wasn't a great sign.

Jax, however, missed the cue on this one, because he said blithely, "Oh, I don't know about that. Every kid keeps things from their parents, right? Ari plays things pretty close to the vest."

"Are you implying I don't know my son as well as you do?"

Jax blinked, obviously taken aback. "I'm just saying most of the time we don't know as much about other people as we think we do."

When the tension didn't entirely dissolve, Jax cleared his throat. "I'm sorry, could you direct me to your restroom?"

Nader gave the directions, and Ari tried not to panic at being left alone with his parents. He couldn't blame Jax for needing a break, but....

"Well," said his mother, "Jax is certainly a character."

"Maman—"

"He *is* handsome," his father interrupted, talking over both Ari and whatever his mother had been about to say.

Unfortunately this did not prove to Ari's advantage. "Yes, of course he's *handsome*," Ari's mother said dismissively. "But Ari, sex appeal is not enough to build a relationship on. What do you and this man have in common, really?"

Ari had considered attempting to eat through Jax's absence in an effort not to have to speak, but now he was glad he'd decided against it. "Maman, you're being ridiculous."

"I'm being a parent," she corrected. "It's my job to ensure your future happiness. And I don't see how you'll be happy with a bartender, sweetheart. He is basically a frat boy."

"Maman," Ari bit out. He'd known she would be judgmental. Thank God he'd prepared Jax. "That's enough. He'll hear you." If she was going to insult him, she could at least have the courtesy to do it in Farsi to spare Jax's feelings.

Of course, maybe she was hoping he *would* overhear.

"And anyway, it's not—" *It's not your business to ensure my happiness. It's mine.* But Ari didn't finish, because Jax reappeared in the dining room doorway.

"Sorry about that," he said with false cheerfulness. He had the same look in his eyes that he got when he was determined to play through a song he hated. "That tea went right through me."

Ari bit the inside of his cheek. An oblique reference to bathroom activities was a tiny infraction compared to the ones committed by his parents in Jax's absence.

"Oh, it's fine," Ari's mother said, suddenly all light again. Ari wanted to relax, but he knew better. "Anyway, Jax, why don't you tell

us about yourself? Ari mentioned you're a bartender. That must be…
interesting work."

Ari wished he'd insisted on bringing wine to serve with dinner.
At least alcohol could dull some of this pain.

"Yeah, I love it," Jax replied. "Who doesn't like a good party?
Work's never boring. Ari probably remembers what it was like—you
worked there for a while, didn't you?"

"For three summers, when I was home from college," Ari
confirmed stiffly. Surely his parents remembered this.

Surely Jax had some reason for asking him to verify the
information.

"That's right," Ari's father said. "And Sean was kind enough to
allow Ari to host a concert there so that local fans could attend."

Thank you, Baba. Perhaps together the two of them could keep
this meeting from derailing too spectacularly.

"That's the night we met, actually." Jax smiled and reached for
Ari's hand on the table. "I'm so glad I was able to bail him out when
his pianist couldn't make it. Call it Fate."

What is he doing? But Ari couldn't question Jax without making
everything that much worse.

"That's right, you play piano as well," Baba put in. "Did you
take lessons?"

Oh no. He was probably trying to help, but he'd just led them
obliviously into a whole new minefield.

"No, no." Jax reached for his water glass with his free hand. "I
mean, not unless you count the six months of lessons I had when I
was, what, eight? No formal musical education. But education's not
everything, right? Life experience counts for a lot."

Once, several years ago, Ari had been in the passenger seat
when his sister had no choice but to run into another car trying to
cut them off. The only other option had been to fail at a lane change
on the busiest highway in Ontario. She slammed on the brakes and
they braced for impact. The seconds right before the crash had been
some of the longest of his young life—knowing what was coming and
unable to do anything about it.

It felt like this moment right now. Watching Jax implode the meeting with his parents while Ari could do nothing to fix it and couldn't understand why it was happening to begin with.

"Nothing can make up for a solid education in a field one is passionate about," his mother said stiffly.

Jax waved the idea away. "Education is great if you want it, but I've found it totally unnecessary for music. I can play most of the music I need through a bit of practicing and a lot of winging it. Most people don't care if you fudge the chords."

Ari stared at Jax. What was happening? He knew Jax didn't actually think Ari's degrees and training were useless. He'd never so much as hinted at such a thought. In fact he had admired the techniques and understanding Ari had learned at the conservatory. But the subtle dig still had Ari's heart squeezing.

His mother narrowed her eyes. "I see. Well, I suppose if you feel education is a waste of time, then who am I to argue." His father looked stunned and uncertain of what to say.

"Oh, not entirely a waste of time. In our overeducated society, an education to some degree is often needed for a job. But happily there is none required to pour drinks for drunkards, so I'm just fine." He gave a dazzling and rather vapid smile, as if he had no idea what he was doing.

Ari wasn't the least bit fooled, but he was absolutely flummoxed. He licked his lips and was about to say something, anything to just stop this, but his mother was faster.

"Well, I guess you must consider us a bunch of overeducated fools."

"I would never say that," Jax reassured her with a mock earnest face.

His parents definitely did not miss the implication that Jax might still think it.

"It seems that there isn't much you wouldn't say."

Jax shrugged. "I've always been pretty good at opening my mouth."

Ari almost dropped his jaw. Did Jax just make blowjob innuendo?

"Yes. That is a skill you seem to have perfected," his mother said waspishly.

Ari was wrong—this wasn't like watching a car pull out in front of you. This was like watching two cars driving at each other head-on and knowing you were in the path of the fallout and you couldn't stop it.

"So I've been told." He flicked his eyes in Ari's direction. Ari wanted to die.

This dinner was pretty thoroughly ruined, and he was starting to wonder if this relationship—Jax's with his parents—could ever be salvaged. The prospect of being caught between them for years to come turned the ball of anxiety in his stomach into a rock. "Jax," he croaked helplessly, wanting to do something to make this stop.

Jax looked at him, and his eyes burned with anger and hurt. Ari nearly swallowed his tongue. He wanted to reach out and soothe that hurt, but the set of Jax's shoulders told him that was a no go.

"Well, if you have no other skills," his mother started, and God, Ari couldn't take any more of it.

"Maman! Jax isn't stupid." He wasn't, and he needed her to know that she wasn't outsmarting him in this game. He fully understood her not-so-hidden subtext. "He got into an MIT doctoral program," he added to underscore the point.

His parents' jaws dropped—but Jax went even more rigid.

"Jax is brilliant," Ari added, because he was, and it frustrated him that his parents couldn't or wouldn't see all the ways in which Jax was wonderful.

"MIT." Ari's father recovered first. "That is impressive."

His mother was eyeing Jax critically, as if trying to make this new knowledge fit. "MIT," she said. "In what program?" Her tone was less nasty, and Ari began to hope that this could be salvaged—that he could get his parents to see the Jax Ari saw.

Jax threw his napkin on the table. "You know what? That definitely doesn't matter. I think I'm done here." And he stood up and walked out.

For a long moment, Ari stared after him, shocked. The front door slammed shut, and each Darvish jumped.

His mother huffed. "Well, I never—that… *boy*—" she gasped, working herself up into a rant.

Ari threw down his own napkin and bolted for the door. He couldn't let Jax just *leave*.

Jax was striding down the sidewalk, tapping his phone, and Ari ran after him. "Jax!"

"Go back inside," Jax snapped without looking back.

Ari ignored him. He grabbed his shoulder and turned him around. "Jax, wait, please."

Jax's eyes were dark with anger. "I'm pretty sure that we have nothing good to say to each other right now, Ari, so why don't you just turn around and go back to your *parents*." He spat out the word like it was dirty, or maybe like he'd rather have replaced it with *assholes*.

That didn't feel true—Ari had a hundred things to say, like *what the fuck were you doing* and *please stay*—but he didn't think Jax would hear them. "I told you they would be like this," he said helplessly.

Jax laughed sharply and jerked out of Ari's grip. "Yeah, you did. But you didn't mention you'd be letting them walk all over you. And me. You were supposed to be my ally."

That was rich, considering the lengths Jax went to provoke a response. "*Allies*? You didn't exactly consult me before you started poking the bear!"

"You never stood up for me even *once*!" Jax shouted. "Not one time! If that was a preview of what I can expect in the future, count me out. I have no interest in fending off your asshole parents on my own—"

"Jax!" Ari protested, frantic. He needed Jax to stop talking, needed enough time to gather a reason Jax should stay. "Would you keep your voice down?"

"Oh, right, I forgot," Jax snarled. "It's okay to say whatever horrible thing you want, as long as nobody hears it."

Ari's heart sank.

Jax *had* heard.

"Like I said, I don't think we have anything to say to each other." Jax's mouth flattened into a thin line. "Do we?"

What could Ari say? He didn't want Jax to go. "I told you they would be like this," he repeated hoarsely. He hadn't invited Jax to meet them because he knew they would hurt him. "You said you could handle it. Instead you drove the train right off the cliff!"

Jax's eyes went hard, and he half turned away from Ari. He shoved his hands in the pockets of his coat as the wind picked up. "Yeah, fair enough," he said. "You told me your parents would be like this. Just like I told you the one sure way to hurt me is to point out all the ways in which I didn't live up to my potential."

Ari knew in the moment he shouldn't have brought up MIT, but he was so desperate to keep dinner from crashing so spectacularly—

"Go back inside, Ari," Jax said hollowly. He was already turning the rest of the way, giving Ari his back. "You'll catch a cold."

He didn't even have a car. No way to get home. Except that wasn't true, because as Ari stood rooted to the spot, a Lyft pulled up to the curb and the driver rolled down the window.

Jax got in, and the car drove away.

The sky, which had been threatening the kind of nasty weather London winters were famous for, darkened another half a degree. By the time Ari closed the door to his parents' house behind him, the front step was dusted in white.

Chapter Eighteen

JAX WAS three-quarters of the way back to his place before he realized his house keys were still on Ari's counter, next to his bike helmet. Just one more cherry on the shit sundae of his life.

Well, fine. Hobbes was probably home, so the door would be unlocked. He wouldn't be stuck outside. Jax had a spare key to his bike in his room somewhere, and an extra helmet. If the snow coming down was any indication, his days of riding the motorcycle were done for the season anyway.

It would be fine.

"Thanks," he told his driver as she pulled up. His voice was rough as he opened the door and got out. "Have a good one."

It was bound to be a better day than Jax's, anyway.

There was already a puddle of ice forming at the corner of the garage, where the driveway wasn't graded properly—as he hunched against the cold, his foot slid forward several inches and he pulled a muscle, but he caught himself on the brick before he could fall.

With a sinking feeling as he reached the doorstep, he realized the house was dark—no lights on upstairs except the one over the stove, which they left on in case the Captain woke them up with a diabetic episode in the middle of the night.

Could this day get any worse?

Of course, Jax should have fucking known how this would go. He should have canceled on dinner when he realized at the post office that he hadn't taken his pill. He knew he would be extra irritable, extra sensitive. He knew that was a bad combination to take with you to dinner at your boyfriend's parents' house when you were already expecting a goatscrew.

But there was no way he could have anticipated the level of clusterfuckery. And if he'd thought Ari was going to leave Jax to fend off the wolves on his own—

He would have broken things off weeks ago.

Without much hope, Jax tried the door. Locked. But maybe Hobbes had just gone to bed early. He rang the doorbell and shoved his hands under his armpits. Maybe Hobbes would answer, he thought, closing his eyes. Maybe Hobbes was home, and Hobbes would let him in and not ask any questions and make him hot chocolate with a medicinal slug of bourbon in it. Hobbes would sit him down in front of the TV and put on a comfort movie like *Star Wars* or *The Fifth Element*, and they'd make popcorn and absolutely not talk about it. And if Jax was extra pathetic, Hobbes would hug him, and it would be even better than before, because it couldn't be bittersweet if Jax wasn't in love with him anymore.

At least one good thing had come of this catastrophe.

But Hobbes didn't answer.

"Fuck," Jax said under his breath. Out of sheer frustration he rang the bell again, again, again, like an obnoxious kid playing nicky nicky nine door. Then he leaned his head against the door.

Goddammit.

A light went on inside, and after a moment, the bolt on the door was flicked and Jax had just enough time to scramble his weight off the door before it was flung open.

By a sleepy-looking half-dressed Naomi.

"Jax?"

"Naomi?" What was she doing here at… whatever the hell time it was? Without pants?

"What are you doing here?"

"I live here."

"I know that, but aren't you supposed to be out with Ari?"

Jax opened his mouth, but no words came out. Instead, his teeth chattered.

"Jesus." Naomi grabbed his sleeve and hauled him into the house.

"Sorry." Jax couldn't seem to stop shaking.

"Don't apologize," Naomi said, somewhat exasperatedly. "God, you're freezing. You need to warm up, get some dry clothes."

"Naomi?" Hobbes's groggy voice called down the stairs. "Where did you go?"

"To answer the door! You sleep like a log." She pushed Jax toward the steps. "Seriously—warming up."

Jax stumbled at the first riser, his feet clumsy.

"Jax? What the fuck?" Hobbes came crashing down the stairs. Seeing Jax shivering and spaced-out sent him into doctor mode, and he tried to check for pupil dilation, tracking, and temperature in quick succession. "What the hell happened?"

Jax didn't exactly want to talk about it. Especially since he suspected the answer was *I'm having a severe reaction to a bad breakup.*

Hobbes glanced at Naomi, who said, "Hell if I know. But he's freezing."

"Right." Hobbes wrapped one of his arms around Jax and practically carried him up the stairs. He brought Jax to his bathroom and stripped him—a former dream come true—and gently nudged him into a warm shower. Oh, the irony. Jax slowly turned under the spray, relishing the sting of the warmth on his chilled skin. He tried not to think, not to relive the evening. How could Ari just sit there when—

Jax ducked his head under the spray and wished he could wash away his thoughts. Why did he always fall in love with people who couldn't love him back?

Hobbes came back with soft sweats and told Jax to get out of the shower. Then he stuck around to make sure Jax did. Normally being treated like a child who couldn't be trusted to dress himself would piss Jax off, but today Hobbes's judgmental company was a comfort.

After Jax was dry and dressed, Hobbes guided him back downstairs, where Naomi was waiting with a pot of herbal tea and three mugs on the coffee table. They settled around it, Naomi and

Hobbes on the couch and Jax in an armchair. He wrapped himself around his mug and tried to think of anything but this evening.

Except the best distraction sat right in front of him, and the sight of Hobbes and Naomi side by side made his heart ache. Everything about their body language—the press of their shoulders and knees together, the slight angle toward each other—suggested familiarity. *Intimate* familiarity.

"So," Jax broke the silence. "How long has this been going on?"

"Jax," Hobbes huffed.

With a toss of her hair over her shoulder, Naomi said, "Since the barbecue." She cast a look at Hobbes. "He looks pretty good in a soaked T-shirt."

Jax smiled, albeit weakly, into his drink. "Don't I know it." Months. Hobbes had been dating someone for months and hadn't told him.

"Is this what it's going to be like now, you two ganging up on me?"

Naomi hummed. "Probably."

Hobbes grumbled. "So, kid, you gonna tell us what's going on?"

The thought of telling Hobbes about his Ari troubles when Hobbes was apparently happily coupled with Naomi, who was one of Ari's oldest friends, filled Jax with dread. He ducked his face back into his drink.

"You know what, I'm going to go back to bed. Seems to me this is a you-two thing." She bussed Hobbes's cheek and then left with her tea.

Jax and Hobbes sat in silence as she worked her way upstairs.

When the sound of Hobbes's bedroom door shutting floated down to them, Hobbes turned to Jax once again. "Start talking. Aren't you supposed to be meeting the parents this evening?"

Jax's face crumpled. "It was awful. They're such snobs! His mother all but called me a dumb slut. They kept looking down their noses at me for being a bartender." He curled tighter around his cooling mug.

"Okay. But they're not exactly the first parents to not approve of your work," Hobbes pointed out gently, as though making this about Jax's mom's disapproval would help at all.

"He just... sat there. He didn't even say anything." Jax pressed a hand to his eyes. He'd felt so alone sitting at that table, being attacked for his life choices while Ari did *nothing*—except betray him.

Jax heard Hobbes shifting, his mug set on the coffee table, a step, and then strong hands took Jax's drink and pulled him out of his chair. Jax sagged into the hug and tried not to cry into his shoulder. Hobbes gave the best hugs—warm, firm. Jax burrowed in and let Hobbes comfort him.

After several long moments, he pulled back and Hobbes tugged him down onto the couch. Hobbes picked up his mug and took a sip—then made a face. "Cold." He set it back down. Jax gave a weak smile.

"So, what's next?" Hobbes asked.

The smile fell away. "Nothing. I can't be with someone who can't—" He choked on the next words, but Hobbes understood.

"Well, shit. I'm sorry, kid. I really thought...." He shook his head.

Jax wrapped his arms around his chest and eyed his friend. His face was all compassion and understanding. Suddenly Jax didn't want to talk about Ari anymore. "Why didn't you tell me about Naomi?" Oh, great idea, Jax. Poke at *this* hurt instead.

Hobbes flushed and smoothed a hand over the back of his hair. "Ah, well... it's complicated."

Jax had arrived home from dinner at Ari's parents' to find them asleep in bed at just past eight in the evening. It didn't *sound* complicated. "Really," he said dryly.

The flush deepened. Maybe this wasn't the worst idea after all. Jax did love to tease, and Hobbes was an easy target.

"Because I know I call you 'old man,'" Jax continued, "but it's a little early for bedtime even for you, isn't it? Unless she wore you out, I mean, I wouldn't judge—"

"Jax."

Yeah, fuck, okay. Jax knew he was being an asshole.

"Thank you." Hobbes shifted and looked like he wished he still had something to occupy his hands. "Considering the circumstances, we figured we'd make sure this was going somewhere before we told… anyone."

By *anyone*, Jax read *you*. Still— "Circumstances?" he asked cautiously.

Hobbes was a pediatrician. Jax knew he had a lot of experience with difficult conversations. But it wasn't something he thought about most of the time, because Hobbes wasn't *Jax's* doctor, he was Jax's friend.

So he didn't appreciate how sensitive Hobbes could be, how delicately he could convey difficult news, until he looked in Jax's eyes with sympathy but not a trace of pity and said, "Kid… we didn't want to hurt you if it fizzled out after a week."

And Jax had thought his day couldn't get any worse.

Hobbes knew about Jax's feelings for him. Hobbes had probably known for ages, and he'd never said a word. He'd treated Jax with the same rough-edged kindness he had since Jax was a terrified student trying to make sense of medical software.

"Jeez." Jax wiped a hand over his face. "I honestly thought this conversation could not get any more awkward."

Hobbes snorted gently. "Don't underestimate yourself."

Jax actually did laugh at that. Okay. *Sometimes* his taste in romantic interests didn't completely suck, even if things didn't work out. And that led him back around to things with Ari's parents, because talking about that was actually the lesser of two evils. He wondered if Hobbes studied conversational strategy the way people studied chess. "I forgot my fucking pill today. Didn't think about it until I was already on my way to Ari's, and then it was too late."

"That probably didn't make things any easier."

"No, I—" He huffed out a frustrated breath. "If I don't take it, I don't feel like I did before I started taking them. It's so much worse, I feel… raw. I take everything too personally. My judgment's not what it could be."

Hobbes waited, but when Jax didn't volunteer any more information, he must have figured out where he was going with it. "Said a few things you wish you could take back, huh?"

Jax shook his head. "I don't know. Maybe." He definitely could've handled dinner better. Yeah, Ari had hurt him with his lack of defense, but there was no question Jax had overreacted. Jax was the one who'd stuck a screwdriver in the fissure between himself and Ari's parents and whacked it with a sledgehammer, then shoved in a stick of dynamite. "If it was going to implode anyway, better to know now, right?"

Then again, maybe if he hadn't escalated—maybe if they'd given each other a chance—they could have found enough common ground to avoid this.

And maybe Jax would go back into academia and win the Millennium Prize.

"Don't ask me, kid, I'm not any better at this than you are."

Jax knew that wasn't true, and even if it were, you didn't have to be better than Jax at relationships to have successful ones, if you had less baggage. He mustered a smile. "Well, do me a favor and don't fuck this up, okay? You literally cannot do better than Naomi. Sorry not sorry. You're punching out of your weight class." Jax knew something about that.

"I know," Hobbes said wryly. "No pressure, right?"

"You survived med school." Unlike Jax, who'd never finished his PhD. "You'll be fine." He gestured with his head toward the stairs. "Now go put your expensive education to good use."

Hobbes buried his face in his hands. "Jax—"

"Yeah, all right." Jax raised his arms in surrender. He wasn't fit company for anyone tonight. "I think I'm just—going to go to bed too. With noise-canceling headphones. But thanks, Hobbes."

Hobbes emerged from his finger cocoon. "Anytime."

ARI WENT home.

He didn't bother going back inside his parents' house for more than to put on his shoes. He could hear his parents mumbling in the

215

other room, but when his mother tried to talk to him, for the first time in his life, he ignored her.

Even seeing, briefly, the Tupperware container of Jax's homemade cookies filled him with rage.

Damn it. If he'd just—if he'd remembered to use the stupid safeword, or if Jax had…. What? They could have gone on forever walking on eggshells around his parents, who would never accept Jax? Ari could go on accepting that his parents didn't care about what he valued in a partner, or his partner's feelings, unless they'd preapproved of him?

No.

Driving home took all of his attention. London's roads were treacherous in the snow, and the first snowfall of the year brought out idiot drivers everywhere, people who hadn't yet put on their snow tires and people who had forgotten it took longer to stop in icy conditions. By the time he pulled into his parking spot, his nerves were shot. His sister and his parents had called four times apiece. He turned the phone off as he threw the car into Park. Then he picked his way across the parking lot.

His apartment was lit only by the glow of the orange sky through the picture window. He toed off wet shoes and hung up his coat, but when he went to set his keys on the counter, there was something in the way. He flicked on the light.

Jax's helmet.

Ari wanted to throw it across the room. He wanted to hold it to him and curl up around it. Too many emotions—rage, sorrow, helplessness—flowed through him.

He should have known that this relationship would end like all the rest: Ari's lover staring at him sad or angry or resigned and pointing out how bad Ari was with words and actions, never saying or doing the right thing at the right time. It seemed inevitable that Jax would come to the same conclusion.

Ari strode across the apartment, settled at the piano, and began to pound the keys. He wanted to drown out the noise in his head, to serenade his feelings into submission, to forget for one moment that the best thing that ever happened to him was now ruined.

So he bent over his piano and stayed there for almost two days straight. Sometimes he moved to the violin, but he spent most of the time furiously composing, trying to purge his emotions.

He wrote a sad song about not being good enough for your lover. Then, after remembering how Jax had promised he understood, that he could handle it, only to spectacularly sabotage the evening, the chords came out angry, confused, discordant. Why had Jax done it? Why had he deliberately made things worse? Why not just retreat?

Of course, then Ari remembered the hurt on Jax's face as he'd gotten into the car, and his next melody came out longing, wanting to fix something but knowing you couldn't. You couldn't fix a relationship when one of you didn't want it fixed. Because Jax was done with Ari.

Ari poured that heartbreak out onto the page.

Toward the end of the forty-eight hours, Ari stumbled away from his piano and collapsed fully clothed onto his bed.

He awoke to the sounds of banging on his front door and then the jangle of keys in the lock.

"I swear to God, Ari, you better not have choked to death on your own vomit."

Ari managed to get upright before she came stomping into his bedroom. She sagged when she saw him, relief stark on her features, before she straightened up and stomped closer. She wrapped him in a hard hug, her arms tight around his ribs.

"Don't you ever do that to me again! I have been going out of my mind—stuck in Toronto, you not answering your phone, and Maman and Baba calling to demand if I knew about your harlot. What the fuck happened?"

Ari pressed his face into her shoulder—even if it hurt a bit to bend that far—and took deep breaths. She still smelled reassuringly of mangos from the scented bodywash she started using in college.

"What's wrong? Not even you normally go dark for two days. Ben thought I might wear a hole through the hotel carpet," she chided.

"Sorry. I know you were looking forward to that trip." She'd had to go to Toronto on business with the label, but she'd convinced Ben to come along to turn it into a romantic long weekend afterward.

"Forget about the trip. You look like you haven't showered. And your piano looks like you exploded a filing cabinet on it."

It was covered in reams of sheet music. He had pretty much finished the album at this point. At least his broken heart had productivity going for it. "Good for songwriting," he mumbled.

She combed her fingers through his hair. "What is?"

With a sigh, Ari pulled back—he was getting a crick—and said bleakly, "They don't have to worry about me bringing my harlot around anymore. Jax made that pretty clear." He slunk into the kitchen. He'd feel better if he drank some water. Probably.

"What the fuck?" Afra demanded. "I thought you guys were okay."

"Me too. Guess he wasn't actually ready to meet the parents." He downed his glass, and Afra frowned at him. "No, that's totally not fair. He hadn't really done anything when Maman implied I was using him for sex."

"What?" Afra's deadpan sounded dangerous.

"That might not even be the worst of it." Ari put down the glass and buried his face in his hands. "It turned into a fucking war. Jax and Maman taking jabs at each other." He pulled his face out of his hands and looked at her. "There was blowjob innuendo in the veiled barbs."

Afra's eyes just about popped out of her head. "From *whom*?"

"Both of them," Ari groaned. "It was fucking awful, and I couldn't stop it from happening." Ari's laugh turned bitter. "Which I guess was too big a failing for Jax."

Afra's eyes, her whole body, softened with compassion. "Oh, Ari."

"Why can't I make them stay? Why can't I make them want to?" Maybe he was being overly dramatic, but Ari had been so *sure* this time. And he was heartbroken, and his big sister always knew how to fix things.

She wrapped him up in another hug.

When he pulled away again, she gave him her best no-nonsense face and told him to go shower and shave. "We'll both feel better for it."

He didn't have the energy to argue, and he had to admit that he did feel marginally better once he was clean. The clean clothes helped too.

He found Afra standing by his piano, looking at the sheet music. "Looks like lots of writing."

"Another six pieces, I think. I'll have to take a look at them, record something and send it to Noella, but they're pretty much done."

"Six songs in two days?" she asked, her eyebrows high.

"Told you it was good for productivity."

She looked down at the sheet music. "These are gonna make me cry, aren't they?"

He shrugged. "Probably."

"All right, well…." She held up her phone. "I'm gonna call Noella and give her an update, because she'll tear you a new one for having your phone off." Ari took that to mean Afra would be giving at least some details of why Ari had been in a hole without cell service. He winced. "When will you be ready to record? Not just demos, I mean. Noella's going to want you in the studio ASAP."

Most of the pieces were as polished as they could be without the help of professional musicians who played instruments other than piano and violin. "A week, probably?" That would give him time to practice, pack… clean up the mountain of takeout containers that had accumulated….

"Great. Meanwhile…." She surveyed him critically. "I'm going to open a window. It reeks in here. And then when I'm off the phone with Noella, we're going for a walk, because you haven't been outside since Sunday and that's horrifying. Deal?"

Ari glanced out the window. "But there's snow out there."

Afra gave him a flat look. "It's London in November. That doesn't mean we pretend outside doesn't exist. Go find your boots."

Chapter Nineteen

IN THE weeks following the breakup, Jax was grateful he worked late six nights a week. And as November ticked over into December, six became seven again, with the bar rented out for holiday parties.

On the plus side, this meant Jax had plenty to occupy him at work, a boosted income, and an excuse to sleep late. On the downside, if he had to sing one more Christmas carol, he was going to snap. At least Murph flat-out banned them from non-private events until the week of Christmas itself.

On this particular Friday night, Naomi picked a request out of the jar, raised an eyebrow, and handed it to Jax. "You up for this one?"

He'd seen a lot more of her over the past two weeks, which was kind of impressive, considering they worked together several nights a week and she spent the rest of the time studying for her last set of music-therapy finals. Well, the rest of the time she wasn't spending naked with Hobbes, which Jax was endeavoring not to think about.

He took the paper. "I Will Survive." Jax gave Naomi a look.

"What?" she protested. "I just want to make sure it's not too soon."

"As if," Jax said with more conviction than he felt. "It's never too soon for Gloria Gaynor."

Truthfully, Gloria should have been a pretty good distraction. The Rock in general should have been a good distraction. But half the time when Jax turned around, he expected to see Ari—in the audience, sitting at the bar with a shy smile, asking for a Sparkling Conversation, standing across the stage from him, lifting his bow as he prepared to accompany Jax on "Señorita."

Eventually Murph called last call and Jax went home.

The nice thing about Naomi and Hobbes dating was that she didn't mind giving him a ride, so Jax didn't have to choose between his bike—which he'd managed to convince a friend to pick up for him so he didn't have to go back for his helmet—or a Lyft. The less nice thing, obviously, being that he'd never get to share that easy closeness with Ari again, and now he had it in his face multiple nights a week.

Win some, lose some.

He must have zoned out on the drive home, because Naomi nudged his arm and he suddenly became aware they were sitting in the garage. "Come on," she said. "Time for all good musicians to go to bed."

But Jax knew he wouldn't be able to sleep. He went inside and closed the door to his bedroom, then stood under the spray of the shower, as hot as he could stand it, and let the water soothe his muscles.

Too bad it didn't do anything for the ache in his heart.

Finally, he dried off and fell into bed long after midnight. Somehow, miraculously, sleep found him, but wakefulness found him much too soon after that.

Jax startled to awareness at the sound of the doorbell, and he blearily lifted his face from the pillow. He'd gone to bed somewhat damp, and the pillowcase stuck to his cheek.

What *time* was it?

The doorbell rang again.

Apparently it didn't matter what time it was, or rather, either way it was time to get up. Jax wiped the last of the sleep from his eyes and tugged on a T-shirt from the pile on the floor. Then he trudged down to the door in his pajama bottoms. Where were Hobbes and Naomi, anyway? God, maybe they'd gone on a date to some horrible Christmas market? Or.... Jax frowned. He was pretty sure Naomi didn't have a final this morning or surely she wouldn't have worked last night.

He was still trying to figure it out when he opened the front door to find a tall woman in her sixties, graying blond hair wisping out from beneath a knit toque, overnight bag at her feet.

Jax gaped. "*Mom?*"

When he didn't move right away, she took the initiative and stepped forward to wrap him in a hug. Jax let it happen, too stunned to do otherwise, hugging back by reflex.

"Hi, sweetheart."

"What are you *doing* here?" he asked when she pulled away.

His mother looked pointedly at her overnight bag.

"I mean," Jax amended weakly, "come in?"

He got her things settled into the guest room, made sure her car wouldn't be blocking the wrong side of the garage when Hobbes and Naomi got home from… wherever they had gone… and then ran out of excuses not to talk to her.

Unfortunately, that did not actually furnish him with intelligent things to say. *So, Mom, no offense, but seriously, what the hell are you doing here* was kind of rude.

"Uh," he said instead. Then he glanced at the clock in the kitchen, and—wow, it was only noon. "Jeez, Christine, what time did you leave Kingston?"

"Early," she said dryly. "You don't happen to have any coffee?"

Under the circumstances, Jax didn't think Hobbes would mind.

"So," Jax said when she was happily curled around the largest mug she could find in the cupboards, "what brings you here?"

His mother gave him the same look she'd given him when he asked her if she was sure he had to go to school in grade five. Jax had claimed he didn't need to go, because he already knew all the math. She pointed to his poor spelling, but then talked to the school about giving him enriched math content. In retrospect, ten-year-old Jax should have known he'd lose a battle of logic against a mathematician.

"I'm here because my son is hurting."

Jax stared at her. "What?"

Her eyes were warm and compassionate. "I talked to Sam," she said pointedly. By which she probably meant, *Sam called and told me some version of the story of your breakup and how, last week during family dinner, you had a minor breakdown and tried to cover it by hiding your face in your niece's beautiful angel curls.* Embarrassing.

Jax cleared his throat. "So you've heard about Ari."

"I've heard about Ari. Sam was a bit stingy on the details, but she mentioned that it was pretty serious seeming until it suddenly ended." She sipped her coffee and waited for his response.

He swallowed. "Yeah. But it ended, so no point on dwelling." He turned away to… do something. Water. He should get some water.

He grabbed a glass and filled it from the sink.

"Jax, it's not dwelling to take time to fix a broken heart."

He tightened his grip on his glass and pressed his lips together to keep the petty response of *How would you know?* from spilling out. For one, being nasty to his mother, who'd clearly come down here just to see him, was low. For another, just because she hadn't had *romantic* heartbreak in her life didn't mean she hadn't had any. He closed his eyes and then opened them again. He turned back to her. "Thinking about other stuff does help, though. So I'm mostly doing that."

"What kind of stuff?"

"Like work. We're pretty busy these days, what with the lead-up to the holidays. I'm working every night."

"Tell me about it?"

She'd never asked about his job before, too upset with him for "wasting his potential." Maybe she was too worried about his recent heartbreak to needle him, or maybe he looked so pathetic she didn't want to take him on in a fight. Whatever the reason, Jax decided against looking at the teeth of this gift horse too closely. He guided her into the living room, and they sat together talking about Jax's life until Hobbes and Naomi came back.

A WEEK after the breakup, Ari went to Toronto to record. The experience was even more miserable than the last time. The city was just so… gray. Dull and gray and impersonal. While it snowed in London, Toronto got freezing rain that stung his skin. Ari hated it.

It took a week to record the album—a long, grueling week during which Ari had to listen to the story of his love affair with Jax over and over again.

Linsey and Brian eyed Ari over their respective instruments as they played out the newer unhappy melodies. On the second day, Linsey caved and asked, "So, your muse…?"

Ari glared at her until she held up her hands, mouthed the word *Okay*, and dropped the question.

Aiden, perhaps too young, too new, or too grateful for the exposure, didn't ask any questions about the lyrics for the new pieces. He was as professional as the last time, and his voice gave Ari's heartbreak a haunting, painful quality that raised the hair on the back of his neck and made more than one onlooker teary-eyed.

Ari texted Afra, *If reaction by sound mixer anything to go by, album will definitely make you cry.*

Good job emotionally manipulating your listeners, I guess? she shot back. Ari almost smiled.

By the time Ari returned from Toronto, December was well underway and his heart was still broken.

Back in London, Ari was at loose ends. He had taken to filling the hours of his days with Jax, and without him, he wasn't sure what to do with his time. Especially since he still hadn't spoken to his parents since the breakup and didn't particularly want to see them now either.

He reorganized his closet and deep-cleaned his kitchen. They were hardly satisfactory replacements for Jax either.

Afra sent Theo around with documents to sign, and with nothing better to do on a Wednesday afternoon, Ari let him stay and taught him more musical theory and fed him dinner before sending him on his way again.

On Friday Afra called and said, "They asked if you're coming to dinner tomorrow."

Ari shut his eyes. He wasn't sure he could face them yet. He wasn't sure what he'd say. "Afra…."

"Look, I get being mad at them and wanting to stay away, and you can stay away as long as you'd like. Don't go if you don't want to. But maybe you'd feel a bit better if you cleared the air? They sounded pretty upset about how things ended the other night."

He sighed. He didn't want to go, but maybe Afra was right. Maybe he could at least fix *that* relationship.

On Saturday he arrived at the house long after the set time—he refused to be left alone with them—and was grateful to see Afra's car in the driveway.

He put the car in Park and then sat contemplating the wheel. He'd been here just two weeks ago and had been nervous but optimistic. He glanced at the empty seat to his right, then turned off the car and walked inside—a condemned man on the way to the gallows.

"Ari!" his father said when he opened the door. "There you are." The words themselves should have been cheerful and welcoming. Ari's father's delivery, however, held mostly surprise and desperation.

It was difficult to take this as a positive sign.

"Hi, Baba." Ari hung up his coat and scarf, trying not to notice that his father was basically wringing his hands. His mother must be vibrating at a particularly irksome frequency today.

"You're late," Baba commented.

By what cultural standard? Since their second retirement, his parents were never on time for anything by Canadian ones. Ari let this remark pass without commenting. "Do you need help in the kitchen?" he asked instead, hopeful for anything that would keep him out of his mother's warpath.

"Dinner is ready," his father said almost apologetically.

Okay, maybe Ari was a *little* late, but only by his own standards, not his parents'. "Let me help you bring the food to the table?"

Needless to say, dinner was strained. Ari kept his answers short, his father directed the conversation to mundane topics like the weather and the London Knights, and Afra interrupted whenever their mother made a remark that might be even an oblique reference to the dinner with Jax.

Ari suspected she'd told Ben to stay home just in case. He could feel the argument brewing under the surface of the conversation, and it was only a matter of time before it erupted. Ari's parents would hate for Ben to witness it, and everyone else would hate to feel like Ben was analyzing them. As for Ben, Ari suspected that there were situations therapists stayed away from, and a family dinner at your in-laws', where every new topic was a potential grenade was at the top of the list.

Maybe he should have fallen in love with a therapist. Afra always was the smart one.

"You went with Aiden again?" Afra asked after Ari recounted, in halting words, dinner at one of Toronto's more entertaining venues.

He nodded. "For one more song, and then Maxi Greene for two as well. Noella said she'd be in touch with them about potential tour dates." Well, with their tour managers, anyway, if they had them. If not Afra might end up with a few more clients.

Too late, he realized that was the wrong thing to say. His mother's fork clattered onto her plate. "I wish you wouldn't leave again. Your father and I need you around."

For a moment Ari was so surprised he couldn't say anything. He locked eyes with Afra, who shook her head minutely in warning— *This is going to go badly.*

What else was new?

He put down his own fork so he didn't throw it. "Maman, you know I love you and Baba. But when was the last time you asked me to help you with something?"

His mother looked to her husband, who had apparently decided Ben had the right idea by opting out of the evening entirely and was staring at his plate to avoid eye contact.

"It snowed while you were in Toronto," she finally managed. "Your father and I can't be clearing the driveway at our age. I'm not strong enough, and your father's heart—"

"And yet the snow was cleared," Ari pointed out.

"Because Ben did it."

Ari glanced at Afra again, this time for permission. Raised eyebrows and pursed lips would've meant no. Instead he got a minuscule head tilt. Okay, then. "If Ben did it, then what do you need me for? Ben's work is here. Mine isn't, not always."

His mother slammed her hand on the table. "*Why* can't you take this seriously? Our whole lives, your father and I have sacrificed for you, and now when we ask you to do this one thing—"

"You haven't *asked*!" Ari exploded. "You demanded! And no one asked you to sacrifice for me, Maman. That was your choice."

"And how could I do otherwise for my family? How can I not want what's best for them?"

Ari gritted his teeth. "Of course I want what's best for you and Baba. I will always be in your lives."

"But not when you're on tour," she said bitterly.

He barely resisted the urge to throw up his hands. "What do you want me to do? Music is my profession. I have to play it to make a living."

"You don't. You could teach. Your friend Kayla teaches. If you settled down with Sohrab—he would be a good provider—"

What the *fuck*. He knew she wanted him to stay close at any cost. He just hadn't realized she was willing to suggest to his face that he give up his dreams and become a househusband. "I need more in my life than family! I'm sorry, but I do. You and Baba sacrificed, but you had your work, your passion. Is mine less worthwhile because I don't save lives? Because music does save lives, Maman—other people's, but also my own."

He needed music—the outlet, the expression. Music helped him process his emotions, and sharing his music let him connect with people in a way he had trouble with when it came to words.

Music had let him connect with Jax.

And now he was angry again.

"Ari…." She sighed, and for a moment he thought she might back off. "I don't mean to make you feel as though your work isn't important. But we're your family. Surely that must mean something to you too."

"My family," Ari repeated. "My *family*."

Ari's father put a hand on his forearm. "Ari—"

The fury inside him boiled over. "It's funny you should say that, Maman, because family is important. And I think you would actually like for me to have one of my own one day."

Afra reached for her water glass, presumably so she had something to do other than look at anyone.

Ari's mother was on the defensive now. "If this is about that young man you brought by—"

"His name is Jax, Maman."

"He was hardly suitable."

Ari gaped at her. "I love him, and he makes me happy. How much more suitable does he need to be?"

"Just because he's pretty—"

"So what if he is? He's more than a pretty face. And not because he's probably a genius, but because he makes me laugh and he understands me." Ari stared at his water glass and bit out, "He thinks my music is beautiful and understands what it means. Even when it's 'overly cerebral' and 'technically stunning.'"

"Ari, your music *is* beautiful," his father said softly.

"What does it matter if he thinks your music is beautiful— it is!—when he's clearly an irresponsible man-child, living with a roommate at his age."

Ari pushed away from the table to avoid hurting something or himself. Opposite him, his mother stood too. "Why are you like this? Always so judgmental! If you'd bothered to ask instead of just judging all the time, then you would know that he met his doctor roommate during the pandemic and moved in because his friend got sick, first to take care of his cat and then to take care of him. And if you'd bothered to ask, you might have learned that they met when Jax was doing work creating statistical models to predict rates of infection."

His parents stared at him.

"But you know what? None of that matters. Because so what if he has a roommate? Lots of people hate living alone or can't afford it. It doesn't make them failures. But even if he were the biggest failure ever, an idiot, and just a pretty face, what does it matter so long as he makes me happy?" He pressed a hand to his face. "Jax was right."

"Oh? And what's Jax's opinion on the matter?" his mother asked icily.

"That you're snobs who were rude to him because of his job." His mother huffed and stood straighter. Ari saw red. "You deliberately tried to—succeeded in—ruining the best thing that ever happened to me, and you can't even—you're not even sorry!"

"Well, if he's going to be chased away by one little dinner...," she blustered, though her shoulders looked less firm.

"You basically called him a whore," Ari snapped. His shoulders slumped. "And I'm the idiot who just let you."

"Ari," Afra said softly.

He turned to her and gave her a watery smile. "I'm not doing it again. I'm not sure I'll ever—" His voice broke. "—meet anyone... but I sure as hell won't be bringing him around here to meet you. I am done letting you chase them away. Because I have been letting you. But I'm not doing it again."

"So you will just keep your partner a secret from us?" His father looked distressed.

"Better that than to have you judge and pick until they leave." He was so fucking tired.

"So your plan is to find some unsuitable boy and marry him without us there just to spite us? You are so dramatic. We never had these problems with your sister."

Afra stiffened, her fingers clenched on her fork. If she were a cartoon, steam would have shot from her ears. She glanced his way, and Ari stepped back and ceded the floor. Their mother wasn't listening to him, but maybe she would listen to her perfect daughter.

"And how would you know?" Afra started softly, dangerously. "If I were keeping things secret, how would you ever know?"

"Parents know—"

"I had nothing but secrets as a teenager. A secret boyfriend who dumped me because he didn't want to be a secret, a secret heartbreak

I couldn't tell anyone about, a secret one-night stand because of the heartbreak"—their parents went white—"and then a secret baby."

A still, shattering silence descended, broken a split second later by Ari's parents inhaling sharply.

"What?" their father asked, as their mother slumped back into her seat.

"My first year of university, I got pregnant. The baby was born healthy and perfect that May, and I never even saw it because I was too goddamned afraid I would want to keep it. I wanted to keep it so badly, but I knew you'd never let me out of the house again if I did. So I made the best decision for me and for the baby." Her fists trembled on the tabletop, but she stared their parents down like a righteous avenging angel. "Ben and I have been trying to have a child for years. I did two rounds of IVF, but it didn't work. We are going to adopt a baby, and we will be fantastic parents. But not being able to have kids took us totally by surprise. It never occurred to us that we might not be able to, because I had been there, done that. But we can't, and now I will never see the only natural child I will ever have."

Their parents sat stiff and pale in utter shock. They didn't try to speak.

"So congratulations. Your limited ideas about acceptable life choices have lost you a frankly fantastic potential son-in-law and perhaps the only natural grandchild you'll ever have." She stood up and looked at Ari. "I think we're done here."

Ari couldn't disagree.

On the porch step, she turned to him and asked, "Drink?" He couldn't disagree with that either.

A WEEK and a half before Christmas, Jax's mother sent him to the grocery store to get a few "necessities." Even in his younger days, Jax had never called pinot grigio and a couple pounds of Lindt chocolate necessities, but to each their own. He hopped in her car—a fancy hybrid that was actually kind of fun to drive—and went to the good grocery store a little farther out.

He had already snagged the wine and the chocolate and was touring up and down the aisle looking for anything else they were missing in the kitchen—he hadn't yet broken the habit of buying in bulk to limit grocery trips—when Ari appeared around the corner.

Jax's heart lurched in his chest.

When they were together, they never ran into each other by accident—not with Jax's work schedule and Ari's tendency to shut himself away with his piano. They had to coordinate every meeting.

He was utterly unprepared to come face-to-face with Ari in the wild.

Not that the international aisle of the grocery store could really be considered the wild, but—

Jax didn't have time to strategize. Before he could even weigh his options—continue forward or attempt a strategic retreat—Ari looked over from his perusal of the imported honey and caught his gaze.

Fuck. Now what?

"Jax," Ari said quietly. "I... hello."

Now forced and awkward small talk, apparently. Had Jax been a puppy-kicker in a past life? "Hey," Jax replied. "You look... uh...." The usual thing was to say *you look good*, right? Except Ari didn't look good. His hair was still as glorious as ever, glossy black curls falling to his chin, sharp cheekbones, beautiful dark eyes. But he seemed gaunt. Had he lost weight? His shoulders were hunched.

Maybe it was just the winter coat.

"You don't have to lie to spare my feelings," Ari said, a little stiffly.

"That's not really my forte," Jax agreed, his mouth once again lurching ahead of his brain.

Once upon a time, Ari might have laughed. Now he only grimaced. Jax desperately wanted to flee, but his feet seemed rooted to the floor. "Nor mine, apparently," Ari said. "Jax... I know our relationship is irreparably damaged, but I—"

Jax's phone rang at full volume, interrupting both of them with an old Spice Girls B-side. Grateful for the excuse, Jax said,

"Sorry, I better…." and picked up. "Hey, I'm almost done at the store. What's up?"

"Did you get marshmallows?"

"Marshmallows," Jax repeated, half turning away from Ari. Well, there definitely weren't any of those in this aisle. "They weren't on the list. What do we need—"

"For hot chocolate, obviously." He could practically hear his mom rolling her eyes, though at least she didn't add *duh*. He bet this was what the fancy chocolate was for too.

You know I'm mostly done wallowing, right? he wanted to say, but then he glanced at Ari and… okay, maybe there were a few more weeks of wallowing in his future. "Obviously," he agreed and let his voice go teasing instead. "Hey, Christine, just wondering—you do remember which one of us is—"

"Finish that sentence and you can forget about me making you cocoa," she threatened.

"Shutting up!" Jax said cheerfully. "Anything else?"

She paused as though considering. "Is *Die Hard* on Netflix?"

"Hobbes has it on DVD."

"Perfect. See you soon, then." And she hung up.

She never was one for lengthy goodbyes. Jax slipped his phone back into his pocket and turned back to Ari, but as soon as he did, Ari turned away as though he'd just remembered a critical shortage of harissa back at his place. Plausible, Jax supposed, but then Ari didn't exactly cook much.

"I'm sorry," Ari said finally. "You must be busy…."

Jax was, actually—he only had a few hours to spend with his mom before he had to be at work—but also he was ready to be out of Ari's immediate presence. His palms were sweating and his chest felt tight. "Yeah, sorry, I can't really… chat." Not that they had much to say to each other.

"Of course. I understand." He cleared his throat. "Ah… but I should mention I still have your keys and helmet. I could drop them off? I was going to bring them to the Rock, but I didn't think you'd want to see me at work."

He wasn't wrong about that. Jax realized with a pang that Ari had never been to his house. Did Ari even know where he lived? "It's okay, I… I'll come pick them up." Call it closure, or whatever. "I'll text you to arrange a time?"

Ari inclined his head. "That would be fine. It was good to see you."

Jax didn't bother attempting a smile. He was pretty sure it would have made him throw up. "You too, Ari. See you around."

He was halfway home before he realized he'd forgotten the marshmallows.

Chapter Twenty

"... AND THIS is Murph," Jax said finally, gently nudging his mother down onto a barstool. "Murph, this is Christine, my mom."

"What are ya at," Murph said, nodding. "Get ya a drink? On the house."

"Avoid anything that sounds like moonshine," Jax advised. "Because it is. I have to go check in with the other musicians, but I'll be back. Please don't seduce my boss."

"Yer boss can look after hisself," Murph scolded. "Get gone, b'y."

Jax turned, but not soon enough to avoid hearing his mother say, "Jax said something about moonshine?"

Honestly, and people wondered where Jax got it.

Kayla, Naomi, and Rosa were clustered around Naomi's phone when Jax came into the break room, but they looked up and turned away from it as he sat at the practice keyboard. "All right, sorry I'm late. Are we working on anything new?"

Naomi had puzzled out a new Billie Eilish hit, which they ran through twice—maybe not smoothly enough to manage tonight, but later in the week they could add it to the repertoire. Jax ran them through Dua Lipa's "Don't Start Now," which earned him an empathetic side-eye from Naomi. He thought Kayla might be considering sharpening a drumstick into a shiv. Then Rosa brought up Bieber's latest pop earworm, which was brainless but fun and easy enough to play stripped down. They could add more complexity as they got familiar with it.

Jax was banging happily away, getting into the feel of it, bullshitting the lyrics because the real ones were absolute nonsense, when the door opened and his mom stuck her head in.

A few months ago, Jax would've faltered or stopped, but he was done being ashamed. So he'd never be Ari, and he'd never be his mom. He was having fun. His job wasn't to be a musical genius; it was to entertain. And Jax was *great* at entertaining.

When he finished, with an over-the-top musical flourish, his mother burst into applause. "That was delightful," she said with a glance at them all, but her gaze rested on Jax. "I had no idea you'd gotten so good at the piano." She gave a mock frown. "Where have you been hiding that talent all these years?"

Jax played along. "Probably under my undiagnosed, unmedicated ADHD."

She smiled. "Probably."

Naomi glanced at her phone and announced practice time was over. "See you out there in five minutes," she said with a warning glance at Jax. He pressed a hand to his chest and mouthed, *Moi?* She flicked her hair over her shoulder and swanned out.

Kayla and Rosa followed, and Jax was left alone with his mother.

"I'm sorry," she said into the quiet, "for not realizing how much joy this was bringing you. You look so happy performing. I should've listened when you told me that months ago."

Jax stared hard at his hands. "Thanks. That means a lot."

"I know that I tend to get fixated and stubborn—sorry for handing that on to you, by the way—but I still should have realized you needed something out of life that wasn't math. I should have seen that need. I didn't have two children by accident, you know. But I'm sorry I didn't recognize that this"—she waved a hand about the room—"was a similar thing."

Well, that deserved a hug. He wrapped her tightly in his arms and squeezed. He couldn't remember the last time they'd had a *proper* hug. Probably before he'd told her about MIT.

As they released each other, his mother cupped his face. "Now, I think it's time for you to go be fabulous."

Jax grinned and winked. "Christine, I am always fabulous."

He led her back out to the bar and watched her settle into a comfortable out-of-the-way table. Jax didn't blame her; the chairs closer to the stage were usually occupied by the bar's drunkest patrons. *Or the flirtiest*, his mind supplied, with memories of Ari watching him from a front-row seat. Jax pushed the image away. He couldn't think about Ari and the myriad emotions he churned up for Jax: longing, love, guilt, hurt, resentment, affection.

On stage, Jax pasted on his performer's smile and bowed when Naomi introduced him. "I'll be your favorite this evening," he said into the mic.

Naomi rolled her eyes and told the crowd not to encourage him.

They were halfway through a duet adaptation of "Take Me to Church" when Jax spotted her. Fortunately Naomi was singing at the time, because Jax almost swallowed his tongue.

Nasreen Darvish stood awkwardly at the bar with a glass of something that looked like straight ginger ale in her hand and her purse clutched close to her stomach.

Jax fumbled the chords and turned away. He couldn't focus on her right now.

What the fuck was she doing here? Why come in now after she had successfully broken up his relationship?

He ignored her until the end of the song, but as soon as the chords were done and the patter started up as they figured out the next piece, he couldn't help but search her out. She still stood awkwardly near the bar, watching. Jax forced himself to look away and tried to catch Naomi's eye—surely she knew Nasreen and maybe would have some clue as to what was happening right now—but mindreading was apparently not one of her talents.

Well, fuck. He was a professional. Sort of. He kept his eyes on the tablet in front of him as they worked their way through some Taylor Swift. When he next looked over at the bar, she was gone. Jax's shoulders started to fall, but they rose right back up when he spotted her again—sitting with his mother.

Would now be a good time to hyperventilate? Why was Ari's evil mother talking to his own?

He felt like he was shaking apart, but his hands never faltered on the keys and his voice was strong.

When they called for their fifteen-minute break, Jax stood on shaky legs and headed toward his mother's seat, but as he locked eyes on her, he noticed she was once again alone.

"Where is she?" Jax demanded when he got close enough. He slid into the vacant seat, and Christine arched an eyebrow. "The woman who was just here—where did she go?" He looked around the bar. The bathroom, maybe?

"She left," Christine said. "She said she couldn't stay any longer."

"Did she say why she was here?" Jax demanded. Had Nasreen found Christine on purpose? If so, how? She couldn't have known that Christine was his mom, surely.

Her eyebrows climbed even higher. "Not really. Just said her son told her about the place and she was curious. I got the feeling it wasn't really her scene. Jax, what's gotten into you?"

"What did you two talk about?"

Christine shrugged. "The music, the band. I mentioned you were my son. She said you were very talented."

"She said I was talented," Jax repeated in a weak voice.

"Well, you are. I don't know why this is so shocking."

He made a noise that sounded something like a dying buffalo mixed with a wheezing elephant.

"Jax? Honestly, what—?"

"She's Ari's mom," he gasped.

Christine went still. "*That* was Ari's mother?"

He nodded, winded. Jesus Christ, what had just happened? He might have thought she was there to check him out—exactly as Ari had warned him all those weeks ago—if he and Ari were still dating. But wasn't a visit to check out a prospective son-in-law a little on the late side now? The barn door wasn't so much open as burnt to cinders.

"You know," Christine said slowly, wearing her mathematician-at-work face, "she did seem very curious about you, even before I mentioned you were my son." She looked at the exit. "I invited her to sit with me because she looked like she could use a chair. But I wonder why she never mentioned that after I told her who I was."

"Probably feared a mama bear," Jax mumbled and stole the last of his mother's drink.

Oh well. He and Ari had already broken up. Whatever Nasreen was up to, it couldn't possibly do him any more damage. Right?

"Mr. Hall."

Wrong, Jax thought, almost choking on piña colada. He coughed, and his mother—because he was trapped in a horrible reenactment of his childhood—stood and patted his back until he could breathe. *Jesus.* He hadn't thought she'd *actually* try to kill him. "Ah. Mrs. Darvish. I didn't expect to see you here."

Jax's mother looked between them for a moment. He tried to make an appeal to her—*do not leave me, woman, can't you see she's dangerous?*—but either she didn't get it or she thought he needed to adult up. "I'm going to go powder my nose," she said. "I'll be back."

I'll be dead, Jax thought grimly as Nasreen slid into the seat his mother had vacated. "You know, I'm pretty okay with where we left things. You really want to go another round?"

For a moment she just looked at him, and Jax squirmed under her gaze. She had the same eyes as Ari, dark and warm. Too bad the personality didn't match.

"I didn't see what my son sees in you," she finally said. Which, great, yeah. Duh. Thank you, Commander Obvious. "But he is not normally a foolish man. I thought I should take a second look."

Right. "Forgive me," Jax said, meaning anything but, "but wouldn't it be easier to just take his word for it?" Not that it would make a difference.

"Since you don't have children, I know that you can't possibly understand how it feels to want to protect them, even from themselves."

"I have a niece, and I can't imagine telling her that her choices are wrong the way that you do."

Nasreen didn't flinch, but she didn't argue either. Instead she took in his words and after a moment said, "Sometimes, when we are worried and care deeply, we do not make the wisest choices."

Jax snorted. "That's one way of putting it." They sat in silence for a moment. "So did you enjoy the show? Since you came to get a second look."

"It was… educational. Interesting too. You are very charming on stage, and your friends are very talented also. I found myself enjoying the songs."

"All of them?" He arched an eyebrow. "You enjoy 'S&M.'"

"Yes. Though not as much as the last one, I'm not sure of the name. I never heard it before."

Jax's stomach wobbled. "Don't Speak?"

"Yes, that one. Your performance was very authentic."

If anyone else had made that observation, Jax might have tried to hide his broken heart, but from Nasreen Darvish…. "I think we both know why."

She inclined her head but didn't say anything, which pissed Jax off. "Since you're not here to apologize or even admit your guilt, why are you here?"

"Curiosity."

Jax barked a laugh. "God, I probably should have anticipated the arrogance. But somehow I didn't, even though Ari warned me. I guess I was a fool for giving you the chance to chase me away."

Her eyes flickered, the tiniest of flinches. "I probably deserve that. I love my children, but I can be stubborn."

"You know," Jax said, angry but willing to give her this, "it's too bad you hate me, because we have a lot in common." Nasreen tilted her head in silent question. "We're both dicks who love your son."

Then he stood and walked away.

"Earth to Ari. Come in, Ari."

Ari pulled himself out of his deep contemplation. He was supposed to be deliberating the relative acoustic merits of Buffalo's potential concert venues, but thoughts of Jax kept intruding. Jax had said he fell in love easily, and their relationship was over now. Ari wasn't allowed to be upset he was seeing someone else seriously enough to do a grocery run for them.

He definitely wasn't allowed to ask Jax about it when he arrived to pick up his things.

He took a deep breath and tried to engage his memory, but for the life of him, he had no idea what Afra had been asking him. "Sorry," he said. "Coffee?"

"*Yes*," Theo said fervently.

The three of them had been sitting at Ari's kitchen table, Ari and Afra mostly planning a tour, Theo learning through osmosis while studying for his final exam, which seemed to be mathematical in nature. Every so often he uttered a curse under his breath. Ari could relate.

"I was asking if you want to go to Tennessee," Afra repeated. "Because Noella forwarded your rough cut, and you've got an invitation to play Bonnaroo."

Theo swore again; apparently Ari wasn't the only one who hadn't been paying attention. "Are you kidding me? That's incredible."

It was certainly the biggest festival Ari had ever been asked to play. He tended to prefer low-key events, but he couldn't deny that the opportunity to perform for an audience of that size appealed—if only from a professional standpoint. And maybe if he played there, his parents would finally realize he was serious about his work. "Do you think I should?"

"*Yes*," said Theo emphatically, pulling his textbook closer and highlighting something, though Ari couldn't tell what the purpose was, because the entire page was yellow. Then he lifted his head again. "Also, coffee?"

Ari didn't bother pointing out that Theo was the intern here; he looked like he hadn't slept in three days. Besides, Ari was fussy about his coffee maker. He got up to start a pot.

Afra picked up the thread. "Do I think you should play one of the most popular music festivals in North America? In a word, yes." She rolled her eyes. "We'll have to reschedule a few of the other tentative tour dates, but it'll be fine."

All right. Afra could work out the details. "Fine." He paused and watched the carafe fill. "But… can we do a few smaller events on either side of it?"

"Smaller ones?"

He didn't need to look to know Afra was rolling her eyes. "You probably didn't notice last year because you weren't on board for the actual planning stage, but Ari can only take large crowds in small doses. So when we're planning a tour, we pick a handful of large venues and those are our tentpoles, and then we use more intimate concerts as stakes. Bonnaroo's a really big tentpole, so he wants some really small stakes."

Ari took down a few mugs and poured. Afra took hers black, and Theo liked his to look and taste like caramel. He turned around to comment, but Theo was head down in the textbook again, this time on a fresh page with barely any highlighting so far. Ari put the mug down in front of him, but he didn't even grunt in acknowledgment.

Afra took her mug directly from his hands, and they stood together at the counter, leaning back against it and stretching their legs. They'd been at this for long enough that Ari's back was sore. "Actually there's a bar in Nashville that would be a great venue, and they've got an available slot…. Fuck."

Ari looked up from his drink to see Afra frowning at her phone, coffee forgotten in her other hand.

"Problem?"

She winced. "The date they're available, uh… I was hoping to take a few days to be back here."

He shrugged. "We could get someone else in for a few days, have them handle things." They'd done it before, when Afra had appendicitis on Ari's first tour. He didn't like it—Afra knew his quirks better than anyone, and he didn't bristle when she tried to handle him the way he did with strangers—but it couldn't be helped.

"The intern could probably handle it," she mused. "I mean, by then he'll have one and a half whole tours under his belt...." Her leading tone and the use of his title didn't prompt Theo to raise his head as he tapped the end of his highlighter under a graph that looked like an upside-down *U*.

Then she sighed. "Except if we're going to do this at a bar, he's got to be twenty-one—hey, Theo, when's your birthday?"

"May third," he said absently. "Hey, do you have any food?"

"Depends. Are you feeling up to trying properly spiced food again?" The looks on Ari's parents' faces when he'd revealed he was twelve before he ate anything spicier than garlic had been priceless.

"I will eat literally anything. I'm not going to taste it anyway. This textbook is all that exists." As he turned the page, though, he knocked into his coffee mug, and suddenly the kitchen became a whirlwind of activity in an attempt to save said textbook.

They got everything cleaned up, and Ari washed his hands in the bathroom to remove the lingering stick of coffee and milk, since the textbook was drip-drying over the kitchen sink while Afra attempted to talk Theo out of a panic attack. At least Ari thought that was what she was doing, but he couldn't hear much over his rough-cut album. As per his habit, he was in the midst of playing it on repeat in the background, a process that helped him catch any defects.

When he stepped out of the bathroom, Jax was standing in the doorway, staring at Afra, poised awkwardly like he didn't know what to do with himself. Afra was eyeing him back warily.

Afra had agreed with Ari that he'd probably screwed up at the dinner, but Jax was the one who'd torpedoed it. Afra was still Ari's big sister, and part of her, she said, would never forgive Jax for making Ari unhappy.

"Sorry for interrupting. I'm just here to get some stuff?" He looked spooked. What had Afra said when Ari was in the other room?

Ari motioned to Afra that he could take it from here. She looked dubious but stepped to the side anyway.

"Sorry," Ari said. "We're a bit—tour planning. You know." He didn't, of course, but Ari wasn't going to air Afra's personal business to Jax. It was none of his now.

Just like the mysterious Christine was none of Ari's.

Silence fell over them as Jax shifted awkwardly from foot to foot.

"Oh, right, your helmet." Ari looked around and realized he'd left it… not here. Where had he put it? He'd meant to shift it next to the door. "Let me just…." He waved a hand over his shoulder and stepped away.

"Right, sure, no problem," Jax said distractedly.

Ari hurried to find the helmet tucked in the closet he'd shoved it into, unable to bear the sight of it on his counter any longer, a painful reminder that Jax hated him now too much to even ask for it back.

When he returned, Jax's face was flushed and he wouldn't meet Ari's eyes.

"Here." He held out the helmet upside down. Jax's keys were nestled safely inside.

"Thanks," Jax said. He looked at the helmet and keys for a long moment. "Is this—" He stopped, then shook his head. "Never mind."

Ari tilted his head. "Yes?"

Jax gave a pathetic smile. "It's nothing." He lifted the helmet. "Thanks. I better let you get back to…." He waved a hand. "Yeah. Bye."

"Bye," Ari said, bemused, as Jax hurried away. He watched him disappear into the stairwell—didn't want to wait for the elevator, it seemed—and then closed the front door. He pressed his face against it and took a deep breath.

Would it never not hurt to see or think about Jax? Every reminder of him came with a deep certainty that Jax was "the one." Except how could he be when he'd behaved the way he had? When he'd gotten over Ari so easily?

He took another deep breath and then returned to his sister and intern, reseated at the table, pretending they had no idea what was going on at the door.

Ari took his seat.

And then noticed the music playing through the thousand-dollar speaker system—a violin begging for forgiveness and a piano demanding an apology.

Well, fuck.

Chapter Twenty-One

JAX RETURNED to the house and pulled his mother's car into the garage. With Hobbes and Naomi visiting Hobbes's parents for the holiday, there was no point parking outside.

He expected his mother would be there, especially without a vehicle, but a note on the kitchen table informed him she'd gone for a walk to appreciate the mild weather. Jax supposed it was milder than Kingston, at least, and no Cambridge either, but the idea of hoofing it through calf-high snowdrifts didn't appeal to him.

Unfortunately his mother's absence left him alone with his thoughts. Sitting in the glow of the Christmas tree, he took out his phone.

He'd unfollowed Ari's social media accounts after the breakup. Coming across him while he was innocently scrolling through Instagram was a lousy way to start a day or end one. But now he found himself searching for the account again.

He couldn't get that song out of his head. Hell, *either* of those songs.

He wasn't an idiot, at least not most of the time. And it didn't take a genius to figure out artists drew inspiration from real life.

So Jax was feeling… *things* about Ari writing music about him.

That was what he'd done, wasn't it? He'd written a song about his feelings for Jax. Possibly more than one song. Jax felt a little stupid for not noticing earlier, considering the number of nights Ari crawled out of bed after leaving Jax a pile of nerveless goo and went to make love to his piano instead. And Jax—okay, maybe Jax *was* an idiot, because it had never occurred to him that Ari, *his boyfriend who was a professional musician*, would write songs *about him*.

What kind of fresh hell was this going to be? Would he be innocently grocery shopping, minding his own business, and

246

then *wham*, all of a sudden, over the store's radio would come the inescapable reminder that Ari used to have feelings for him, but now he didn't?

Worse—shit—what if someone requested one of his songs at the Rock? What if someone requested one of Ari's songs at the Rock while Jax was playing *and Ari was in attendance*? That was, like, a special *Inception*-level cross-section of Jax's nightmares.

Of course, Ari probably wouldn't come to the Rock anymore.

After next week, Jax wouldn't be going to the Rock anymore either.

One of the good things to come out of his mother's visit was that their reconciliation had included Jax's admission that he wanted to go back to MIT to defend his thesis, once he'd saved up the money. When he tried to turn down his mother's offer of a loan, she threatened to give him the money for Christmas instead, and he was forced to accept a loan as the lesser of two evils. With her help, he'd even be able to rent a place that wasn't a complete shithole. He didn't have to be in Boston long. He'd already submitted the work to Grayling's successor for evaluation. He was just waiting on the committee to decide on an official date.

It was for the best. He needed to close that chapter of his life. But he didn't want to close *this* one—his friendship with Hobbes, with his coworkers at the bar, being Uncle Jax. But he didn't want to do a postdoc, so continuing in academia was out. He was no longer certain he wanted to work at a think tank either.

And—

And all of that went right out of his head when he got to Ari's Instagram, because there *was* new content there. Jax scrolled until he found the first post he hadn't seen—an image of the track listing on the back of the album—and clicked on it.

The background image was a geometric black and white—a smooth, sinuous soft-focus parabolic curve that looked like nothing so much as an artistic ass shot. At least, that was how it struck Jax, though of course it wasn't. He suspected it was computer-generated.

Alice, said the track listing. *1.618. First Sight. September 27. Push/Pull. Solo.*

Jax's face went hot. Wait a minute. September 27 was the day they first… wasn't it? He wasn't going to check a calendar to make sure.

He was pretty certain he'd know if he ever heard the song. Shaking himself, he scrolled past the rest of the image and over to the description.

String Theory. Coming March 17.

Jax put his hand to his mouth.

There were a few more pictures. Ari in the studio, handsome and serious with his chin on the chinrest of his electric violin, his eyes closed, obviously lost in the music. A few of the musicians he recorded with—two more with Aiden Lindell and one with a sweet-looking blond girl named Maxi Greene.

As Jax had hoped—dreaded—there were a few videos with song clips.

The first was a clip of Aiden Lindell singing a few bars of "Alice"—the song that had been playing when Jax knocked on Ari's door today. At first Jax had thought it was a coincidence when he heard the name, but as he stood waiting for Ari, the song spun out a story about the Cheshire Cat guiding Alice, seeing the world for what it was and loving it for its infinite complexities. And Jax had just *known* on a level he couldn't fully explain that he was the cat in question. He'd wanted to break down in Ari's doorway, demand that Ari tell him everything.

But then the song had changed to something angry and volatile, and Jax realized "Alice" must have been composed weeks ago. It didn't mean Ari still felt the same.

The "Push/Pull" post had a snippet of intense dialogue between the piano and the violin. It was electric and left chills down his spine—an argument in song.

"Solo" made his lip tremble. There was no violin in this piece, just a piano, and it sounded sad.

So Ari had basically written him an entire album, every song either about Jax or their relationship. And he hadn't told Jax. Why? What did it mean?

Was it meant to be a surprise? A secret forever? Surely Ari hadn't thought Jax would never notice.

Jax didn't know whether to be grateful or not that "September 27" wasn't sampled on Instagram. He wasn't sure he was ready to listen to Ari describe their sex life with a violin.

His mother found him on the couch, watching the "Alice" clip on loop.

"What are you doing?"

Jax jumped and stared at his mother for a long moment, then finally admitted, "Listening to a clip from Ari's new album."

"Jax...."

"It's called 'Alice.'"

"Oh," she said. For a moment she looked too taken aback to say anything else. Then she shook herself and said, "Right. Turn that off—it's not helping—and come help me make cookies. We have a lot of baking that needs doing before we go see your sister tomorrow."

"Yes, ma'am," Jax said with a mock salute, and she threw one of her cold gloves at his face.

Laughing, Jax set his phone on the coffee table, lobbed the glove back at her, and ducked into the kitchen to escape retribution.

"CHRISTMAS" DINNER was a strange one that year, not that these dinners didn't always strike Ari as odd. He'd never had a Christmas with a Christian family, but he was pretty sure that the TV-inspired mashup his family did wouldn't feel authentic to most Canadian families.

Still, this year was weirder than normal, since they'd decided to delay until the twenty-eighth in order to invite Theo after his return from his family home. He'd expressed an interest in experiencing Persian family life, even if he didn't know his own ethnic heritage exactly— "23AndMe is terrifying," he once said apropos of nothing before diving back into his textbook—though Ari found it hilarious that his first full Persian family dinner was a holiday no one else celebrated.

Ari was the last one there again, once more by design. Afra had asked for some time to prepare their parents for the news that she and Ben had started the adoption process. By now, though, she'd had plenty of opportunity.

Ari could tell as soon as he went inside that no one had tried to cook the North American classics this year, for which he was grateful. He'd never forget the turkey dinner debacle of '04. The poor bird had been black on the outside and raw on the inside. In its place, his father appeared to have cooked every Persian holiday food known to God and man.

Whatever their other shortcomings, his parents welcomed Theo with open arms, and though, as Ari had surmised, there was no turkey, it seemed they were simply trying to stuff Theo instead.

After dinner his mother took him aside. "Ari... I'd like to talk to you privately."

He'd eaten too much to fight her on it.

When the door to her study closed behind him, she reached for his hands, but when he didn't reach back, she stepped away and clasped hers in front of her. A flicker of hurt showed on her face, but it quickly disappeared under her usual put-together mask.

Ari put his own hands in his pockets in order to avoid the urge to fidget. "What did you want to talk about?" He glanced behind him at the door. It felt strange to be closed in a room with her. They were a tight-knit family; they didn't often keep secrets.

Or at least, until recently he'd thought they didn't.

She sighed and gestured to her desk, but instead of sitting behind it as she had when he was a child, she sat in one of the two armchairs on the opposite side.

Ari was thankful, a moment later, that she waited until he was sitting down to say, "I owe you an apology."

He was so taken aback he couldn't form words. In his entire life, his mother had never apologized for anything. It took him a moment to manage, "Oh?"

She broke his gaze, her hands still twisted together in her lap so tightly that the brown skin was turning pale. But she took a deep breath and persevered, once again meeting his eyes. "One of the most important parts of raising a child is making decisions that are in the child's best interest. It's part of why we moved to Canada in the first place, because we knew we wanted our children to have more choices than we did. It's part of why Afra gave her baby up for adoption when he was born." She let out another long breath. "And it's a very difficult habit to break when our children grow up enough to make their own decisions about what's best for them."

It was more of an apology than Ari had ever hoped for, but it didn't explain everything to his satisfaction. Honestly, now he had more questions. "I don't understand why it's so important to you that I stay in London. You always said you wanted me to be happy. You supported my dream of playing music professionally. You didn't think, when I went to college in Boston, that I'd come home and sign up with the London Symphonia?" The London orchestra didn't have the budget or the schedule of a larger orchestra, and most of the members taught or performed with several groups in order to support themselves.

Before she could answer, he added in frustration, "And I don't see why it's so important that I marry a doctor, Maman." *I wish you could have loved Jax as much as I do.*

And he wished he'd behaved differently. He wished he'd told Jax how he felt when he had the chance. Maybe then they could have salvaged things.

She took a deep breath. "Lately I have been letting my own fears guide me." Ari frowned. "My prognosis is good, but I have breast cancer."

He felt dizzy. "What?"

"There are two lumps. The surgeon will remove them, and after some additional therapy, probably radiation, I should be absolutely fine. You're not losing me yet." He could hardly reconcile the words coming out of her mouth with the smooth composure of her voice and face.

"You're sure?" His throat felt tight. This conversation barely felt real.

"As sure as a medical professional can be about this." Her tone reminded him that medicine did not deal in certainties. "My prognosis is excellent. It was caught in a routine checkup, nice and early. They will do a lumpectomy, and I should be around for years to come."

"Good." He might be mad at her, but he couldn't imagine losing her.

Now the smoothness on her face disappeared, replaced with tight lines at the corners of her mouth, her forehead, her eyes. "But cancer has a way of putting things into perspective, or maybe warping it. I suddenly felt very old and very worried about what I would and wouldn't live to see. I wanted you to be comfortably established, to know that even if I wasn't here, you would have someone to love and to love you. To look after you." Was *that* why she'd wanted him to marry a doctor? "But I lost perspective about what was important on that front."

That was putting it mildly, but it felt like it would be rude to point that out. "Thank you for telling me. When are you…?"

"The surgery is set for January third."

"Oh." So soon? Was that a bad sign?

"I should have told you weeks ago, but I didn't want you to worry."

Ari gave her a look. "So you decided to be weird instead?"

She made a gesture that Ari interpreted as *mea culpa*. This was truly the strangest family dinner in history. "I deserve that. Afra read me the riot act when I told her. You can rest easy, though—your Jax did worse."

Hearing her say his name, suggesting that she'd talked to him, blindsided him almost as badly as the word *cancer*. "Jax?"

"Hm." She smoothed her pants and avoided his gaze. "Yes. I went to that bar."

"*You* went to the Rock?" Was the bar still standing?

"Yes."

"Why?"

"Honestly?" She lifted her gaze and shrugged. "I'm not entirely sure, except I wanted to see him how you saw him. He was very charming on that stage. And as good-looking as ever," she added somewhat slyly. It didn't feel like a dig this time.

252

"Maman," he warned.

"I didn't intend to talk to him, but, well, I accidentally sat down next to Christine and got talking."

"Christine?" Jax's new… girlfriend? Lover? Paramour?

"You can imagine how I felt when she said she was his mother."

Ari choked. "His *mother?*"

"Yes?"

"I never knew her name," Ari managed to strangle out, reeling.

"It was an awkward conversation, given the things I'd said to Jax's face and vice versa." She let out a sharp laugh, and Ari stared at her. "You know, I think I like him. He told me we had a lot in common. We're both awful people who love you. Well, actually he used the word *dicks*."

"Love?" He didn't know where to start. Jax hadn't started dating someone else? Jax had talked to his mother? And called her a dick?

And that was them, for lack of a better term, making up?

"Well, of course, dear. No one can sing a love song like that if they don't mean it." She rose. "When you're both ready, I'd like to retry that first meeting."

Stunned, Ari watched her leave. He had no idea what to do with all of this information, except maybe to get in his car and go see Jax right now and ask to talk.

Only, he had a family dinner to get through, and he couldn't just leave. Afra would never forgive him.

Tomorrow he would call Jax and ask to meet him, and then they could have a proper conversation.

Tomorrow he could get his life back on track.

ARI'S PLAN had only two kinks—Jax was not answering his damned phone; every call went straight to voicemail, and he didn't know where Jax lived.

The first issue, the thought that Jax might be ignoring his calls, was disheartening but did not dissuade him. Even if Jax really was done with him, Ari needed to know for certain.

The second was a bigger hurdle. Because if Jax was ignoring him and not simply busy, Ari couldn't even leave him a note if he didn't know where to find him.

Well, he knew of one place, but showing up to Jax's work would be a dick move. Even Ari knew that.

Which left Ari with only one recourse, aside from morally dubious ones involving private investigators—Naomi.

"Ari, to what do I owe the phone call so early on a weekday morning." She did not sound pleased.

"Hello, Naomi. I'm sorry for disturbing you, but you're probably the only person who can help me with this."

"You're lucky my practice isn't opening till next week," she grumped. Perhaps Calvin was rubbing off on her. "What do you want?"

"I need to speak with Jax, but he's not answering his phone, and I don't know his address."

"And you didn't think that was a hint to stay away?"

He blew out a breath. Of course he had. "Yes. But I need to speak to him anyway. I owe him a lot."

"What are you going to say to him when you see him that you can't tell his voicemail?"

He winced. That was a good point. But he was coming full circle with the "bad at words" thing.

Maybe that was a sign this was a time for feelings. "That I'm sorry." He swallowed hard and forced himself to say the next bit. "That I love him. And I want to try again, if he does."

"Good," she said with no small amount of satisfaction. "Though your timing sucks. He just left for Boston."

He blinked, taken aback. "Boston?"

"Yeah, apparently he's got to actually be at MIT if he wants to convince them to give him a PhD."

Ari hadn't even known he was thinking of going back. "Do you know how long he'll be gone?"

"No, but he doesn't either. Depends on his advisory committee, but Jax thought probably a couple months. Maybe the whole semester."

Ari couldn't wait that long. He'd be on tour before the semester ended. "Do you know his address in Boston?"

Naomi stayed silent for a long moment. "I do not."

Ari closed his eyes. If Jax kept refusing his phone calls…. He thought about flying to Boston anyway, haunting the MIT math department. He'd probably get arrested for being a creep, and he'd deserve it.

"But I know someone who does."

Chapter Twenty-Two

THE DAY he saw his mother off at the airport, Jax went home and surveyed his realm with a critical eye.

It wasn't glamorous.

The Boston rental market being what it was, Jax's apartment consisted of a single room large enough for a bed, a desk, a couch, and a kitchenette—no baking in his future—with a bathroom the size of his closet in Hobbes's place. The hardwood floors were scuffed and uneven, and the double-hung windows were drafty and yet somehow still difficult to pry open. He definitely didn't have room for his keyboard. But he had a place for his laptop and a place to sleep, so he couldn't complain. It was only temporary.

He repeated that to himself as he dragged his suitcase out from under the bed and hung his clothes in the closet. He was an adult now. Adults didn't live out of suitcases for months at a time.

Adults did, however, consider hanging an extra blanket in front of a window because the window was drafty. Fuck Boston winters. Why couldn't Jax have decided to defend in summer or fall?

In any case, now that his mother was gone, he didn't have an excuse to eat out all the time, so he needed something to fill his cupboards and the mini fridge. There was a corner store a handful of blocks away. He could get the basics there and worry about fancier things when he was settled.

It wasn't currently snowing, which was as good as he could hope for in terms of weather, so he put his gear on and went outside.

His neighborhood wasn't far from campus, in Fenway-Kenmore. There were maybe too many bars per capita in the neighborhood, but maybe that was a good thing. They could be home away from home when Jax got nostalgic for the Rock. One of them probably even had decent live music. He was within walking distance of a Target, or at least he would've been if it weren't twenty below.

He took his time at the store, not eager to go back out in the cold. Bread, milk, eggs, peanut butter, some instant ramen that he added to his basket with a wry twist of a smile. He hardly felt like a college student anymore. Rice, deli meat, carrots, onions, tea. That was probably all he could carry without risking the bags breaking and spilling his groceries all over the icy sidewalk, so he paid, tucked the ends of his scarf back inside his coat, and went home.

At just past four, the sky was already a deep, bruised blue. Soon it would be fully dark and Jax would be alone in his sad apartment, eating instant noodles.

But it was fine. It was *necessary*. In a few months, he could go back to London and be with Sam and George and Alice and Hobbes…. At least he'd made up with his mother.

He wondered how Ari was faring with his.

It had been a month since their disastrous dinner, and Jax felt no closer to getting past it. What if he'd taken his pill that morning? What if he'd called off the dinner when he realized he hadn't? What if he'd taken Ari's warnings more seriously? What if they'd waited longer for Jax to meet them and they'd met on more neutral territory, like a restaurant, somewhere they'd have had to stay civil?

There was no excuse for how Nasreen treated him. He wasn't denying that. But Jax could have put up with it for Ari, if Ari hadn't left him high and dry to deal with it.

If Jax's own mistakes hadn't made him overreact to her petty insults and lash out to hurt her and Ari in turn.

If they were still together, Jax would be… what? Hurrying home to do the same thing he was doing now, probably, except with the promise of a phone call with Ari to keep him warm.

Thinking of that led to remembering the strange moment he felt when the plane touched down in Boston, when he turned his phone on to find multiple missed calls from Ari. But he hadn't left a message, and he hadn't texted…. Jax had concluded that it must not have been important. That had been days ago, and Jax hadn't heard anything since.

A car slushed past down the street, kicking dirty snow onto the sidewalk. Jax grimaced and shifted to walk closer to the buildings. Next time he decided to get a PhD, he was applying to the University of Hawaii.

The wind kicked up when he rounded the final corner back to his building, and he grimaced and buried his face deeper into his scarf. Definitely Hawaii. Maybe even Australia. Except everything killed you in Australia. That was no good.

He was deliberating the relative merits of New Zealand when he came within a block of his apartment... and froze.

There was a familiar figure standing on the step, flyaway hair stuffed under a knitted hat, one hand pressed to the side of his head.

Somewhere in the depths of Jax's multiple winter layers, his phone rang.

He dropped one of the grocery bags.

The sound of a full aluminum can hitting the pavement must have reached Ari, because he looked over, his cheeks red from the wind, the color just visible in the light from the streetlamp.

It probably wasn't cold enough that Jax had started hallucinating. Numbly, he bent to pick up his grocery bag and walked the rest of the way to the door.

Ari still had his phone to his ear, but when Jax grew close enough that he could hear the phone ringing, he blinked and pulled it away.

What the hell did Jax even say? *What are you doing here* seemed like the obvious choice, but it was also kind of confrontational. Jax didn't want to fight. The sight of Ari filled him with a bone-deep longing. He just wanted to erase the past month from his life and go back to how things were.

"I had to see you," Ari said before Jax could ask the question. "I'm sorry, I know it's... creepy."

Laughter bubbled out of Jax in a sharp bark. "Maybe a little. But I don't mind."

Ari smiled slightly. "Good." His eyes flicked about as he attempted to take in all of Jax. Jax was doing the same. He wanted to take in every inch of him too.

"We should go inside," Jax finally managed, and he unlocked his door and brought Ari upstairs.

As Jax shoved some of his groceries away—he didn't want anything to go bad in case he got distracted—Ari looked around the apartment. Jax bit his lip against defending his choice. Ari knew how expensive Boston was, and he could probably guess how short-term Jax's needs were.

Jax put the milk and eggs in the fridge and shut it. The last of the groceries. He took a deep breath and stepped closer to Ari.

"So—"

"I'm sorry," Ari blurted. He flushed slightly and looked away. "There is a lot I wanted to tell you, but that was at the top of the list. I'm sorry. You were right, I was useless at dinner with my parents. I shouldn't have just sat there."

Jax sighed and rubbed the back of his head. "Yeah, well. I was also an ass. I should have believed you about how intense it would be. Also, being an ass just to prove a point wasn't very productive. I forgot my pill that morning."

Ari's expression of dawning realization made him feel worse. "You know I would have understood if you'd wanted to cancel."

"I know." Jax huffed out a shaky breath. "Only I didn't want your parents to think I was a flake. Ironic, I know."

"A little," Ari admitted. "Though somehow you've won over my mother. Not that I care, because I don't need her permission to date anyone, but she's decided she likes you."

What on earth could Jax say to that? His mouth dropped open and he stared at Ari, flabbergasted. "What?"

"Did you really call her a dick?"

"Oh my God, she *told you that*?" He was going to die of mortification.

"Yes. She apparently respects you for it."

Who knew giving zero fucks could convince Nasreen Darvish to give him a second chance?

Ari waited for him to say something else. Jax licked his lips. "So did you come all the way here to apologize?"

"No." Ari shook his head and took a step closer. When Jax didn't back away, Ari took his hands. "I came here to tell you that I love you."

Jax's breath hitched. After all this time, had he really not gotten it so wrong after all? Was he really getting a second chance?

Ari wasn't finished speaking. "And I want to be with you, and if you're willing to try, I—"

"Yes," Jax rasped before Ari got any further into what Jax was recognizing as anxious babble. "I mean, we totally have to talk stuff out and figure out how to avoid something like that dinner ever happening again." That meant no sparks from Ari and no gasoline from Jax. Ari nodded. "But I've missed you."

Ari stepped closer. Jax inched forward too.

"How much?" Ari asked.

"Huh?"

"How much did you miss me?"

"Enough to Instagram stalk you."

Ari was closer still. "Yeah?"

"Enough to sing stupid breakup songs."

"Angry ones at the bar?" Ari's face was within touching distance now.

Jax nodded. "Enough to leave London a few days earlier than planned."

"I tried calling you the day you left. I wanted to see you. To tell you how much I love you."

Jax launched himself into Ari's arms.

His mouth was as warm and giving as always, as Ari eased Jax's lips apart and slid their tongues together. Every press, slide, and lick seemed to say *I'm sorry*, and *forgive me*, and *let's try again*. Jax whimpered and tried to reply *me too* and *me too* and *yes* and *yes* and *yes*.

Ari slipped his arms around Jax's waist and held him close while Jax tangled his fingers in Ari's hair.

As they pulled apart, panting into the short space between their lips, Jax breathed, "I love you too. I love you, of course I—fuck, Ari, you wrote me a *whole fucking album*."

Ari stilled in his arms, his shoulders at attention, and pulled back enough to see Jax's face. Whatever he found in Jax's eyes apparently reassured him, as his shoulders stood down. "Ah. I had wondered if you noticed."

"Not until I heard 'Alice' at your place. Because I'm an idiot and didn't even think about it before. But I looked up the track listings on your Instagram."

"Oh, have they posted that?" Ari asked, sounding distracted. He seemed more interested in rubbing his thumb over Jax's cheekbone.

"Yes." Jax leaned into the touch. "Did you really write a song about the first time we slept together?"

Ari froze once again and flushed bright red. "Um."

"Ari!" Jax choked on a laugh.

"You are very inspiring?" he offered weakly.

"Oh my God. Please tell me not everyone is going to know."

"It doesn't have lyrics," Ari offered.

Jax hummed, relieved. Not that he wasn't flattered, but his mom was going to buy this album. "But it is an ode to my perfect body?"

Ari's face softened. "More like an ode to how wonderful you are in all ways."

Jax laughed. He hoped Ari wasn't offended, but he couldn't accept that kind of compliment just then. "Right. Or an ode to how much you love my ass."

The hand on the small of Jax's back dipped slightly, and Ari brushed his fingers along the top of Jax's ass. "Well, it is a rather nice one."

"You know it," Jax murmured and kissed him again. Everything else could wait.

MUCH LATER, curled safely under every blanket in the terrible apartment, Jax said, "How long do I get to keep you here, anyway?"

Ari had been toying absently with the hair at Jax's nape—he needed a cut—but at the question he froze, feeling caught. Which was silly, because he'd already admitted to getting on a plane with only a slim hope that Jax might forgive him. And grand romantic gestures weren't in his makeup. He couldn't remember the last time he'd been so impulsive. "Ah, well...."

Jax looked up, eyes shadowed in the dim orange glow of the streetlight. He narrowed them and pressed his hand against Ari's chest. "What?"

"I booked a one-way ticket," Ari admitted, his ears burning. "It was a bit... last-minute."

He didn't regret it when Jax smiled. "That's... sweet, actually. Although I do foresee one problem."

Still pleasantly postorgasmic and basking in Jax's attention, Ari had a difficult time conceiving of any such thing. "Hmm?"

Jax half sat up and gestured around him. "We're going to drive each other nuts if we're stuck hanging out here together all the time."

Ah. "Yes, I see your point."

"Also—and please don't take this the wrong way—"

"It's far too soon for us to live together, even short-term," Ari finished for him.

"Especially after...."

"Yes." Neither of them was particularly suited to a slow relationship progression, but they could at least pretend. "Also, there's no room for a piano in here."

Jax snorted and flopped back down next to him. "You noticed that, huh?" He turned onto his side. "Besides, I do actually have work to do prior to my defense. So, what's the plan? Are you going to fly back, or...."

"I'll have to eventually." He was done with the album, but his mother was still recovering from surgery, and there would be tour details to work on. When Jax's smile faded, he added, "But...."

"But?" Jax asked hopefully.

Ari kissed him quickly. "But I'm certain there's another short-term rental available *somewhere* in the city. Perhaps closer to the conservatory. I'm sure I could get access to a practice room in exchange for a few guest lectures."

"Yeah?" Jax shifted closer, until Ari had no choice but to roll onto his back. Jax moved with him, half lying on his chest.

Ari traced a thumb over Jax's lips. "Yes."

Jax sighed and leaned his face into Ari's palm. "I can't believe it took us this long to make up. We could've had another whole month together." He shook his head. "And you said your mom was the one who convinced you to come?"

Ari felt a pang. There was so much they had to talk about. "Well, actually, it's a funny story."

"Uh-oh, serious talk." Jax kissed his thumb and then sat up and gathered the sheets in his lap. His skin immediately pebbled into goose bumps, and he grimaced and reached over the side of the bed for his sweatshirt. He pulled it on, then grabbed Ari's too. "Maybe we should move to the couch."

"I'll make tea," Ari agreed.

They settled on the sofa, which was a hideous worn brown velvet, though free at least of any stains and surprisingly comfortable. Jax spread one of the blankets over their laps, and they sat facing each other, their legs entwined.

"All right," Jax said, tucking his feet under Ari's leg and cupping his mug under his chin. "Start at the beginning."

"Would that be the furious fight with my mother where I blamed her for my own spinelessness, the phone call you took at the grocery store that I somehow thought meant you were seeing someone else already, or the *other* parental bombshell—"

"Whoa, I can see I should have gotten a bottle of something stronger than milk at the corner store."

Ari acknowledged that with a tilt of his head and sipped his tea. "Well, the fight was self-explanatory. The phone call... why *do* you call your mother Christine?"

"'Cause it's her name?" Jax said wryly. "Wait, you thought I was dating my mom?"

"In my defense, I'd never seen her, and you never mentioned her name. And who calls their mom by their first name?"

Jax smirked over the rim of his mug. "Got in the habit in undergrad. Every time I went to see my mom on campus, I'd get these looks if I asked if people had seen Professor Hall. She mostly teaches grad students, so everyone thought I was about to get eaten. One day someone asked if I was there to see Christine and I realized that was what her students called her. What a revelation. Moms have first names? So every time I was on campus, I'd call her that. She thought it was funny."

If she was anything like Jax, Ari supposed she would. "I should have talked to you before that, but afterward...."

"You thought I got over you that quickly?" Jax seemed a little hurt, but not as much as Ari had expected.

Ari lifted a shoulder sheepishly. "You did mention that you fall in love at the drop of a hat."

Jax accepted this with a wobbly nod. "That's fair." He dropped his gaze to his mug, then lifted it again and smiled slightly. "Though maybe not anymore."

Ari went warm all the way through, despite the draft. "Perhaps just one more time."

Jax nudged his thigh. "Yeah. That sounds nice." He put his tea on the coffee table. "You mentioned another parental bombshell? Dare I ask?"

Well, that was a mood-killer. "I'll tell you." Ari put down his tea as well and held his hands out for Jax. "But first you have to come here."

His mother's surgery had gone according to plan, and she was recovering well, but that didn't mean reality wasn't easier to face with Jax's weight a solid, warm comfort against his chest.

GETTING BACK into the swing of going to school—even if he didn't technically have classes—took some getting used to. Ari's presence didn't help. Although he'd rented a hotel room while he looked for a longer-term solution, it had been so long since Jax dated someone and went to school at the same time that it didn't feel like going *back* to school so much as starting a whole *new* chapter.

Thank God for ADHD meds, because he already felt like he was writing three different parts of the same book all at once without knowing how anything ended.

Since Ari couldn't stay in Boston past January, Jax found a new drive to work hard and get his defense scheduled as early as possible. Unfortunately MIT was like every other college around—a big, slow bureaucracy with lots of paperwork to fill out. Jax hated forms.

But the potential of leaving Boston behind *with* Ari was an excellent carrot, so when the department administration asked him to come down to get some things taken care of, Jax didn't argue. Instead he put on his big-boy pants—actual jeans instead of sweats—and headed down to the college.

The woman heading up the mathematics department's admin was an unfamiliar face, and she seemed immune to Jax's charm. Then again, he probably wasn't the only good-looking young person trying to flirt his way through this maze of forms and applications.

"I understand that I need to fill out form 35-B before I can schedule the next bit, but the form wants to know information I don't have yet."

"And what is that?" She looked at him over the rim of her reading glasses. She was forty and had the strongest strict-librarian vibe Jax had ever encountered. Part of Jax—a small part who was still a seventeen-year-old boy—wondered if she'd punish him for being naughty.

"My advisor. The college hasn't cleared that up yet—whose name I should put, Grayling's or Greenwood's—and I don't want to put in the wrong name and have things delayed."

"Surely that's a question for Greenwood. She has, after all, taken over his workload."

"Yes, but she doesn't know either—"

"Jax?"

He turned to see Rebecca Grayling standing in the doorway to the admin office.

She looks old. Her dark brown hair was shot through with gray that hadn't been there two years ago, and lines were etched near her eyes and mouth. But though she looked tired, a bright smile slowly transformed her face.

"I thought I heard your voice."

"Yup, it's me."

"Are you busy? Why don't you come see me in my office?"

"Well." Jax looked at the admin and then back at Rebecca. "I'm filling out forms, but I've hit a wall. So…."

"You're all mine. Come." She motioned for him to follow her out of the office, down the hall, and into hers.

Jax hadn't spent much time in her office on campus—he'd seen it, of course, and spent too much time in her home, but he hadn't had much cause to spend time in the department head's personal office when she wasn't his advisor.

"How have you been?" She settled into one of the chairs in front of her desk, and Jax took the other.

"Oh, you know, same as everyone else, probably. Busy and then not busy."

She gave a wry smile. "Yes. I heard you did good work on statistical models up north."

Jax snorted. "You know, London is barely farther north—"

She narrowed her eyes. "*Barely* means that it is. Don't try to outpedant me, kid."

"Never." Jax, Rebecca, and Chris had spent more than one evening, after the kids had gone to bed, debating the semantics of pretty much everything. The devil was in the details, and they all loved to debate the absurd as much as anything else.

She asked more about his life in London until, several minutes later, he'd exhausted that topic almost entirely. He looked down at his knees, took a deep breath, and said, "I'm sorry. For not—" Calling? Coming back sooner? He shrugged helplessly.

"Not what?" she asked softly.

"I don't know. Being here?"

"Oh, Jax. I don't blame you for going home or for not calling. I know how much Chris meant to you."

"Thanks." He blinked furiously. "But I should have—you were alone—"

She held up a hand. "Jacob Stirling Hall, you stop thinking that right now. You did not leave me alone. I have a fantastic brother and sister-in-law who basically moved into my house to help me cope. I had all the support I needed during what was the worst time in my life, and I made it through that awful first year."

Jax hadn't known that. Probably because he hadn't talked to Rebecca since days after he fled the country.

"Yes, I missed you and would have loved to have you around. But don't think for a moment that I wasn't relieved that you were north of the border." She clenched her hand into a fist. "Chris was too. We didn't have to worry about you too much."

Jax's mouth trembled. "Rebecca...."

She stood and he followed suit, and then she was wrapping her arms around him. "I missed you, but I didn't *need* you here."

Minutes later they settled back into their seats, both of them rubbing their faces. "Now, tell me about your admin troubles."

Jax raised his eyebrows.

"You think I couldn't recognize the look on Miranda's face? What's the problem?"

Jax outlined everything, and Rebecca laughed. "Oh, is that all? Well, I think I might know a few people and can pull some strings."

"Yeah?"

"On one condition."

"What's that?"

"Come for dinner."

"Oh, I can definitely do that." Jax thought of Ari, with whom he'd had dinner every night for the past week. "But uh, only if I can bring someone along."

"Oh?" One of Rebecca's eyebrows arched high. She looked positively eager for some gossip.

"Yeah." He rubbed his neck. "Have you ever heard of Aria Darvish?"

Chapter Twenty-Three

JAX LEFT the math department with a spring in his step. He wouldn't have thought it possible when he arrived two hours before, but Jax actually felt light in this space. As he hurried down the steps and out of the building, eager to burn some energy, he fished his phone from his pocket.

Ari had tried to call him half an hour ago and left a text asking Jax to call him when he could. *Nothing serious.*

"Jax," Ari said, all warmth and affection. "What are your plans for the day?"

"Well, now that I've slain some bureaucratic dragons, I thought maybe I would see what my handsome and talented boyfriend is up to tonight."

"Handsome *and* talented? Anyone I know?"

Jax smiled despite himself. "Maybe I'll introduce you later… if you finish what you were going to ask me."

Ari cleared his throat. "I ran into one of my old professors at the conservatory this morning. Several of the faculty are going out to dinner tonight, and they asked if we might want to join them."

Jax's heartbeat sped. On the one hand, he was pleased to get a chance to meet some of the people who had shaped Ari into the musician he was. On the other hand, the last time they'd had a dinner with outside influences had been an absolute shitfest.

They'd only just found and forgiven each other again. Did he want to risk it so soon?

Then again, if it was going to be a nightmare, better to find out now. Right?

"Jax?" Oops. Apparently he'd deliberated for too long. "If it helps at all, I promise to throw the first punch if any of my old acquaintances call you a whore."

That startled Jax into a laugh. "Don't you dare. You'll break your fingers." He paused. "Kick them in the privates instead."

"Joking aside, you have my word that this won't be like the dinner with my parents. I don't know everyone who's coming, but I like and trust the majority of them. I think they'll like you."

Jax was getting pretty good at decoding what Ari didn't say, and the subtext here was pretty clear—*they'll love you because I do.* In the end, that decided it for him. "All right," he agreed. "What time, and what do I wear?"

ARI HAD originally planned to pick Jax up at his apartment, but Jax texted him an hour beforehand that he was on the phone with the admin at the college, and since he might be late, he'd meet Ari at the restaurant.

Part of Ari wondered if he didn't have cold feet—he couldn't exactly blame Jax if he did—but in the end, he decided the least Jax deserved was the benefit of the doubt.

It turned out he needn't have worried. Their group was still congregating in the lobby of the restaurant ahead of their reservation when Jax blew in, liberally dusted with snowflakes, cheeks red with the cold.

He lit up further when he saw Ari, and Ari knew that he must be doing the same, but as much as he found public displays uncomfortable, he couldn't help himself. When Jax was close enough, Ari grabbed his hand and pulled him in to kiss his cheek. "You made it."

Jax was even redder now, but he squeezed Ari's hand and grinned. "Wouldn't miss it."

"Ari!" Professor Marston cut through the milling crowd, eyebrows first. "You made it. And this must be Jax."

"It is," Ari confirmed, tugging Jax forward. "Jax, this is Professor Marston. He taught me almost everything I know about composition."

"It's Chuck, Ari, I keep telling you. And he flatters me, Jax. I taught him half of what he knows at best."

"It's nice to meet you."

The host called them to their table before Ari could make further introductions, and they were led to a private room near the back of the restaurant, where they had the opportunity to hang up their coats. Jax had chosen a fitted charcoal collared shirt and tailored gray trousers Ari had never seen on him and which he planned to remove at their earliest mutual convenience.

As Ari and Jax were the out-of-towners—and as Ari had some degree of celebrity, much as it pained him—they were cajoled into the seats in the middle of the table, where everyone could hope to have a turn talking to them. Jax hooked his ankle around Ari's under the tablecloth, where no one would see, either as a gesture of support or a request for comfort, and the proper introductions commenced.

Apart from Professor Marston—Chuck—Gianna Handel, the piano chair, and Tomas Markovic, who taught music theory, Ari knew two other faculty—Janie Cheng, a violinist who'd been finishing up graduate studies when Ari was at the conservatory, and Marco Cervini, who also played violin but wasn't in Ari's cohort. Two others, Marisa Lopez and Adi Singh, he hadn't met before.

"I'm a vocal instructor," Marisa said, smiling. "So if you ever decide you'd like to sing on your own album…."

Chuck and Gianna both laughed. "Don't think we haven't tried that before, but he is very determined."

"I'm very aware that my singing voice is average at best," Ari corrected. Besides, sometimes the emotion in his own music got to him. It made singing challenging. "What about you, Ms. Singh?"

"Just Adi," she corrected. "Contemporary improvisation and musicology." She darted a glance at Jax. "Forgive me, but I feel like I may have seen you somewhere before…."

"You don't look familiar," Jax said apologetically. "Have you been in Boston long?"

"This is my second year teaching." She tapped a finger against the edge of her water glass. "Well, never mind. It'll come to me."

The server came by to take their drink orders, interrupting the flow of conversation. Jax got only one raised eyebrow for opting to stick with water, from Marco, who had never been able to mind his own business when they were undergraduates either. Ari hoped that the presence of his coworkers would prevent him from acting on the same misguided impulses that had driven him to needle Ari back then.

"You don't like wine?" Marco asked, and Ari squeezed Jax's leg under the table—both a warning that Marco could be unpleasant and a show of silent support.

"Interferes with my medication," Jax said smoothly, "so I limit consumption."

Ari hid his smile by taking a sip from his own water glass. He should have known that Jax could defend himself while making Marco look like an asshole without drawing even the slightest scrutiny.

The server disappeared and Chuck turned to Jax. "So what is it that you do?"

Since Jax had just lifted his glass to his mouth, Ari said smoothly, "He's a bartender. It's how we met."

"Do you enjoy it?" Chuck asked. "I hated my months as a waiter."

Jax shrugged. "I do, actually. I like people and making them happy." Chuck nodded and smiled, and a look around told Ari that only Marco was being judgmental.

"It's the same bar I worked at years ago. Murph is a good man," Ari added.

Adi smacked the table. "That's where I know your face! The video!" She pointed a finger at Jax and continued happily, "That was some truly impressive ivory-tickling."

"Ari was the impressive one. I was just trying to keep up."

"So you play piano at this bar?" Marco said between sips of wine. "I commend you. I'm not sure I could survive playing that many renditions of 'Piano Man.'"

"Ehh. I don't play it as often as you'd think. I'm more of a Beyoncé and Taylor Swift man." Jax smiled beatifically. Ari wanted to kiss him.

Adi grinned. "You do covers of Beyoncé?"

272

Jax shrugged. "My 'Bootylicious' is legendary."

"I thought," Ari said with a smile, "that your version of 'Single Ladies' was more impactful."

"You just like my dance moves." Jax fluttered his lashes outrageously.

"Yours? I thought they were Beyoncé's?"

Jax laughed, squeezed Ari's thigh under the table, and turned to Adi to continue their conversation. His recounting of bar stories got them to their drinks, and for several minutes, everyone was distracted giving their orders.

"I cannot imagine having to play such derivative music every night is very entertaining for you," Marco said into the silence after the server left.

Ari wondered if Jax would let him start kicking yet, but Jax gave another almost vapid smile and said, "It's not to everyone's taste, I'm sure. But like I said, I like entertaining people, and most people are entertained by derivative pop music."

"Jax is very good at it too. The patrons at the bar love him."

"I'm sure they do," Marco said.

Jax squeezed Ari's thigh once again, and when the server stepped back up to the table to inform Marco that they were not able to make the alterations on the dish he requested, Jax leaned in to murmur in Ari's ear, "That definitely isn't a kickable offense."

For a while the conversation eased away from them, but Jax quickly became everyone's darling—well, except Marco's—as he charmed them all.

"It tends to be above the layman's understanding," Marco said when Jax asked after Marco's advisory work at the conservatory. "I'm working with students who are heavily steeped in compositional theory."

"That sounds intense," Jax agreed. "I've barely taken piano lessons, so I have very little knowledge about theory."

Adi's eyebrows flew high. "I'm even more impressed at your improv now."

Jax flushed. "Well, you know, if you don't know the rules, you don't have to worry about breaking them. Besides, I was mostly flirting with Ari."

Ari might not be one for PDA, but how could he resist? He lifted Jax's hand to his mouth and pressed a kiss to his knuckles.

"So what kind of work do you do with your students?" Jax asked Adi, and spent several minutes asking her follow-up questions about teaching musical improv. Soon he was leaning across the table asking if she had any advice for his job, nodding along with her answers.

"You look very happy," Chuck said softly to Ari.

"I am. Jax is… special."

"He is that, and very good for you too."

"He is indeed very good for me," Ari agreed as he considered how loose he felt at this meal, how natural it was to be in public with Jax, introducing him to friends.

After their dishes were carted away, when Jax was making noises about dessert while Ari gently urged him on, Chuck asked what had brought Jax to Boston. "Ari has said he followed you here, and from your accent and your job, you're obviously not local."

"Oh," Jax said, looking up from the menu. He'd made drooling noises over the chocolate gateau. Marco was looking down his nose so hard, Ari could practically see up it. "Needed to come back and finish the PhD."

Chuck blinked but barely missed a beat. "Oh?"

"Yeah, I got interrupted a couple years ago. I was putting it off—going back to school and all—but MIT's letters were getting kind of angry."

Marco choked on his water.

"What is it about?" Chuck asked.

"Statistical models. Applied mathematics," Jax added with an almost apologetic smile that seemed to say, *Don't worry, I won't bore you with details.*

"*You* are earning a PhD in mathematics at *MIT*?" Marco said, the disbelief so clear that the whole table fell into an awkward silence.

Except for Jax, who blinked guilelessly and said, "Everyone needs a hobby."

Ari briefly contemplated crawling under the table to blow him.

Marco turned red. "Going to MIT was a hobby."

"Massachusetts is a nice place to live when it's not winter. No one wants to live in New Jersey, even if Princeton is beautiful."

Chuck barked out a laugh. "Ari was right—you are definitely entertaining, Jax."

Jax raised his water glass to Chuck in acknowledgment.

Ari ordered dessert too, took two bites and declared it too sweet as an excuse, and slid it in front of Jax, who gave him a look that said he wasn't fooled but also wasn't going to look a gift gateau in the mouth.

The party broke up in the lobby, and Ari and Jax shook hands with everyone as they went their separate ways.

"I hope you'll be making another stop in Boston for your next album tour?" Chuck inquired as Gianna and Adi waved goodbye to get into an Uber. "I'd love to get dinner again."

"April twenty-seventh," Jax said absently, watching the snow come down out the main doors. Then he seemed to realize he'd spoken aloud and added, "Uh, unofficially."

Ari fought not to gape at him. The dates wouldn't officially be released until next week. "How did you even—?"

Jax flushed. "Afra sent me your itinerary, just in case I might still be here?"

That sounded like an incomplete truth, but Ari wasn't going to call him on it in front of Chuck. "I'll be sure to text when the dates are confirmed," Ari said instead.

Chuck clapped his shoulder, and then his car pulled up and he too disappeared into the night.

Now that they were alone—or at least their group had gone—Jax slid his hand into Ari's. "So that was a much better time than the last time we did this."

Ari laughed helplessly and leaned his head against Jax's. "Call it a trial run?"

Jax squeezed his fingers. "Let's not get ahead of ourselves." But his voice was warm and wry.

Another car pulled up at the curb, and Ari checked his phone—this one was theirs. He tugged Jax along with him into the night and bundled him into the car. "Come back to the hotel with me?"

"Hmm," Jax said as though he were considering. "I should probably go to the lab. I want to double-check some calculations—"

Ari put a finger to his lips. He wouldn't kiss Jax in someone else's car—that was too much when he didn't know the driver personally—but he met Jax's eyes as seriously as he could.

"—which I can absolutely do in the morning. Yes, good point," Jax finished against Ari's fingertip.

He didn't let go of Ari's other hand until they were in the hotel room.

NOW THAT Rebecca had wrangled together his defense committee once more, with a substitute advisor in the place of her late husband, Jax really did have work to do in the lab. A day after his dinner out with Ari's professors, he got an official defense date: February 23. And suddenly he remembered why he hadn't dated much when he was doing his PhD.

Most of Jax's work was in the program itself, which allowed the input of growth factors and various conditions like temperature and humidity. He'd even built in a widget that could take raw data and spit out functions that defined the variables in terms of each other so the user wouldn't have to guesstimate. Unfortunately he couldn't prove that it worked well without spending hours in the laboratory, carefully calibrating bacterial cultures under strict controls with the help of two other researchers, who were both thankfully studying biology and better at this type of lab work than Jax.

When he wasn't at the lab, tweaking code, or revising sections of his thesis, he was eating or passed out in bed under every blanket in his apartment because it was frigid and Ari wasn't around to keep him warm. On Jax's good days, he remembered to call. On the bad days, it was nine thirty before he remembered to check his text messages.

And it was a hell of a lot easier to concentrate now that he had medication.

"What are you *listening* to, anyway?" Bokyung asked one afternoon—evening?—when she breezed into the lab to find Jax up to his eyeballs in growth medium.

"Boyfriend's last album," Jax answered as he cast around for the damn pipette. Where—there it was. "New one's not out yet, but there's too many songs with lyrics anyway. Distracting."

Bokyung was quiet for a moment and then asked, "Your boyfriend's a classical musician?"

Jax finished what he was doing, put the petri dish in the incubator, set it at precisely 30 degrees Centigrade, and noted the time in his log. "Uh, sort of?"

She shrugged. "Cool. I like it."

It turned out she must mean it, because the next time Jax entered the lab, he found her listening to the same album, bobbing her head gently to the rise and fall of Ari's violin. He snapped a picture—without any personal identifying information—and sent it to Ari with the caption *the lab is now an Ari Darvish zone.*

An hour and a half later he remembered to check for a reply. Ari had written *Careful, or Noella will try to add you to my "hype team."*

Please. As if Jax were not Ari's number-one hype man.

The weeks passed in a blur, until one day Jax looked up at a knock at the door of the computer lab to find a walking bouquet of roses. "Delivery for Jax Hall?" the roses said.

"Uh?" Jax answered. They had to be from Ari, right? But why?

The roses shifted to one side, revealing arms. The arms set them down on a table near the door, thankfully far away from any equipment. Then the feet stepped back and a full person emerged from behind the flowers. "Sorry, pal, but we don't deliver after five, and we had special instructions. You got a way to get these home?"

"I think I'll get an Uber," Jax said faintly.

"Good call. Happy Valentine's Day, buddy." And the guy saluted and left.

Oh. Well. That explained the roses. They sat like a beacon at the door, drawing Jax's eye, and his lab partners' as well. They kept smirking and shaking their heads.

Jax gave up working an hour later. He booked an Uber and carried his ridiculous bouquet out of the building. At least the sheer number of petals hid his burning face.

At home, he searched the flowers for a card. It was small and said only, *Since we cannot be together today, this will have to do. —A.*

Jax dialed up his boyfriend.

"So a plant walked into my lab today," Jax said in greeting.

"Did one?"

"Yes, a rather large red one. It wanted me to know my boyfriend is a sap of epic proportions."

"Maybe, maybe not. It could just be that you inspire romance in others."

Grinning ear to ear, Jax said, "Now that is ridiculous."

"Only with you," Ari murmured.

"Happy Valentine's Day," Jax said back. They sat in warm silence. Jax only wished that Ari were with him so he could lean into his space and get all the comfort he needed.

"Tell me about your day," Ari said, and Jax curled himself under a blanket and started to talk.

Unfortunately, Jax's days were mostly the same. At least after talking about how boring but productive the lab was, Jax was able to offer, "I heard from Afra today."

"Oh?"

"Yeah, she wanted to send me the most recent tour schedule. She mentioned something about the fostering stuff being stressful, though."

Ari hummed. "Yes. They have had a relatively smooth experience with getting themselves onto fostering lists. Things are happening much more quickly than Afra anticipated, I think. She's trying not to panic."

"Oh, yikes."

"It would seem there is a need for foster parents."

"There usually is," Jax murmured.

Ari blew out a breath. "They could end up with a child before the end of the year. I have attempted to ask her what her plan is for touring, but she is being… reticent."

"Maybe she and Ben need to talk more about how they want things to work?" Jax suggested. His heart thundered and he hoped he didn't sound guilty. "Anyway, it's not like she's gonna leave you in the lurch. She's your sister."

"I am aware. Only… I find touring very stressful, and knowing she has my back…."

"Hey, Ari. Everything will work out just fine. You know it will."

"Well—" Ari cleared his throat. "—if you say so, it must be true."

"Of course. I'm right about everything."

"That has generally been the truth of my experience."

And what could Jax say to that? "Long-distance is terrible, because that deserved a kiss." Ari hummed, and Jax got a great idea. "Hey, Ari? What are you wearing?"

Ari choked and sputtered, but he did eventually answer the question, so Jax counted Valentine's Day a success.

The next week passed in a blur of research and writing, and then it was the twenty-third and Jax brought his findings before a committee.

Jax walked into the room, and an hour later he stumbled out again. Rebecca stood waiting in the hallway. She'd told him he could have a cup of tea with her while he waited for their decision.

"How are you feeling?" she asked.

He shrugged helplessly. "I… have no idea." He rubbed his head. He was pretty sure that he answered questions of some sort? "I said stuff?"

Rebecca slung an arm around his shoulders. "Well, I'm glad to hear that you said stuff." She guided him down the hallway and into her office. Jax let her lead; his brain was not up to tasks more complex than basic locomotion.

Which he proved when the office door opened and Jax made an extremely obvious observation out loud. "Christine? Ari?"

His mother glided across the room, her long coat-like sweater ballooned out behind her like wings, and enveloped him in her arms. "I wanted to be here to support you on your big day, but I didn't want to distract you beforehand."

Still kind of numb, Jax clutched her tightly. "Thanks."

When she released him, Jax turned to Ari, and some of the numbness faded. Jax flung himself into his arms.

"Oof," Ari grunted but held him close.

"Shut up," Jax murmured. "I thought we agreed to meet at my place tomorrow? Did I hallucinate that?" He was sure Ari had insisted on coming to town for his defense, but Jax had insisted even louder that there was nothing Ari could do and Jax didn't have the time or energy to see him until it was over. Besides, he didn't want anyone to see him while he was a nervous wreck, awaiting a decision that would let him know whether four years of schooling had been for nothing.

He'd obviously been wrong about that, because he couldn't seem to make his arms let Ari go, and now he was trembling a little. Good thing Ari had ignored his directions.

Ari had the grace to look somewhat chagrined. "I couldn't not have a celebratory dinner with you tonight."

"I found him loitering in front of the building," Rebecca said.

Jax found the strength to pull back somewhat from Ari's arms and arch his eyebrows. "Hooligan."

Ari flushed.

"He was trying to appear inconspicuous, but it's hard to hide when you're that gorgeous." Rebecca smirked, and Jax laughed a little too loudly. He felt like he'd taken one too many pills this morning—his heart racing too fast, everything a little too sharp, too bright, too *much*.

Well, people got punch-drunk when they were stressed out and sleep-deprived. And Jax didn't know anyone with a PhD who'd made it there without a crippling caffeine addiction. But he tried to act normal, for Ari's sake, and he reached up to stroke his cheek. "Aw, did you get spotted by an adoring fan?"

Ari turned his head to kiss Jax's palm, which had the effect of bringing Jax's anxiety down at least three points. "Hardly."

"More like some lustful undergrads were trying to figure out if he was famous. Luckily for him, we're old friends." She winked. Rebecca had been instantly enamored of Ari when Jax brought him over for dinner.

For the first time since he'd begun his defense, Jax felt like he could breathe. *Fake it till you make it.* "What about Christine? She loitering too?"

Christine settled in a chair and put up her feet. "Please. As if I couldn't use a directory to find Rebecca's office."

Christine hadn't exactly gotten on with the Graylings before, but academia was a small world, and Christine and Rebecca had known of and been acquainted with each other for longer than Jax had been a postgrad. They were both scary-smart women who respected the hell out of each other and loved Jax—

Rebecca's desk phone chirped.

And there was the anxiety rushing back. Jax felt the blood flow out of his face, and he might have actually staggered if Ari hadn't been there to steady his elbow.

"I think that means they've made their decision," Rebecca said. "Time to go back, Jax."

Okay, but what if he just stayed in this office forever? It held a few of his favorite people. They could get pizzas delivered!

But Ari was already leading him to the door, because once again Jax's navigation function had crapped out and left him with ambulation only. Figured.

"Hey, Jax," Bokyung said when they reached the corridor. She'd replaced a researcher on his advisory committee who had moved on while Jax was away. "We're ready for you. Come on in."

Ari paused at the door. "Do you want us to come in?"

Jax thought about it. No matter what, he wouldn't be alone— not really. But part of him felt like he had to stand on his own two feet for this, see it through to whatever end, just to prove to himself that he could. "No," he said firmly, dredging up a smile. "Thank you, though."

On legs that felt like they might melt into the floor, Jax walked into the room and faced his committee.

Marie Greenwood, his advisor, looked up from her place in the middle and smiled. Relief flooded through him so fast it almost swept him away. "Congratulations, Dr. Hall."

Rebecca insisted on taking them all out for dinner to celebrate. Ari glanced dubiously at what Jax knew were deep and unattractive circles under his eyes, and suggested that it be an early one.

It turned out she'd made a reservation at a little place down the street from Ari's hotel, where Jax celebrated by allowing himself to drink two and a half cocktails, since he'd woken up at five and decided he might as well take his pill.

He couldn't have said what he ate or even what he drank or given any details of the conversation. But he came back to himself when the door to Ari's hotel room opened and he nudged Jax into it, and Jax saw the enormous bed.

"Ari," Jax said.

"Hmm?" Ari asked, pressing his lips to the side of Jax's head, just over his ear.

"I really wanna have sex with you."

Jax would've sworn he could feel Ari smiling against his scalp. "I'm not into somnophilia," he said wryly.

"Yes!" Jax said. "That's the problem!" He turned around so he could face Ari and pressed his hands to his chest as he pushed him toward the bed. "You have coffee, right?"

"Coffee you're not supposed to drink on your medication," Ari reminded him.

Yeah, that rule had been bent to the breaking point in the past five weeks. "But—" Jax began.

"No buts," Ari interrupted.

Jax's lips twitched.

"Yes, very funny. None of that type of butt either. At least not until you've gotten some sleep." Jax wanted to pout, but it was difficult when Ari was gently kissing his lips, carefully removing his clothing, turning down the covers. "Go wash your face and brush your teeth, and if you can keep your eyes open for that, we'll talk."

Jax marched into the bathroom with renewed determination but unfortunately fell asleep standing up with the hotel toothbrush in his mouth. He stumbled back into the bedroom, all but collapsed onto the mattress, and sighed as Ari tucked him in. "Okay," he said, admitting defeat, "but after this, sex."

"I promise," Ari said solemnly, and Jax let the darkness take him.

KNOWING HOW exhausted Jax was and how hard he'd been working, Ari expected him to sleep for at least twelve hours.

He should have known better than to underestimate Jax's sex drive.

Perhaps three hours after they'd gone to bed, Ari woke to find Jax had gotten up to use the washroom. He glanced at the clock and saw that it was just after midnight. Jax would probably go right back to sleep—

"Oh good, you're awake," Jax said, and he swayed right back into bed and entwined his body with Ari's.

From the slight incoordination of his movements and the heat coming off his body, Ari deduced he was probably still a little drunk. That didn't dampen his arousal any; it had been weeks since they'd been together like this, and he'd missed....

Jax lifted his head and brushed his nose against Ari's.

He'd missed this.

Ari kissed him, and Jax groaned into it He lifted his hand to Ari's shoulder, then his chest, his waist, his ass. His cock was hard against the meat of Ari's hip, and Jax rubbed against him.

They needed to be naked. Ari bit at Jax's lower lip and tore his hands from Jax's hair to paw at his boxers. "Take these off," he ordered, voice rough but quiet. "Come on."

"You too." Jax batted Ari's hands away to take care of his own clothing.

Once they'd shimmied out of their boxers, they came back together and pressed their naked bodies head to toe.

Jax fumbled to settle himself on top of Ari and lifted his face for a kiss as he began to grind his hips. The drunken coordination might have been amusing if Ari hadn't been Jax-deprived for a month. But then Jax found his rhythm, braced his hands and knees on the mattress, and rubbed his cock into the hollow of Ari's hip. Since that also had Ari's dick rubbing against Jax's hip and belly, Ari could hardly complain.

He grabbed Jax's ass and held on.

Jax pressed his face into Ari's neck, rubbed his nose and lips against the tender skin where it connected to his shoulder, and moaned into the hot, humid space. Ari tangled his fingers in Jax's hair and breathed him in while Jax thrust his hips and let out happy, desperate noises as he moved. He was, Ari realized, almost unaware of Ari or what he was doing—Jax was chasing his orgasm, sleepy and horny, and anything else, including Ari's own orgasm, was incidental. Which was hot as fuck.

Usually Ari would have flipped Jax over and either taken over the thrusting or swallowed his cock. But watching Jax single-mindedly get himself off was a new kind of pleasure Ari hadn't known he wanted.

He pressed a free hand under Jax's chin and lifted him up for a kiss. Ari needed that mouth right now, so he pressed his tongue inside and swept it against Jax's to discover all his secrets, devour him, communicate to Jax just how much he was wanted.

"Ari!"

Jax came shuddering, gasping into Ari's mouth, and Ari ran his hands over Jax's body to ease him through it. Jax slumped and pressed his mouth to Ari's neck again. He hummed softly, content, sleepy. And fuck no, Jax was not going to sleep just yet, not after that show.

Ari flipped them and settled over Jax's body. He reached for Jax's hand, and a fraction more awareness settled into Jax's eyes as Ari guided his hand through the mess of come and down over his cock.

"Oh fuck."

Jax was perhaps too tired to do the work himself, but that was okay. Ari wrapped his fingers over Jax's and used his hand the way Jax had used his body, until Jax murmured, "Yeah, come on. Come on me, Ari."

What else could a man do? Ari redoubled his efforts until he came all over Jax's belly and cock, worsening the mess between them. He swooped in for another long, filthy kiss as he came down from the high.

"That was awesome," Jax slurred. Now that Ari had also come, it seemed that Jax was no longer able to keep his eyes open.

Ari wanted to follow him into sleep, but he forced himself to get out of the bed to clean up. Jax was snoring by the time he brought back a washcloth. Thankfully he was still spread out on his back. Ari cleaned him up, disposed of the dirty laundry, then climbed back into bed and cocooned them both under the covers.

Chapter Twenty-Four

"I LIKE him," Christine said over her cup of coffee.

She had checked into a hotel not far from Ari's, and after Jax finally responded to her text that morning, she suggested he meet her for a coffee. She couldn't stay long, she reminded him, as she needed to get back to her own teaching. So Jax tore himself away from Ari's very nice hotel bed and headed out into the wild.

"Hm?" Jax eyed her over his hot chocolate.

"Ari. I like him. I wasn't sure that I would after I saw you crying into your cereal over him, but he's a good man. And it's clear that he adores you."

Jax blushed and tried to hide his face in his drink. "Good. Because I'm pretty sure he's sticking around."

"Good," Christine parroted. Silence stretched between them. Hopefully that would do it for Christine's awkward-mom conversation. "You're looking good today, settled. I don't think I've seen you so comfortable in your own skin in, God, years. Maybe not since you hit your teens."

Jax refused to think about how painful those early years had been. Thirteen, skinny, too smart for his own good or for his peers, younger than everyone in his classes, and newly discovered pansexual. Not Jax's best years. "Gee, thanks."

Christine laughed. "I'm trying to say that you look happy in a way I've never seen. This is a good thing."

"Yeah, well. I feel like I know me and what I want for the first time in a long time."

"Oh?" She sipped her coffee. "Care to share any of your revelations with the class?"

"Well, for one, I'm done with academia. Maybe one day I'll go back, but right now, I know it's not what I want. Or what I will want in the near future." He lifted his chin and looked her in the eye. He needed her to know he was serious.

She nodded slowly. "Okay. I can't say that I'm surprised."

"Good." He swallowed. "I'm not sure what I'll end up doing more long-term, but right now, for the immediate future, I just want to be with Ari, figure us out. It's been a weird few months." Between getting together, breaking up, reuniting, and Jax's PhD, they hadn't had a post-honeymoon domestic period to test out their relationship. "So I'm thinking I might just follow him around on his tour for a while." He grinned cheekily. "Be a groupie."

Christine snorted. "Well, if that's what you want, dear, then I support your decision to be a full-time groupie."

The tacit approval—finally—to make his life his own unwound something in Jax's spine that had been ratcheting for years. He let the lassitude seep into his posture and spread to his extremities, and he breathed unencumbered for the first time in ages. Maybe *groupie* wasn't exactly right—but then, bartender-slash-musician hadn't been either, and he didn't regret that choice.

He had time.

"ARI? MAMAN?"

Ari looked up from the mirror in his parents' foyer, where he'd been adjusting his shirt, and turned around to see his sister behind him. "Afra. Hi." He glanced at the clock. "You're early." And if *that* didn't set off alarm bells.

"You think you're so funny." She huffed, but he could tell it was put on—she looked… *happy*, but nervous underneath that. "I was hoping to talk to you and Maman and Baba before we leave."

That would probably make them *late* instead, but considering what the atmosphere at the bar was likely to be on the event of Jax's PhD celebration, he doubted that even the guest of honor would notice. Besides, this seemed serious. "They're upstairs. Do you want me to—"

But before he could finish, their parents appeared at the top of the stairs. Unlike Ari, they seemed to have expected Afra's presence. "There you are." His mother smiled. She had been doing more of that in the past week now that her radiation therapy had finished. "Right on time."

Was Ari the only one who thought that was spooky instead of something to smile about?

"Let's go into the study," Baba suggested, including Ari with a gesture of his hand.

"Now." Ari's mother settled in her desk chair this time, because there were only four chairs total. "What did you want to talk about, Afra? It sounded important."

She looked down. "It is. I—" Finally she met their gazes, each in turn. "I've been doing a lot of thinking…."

By the end of the impromptu family meeting, Ari felt shell-shocked and Afra and their mother were both dabbing away happy tears.

"You're sure this is what you want?" he asked for what felt like the hundredth time.

He almost died of shock when his mother echoed his concern. "This is a big decision. You've always been my independent daughter…."

Afra laughed and nodded as she wiped away a tear. "I'm sure, Maman, Ari. I hope… I know it's a big change."

And Ari didn't always take well to change. Yes, he understood the subtext. He took his sister's hands in his. "I could not be happier for you. If this is what you want, you should do it."

Baba slapped his hands on his thighs and stood as though this closed the issue. "Well! It seems as though we have one more reason to celebrate tonight."

"Maybe two more reasons." Their mother beamed as she stood, less smoothly than she used to but already looking stronger than she had a week before. "But let's not forget that tonight is about Jax."

And speaking of Jax— "We'd better get going," Ari said, noting the time. Good thing Ben had volunteered to pick up the cake on his way over from work.

Murph had offered the Rock for the afternoon for their private party, with all Jax's friends and family and former coworkers in attendance. When they went in, Jax was center stage, banging away at "School's Out," hamming it up in a velvet top hat that kept falling down over his eyes. Kayla was barely keeping it together.

"You know," Ari's mother said at his elbow, "I was wrong about him."

He offered her his arm out of habit, even though she hadn't needed it for support for weeks now. She took it anyway. "I know, Maman. I'm glad you figured it out."

"Laughter is its own kind of medicine." She sighed happily as Ari deposited her at a table far enough away from the stage not to be overwhelmed by the sound from the speakers. Then she looked up, her eyes full of a mischief Ari couldn't ever recall seeing in her, though her expression was smug. "And it looks like I'll have you married off to a doctor after all."

"*Maman*," Ari protested, his face heating.

He was saved from further embarrassment by Ben's arrival with the cake, which prompted Murph to hop up on the bar and call for everyone's attention. Jax was one of the last to give in, possibly because he couldn't see anything with the enormous hat over his eyes or hear over his own repeated refrains that school was out forever.

"All right, shut yer pie holes," Murph shouted. "We're here today to celebrate the accomplishments of Dr. Jax Hall—one of the finest bartenders ever to pull a beer. Even though he left us for two months to freeze his arse off in Boston." He hefted an enormous bottle of champagne. "So!"

The cork hit the disco ball when he popped it, then somehow managed to land in the tip jar on top of the piano.

"Come and grab a glass and we'll have a toast!"

Even a giant bottle of champagne wasn't actually enough for everyone, though of course there was more behind the bar. As Murph,

Bruce, and Naomi poured, Ari maneuvered through the crowd until he found Jax.

"Has it sunk in yet?"

Jax shook his head ruefully. "It's starting to, but I think I'm still about twenty hours of sleep under par. Hard to say."

"I understand." Ari often felt that way at the tail end of writing an album.

Naomi and Calvin found them then, with an extra glass of champagne each. Calvin handed his to Jax, while Naomi gave hers to Ari.

"Everybody got a glass?" Calvin shouted.

It seemed that everyone did.

"All right, then." He was beaming as he raised his glass. "To Jax!"

HALFWAY THROUGH the party, it finally started to feel real. Jax was done.

It felt great.

"So, not to spoil the party," Hobbes said, promptly spoiling the party as he sidled up to Jax in a rare moment without Ari, who had volunteered to play the piano, "but there's something we should talk about."

Jax stared at him. "Oh my God, Naomi's pregnant?"

"What? No. Did you see the way she's putting away the champagne?" Hobbes huffed, his cheeks red. "Way to take the wind out of my sails."

Jax gave him a flat look. "I haven't slept properly in, like, three months. I couldn't pass a blood test right now. Just spit it out."

"I'm selling the house."

No wonder he was worried Jax might panic. Fortunately it wasn't as though Jax had long-term plans for living there anyway. "Yeah?" He glanced at Naomi, who was at the bar doing shots with Theo—that was going to end badly. "Shacking up?"

"Yeah." He was still blushing, but now he had a helpless smile too. Aww. Adorable. "Naomi doesn't want to sell a house that's been in her family for three generations, so…."

"Good. Maybe she can get you to stop working so much."

Hobbes furrowed his brow. "Did I forget to tell you, or did I tell you and you forgot?"

Oh great—now what? "Forget what?" Jax asked, alarmed. Hobbes hadn't proposed and decided to ask Jax to be his best man or something, had he?

"I left the hospital in January. I'm doing family practice at a clinic on Wonderland Road."

Well, shit. "No wonder you look so well-rested," Jax quipped, then easily dodged Hobbes's halfhearted swipe. "Come to think of it, no wonder Naomi's looking so smug—"

"Jax—"

He grinned. "Congratulations, though, really. Let me know when I need to move my stuff."

They talked a little about the details—Hobbes wasn't in a hurry to get the house on the market, so there was no rush for Jax to make a decision before the tour started up in April—and then Afra came over with a couple plates of cake, and Hobbes retreated to the bar to get fresh with Naomi.

"So," Afra said, handing him a plate, "I talked to Ari."

And there it was: the first piece of the new chapter of Jax's life falling into place. Or maybe not.

Jax cleared his throat, trying not to let on how fast his heart was beating. He forked off a big chunk of vanilla cake with chocolate buttercream. "And?"

"And I told him Ben and I have a foster placement coming up and I'm officially retiring from going on tour."

Jax nodded and licked frosting from the corner of his mouth. He and Afra had been over this by email. "And you really think it's a good idea for me to take over?"

"Well, you won't really be taking over," she pointed out. "Most of the organizing is still going to happen on my end. You'd be more of a deputy. But as for whether it's a good idea... you'd have to ask Ari."

"Ask me what?"

Jax almost dropped his cake. He hadn't noticed the music tapering off. Afra made a quiet exit as he turned around. "Do these pants make my ass look big?"

"Absolutely not," Ari answered immediately. "It looks perfect."

Flatterer. Jax took a deep breath. "Actually I wanted to ask you... what would you think about me coming along on tour with you?"

Ari smiled, gently took Jax's cake plate and set it on a table, and curled his hands around Jax's. "I think nothing would make me happier."

Jax exhaled a laugh that was part relief and part sheer joy. "Good, because Afra thinks I should be your handler—carry out her orders, charm hotel and venue staff, keep you from losing your cool when you're playing for twenty thousand people... sell a bunch of T-shirts with your face on them—"

Ari cut him off with a chaste kiss. Jax, surprised at the public display even though they were among friends, found himself blushing.

God, he hoped no one saw him. He'd never live down a blush from something so innocent.

"You're perfect for the job," Ari said. "But is it what *you* want? You're somewhat overqualified."

Jax shrugged. "It's not like I'm going to be your PA. And honestly, I don't really know anymore what I want to be when I grow up, but I know I want to be with you. That's more than good enough for now." He allowed himself a moment to speculate. "You know, I bet I can come up with a way to optimize scheduling, accounting for travel time, airfare, important festivals...."

Ari laughed and squeezed Jax's hands. "You haven't been Afra's deputy for five minutes and you're already planning to usurp her."

"Not *usurp*—"

Ari cut off Jax's weak protest with another kiss. "So. What shall we do to celebrate?"

Jax did not swoon. He did come up with several ideas, but most of them were best saved for later.

Then he smiled. When in Rome…. "Wanna go play a duet?"

ASHLYN KANE likes to think she can do it all, but her follow-through often proves her undoing. Her house is as full of half-finished projects as her writing folder. With the help of her ADHD meds, she gets by.

An early reader and talker, Ashlyn has always had a flare for language and storytelling. As an eight-year-old, she attended her first writers' workshop. As a teenager, she won an amateur poetry competition. As an adult, she received a starred review in *Publishers Weekly* for her novel *Fake Dating the Prince*. There were quite a few years in the middle there, but who's counting?

Her hobbies include DIY home decor, container gardening (no pulling weeds), music, and spending time with her enormous chocolate lapdog. She is the fortunate wife of a wonderful man, the daughter of two sets of great parents, and the proud older sister/sister-in-law of the world's biggest nerds.

Sign up for her newsletter at www.ashlynkane.ca/newsletter/
Website: www.ashlynkane.ca

MORGAN JAMES is a clueless (older) millennial who's still trying to figure out what they'll be when they grow up and enjoying the journey to get there. Now, with a couple of degrees, a few stints in Europe, and more than one false start to a career, they eagerly wait to see what's next. James started writing fiction before they could spell and wrote their first (unpublished) novel in middle school. They haven't stopped since. Geek, artist, archer, and fanatic, Morgan passes their free hours in imaginary worlds, with people on pages and screens— it's an addiction, as is their love of coffee and tea. They live in Canada with their massive collection of unread books and where they are the personal servant of too many four-legged creatures.

Twitter: @MorganJames71
Facebook: www.facebook.com/morganjames007

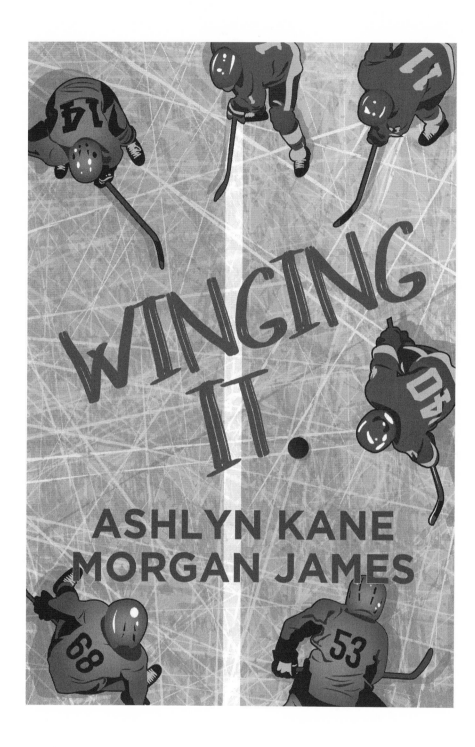

Gabe Martin has a simple life plan: get into the NHL and win the Stanley Cup. It doesn't include being the first out hockey player or, worse, getting involved with one of his teammates. But things change.

Dante Baltierra is Gabe's polar opposite—careless, reckless… shameless. But his dedication to the sport is impressive, and Gabe can overlook a lot of young-and-stupid in the name of great hockey. And Dante has a superlative ass in a sport filled with superlative asses.

Before Gabe can figure out how to deal, a tabloid throws him out of his comfortable closet into a brand-new world. Amid the emotional turmoil of invasive questions, nasty speculation, and on- and off-ice homophobia, his game suffers.

Surprisingly, it's Dante who drags him out of it—and then drags him into something else. Nothing good can come of secretly sleeping with a teammate, especially one Gabe has feelings for. But with their captain out with an injury, a rookie in perpetual need of a hug, and the race to make the playoffs for the first time since 1995, Gabe has a lot on his plate.

He can't be blamed for forgetting that nothing stays secret forever.

www.dreamspinnerpress.com

Ashlyn Kane
and Morgan James

HARD
FEELINGS

Rylan Williams hates conferences: too many people, not enough routine, and way too much interaction with strangers. When he gets stuck in a broken elevator with Miller Jones, the kid who fell asleep in his lecture, he figures things can't get worse. Then Rylan realizes he's the same guy he just spent an hour perving over from afar.

Rylan wants to await rescue in silence, but Miller insists on conversation, or at least banter. But just because they don't get along doesn't mean they don't have chemistry, and Rylan breaks all his rules about intimacy for a one-time-only conference hookup. He'll probably never see Miller again anyway. So of course, two months later Miller shows up at Rylan's office, having just been hired to work on a new computer program—with Rylan.

And Rylan thought being stuck in an elevator with him was bad.

Soon Rylan and Miller learn that they get along best when they take out their frustrations in the bedroom. Their arrangement goes against everything Rylan believes in, but the rules are simple: Don't stay overnight. Don't tell anyone. And don't fall in love.

This is probably a bad idea.

www.dreamspinnerpress.com

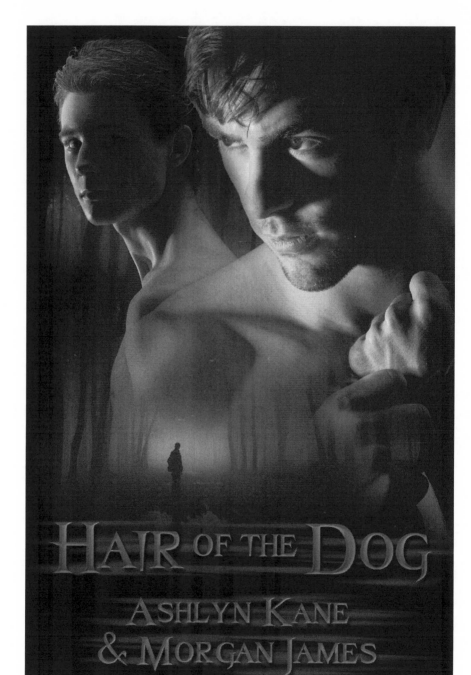

HAIR OF THE DOG

ASHLYN KANE
& MORGAN JAMES

It's nine o'clock the morning after his father's funeral, and Ezra Jones already knows it's going to be a bad day. He wakes up hungover, sore, and covered in blood. Then it gets worse: the handsome and compelling Callum Dawson shows up on his doorstep claiming Ezra's been turned into a werewolf. Ezra wants to be skeptical, but the evidence is hard to ignore.

Ezra doesn't have a lot of time to get used to the rules Alpha Callum imposes—or the way his body responds to Callum's dominance—as he's busily working for the CDC to help uncover the origins of a lycan epidemic. When the sexual tension finally breaks, Ezra barely has time to enjoy it, because a new danger threatens. Someone wants Ezra for their own unscrupulous purposes and will do anything to get him.

www.dreamspinnerpress.com

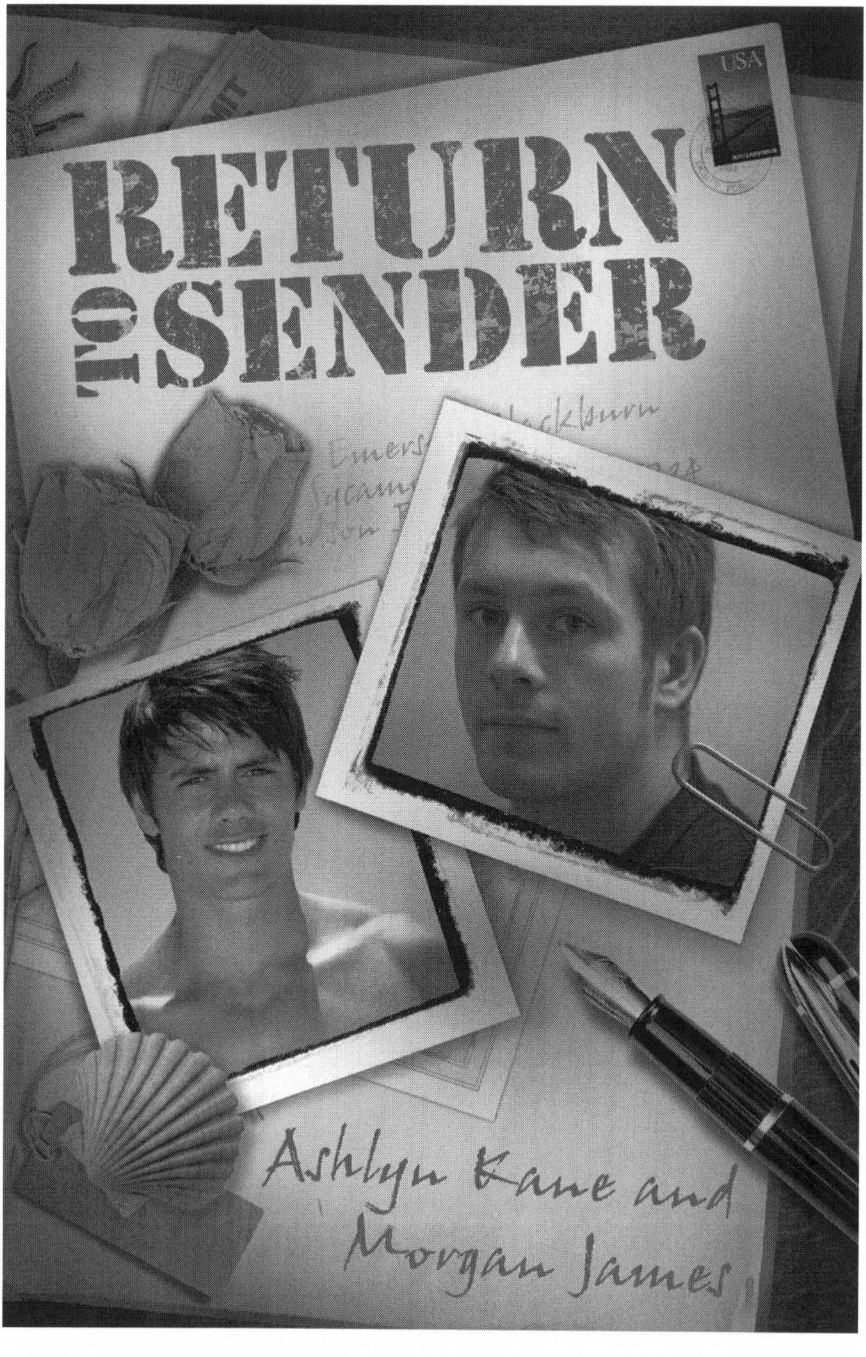
RETURN TO SENDER
USA
Ashlyn Kane and Morgan James

Emerson Blackburn really screwed up this time. He's finally pissed off Jonah, the sweet, patient, funny boyfriend he's loved as long as he can remember, to the point that Jonah isn't even speaking to him. Emerson hasn't felt this awful since the summer after graduation when Jonah ruined their college plans by running off on a cross-country trip without even saying goodbye.

Jonah isn't just angry. He's furious and hurt. Devastated, even, because he's completely in love with Emerson, but although they've been together for a year, Emerson still doesn't trust him.

The full weight of their past mistakes drags Jonah and Emerson into memories of happier—and lonelier—times, but wallowing in their guilt isn't solving the problems. The only way to move forward is to learn from the past… but someone still has to be the first to apologize.

www.dreamspinnerpress.com

Made in the USA
Middletown, DE
20 July 2021